'Scott Sigler takes us on a breathtaking, hyper-adrenalized

filled with te

racing'

'A talented storyteller who knows how to write scenes that are
graphic, frightening, and memorable. Many veteran horror writ-
ers will be grinding their teeth in envy. A definite must-read,
whether you've read *Infected* or not.'   *Booklist* ★

Praise for Infected

'Sigler is the Richard Matheson of the 21st Century . . . smart
and creepy, *Infected* is a flawless thinking-person's thriller. Bravo
to a bold new talent!'

Jonathan Maberry,
Bram Stoker Award-winning author of *Patient Zero*

'In-your-face, up-to-the-minute terror'   Lincoln Child

'A novel that lives up to its hype . . . the folksy character detail
of Stephen King, the conceptual panache of Clive Barker, and
the oozing, shuddery pathologies of a David Cronenberg movie'
Jay Bonansinga, author of *The Sinking of the Eastland*

'Sigler has a unique talent for keeping readers on the edge of
their seats; I absolutely had to know what was going to happen
next. *Infected* is full of mayhem, action, and gore – and you
won't be able to put it down'

David Wellington, author of *13 Bullets*

Also by Scott Sigler

EarthCore
Ancestor
Infected

CONTAGIOUS
SCOTT SIGLER

HODDER

First published in Great Britain in 2009 by Hodder & Stoughton
An Hachette UK company

First published in paperback in 2009

1

A CIP catalogue record for this title is available from the British Library.

ISBN 978 0 340 96359 3

Typeset in Plantin Light by Hewer Text UK Ltd, Edinburgh

Printed and bound in the UK CPI Mackays, Chatham ME5 8TD

Hodder & Stoughton policy is to use papers that are natural, renewable
and recyclable products and made from wood grown in sustainable forests.
The logging and manufacturing processes are expected to conform to
the environmental regulations of the country of origin.

Hodder & Stoughton Ltd
338 Euston Road
London NW1 3BH

www.hodder.co.uk

To the memory of Mike Lehn, who led by example.

To the memory of Mookie: fourteen years as my
writing partner was not enough.

To the Sigler Junkies all over the world.
The FDO™ thanks you.

Prologue

JANUARY 20

It had to be a joke.

Being hazed on the first day of work was nothing new, but John Gutierrez had never thought someone would have the balls to prank him on *this* first day.

On Inauguration Day.

One simply did not haze the president of the United States.

'Murray, I'm not finding the humor in this,' John said. 'The country has some very serious issues to deal with, and this goes beyond the realm of good taste.'

Murray Longworth looked surprised. 'A . . . joke? This is no joke, Mister President.'

Of course it was. John Gutierrez hadn't been born yesterday.

He looked around the Oval Office, gauging the reaction from his key advisers. Tom Maskill, his twitchy deputy chief of staff, was trying and failing to look nonplussed. Secretary of Defense Donald Martin sat back on an antique couch, his legs crossed. Donald was old-school Washington: tall, white, graying hair, tailored suit . . . looked like he was made of plantation money. Chief of Staff Vanessa Colburn sat on a striped chair. In appearance she was Donald's polar opposite – female, black and young. Her no-nonsense poker face carried a cold stare that could freeze you where you stood. At the moment, that stare was fixed directly on one Murray Longworth, deputy director of the CIA.

Murray also had an old-school Washington look, but different from Donald's. Murray's suit looked expensive, too, but like its owner it seemed a bit rumpled and tired. Murray was past retirement age, slightly overweight, with a scowl permanently etched into his face. His was a familiar image among the dinosaurs of Washington, a look Vanessa had dubbed *Cold War White Man*. He was *a* CIA deputy director, but not *the* deputy director. Murray worked mostly behind the scenes.

'I've heard a lot about you, Murray,' John said. 'I spoke to all five former presidents before I took office. Of the many nice things they had to say, there is only one person they each pointed out by name – you. They said that you are a . . . how shall I put this? A special kind of go-to guy.'

'Yes, Mister President,' Murray said.

'Now it seems they all pointed you out for a reason, to set me up for this ridiculous story about triangular growths infecting Americans and turning them into psychopathic killers.'

'Sir,' Murray said, 'I assure you this is no joke.'

'Then why haven't we heard anything about it before?' Vanessa asked, her voice almost as expressionless as her face.

'President Hutchins wanted this in the black,' Murray said. 'And keeping things in the black is what I do.'

Murray had brought in a large flat-panel screen for his presentation. It looked out of place in the Oval Office, a brash piece of technology in a room designed to reek of history and tradition. John stared at the image frozen on that screen: an old woman, clearly dead, a lumpy blue triangular growth on her shoulder. Each side of the triangle was about an inch long. It wasn't on her skin, or under it, but *part* of it. Beneath the photo, her name – *Charlotte Wilson*.

According to Murray, that growth had made Wilson murder her son with a butcher knife, then attack two police officers before they shot her to death in self-defense.

This wasn't just a joke, it was inexcusable.

Based on the endorsement of the former presidents, John had saved Murray Longworth's 'Project Tangram' presentation as the last of the day. It was the closing act in a mind-boggling cache of the previous administration's secrets: two stealth submarines resting on the bottom of the Sea of Japan ready to rain nukes on North Korea; two more subs sitting off Qatar, ready to first-strike Iran should the new government fall and fundamentalists get their finger on the nuclear button; secret deals with the Chinese government; a Mach-10 skunkworks strike-fighter that could fly forty miles above the Earth; fast-track deals for drilling in Alaska and off the coast of Florida; plus a dozen other tawdry dealings that – under Hutchins's administration – had been business as usual.

'If I could finish the presentation, sir,' Murray said, 'things might be a little clearer.'

John looked at Vanessa, then Donald. They both shrugged. John sighed and nodded for Murray to continue.

'Thank you, sir,' Murray said. 'The disease was discovered about four months ago by CDC epidemiologist Doctor Margaret Montoya and her colleague Doctor Amos Braun. Both are still on the project. Symptoms begin with itching and small rashes that grow into large welts, then finally triangular blue growths. The disease also seems to create extreme paranoia in its victims, to the point where almost all subjects showed a definitive pattern of avoiding hospitals, health-care workers or members of law enforcement. Paranoia toward police and military, in particular, was particularly severe. Most victims either died of unknown causes, committed suicide or were killed by law enforcement as a result of psychotic behavior.'

'Wait a minute,' Vanessa said. 'The parasite *made* them avoid hospitals? Aggressive behavior from some chemical imbalance is one thing, but you expect us to believe that these parasites actually modified a host's decision-making ability?'

'It happens in nature all the time,' Murray said.

'But these are *people*,' Vanessa said.

'Behavior is merely a chemical reaction, ma'am,' Murray said. 'Trust me, there is zero question.'

Vanessa's face showed just how much she trusted Murray's opinion. 'Is this supposed parasite contagious?'

Murray shook his head. 'As far as we can tell, it does not transmit from an infected host to other people. Something spreads the disease, however, and we haven't figured out what that vector is.'

'So Americans can catch a parasite that turns them into killers,' she said, 'and yet you guys kept the people in the dark?'

'President Hutchins opted to keep this information secret, yes,' Murray said. 'He feared that reports could cause panic as well as a flood of false cases into hospitals that could impede our ability to find real victims. There is also the threat of a lynch-mob mentality that could result in grave harm to Americans guilty of nothing more than having poison ivy or psoriasis.'

Vanessa leaned back in her chair and threw her hands up in disgust. 'You see, Mister President? This is why the last eight years have crippled America. The old guard never trusted the people. This is exactly why we're here, to put an end to government run as a web of lies.'

'I understand you're enthusiastic about implementing new policies,' Murray said. 'But if you don't mind a little advice, Miss Colburn, you might want to get the whole story before you dismiss the calculated decisions of a former president.'

Vanessa sat forward again and glared at him. John couldn't suppress a small smile. Murray Longworth was taking a tone with Vanessa Colburn right off the bat? John wondered how long Murray would last.

'By all means,' Vanessa said, smiling her best saccharine smile. 'Please continue.'

Murray nodded. 'Charlotte Wilson was just the first case we discovered.' He pointed a remote control at the screen.
click

Gary Leeland: An old man, very much alive, with hateful eyes that would have commanded full attention were it not for the one-inch-wide bluish triangle on his neck.

'This man checked in to the hospital, then hours later set his hospital bed on fire. He burned alive.'
click

Martin Brewbaker: A corpse on a morgue table, covered with blackened third-degree burns, legs cut off below the knees.

'This man killed three people: his wife, his six-year-old daughter and, when we tried to apprehend him, a CIA agent named Malcolm Johnson.'
click

Blaine Tanarive: A charred, rotted corpse, little more than a skeleton coated with gossamer green fibers.

'This one also killed his family,' Murray said. 'We found him after he'd died.'

John wasn't smiling anymore. He stared at the last picture. 'What happened to him?'

Murray looked at the picture for a moment, then turned back to face John and his staff.

'Once the hosts die, their bodies decompose at an extremely advanced rate. Corpses break down to nothing but a blackened skeleton in less than two days.'

John watched Donald, Vanessa and Tom. That had always been his strength, the ability to watch people, to understand them from facial expressions, posture, movement.

Tom looked like he wanted to vomit. Donald clearly believed. Vanessa was starting to. And in believing, Vanessa grew more and more angry. Most people wouldn't have seen it, but John knew her better than most. A secret like this, kept from the American people . . . she would want someone's head. Unfortunately for Murray Longworth, that head would likely be his.

click

Perry Dawsey: A giant of a man lying on a hospital bed, eyes closed, chest exposed, arms and legs locked down with heavy canvas straps. A black, oozing sore on his right collarbone, white bandages covering his right forearm, tubes going into his nose and arms.

'Perry Dawsey,' Donald said. 'I know that name. Isn't he that football player who went crazy and murdered his friend? "Scary" Perry Dawsey?'

Murray nodded. 'Dawsey is the only known survivor. He had seven parasites, which he cut out of himself, removing the final one five weeks ago.'

'Jesus Christ,' Vanessa said. 'Look at this body count, and you kept it secret? What are you, some kind of monster?'

Now it was Murray's turn to smile a little. John immediately disliked that expression – it was the smile of a hunter. Murray Longworth clearly loved the game, and he was used to winning, no matter what the cost.

'Funny you should mention monsters,' Murray said. 'We put together a team to investigate the situation, led by CIA operative Dew Phillips. Through Phillips's work we discovered that the parasites leave the human host and became free-moving organisms.'

If the Oval Office hadn't had such a nice rug, you could have heard a pin drop.

'Murray,' John said, talking slowly, choosing his words carefully. 'Are you telling us that these triangular growths . . . *hatch* out of *people*?'

'That's correct, Mister President,' Murray said. 'We even refer to them as hatchlings.'

'And then what?' Donald said. 'Do they *walk* on their own or something?'

'That's correct, Mister Secretary,' Murray said. 'Not only do they walk, they operate as a unit. Hatchlings tried to build and activate a construct that we believe is either some kind of gateway or a weapon. This is footage shot by army soldiers in Wahjamega, Michigan.'

Murray cued the video. The quality was fairly good. John saw soldiers, trees and then something deeper in the winter woods . . . something *glowing*. It looked like a big archway, maybe twenty feet high at the apex, an illuminated wedding band half-buried in the muddy forest floor. Inside of that he could see three more arches, each smaller, each farther back. It was like looking into a glowing cone.

And *creatures,* scurrying over the arches like termites on a rotten log. A strange skin growth was one thing, but this . . . this wasn't even remotely *possible*. John felt a cold tingle wash over his skin. If this *was* real, then it had to be . . . what? Aliens? Demons? This just couldn't be happening.

'No way,' Vanessa said. 'There's no way that's real. Why are you wasting the president's time with special effects?'

'It's real, ma'am,' Murray said.

John leaned forward for a closer look, his ass barely on the edge of his chair. 'Just what the hell are those supposed to be?'

'Hatchlings,' Murray said. 'You get a better look, right about . . . now.'

The video grew shaky as the hatchlings suddenly rushed forward to attack. The shot angled sharply before the first creature reached the troops, probably as the soldier shooting the footage dropped the camera. Murray paused it there. John stared at a tilted close-up of a pyramid-shaped creature with angry, vertical black eyes and tentacles for legs.

Again, total silence.

John Gutierrez had made a career out of sizing people up. That innate skill had taken him from mayor to state senator. It had been key in adding Vanessa to his staff. When he met her, he *knew*. Her skill and ruthlessness had guided him from state senate into Congress, and now the White House. An amazing feat, considering that John was forty-six years old and the nation's first Hispanic president. John Gutierrez trusted his eyes, his instincts – and those tools now told him that Murray Longworth wasn't bullshitting anyone.

This was real.

'What the hell are we dealing with, Murray?' John asked. 'You're not going to tell me these are aliens, are you?'

'That's our best guess, sir,' Murray said. 'The technology is way beyond anything we know. We suspect that the hatchlings are a form of biological machine, designed to build the glowing structure.'

John wanted to kill Hutchins. The former president might as well have left a giant, steaming pile of shit on the Oval Office rug. Now the problem rested squarely in John's lap, and no matter what happened, the public would associate this with his presidency, not Hutchins's.

'Wahjamega,' Donald said. 'Wait a minute, that's where the Osprey helicopter crashed back in December. Eight soldiers died.'

'A cover story,' Murray said. 'There was no crash. The eight soldiers died when we attacked and destroyed the gate.'

Donald looked around the room in disbelief, as if he were waiting for Vanessa or John or Tom to say *gotcha*.

But no one said *gotcha*.

'Simply amazing,' Vanessa said. She sounded sarcastic, but also quite shaken, and John couldn't blame her. 'The families of these brave men may never know the truth. They died in battle, and we list it as a helicopter crash. How *patriotic* of us. So what's happened since then?'

'Dawsey needed serious medical care,' Murray said. 'We had him in a VA hospital in Ann Arbor, Michigan. Seems he recovered faster than expected, got access to a computer, hacked into the facility's database and altered his security status. It's a bit embarrassing to say, but on January eighth he just walked out.

'The parasites built something in his brain, some kind of mesh structure that lets him track down infected hosts. He found one that had just murdered three people. Dawsey killed the man in self-defense. Before the man died, however, Dawsey discovered the location of another gate, in—'

'Mather, Wisconsin,' Donald interrupted. 'The Osprey crash in Mather. Twelve men dead.'

Murray nodded.

'Who knows about this?' John asked. 'The whole story, who knows?'

'The Joint Chiefs,' Murray said. 'They had to implement President Hutchins's decision to sequester the soldiers involved and reassign them to a new unit. The soldiers themselves know they fought something unusual, but very few people know the whole story: Phillips, Montoya, Braun, Agent Clarence Otto – who's Montoya's CIA liaison – the CIA director, Hutchins and a few members of his staff.'

'What about the FBI?' Vanessa asked. 'The CIA has no domestic police authority. You shouldn't be doing any of this.'

'The FBI does not have detailed knowledge,' Murray said. 'Once again, we were acting on the direct orders of President Hutchins.'

Vanessa stared at Murray and shook her head. John knew she had her sights firmly set on the man: she was going dinosaur hunting. It would be up to Murray to fend off her attacks and to prove his worth.

But how much more did the man need to prove? A behavior-altering human parasite, at least two military operations on U.S. soil that resulted in casualties, what might very well be alien machines . . . *and no one knew.* The media didn't even have an inkling. John now understood why his predecessor raved about Murray Longworth.

'We still don't really know what we're up against,' Murray said. 'We haven't been able to capture one of those hatchlings alive. The ones we kill disintegrate very quickly, within a few hours. Even the gate material breaks down almost immediately, so that hasn't given us any information.'

'How do we know that these things are truly hostile?' Donald said. 'They attacked our troops, I understand, but could that be a defensive action, to protect this construct long enough for them to . . . I can't believe I'm even saying this out loud . . . long enough for them to make contact?'

'A race that technologically advanced could initiate at least a rudimentary communication,' Murray said. 'The only logical reason they haven't is that they don't *want* to. They build only in remote areas. Why not build whatever it is out in the open? Because if they did that, our military could surround them and prepare for whatever came through. That's not a problem unless you're bringing in *your own* military units. This seclusion indicates they want to insert assets, assets that could be vulnerable during the insertion process.'

'A beachhead,' Donald said. 'They want to control a landing zone.'

Murray nodded. 'That's our assessment, Mister Secretary. And finally, look at the behavior of the infected victims. These parasites represent a level of bioengineering we can't even fathom. Could something capable of utilizing a human host like that *accidentally* create behavior that makes the host *avoid* contact with health-care professionals? Or kill people very close to them, people who might see the welts and call for help?'

Murray stopped talking. He stood motionless, his hands by his sides. Donald, Vanessa and Tom all turned to look at John. He took a long sip of water. What the fuck was he going to do with Hutchins's little going-away present?

He set the water down.

'Donald,' John said. 'In your position as secretary of defense, do you think these things are hostile?'

Donald nodded. 'Based on what we've been told, yes.' He looked at Vanessa. 'And you?'

She looked as if it pained her to say the words. 'I also would agree, but *based on what we've been told*, Mister President, we have to go public with this.'

'Are you fucking *nuts*?' Murray said. He looked at everyone in the room, then stood a little straighter. 'My apologies for my outburst, but this is a bad time to go public. Doctor Montoya is developing a test that will detect the disease. We have Phillips's team in place, and we're actively seeking additional hosts.'

'Trust the people,' Vanessa said. 'We need to tackle this as a nation.'

John leaned back in his chair. Nothing like a major, possibly historical decision to kick off his presidency in style.

'Murray,' John said. 'How long until the test is ready?'

'We can't say for sure,' Murray said. 'At least a week, but we won't know if it works until we find more hosts.'

Opening up this can of worms to the public . . . now might not be the time. Murray Longworth had kept things secret for five administrations; John imagined he could do the same for a sixth.

'Two weeks,' John said. 'I want two weeks to evaluate the situation. Let's get that test working and move from there. And, Murray, keep this thing quiet.'

Murray nodded. He looked pleased, as if somehow he'd known all along that this was how the meeting would turn out. John couldn't miss his small smile.

John could also see that Vanessa didn't miss it, either.

DAY ONE

TAD TAKES A LEAP

They were going to get him.

Tad wasn't going to let that happen, even if he had to kill himself.

The window slid open.

Curtains blew back, thrown by the same nighttime wind that splashed cold rain and bits of ice into the face of Thadeus 'Tad' McMillian Jr.

He hoped his little brother wouldn't wake up. When Sam woke up, he cried loud. Real, *real* loud. His cries always brought Mom and Dad.

Mom and Dad, who wanted to *get* Tad.

Tad got down off of his toy box. He picked up the box and lugged it over to his brother's crib. Carrying it hurt the blisters on his hands, but he had to stand on the toy box to reach inside the crib, just like he needed it to reach the sliding window's latch. Tad set the box down next to the crib, stood on top and reached in to pull the blankets up tight under the baby's chin. That would keep Sam warm. Tad gently brushed his brother's hair, then leaned in and kissed the baby on the forehead.

'Good-bye,' Tad whispered.

He got down and lugged the box to the window one last time.

'Good luck, Sam,' Tad said quietly, looking back at his brother. 'I really hope you don't wind up like Sara.'

Tad held on to the window frame as he put his feet up on the metal sash. Freezing rain instantly soaked his shirt. Bits of wet ice stung his face. A gust of wind almost blew him back, but he adjusted his balance and held on.

It was better this way. *Anything* was better than staying here.

Tad McMillian jumped into the night.

OGDEN GETS READY TO RUMBLE

Not too far outside of South Bloomingville, Ohio, in the hushed darkness of winter woods, Colonel Charlie Ogden stood tall behind a loose line of nine men. The men were his personal squad, Fifth Platoon, X-Ray Company, Domestic Reaction Battalion. X-Ray Company was the unit's official name, but in the usual testosterone-stoked spirit of the military the men called themselves something else.

They called themselves the Exterminators.

The boys had even come up with unit insignia: a lightning bolt hitting an upside-down cockroach. They wore it on the right shoulder. Under it they added small black triangle patches for each combat mission, and decorated the triangle with a white X for each monster killed.

Ogden's sleeve had two black triangles. The first triangle bore two white X's. That was because Colonel Charlie Ogden didn't sit in a Hummer miles from the action. He led from the front. And when you led from the front, sometimes you had to fight.

But that didn't mean he was stupid – his personal squad was the best of the Exterminators, men who could chew rusty Buicks and shit stainless-steel nails. The fifth platoon of any company usually consisted of support staff, drivers, armorers – mostly noncombat troops – but since Ogden could do just about whatever he wanted, he'd given himself a personal guard that could jump into any fight at any time.

On Ogden's left stood Corporal Jeff Cope, his ten-pounds-too-heavy communications man. On his right, the swarthy Sergeant Major Lucas Mazagatti, his top NCO. Behind him, observing, stood the overly tanned Captain David Lodge, commander of Whiskey Company, and Lodge's massive, intense sergeant major, Devon 'Nails' Nealson.

'Give me an update, Corporal,' Ogden said.

'Third Platoon will be in position, due west of the target, in ten minutes,' Cope said. 'Fourth will take up security posture to the northwest of target in twenty minutes. First and Second platoons in position just ahead of us, sir.'

The 120 men of X-Ray Company were almost ready.

'Excellent,' Ogden said. 'Air support?'

'Predator drones to northeast of target,' Cope said. 'Four Apaches on station one mile out. Target is painted, the Apaches can destroy it at any time. Two F-15Es with GBU-31s on station five miles out. Two more F-15Es in reserve, seven miles out.'

'Very well.'

He turned to face Captain Lodge. 'How about you, David?'

'Whiskey Company is a mile due west, Colonel,' Lodge said. 'We're ready to go.'

Nealson leaned forward to speak, or more accurately for his six-foot-three frame, he leaned down. 'Any chance we'll get in on this one, sir?' He said it a bit loudly for Ogden's taste, but for Nealson that was a whisper. His regular speaking voice was three or four times that of a normal man's, and his shout would make you look for a place to hide.

'Nails,' Ogden said, 'the only way Whiskey's involved is if we're overrun and I drop bombs on our own position, then you guys come in to clean up whatever is left. So let's hope you get to take the night off. Lodge, I want you and Nails back with your men twenty minutes before the attack begins.'

Nealson returned to an at-ease stance. He looked disappointed. Lodge tried not to look relieved, but he clearly was. Lodge was an exceptional pencil pusher, but perhaps not a true warrior soul.

Only one question remained – what new tricks did the little bastards have in store?

Ogden looked through night-vision binoculars, taking in all the details of their objective, two hundred yards due north. He stared at the glowing, now-familiar shape. It consisted of two twenty-foot-long parallel objects that resembled big logs lying side by side. The log structures led into a set of four curving arches, the first about ten feet high, the next three successively larger with the final arch topping out at around twenty feet. All of the objects, both logs and arches, had an irregular, organic surface.

But something was different this time.

The last two times he'd seen such a structure, all the pieces had been much thicker: thicker logs, thicker arches. This one looked kind of . . . anorexic.

Mud surrounded the thing, the result of snow melted by the structure's heat. The first two constructs had put off a huge heat bloom. Satellite readouts had measured them both at around 200 degrees Fahrenheit. This one held a steady 110 degrees. And one other key difference: the first construct, in Wahjamega, Michigan, had shown action, something going on *inside* the cone, only an hour after heating up. This one had been hot for almost three hours.

But there was still no movement.

At Wahjamega they'd seemed to catch the hatchlings off guard. The creatures had been crawling all over the construct, and when they'd detected Ogden's men, they'd attacked. The battle had been something out of a nightmare – pyramid-shaped monsters sprinting forward on black tentacle-legs, rushing right into automatic-weapons fire. Some of the monsters made it past the bullets, forcing his men into brutal, close-quarters fighting.

Eight men died.

Three weeks after Wahjamega, Perry Dawsey had discovered another construct in the deep woods near Mather, Wisconsin. Ogden's primary objective was to capture or destroy the Mather construct before it could activate, but the brass had given him a secondary objective: capture a living hatchling. But that time it was the hatchlings that caught the Exterminators off guard. The creatures had actually set up a perimeter about a hundred yards around the construct. They'd been hiding up in the damn trees; his men literally walked right under the things. When the Exterminators closed to about seventy-five yards from the construct, the hatchlings had dropped down and attacked from behind.

As soon as they dropped, the construct activated. In the confusion of hand-to-hand, Ogden had no idea of the enemy's numbers. The whole unit might have been overrun, so he didn't hesitate – he called in air support to make sure he completed the primary objective. Apache rockets tore the thing to pieces.

That hadn't left much to study, not that it mattered; just like at Wahjamega, the broken pieces of construct dissolved into pools of black goo within hours of the Apache strike. His men also failed to capture a hatchling, but Ogden wasn't about to lecture them – it was a little much to expect men ambushed by monsters to worry about anything other than survival.

Twelve men died in that fight.

From a purely tactical perspective, casualties weren't a problem. Charlie Ogden's unit was so far into a secret black budget that even light probably couldn't escape. He needed replacements? He got them. He needed equipment? Whatever he wanted, including experimental weapons, even ten Stinger surface-to-air missiles just in case some flying thing came out of those gates. Resupply? Transport? Air support? Same deal. Ogden took orders from Murray Longworth. Murray interfaced directly with the Joint Chiefs and the president. It was a heady bit of power, truth be told – no requisition, no approval, just tell Corporal Cope to place a request and things showed up as if by magic.

The blank check for men and equipment was key to mission success. So was an open-ended flexibility that let him move instantly, without orders, without approval, to wherever the danger might lie. He had to be flexible and fast, because the Mather engagement showed a clear change in hatchling tactics. They had *expected* an infantry assault. They had *learned* from the first encounter, learned and adapted.

That chewed at Ogden's soul. His men had killed all the hatchlings in Wahjamega, and they hadn't found anything that might be communication equipment. How had the Wahjamega hatchlings communicated with the Mather hatchlings?

Despite the change in tactics, the hatchlings still lost at Mather, which meant they'd likely change tactics again

– so what was Ogden facing this time? His men had scanned the trees. Scanned *everything*. Normal vision, night vision, infrared, advance scouts. Nothing other than the hatchlings on the construct. No picket line, no perimeter. Odgen couldn't figure it out. They seemed to be waiting for his men to come in.

He had his objectives, his attack options. The first option, use infantry to take the construct intact. Should that fail, hit it with the second option —Apache rockets. If needed, the Strike Eagles would deliver the third option: dropping enough two-thousand-pound bombs to turn a one-square-mile patch of Ohio into a burning crater. That would kill all his men and Ogden himself, but if it came to that, they'd have already been overrun.

Should that *third* option fail, the president would have no choice but to authorize what had been dubbed simply *Option Number Four*.

And Charlie Ogden really didn't want to think about that.

He checked his watch again. Fifty minutes. Normally he'd attack as soon as the men were in position. He could still do that if he saw the need, but this time things were going to be a little different.

This time he'd have an audience. A career-making audience, the kind that could move him from a colonel's eagle to a general's star.

Charlie raised the night-vision goggles again and stared at the glowing construct. He hoped Murray could keep things on schedule at his end, because in fifty minutes, president or no president, Charlie Ogden was going in.

TAD, MEET MR. DAWSEY

Tad's shivering brought him out of it.

He rolled on the grass, wondering if he was already dead. His shoulder hurt real bad. He didn't *feel* dead – he was still moving. When people jumped out of windows on TV, they hit the ground and didn't move. He rolled to his butt. Cold water seeped into the seat of his jeans.

Tad slowly stood. His legs hurt real bad, too. He took a deep breath, the rain and bits of ice splashing inside his wide-open mouth. He looked up, at the second-story window open to the night sky. Weird – it seemed like such a big drop from up in his room, but from down here it was about as high as a basketball hoop.

It didn't matter how high it was or it wasn't. He was out. Out of the house.

Okay, so he wasn't dead . . . but he wasn't going back in there, either.

Tad ran. His legs hurt, but they worked, and that was enough. He sprinted out to the side of the road and turned left. He pounded down a sidewalk cracked by tree roots and slick with slush.

He sprinted hard. He looked up just before running headlong into a man.

A *huge* man.

Tad stopped, frozen on the spot. The man was so big that Tad momentarily forgot about the house, his mom, his dad, his sister, even little Sam.

The man stood there, lit by a streetlamp that formed a cone of mist and light and wind-whipped, streaking rain. He looked down out of glowering blue eyes. He wore jeans and a wet short-sleeved, gray T-shirt that clung to his enormous muscles like a superhero costume. Long blond hair matted his head and face like a mask. A big, baseball-size twisted scar marred the skin of his left forearm.

The giant man spoke. 'Are you . . . ?' His voice trailed off. His eyes narrowed for a moment. Then they opened, like he'd just remembered something very cool. 'Are you . . . Tad?'

Tad nodded.

'Tad,' the man said. 'Do you feel *itchy*?'

Tad shook his head. The man turned his right ear toward Tad, tilted his head down a bit, as he might have done if Tad was whispering and he was trying to hear.

'This is important,' the man said. 'Are you *sure*? Are you really, *really* sure you're not itchy? Not even a little?'

Tad thought about this carefully, then nodded again.

The man knelt on one knee. Even kneeling, he still had to bend his head to look Tad in the eye. The man slowly reached out with a giant's hand, placing his palm gently on Tad's head. Thick fingers curled down around Tad's left temple, while a thumb as big as Tad's whole fist locked down on his right cheek.

Tad kept very, very still.

The man turned Tad's head back and to the right.

'Tad, what happened to your eye?'

Tad said nothing.

'Tad, don't piss me off,' the man said. 'What happened to your eye?'

'Daddy hit me.'

The man's eyes narrowed again.

'Your daddy hit you?'

Tad nodded. Or tried to – he couldn't move his head. The man stood. Tad barely came up to his belt.

The man let go of Tad's head and pointed back the way Tad had come. 'Is that your house?'

Tad didn't need to look. He just nodded.

'How did you leave?'

'Jumped out the window,' Tad said.

'Run along, Tad,' the man said. He reached behind his back and pulled out a long piece of black metal, bent at one end. Tad recognized it from when he and his family were on that trip to Cedar Point last summer, when Dad had to fix a flat.

It was a tire iron.

The man walked down the road, heading for Tad's house.

Tad watched him for a few seconds. Then he remembered that he was running away, and what he was running away from. He sprinted down the sidewalk.

He made it one block before he stopped again. Who knew that running away would have so many distractions? First that great big superhero man, now a car accident. A fancy red and white Mustang and a little white hatchback, smashed head-on. The Mustang's trunk was open. The little white car's driver's-side door was also open. The inside light of the hatchback lit up a man lying motionless, his feet still next to the gas pedal, his back on the wet pavement.

The man had blood all over his face.

And he was holding a gun.

There was another man in the passenger's seat, not moving, leaned forward, face resting on a deflated air bag.

Over the pouring rain and the strong wind, Tad heard a small voice.

'Report!' the voice said. 'Goddamit, Claude, report!'

Tad knew he should just keep running. But what if his parents came after him? Maybe he needed that gun.

Tad walked up to the man lying on the pavement. Rain steadily washed the blood off the man's face and onto the wet-black concrete.

'Baum! Where are you?'

The voice was coming from a little piece of white plastic lying next to the man's head. It was one of those ear receivers, just like they used on *Frankie Anvil,* his favorite TV show. Maybe this man was a cop, like Frankie.

Cops would take him away, protect him from Mom and Dad.

Tad looked at the earpiece for a second, then picked it up. 'Hello?'

'Baum? Is that you?'

'No,' Tad said. 'My name is Tad.'

A pause.

'Tad, my name is Dew Phillips. Do you know where Mister Baumgartner is?'

'Um . . . no,' Tad said. 'Wait, does Mister Baumgartner have a big black mustache?'

'Yes! That's him, is he there?'

'Oh,' Tad said. 'Well, he's lying on the ground here, bleeding and stuff.'

'*Shit,*' Mr. Phillips said. 'Tad, how old are you?'

'I'm seven. Are you the police?'

A pause. 'Yeah, sure, I'm a policeman.'

Tad let out a long sigh. The *police*. He was almost safe.

'Tad, is there another man around, a man named Mister Milner?'

'I don't know,' Tad said. 'Is Mister Milner like, really, *really* big?'

'No,' Mr. Phillips said. 'That's someone else.'

'Oh,' Tad said. 'Mister Milner might be the short guy in the passenger seat, but he looks dead. Can you send someone to get me? I'm not going back home.'

Mr. Phillips spoke again. This time his voice was calm and slow. 'We'll send someone to get you right away. Tad, listen carefully, that really big man you talked about . . . is he there with you now?'

'No, he's gone,' Tad said. 'I think he's going into my house.'

'Your house?'

'Yes sir. I live right down the street.'

'Okay, hold on to that earpiece. We'll use it to find you. Give me your address, and then whatever direction you saw that big man walking, you run the *opposite* way. And run fast.'

THE SITUATION ROOM

The elevator opened at the bottom level of the West Wing. Tom Maskill and Murray Longworth walked out. Murray had made many trips to the White House in the past thirty years, of course, but none this significant, and none with this caliber of an audience: the Joint Chiefs of Staff, the secretary of defense, the chief of staff and, of course, the president.

There were actually two Situation Rooms under the White house. The first one could handle about three dozen people. That was the one seen on TV shows, in movies and in newscasts.

They walked right by it.

Tom led him through mahogany doors into the smaller of the two Situation Rooms. Like its more famous counterpart, this room sported mahogany paneling and nearly wall-to-wall video screens. This one, however, was more discreet. One mahogany conference table ran down the middle of the room, six chairs on either side. Very few people even knew that this room existed – it was mostly for situations unfit for public consumption.

Military men filled the chairs on the table's left side (the president's left, of course). Next to the president sat Donald Martin, secretary of defense, then General Hamilton Barnes, chairman of the Joint Chiefs of Staff, army general Peter Franco, air force general Luis Monroe, Admiral

Nathan Begeley, head of the navy, and finally the highly opinionated, buzz-cut-wearing General Monty Cooper, marines.

Vanessa sat on the other side of the table, first chair to the right of the president. Then Tom's chair, then the space for Murray. Empty chairs lined the walls. These were usually occupied by junior officials, assistants, but today everyone was flying solo. They couldn't afford a leak. Maybe Gutierrez still wanted to reveal everything to the public, but at least he understood that until such a time came, they couldn't afford extraneous eyes and ears.

'Mister President,' Murray said. 'The attack is scheduled to begin in forty-five minutes. If I may, sir, I'd like to take advantage of the time to bring you up to date on another development.'

Gutierrez sighed and sagged back into his chair. Murray couldn't blame him for showing frustration – what with the Iranians, increased hostility between India and Pakistan, the Palestinian complications, Russian troops rattling sabers over Arctic oil and, of course, Project Tangram, it had to be the longest first eight days in office any president had ever faced.

Gutierrez stayed slouched for a second, then sat up again and straightened his coat. It seemed a clear effort to look more presidential. He nodded at Murray.

'We've detected another possible host location,' Murray said. 'Near Glidden, Wisconsin.'

'Is that anywhere near Bloomingville, where Ogden is going to attack?' Gutierrez asked.

'*South* Bloomingville, sir,' Murray said. 'And no, it's about seven hundred miles away. Glidden is near Michigan's Upper Peninsula.'

'Is there another construct?' Vanessa asked.

'We don't know yet,' Murray said. 'Dew Phillips is in Glidden, trying to find parasite hosts who could identify the construct's location. He's using Perry Dawsey to track down the hosts.'

'*Dawsey?*' Vanessa said.

'He's under control,' Murray said.

'Under control,' Vanessa said coolly. 'I did a little fact-finding. When infected, Dawsey killed his friend Bill Miller. He killed Kevin Mest, the person who gave him the Mather location, and then it seems you forgot to tell us he burned three little old ladies to death to get the South Bloomingville location.'

Murray blinked. How had she found out about that?

'That was self-defense,' Murray said.

Vanessa raised her eyebrows. 'Three women in their eighties, Murray? Self-defense?'

The president's eyes narrowed. 'Murray, is this true?'

She'd saved this up and sprung it on him, right in front of the president.

'Yes, Mister President, but I'm not kidding about self-defense. Those ladies were infected. They tried to fire-bomb Dawsey with a Molotov cocktail. Apparently, he caught it and threw it back.'

'That's five deaths,' Vanessa said. 'Tell us, Murray, why are you still using him?'

'We don't really have a choice, ma'am,' Murray said. 'As I've explained, the only reason we've found any of the gates is because Dawsey can track these hosts.'

'I understand that,' Vanessa said, her voice dripping with contempt. 'Your bloodhound picked up the scent. Now send in professional soldiers, not Phillips and his pet psycho.'

Donald cleared his throat. 'Vanessa, Ogden's men are already deployed. I don't think Murray has a choice here.'

She shot Donald a glare that spoke volumes. 'Ogden has four hundred eighty men in the DOMREC,' she said, using the military acronym for Domestic Reaction Battalion. 'Four companies of a hundred twenty men each. Ogden is going in with X-Ray Company and he's got Whiskey Company on reserve there, right?'

Donald nodded.

'That leaves Companies Yankee and Zulu on the ground at Fort Bragg,' Vanessa said. 'So why the hell aren't we using them instead of Dawsey and Phillips?'

'We need to be subtle,' Murray said. 'Glidden is a town, not the deep woods. If we drop two companies on Main Street, USA, that might attract a little attention.'

'And a rampaging psychopath won't?' she said.

'That's enough,' Gutierrez said. 'Murray, I'm sure you took steps to keep Dawsey in check, am I correct?'

'Yes, Mister President,' Murray said. 'We have two seasoned agents following Dawsey at all times. Dawsey will locate the hosts, then these men will move in, take Dawsey down if necessary and secure the hosts.'

General Cooper knocked twice on the table. 'This is all good and fine, but we have an attack to monitor here,' he said in a voice so gruff it almost sounded like a caricature of how a marine general *should* talk. 'Not to speak out of turn, Mister President, but there's information we need to share so you know what you're seeing when the attack begins.'

Gutierrez nodded. 'Thank you, General Cooper. Murray, before we focus on Ogden's attack, I want to make something clear. We know that this is a crisis situation and Americans may get hurt, but we don't need them getting hurt by the people who are supposed to be solving the problem. Understand?'

'Yes sir,' Murray said. 'I do.'

Murray did understand the need to control Dawsey – he just hoped Dew Phillips understood it as well. Vanessa Colburn wasn't playing around. She clearly wanted Murray gone. And as much as he disliked that woman, she was right about one thing . . .

That kid *was* a fucking psycho.

YOU SHOULDN'T HIT YOUR KIDS

Dew Phillips ran a red light at the intersection of Grant and Broadway. He'd even put the port-a-bubble on top of his Lincoln, its circling light playing off the sheets of pouring rain. Fuck secrecy. He had two men down. That murdering kid was going after hosts again.

Dew wondered if any of the infected would be alive by the time Margaret arrived.

Thadeus McMillian Sr. sat at his kitchen table, bouncing his five-year-old son, Stephen, on his knee. Stephen wore his favorite fuzzy yellow pajama bottoms and a little Milwaukee Bucks T-shirt. Looked so damn cute. Stephen was the good child. Tad Jr.? Not a good child. Sara? Not a good child.

Thadeus pushed the thoughts away. He didn't want to think about his daughter.

A dozen empty beer bottles stood on the table, leaving wet ring-stains on the map spread across the table's surface. There were more beer bottles on the floor, along with a half-empty fifth of gin. He didn't drink gin. His wife, Jenny, guzzled the stuff.

The fucking alcoholic bitch.

She'd been a three-martini-a-day girl up until Junior started acting up. Since then she'd skipped the martini glasses altogether and started pouring gin right into her favorite Hello Kitty coffee cup. Every time she took a sip, that stupid cartoon cat seemed to stare at him.

Limping along on one crutch, Jenny hobbled into the kitchen. She couldn't put weight on the foot, which was understandable if you saw the thing (and Thad had no desire to ever see it again). Jenny's insistence on keeping Ginny Kitty in hand at all times complicated the crutch-walk even more.

She stopped just past the open doorway between the kitchen and the stairway that led up to the kids' rooms.

She stared at him. So did that fucking cat.

'What are we gonna do about that boy of yours?' she asked.

Thadeus shrugged. 'Dunno.'

'He's a bad influence on Stephen and Sammy,' she said. 'I don't know why you let him run wild.'

'Look, I grounded him,' Thadeus said. 'What else can we do?'

'You can discipline him,' she said. Thadeus looked away, ashamed. He *had* disciplined the boy . . . maybe a little too much. He'd hit his own son. Right in the face. Not *slapped,* but *punched.* How could he do that to his own flesh and blood? And yet the boy was acting so crazy. Something had to be done.

'Thadeus,' Jenny said, 'we have to go, you know we do. They're almost done, and we haven't even left yet. We can't take Junior, and we can't leave him behind, either.'

He nodded slowly. Maybe Jenny was right. For fourteen years, ever since their first date, he'd been able to count on her for sound advice. Maybe she could see the obvious when he couldn't, he didn't know. Maybe she just cared for him enough to give tough love.

He hung his head, stared absently at the back of little

Stephen's head. Junior had always been his favorite. You weren't supposed to have a favorite child, he knew, yet he couldn't change the fact that Junior lit up his heart just a little more than the others. Maybe that was why he'd been so lenient.

'All right, Jenny,' Thadeus said. 'Get him in here.'

Jenny leaned back so she could shout up the steps to the second floor.

'Junior! Come into the kitchen! Your father and I want to talk to you.'

She leaned forward again, resting heavily on her crutch. They heard Tad's bedroom door open. It always squeaked. Thadeus kept meaning to oil the hinges, but hadn't gotten around to it.

'You've got to have a firm hand,' Jenny said flatly. 'You must not waver. You must be strong, just like you were with Sara.'

Sara. He didn't want to think about Sara.

Tad stomped down the stairs, stomped fast.

But how could a little boy sound so heavy?

Thadeus watched Jenny lean back into the hall again.

An arm, a huge arm, lashing down, a hissing sound like a golf club swinging just before it hits the ball.

Then a dull, wet thonk, like the sound of a watermelon dropped on the floor.

Jenny's head snapped down, then limply bounced back up but only halfway. The very top of her head wobbled like shaking Jell-O. She managed one staggering step, then dropped to the floor. Her Ginny Kitty cup landed with a ceramic clank, spilling four shots' worth of liquor onto the kitchen's linoleum.

Thadeus's grip on little Stephen tightened as he stood. He started to come around the table, heading to the kitchen counter to grab a knife, a frying pan, *something*, when the monstrous man turned the corner.

Thadeus McMillian Sr. froze in his tracks.

'Holy fuck,' he said.

The huge, wet, blond nightmare stood in his kitchen doorway. Thadeus had seen a man that big once. *Almost* that big. He'd met Detroit Lions' defensive tackle Dusty Smith in a bar. Dusty was six-foot-four, 270 pounds. More like a refrigerator with legs than a human being.

This guy was bigger than Dusty Smith.

And Dusty Smith hadn't been holding a tire iron.

In one hand the man held the tire iron that had just killed Jenny. In the other massive hand, he held Thadeus's baby, Sam. He wasn't cradling Sam; he was holding the tiny baby the way you might pick up a toy doll that's been left on the floor. Thumb and forefinger circled Sammy's little neck, the three remaining fingers wrapped around Sammy's yellow-pajama-clad body.

Sammy's eyes were closed.

Oh no it's him!

The voices in Thad's head. They had been quiet most of the evening.

It's the sonofabitch!

'I'm here to help you,' the sonofabitch said.

Little Stephen raised an arm and pointed at the man. He spoke in his baby-boy voice.

'Da-dee,' he said. 'Kill dis moderfucker.'

Stephen suddenly squirmed and kicked. Thad dropped him. The little boy fell clumsily, but scrambled to his feet. Stephen's little Milwaukee Bucks T-shirt slid up when he stood, exposing a light blue triangle on the skin at the small of his back. The boy screamed a murderous, gravelly battle cry that sounded almost comical from such a tiny voice, then charged the giant man.

The sonofabitch took a step forward and kicked, swinging his hips into the blow. Stephen made a little staccato sound when the foot connected, a half-cough, half-squeal. His small body shot across the room like it had been fired from a cannon. With a sickening snap, Stephen's right side slammed into the edge of the kitchen table. The impact tilted the table back, spilling beer bottles onto the linoleum before it rocked back to level. Stephen's body, still bent at an odd angle to the right, hit the floor.

The boy's little fingers twitched a bit, but other than that he didn't move.

Thadeus reached the counter, yanked open a drawer and pulled out a butcher knife.

Yesss kill him KILL HIM!

He turned to face the man murdering his family, but as he did, he saw a flash of spinning black, then his head filled with a sudden darkness and pain. He fell to the floor, blinking, thoughts slipping in and out. He tried to spit. A chunk of tooth barely escaped his lips and hung on his right cheek, plastered there by blood and saliva.

Get up, get up!

A hand around his neck, lifting him.

His feet, dangling.

Kill him, KILL HIM!

His breath . . . nonexistent.

Thadeus opened his eyes. The man-monster's face was only an inch away. Two days' growth of reddish beard. A snarl. Thadeus stared into blue eyes wide with madness.

'You shouldn't hit your kids,' the man said.

Thadeus heard an approaching siren, but it was too

late. The hand around his neck might as well have been an iron vise. It squeezed, slow and steady.

'It's okay,' the man said. He smiled. 'I'm here to help you.'

B r e a t h e ! said the voice in his head, the same voice that had made him kill his only daughter.

Fight! You have to breathe!

Thadeus felt his bladder let go, felt the heat of piss filling his underwear and jeans, then felt his sphincter offer up the same betrayal. Even in the act of dying, he somehow had a flash of embarrassment.

He would've liked to have said one last thing. He would've liked to tell the voices in his head to stick it where the sun don't shine, but he couldn't make any noise at all save for a tiny, hissing gurgle.

THE MARGOMOBILE™

Margaret Montoya, Clarence Otto and Amos Braun sat in comfortable seats in the customized sleeper cabin of a semi tractor-trailer. The massive eighteen-wheeler rolled north along Highway 13, followed closely by a second, outwardly identical rig. The two trailers, designed to work together as one unit, were worth about $25 million and had come to be known collectively as the 'MargoMobile.'

The three sat biggest to smallest, a cross section of cultures – Clarence's chocolate skin and tall, muscular bulk on the left; Margaret with her long black hair and Hispanic complexion in the middle; and the diminutive, oh-so-Caucasian Amos on the right. Those two men constituted one half of Margaret's team. The other half drove the rigs. Anthony Gitsham handled this one, Marcus Thompson drove the other. Murray's single-minded mission to keep 'those in the know' to the absolute minimum had landed Gitsh and Marcus this choice assignment, thanks to their rather unique set of skills.

Both men had logged at least a hundred hours driving a semi, had medical-assistant training, combat experience and – the big one – hands-on experience with biohazard procedures and gear. Gitsh had driven army rigs in the Mideast and traded small-arms fire a few times, but Clint Eastwood he was not. Clint wasn't as pale, wasn't as skinny and didn't have a 'fro that made him look like a white Black Panthers wannabe from 1974. Marcus was something of a study in contrast to Anthony, with his deep black skin, shaved head and enough wiry muscle for both men. Marcus's combat experience, apparently, was rather extensive. He didn't talk about it, and no one asked. From what Margaret could gather, being assigned to drive a truck and lug around rotting corpses that might or might not be fatally infectious . . . well, that was like a vacation for Marcus. Maybe it was why he whistled all the damn time.

Her whole team was already dressed in black biohazard suits, completely covering them in airtight PVC material save for their exposed heads and hands. She was so used to the suit that she didn't give it a second thought anymore. A silly, uncontrollable part of her liked the fact that it hid the extra weight on her hips.

When it came time to go in, they'd all don the gloves clipped to their belts and the helmets sitting at their feet, pressurize the suits, and they'd be ready to face the latest horrors in an endless, gruesome parade.

Horrors that always seemed to involve one 'Scary' Perry Dawsey.

Margaret didn't know how or why Perry could still hear the triangles. CAT scans showed a network of very thin lines spreading through the center of his brain, like a 3-D spiderweb or a spongy mesh. While she was fighting to keep him alive, she hadn't dared risk trying to get a sample of the material. Any additional trauma on his ravaged body could have been the final straw. Since he'd regained consciousness, Perry wouldn't even talk about the incident – it was no surprise he wouldn't let anyone slide a drill into his skull.

Even if they could get a sample, it probably wouldn't

do them any good – the National Security Agency, the group that handled signal intelligence and cryptography for the government, detected no signals of any kind. The triangles and hatchlings communicated, yet no one knew how. The NSA's prevailing theory involved some form of communication via quantum tunneling, but that was guesswork at best without a shred of data to back it up.

Whatever the science behind it, Perry's homing instinct had been the only thing keeping them in the game. Unfortunately, when he found infected hosts, he killed them. First Kevin Mest, who had butchered three friends with a fireplace poker. Perry claimed self-defense for that one, and everyone bought it. His self-defense claim for burning three eighty-year-old women alive? Well, that was a little harder to swallow.

But whatever he had done, however ugly, he found the constructs. Kevin Mest's death resulted in Ogden destroying the one at Mather. The three elderly ladies Perry had burned to death? Because of them, Ogden was in South Bloomingville right now, hopefully taking that construct out as well.

Glidden would be different. Dew had said so. His men, Claude Baumgartner and Jens Milner, were watching Perry at all times. They *would* deliver live hosts. When they did, she knew she could operate on the infected and successfully remove the parasites.

Murray wanted live hosts for other reasons, reasons that created a bit of a catch-22. He wanted to interrogate the triangles. Good in theory, but Margaret would operate to remove any growths she found. If that killed the triangle but saved a host, too bad for Murray. Her job was to save lives, not keep someone chained up as a parasite interpreter.

Clarence studied a map resting on his knees. He wiped sweat from his forehead with the back of his hand, then let out an exasperated sigh.

'Come on, Margo, this suit is annoying,' he said. 'I'm taking it off.'

'Clarence, give it a rest,' Margaret said. 'I don't want to go over this again.'

'But there's no purpose for this thing,' Clarence said. 'Dew has been around dozens of corpses – he hasn't contracted anything.'

'Yet.'

Amos smiled. 'You look like a black Stay Puft Marshmallow Man. It's not a good look for you.'

'And you look like a short KKK grand dragon who washed his whites with his darks,' Clarence said. He looked at Margaret again. 'And what about Dawsey? You fixed him up, you didn't start growing triangles. This suit is making me sweat, and sweaty is *definitely* not a good look for me.'

Margaret would beg to differ on that. She'd seen CIA agent Clarence Otto all sweaty, seen him that way up close and personal, been all sweaty herself at the same time, and she couldn't imagine a better look for him.

Amos laughed. 'You serve up a softball about being all sweaty? I'm not even touching that one. Seriously, Otto, you have to make it a little harder to make fun of you two boinking whenever you think no one is looking.'

'That suit will stop microbes,' Clarence said. 'But I'm afraid it doesn't offer much protection against a pistol-whipping.'

Amos laughed again and held up his hands palms out: *okay, okay, take it easy.*

Clarence talked tough, intimidating gravel voice and all, but over the past three months he and Amos had become fast friends. Clarence Otto was just flat-out likable. Witty, helpful, respectful and with a major streak of deductive common sense, he often put a strategic perspective on Margaret and Amos's scientific discoveries. As for Amos, his multidisciplinary expertise and sheer brilliance had helped the team stay one step ahead of the infection. More like a half step, maybe, but at least they were still ahead.

At some point in the past three months, both men had revealed a love for basketball. Otto, a former Division III point guard and a lifelong fan of the Boston Celtics, discovered that short, frail little Amos Braun had a wicked outside jumper. Well, calling it a 'jumper' was a stretch – he came off the ground *maybe* three inches when he shot. Amos couldn't play one-on-one to save his life. At a game of H-O-R-S-E, however, he could beat Otto six times out of ten. Amos was also a lifelong hoops fan, although he preferred the Detroit Pistons, giving the two men plenty to argue about in the many hours when there wasn't a corpse on the autopsy table.

'Clarence,' Margaret said, 'no one has been infected by contact, but that doesn't mean the disease isn't contagious. There could also be toxins we haven't seen yet, or something else that could hurt you. That suit will keep you safe, so it stays on.'

Otto sighed. 'Yes sir.'

'You made her this way,' Amos said. 'I remember when Margaret was a total pushover. You're the one that got her on the Gloria Steinem express, all women-libbed and everything.'

'I know, I know,' Otto said. 'I wish I'd kept my mouth shut. Keep her barefoot and in the kitchen.'

'Don't forget pregnant,' Amos said. 'But you're working on that.'

Margaret felt her face flush red. 'Amos! Knock it off!'

'Amos, my diminutive white friend,' Otto said, 'you're just mad that a fine-looking black man is getting all the action.'

'Fine-looking until you put on that suit and get all sweaty,' Amos said. 'Then you look like a half-chewed Tootsie Roll.'

Margaret sighed. The juvenile name-calling never ceased. She just didn't get men.

Otto smiled and nodded, which meant he had a killer comeback, but his cell phone chirped before he could speak. There was only one person who would be calling. Clarence answered.

'Otto here.' He listened. His smile faded into an expression that was all business. He pinched the cell phone between his shoulder and ear, then looked at the map.

'We'll be there in three minutes.' He hung up.

'What's the matter?' Margaret asked.

'Baum and Milner are down,' Otto said. 'A kid named Tad found them, said Dawsey was going to his house.'

Otto leaned forward to give Gitsh directions.

Margaret cursed under her breath. If Perry got to the hosts first . . .

LESS LETHAL

Staccato gunfire echoed through the woods as Third Platoon opened the engagement, making the dark western tree line sparkle with bright muzzle flashes. First Platoon waited exactly three minutes, then pushed due north, straight toward the construct. Second Platoon swept east and curved north, ready to flank the hatchlings should they flee directly away from Third Platoon's fire.

Fourth Platoon held their position. If the hatchlings fled northwest, they'd run directly into the Fourth. If they ran due north, the Fourth would strafe their flank the whole way.

Predator drones circled low to the northeast, ready to launch Hellfire missiles that would either herd the hatchlings back into the action or kill them outright.

There was nowhere for the creatures to run.

Ogden watched through night-vision goggles, ready to adapt his strategy if something unexpected popped up.

But nothing did.

'Corporal Cope, status of air support?'

'Apaches, Predators and Strike Eagles still on station, sir,' Cope said. 'Ready if you need them.'

'Very well.' Ogden watched as First Platoon moved in, methodically marching forward in a squad-after-squad leapfrog style that allowed a steady advance with constant fire on the enemy position. As First Platoon closed in, Third Platoon ceased fire to avoid any friendly casualties.

Two soldiers in each nine-man squad carried a less-lethal weapon. Like all the platoons, First had three squads, putting six less-lethal weapons into the initial infantry assault.

Such weapons had once been called *non*lethal, but in combat there was never a guarantee of preserving life. If you killed half the people you fought instead of all the people . . . well, then that wasn't actually *non*lethal, now was it?

They didn't know what would work against the hatchlings, so they'd brought two less-lethals: the sticky gun and ShockRounds.

The sticky gun fired jets of foam that would, theoretically, tangle the hatchlings' tentacle-legs. The guns had been used with mixed success against people in Somalia – the 'mixed' part was that the foam sometimes got in the targets' eyes, blinding them, or clogged up their mouths. Put a clogged mouth together with hands immobilized by that same foam, and within minutes you had a dead target. Somewhat unacceptable against human targets, but hatchlings were a different story – it was worth the risk.

Compared to sticky guns, the ShockRounds seemed almost normal – 5.56-millimeter bullets that delivered a concentrated electric charge. These were untested, but his men didn't have to do anything different from what they were trained to do – point their weapons and fire.

He'd avoided Tasers. Their range was just too short for his comfort. If electricity even worked on the hatchlings, he had that covered with the ShockRounds.

He'd brought the less-lethals assuming that the hatchlings would behave the way they had in the last two engagements – once the fighting began, they would rush the ground troops and force hand-to-hand fighting. He hoped the lead hatchlings could be taken down with a less-lethal, then the rest could be slaughtered with concentrated conventional fire.

But this time the hatchlings didn't attack.

Ogden watched the construct. The little monsters moved around the structure itself, scuttled across the ground surrounding it, but they didn't come out to engage. One by one they shuddered as bullets tore through their plasticine skins. Gouts of their purple blood looked gray through the night-vision goggles, spraying on the ground in stringy strands before the hatchlings collapsed into twitching heaps. If any of those bullets were ShockRounds, they punched through the hatchlings just like normal ammo.

Why the hell weren't they fighting back?

He had a bad feeling he knew why – another trap. Something new. He had no choice but to push forward and hope his attack plan allowed enough flexibility to react when that trap was sprung.

Corporal Cope lowered the handset and held it against his chest.

'Colonel, First and Second platoons report no resistance. Nothing is coming out to attack. They estimate enemy forces are down to maybe five or six individuals.'

'Order immediate cease-fire of lethal weaponry,' Ogden barked. 'Less-lethals move in slowly. Sticky guns first, but tell them to also try the ShockRounds and see if they have any effect. All squads are to try and take one alive. Tell the squad leaders no lethal fire unless they specifically order it.'

The last shots echoed through the woods as soldiers stopped firing the M4 carbines and M249 squad automatic weapons.

Ogden turned to face Mazagatti. 'Sergeant Major, let's move in. I want to see this thing up close.'

'Sir,' Mazagatti said, 'I wouldn't be doing my job if I didn't say that it's a stupid idea for you to get that close. Again. Sir.'

'Understood,' Ogden said. 'I'm feeling lucky. Again. Proceed.'

Mazagatti flashed hand signals to Ogden's personal squad. Ogden drew his sidearm and followed. Corporal Cope trailed a step behind and to the right, radio at the ready.

With the gunfire gone, Ogden heard the nonlethals: the *whoosh* of the foam guns and the normal-sounding reports of ShockRounds. He followed the platoon to within seventy-five yards of the construct before he ordered all platoons to halt. First Platoon was only forty yards away now; a quick sprint would take them right into the construct.

Ogden saw the hatchlings scurrying around inside the glowing arches. Triangular bodies, three tentacle-legs that looked like muscular black pythons. The point of the shortest hatchling would come up just to his knee, the tallest one to his chin.

The sticky foam seemed to be working, reducing two hatchlings to weakly wiggling lumps on the muddy ground, unable to pull those tentacle-legs loose. He counted another five hatchlings moving freely, but they didn't engage. Did they fear the weapons? Were they aware that the less-lethals might isolate them? If so, why didn't they at least run north? Why didn't they try *something*?

Ogden again sensed a trap – the enemy wasn't behaving rationally or consistently with the previous two encounters. But trap or no trap, he had his orders.

'Corporal Cope, tell First Platoon to move in. Capture the enemy by hand.'

Cope spoke into his handset and relayed the orders.

Thirty-five yards ahead, Ogden watched a line of men rise up and silently walk forward. The three foam-gunners led the charge, each flanked on the immediate left and right by comrades carrying M4s. The rest of each respective squad fanned out on either side of this lead element.

Ogden watched. The hatchlings seemed to sense the advance. They clustered tighter around the base of the smallest arch.

First Platoon closed to thirty yards. Then twenty. The line of men rushed forward through the snow, moving in. . . .

A spark flashed somewhere beneath the hatchlings, at the base of the arch. Was this it? Was it opening up?

Another flash, then a steady glow backlit the hatchlings. This new illumination showed only at the base of one arch. It flickered, jumped, then Ogden recognized it for what it was – fire.

Blue-flamed, not orange, but fire nonetheless. The flames crawled up the arch as if it were made of tinder, shooting along the curve almost like a flamethrower.

All five of the free-moving hatchlings jumped into the flames, igniting themselves. They scampered toward the stuck hatchlings, setting them aflame before running into the other arches and the loglike things, spreading the blaze. Within seconds the whole construct danced with crackling blue flames.

Heat pushed his soldiers back, stopping their advance as surely as a wall.

'Tell the men to fall back and set up a perimeter at

fifty yards,' Ogden said. 'And don gas masks – we don't know what kind of fumes that thing might put out.'

It wasn't an ambush. He had a feeling it was something worse.

Not a trap . . . a *decoy*.

STIMULATING CONVERSATION

Dew arrived at Tad's house only a few seconds behind two unmarked gray vans. The vans parked on the street while he drove his Lincoln onto the wet lawn just before the vans unloaded hazmat-suited gunmen. No one parked in the driveway; they needed to keep that open for the MargoMobile.

Dew got out and instantly felt cold rain splattering the bald top of his head. He hadn't made it fifteen steps before his suit jacket was soaked through. He walked briskly but didn't run – the two young bucks in full black hazmat suits took care of that. Each toted a compact FN P90 submachine gun, as did their two hazmat-suited comrades who took up positions on the lawn.

One of the young bucks hit the front door with a hard kick, smashing it open. He went in, followed by his partner.

Dew slowly counted to ten, giving the young men time to secure the house. Hearing no gunfire, he walked inside.

The two men were in a living room that stood between the front door and the kitchen. Neither of them moved – they had their P90s pointed at a huge, wet man sitting at the kitchen table.

A man drinking a Budweiser with his right hand and holding a blinking baby with his left.

A tire iron sat on the table. Where it bent ninety degrees, it shone with wetness. A clump of scalp and long brown hair clung to the black metal.

A dead woman lay in the open doorway that led out of the kitchen. Dead, Dew knew, because living people's heads just didn't look like that, living people's eyes didn't hang open with a blank expression, and living people usually weren't lying in a big puddle of their own blood.

A dead toddler lay on the ground at the edge of the table, only a few feet from Perry's canoe of a foot. The kid's back was broken, his spine bent in the middle at a forty-five-degree angle.

The place smelled like someone had shit their pants.

Dew drew his Colt M1911 pistol. He held it at his side, pointed to the ground. 'How did you get in here?'

'Back window,' Perry said. 'Only about ten feet up. I can still jump pretty good for a guy who once got shot in the knee.'

Dew ignored the dig. 'You crazy fuck. We needed these people.'

'I helped them,' Perry said.

'I wish I could just shoot you and put you out of your misery.'

'Gosh, I *am* awful miserable,' Perry said. 'So go ahead.' He took a swig.

'You gonna kill that baby?' Dew asked, as calmly as you might ask someone to please pass the salt.

'No, the baby is clean,' Perry said. He casually tossed the baby toward one of the soldiers. Dew twitched reactively as the child softly arced through the air. The soldier dropped his P90 and awkwardly caught the kid, who started crying immediately.

Crying *loud*.

The baby hadn't cried when he was sitting with the psycho who had just butchered his family, but as soon as he was safe, he fired up the air-raid siren. There's just no figuring kids.

'Both of you, get that baby out of here,' Dew said to the soldiers. 'Get him in a van and keep him there. I'll send a guy to check him out. Doc Braun, real short, you'll know him when you see him.'

The men left, leaving Dew alone with Perry.

Dew started to shiver from his wet suit and shirt. The weather in Wisconsin was much like the weather in Michigan – both fucking sucked, and both made his bum hip ache.

'Any others?' Dew asked.

Perry pointed to a place inside the kitchen. Dew carefully walked to the living room's edge, leaned in a little and looked around the corner.

Another corpse, a man, lying on the floor in front of the refrigerator. A big dark spot covered the crotch and legs of his jeans. He was the source of the shit smell.

Three more hosts, dead. Murray Longworth was going to crap a canary when he found out. Three murders. Just like that. And Dawsey sat at the table, sipping a Bud.

It would be so easy to just put a bullet in the psycho's head.

Perry pulled a second beer from the six-pack and tilted it toward Dew. *Want one?* the gesture said.

'Drink up while you can,' Dew said. 'If Baumgartner and Milner are dead, I don't care how important Murray thinks you are.'

'Were those the dumb-shits following me in the little white car?'

Dew nodded.

Perry shrugged, drained his beer, then opened the one he'd offered Dew.

'Control, this is Phillips,' Dew said. The microphone in his earpiece picked up the words and transmitted them to a control van some five or six blocks away.

'Copy, Phillips,' the tinny voice said.

'Status on Baum and Milner? Anyone find them yet?'

'Let me check,' the voice said.

Dew waited.

Dawsey took a long swig. 'I bet you want to shoot me. I bet you want to kill me.' He tossed the gold Budweiser cap up and down in his free hand.

'Maybe I just want to *help* you,' Dew said quietly.

Perry grinned and nodded. 'That's pretty good.'

The tinny voice returned. 'Baumgartner and Milner are alive. Agent Revel says they're roughed up a little but will be okay. Ambulance en route. Their car and Dawsey's Mustang are totaled, by the way.'

Dew put his .45 back in its shoulder holster.

Dawsey smiled. 'I told you not to have anyone follow me, Dew. I could have killed them if I wanted do.'

'What the fuck is wrong with you, Dawsey? We've told you a million times we need a live host.'

'I'm not a soldier,' Perry said. 'Your orders don't mean dick to me.'

'We need information, you murdering piece of shit. These people had information.'

'I have all the information you need,' Perry said. He cleared away the beer bottles, revealing a ring-stained map spread across the table. His sweeping hand also brushed aside a clump of hair that had fallen off the tire iron, leaving a long, bloody arc on the paper. He wiped his hand on his pant leg.

'The next doorway is northeast of here,' Perry said. 'Across the border into Michigan. Nearest town is called Marinesco. That's where these people were going. If anyone else around here is infected, that's where they're headed, too, or they're already there. That's the information you really need, and now you have it, so why would you need these losers alive?'

'Losers? That one you snapped in half couldn't be more than five years old.'

'Sure,' Perry said. 'And any knife he could pick up, he'd put it right in your belly. *Why* do you need him alive?'

Dew ground his teeth. 'Because the eggheads say so, that's why.'

Perry nodded. 'Right. They need to watch someone suffer. They need to watch someone go crazy. They need to watch someone go through what I went through, right?'

Dew said nothing.

'You're stuck with me, old man,' Perry said. 'I'm the only one who can hear them. I'm the only one who can *find* them. My ass is made of gold.'

Dawsey was completely out of control. Dew understood the kid being messed up, sure. Only five weeks ago, Dawsey had snipped off his own jumblies for fuck's sake. Dew could sympathize with some anger, some depression, even post-traumatic stress disorder, but *this*?

Still, part of Dew couldn't shake the thought that if he treated the infected the same way Perry did, his partner, Malcolm Johnson, would still be alive.

'Perry, you have to stop this,' Dew said. 'Margaret thinks she can save these people. How can she do that if you keep going apeshit?'

'She can't save them,' Perry said. He drained the bottle in one pull and opened a third. 'Trust me, I know what I'm talking about. I'm all the help these *people* need.'

Dew stared at the gigantic man for a few more moments. For the third time – and the second in the past three days – Dawsey had located a construct.

Dew remembered the horror of that first construct. So hot it melted the snow around it. Watching it light up, the whole thing glowing brightly, then the vision of thousands of creatures coming *through* the gate, almost pouring into the woods before a dozen HEAT missiles launched from Apache attack helicopters blasted the thing to bits.

'That's two new doorways in a pretty short time,' Dew said. 'You think there's more?'

Perry shrugged. 'I dunno. I can't really explain it. I hear – what's the word you spy guys use? I hear *chatter*. More might be coming. I can't say. But you better get it in gear, old man, instead of sitting here with your thumb up your ass – I think the Marinesco one is well under way.'

Dew pointed at Dawsey. 'You stay *right here*. I'm going to call this in, then I'll take you back to your hotel.'

'Thanks, Pops,' Perry said. 'Oh, and have your peons get my bag out of the Mustang's trunk. And speaking of Mustangs, I'm going to need another one. Make sure it's a GT. I'd prefer blue with a silver strip this time, but I'll take whatever color you can get. I wouldn't want to be difficult.'

Not only was Dawsey a freak, a killer, he was a smart-ass as well. Dew stared at him, wondering if maybe he should just pull the gun out again and end it.

The gun . . . that brought up an interesting question.

'You had Baumgartner and Milner down,' Dew said.

'They're both packing. Why didn't you take their weapons?'

He saw something flicker in Perry's eyes, a flicker that only appeared in the rare, brief instances when he talked about triangles or hatchlings – was it fear?

'Guns are for pussies,' Perry said. 'I find a tire iron has more of a Charles Bronson flair.'

Dew stared for a few more seconds, then picked up the map and walked out of the house. As he left, he saw the first of the two MargoMobiles pulling up into the drive. When Margaret found out she had nothing to work with, she would not be happy.

WHIPPED

The semi's air brakes hissed as the tractor slowed and stopped.

The McMillian house wasn't much to look at, a typical boxy three-bedroom, two-story affair, once-white paint now cracked, peeling and speckled with dark spots of exposed and well-weathered wood. Big yard, old trees devoid of leaves. Two gray vans were parked on the street, and she guessed that the nondescript black Lincoln in the lawn belonged to Dew.

The downpour was actually a welcome break – icy rain would keep curious neighbors inside. A few might peek outside at the commotion, but as long as they didn't try to cross the perimeter, that was fine.

Gitsh craned around the driver's seat to look at Margaret, his 'fro bouncing a bit with each movement. 'Should Marcus and I go ahead and connect the trailers, prep the examination room, ma'am?'

'Yes, Gitsh,' Margaret said. 'Thank you.'

He got out and closed the driver's-side door. *Examination room* was a funny phrase. That's what they all called it, of course, but so far they hadn't done any examinations – only autopsies. Not exactly ironic, considering that this two-trailer setup had originally been designed for on-site postmortems of infectious-disease victims. If you had an unknown, lethal contagion, it made more sense to analyze the corpses where they died rather than haul them to a Biohazard Safety Level-4 lab. No matter how secure the transportation, you were still at risk of spreading the contagion somewhere along the route. A portable BSL-4 autopsy facility, on the other hand, let you not only analyze the body on the spot but incinerate it as well.

A few seconds after Gitsh shut the driver's door, the passenger-side door opened and a soaking Dew Phillips climbed in. Bits of ice clung to his bald scalp and the ring of red hair that circled around the back of his head from temple to temple. He looked tired, wet and pissed off.

'One survivor,' Dew said. 'An infant boy, in the van on the right. Doc Braun, can you check him out? He's not infected.'

'How do you know?' Margaret asked.

'Because if he was, Perry would have killed him. Just like he did the three people that were.'

Margaret sagged back into her chair. They were too late. Again.

'I'll check out the child, Dew,' Amos said. 'But I have to wonder why you government types can't control Mister *It Puts the Lotion in the Basket.*'

'He put Baum and Milner in the hospital,' Dew snapped. 'Maybe *you'd* like to try and control a six-foot-five murderer who can probably bench-press this whole rig?'

Amos shook his head. 'No way. That alkie scares the fu-schnickens out of me. Make sure that psycho is gone from the house before I go in, or I'm not even getting out of this vehicle.'

'Tiny white man makes a good point,' Clarence said. 'Dew, can your guys get the eunuch out of here?'

Dew nodded, tiredly. Margaret sat forward.

'No,' she said. 'I want to talk to him first.'

'Forget it, Margo,' Clarence said. 'What the hell is wrong with you?'

'First of all, the man's name is Perry, not *the eunuch*, not *Mister It Puts the Lotion in the Basket* and not *that psycho*. Second, nothing is wrong with me.'

'*Something* is wrong with you,' Dew said. 'Didn't you hear me say he just killed three people?'

'Yes, and I also heard you say he didn't kill the baby because the baby isn't infected. He didn't kill the boy who found Baum and Milner, and, I might add, he didn't kill them, either. I'm not infected, so I'll be fine.'

'No way,' Clarence said. 'He's probably drunk again. Dew, is he drunk?'

'If not, he's on his way.'

'See?' Clarence said. 'That's it, Margo, you're not going in there.'

'He's right,' Dew said. 'Forget it.'

'Quorum carries,' Amos said. 'Moving on to new business, the chair recognizes Senator Gonzales from Topeka.'

'All of you just *shut up*,' Margaret said. 'We can't have Perry killing the hosts. Someone has to get that through to him.'

'Don't worry about that,' Dew said. 'You can bet the next time he gets a sniff, he'll be in handcuffs and leg irons before we track it down.'

Amos laughed. 'Handcuffs? He'll probably just eat them.'

'Handcuffs?' Margaret said. '*Leg irons?* After the tortures that man has faced, you think you can get through to him by putting him in chains?'

'He just *killed* three people,' Clarence said. 'Someone please tell me I'm not hearing this bleeding-heart-liberal bullshit.'

'Margaret,' Dew said, 'you need to pull your head out of your ass.'

'*Stop it!*' Margaret shouted. 'All of you, just stop it! We need to figure out why Perry is doing this, and we need to figure it out now. He's my patient, did you guys forget that? I'm the one who kept that rot from killing him.'

'Hey, I helped,' Amos said.

Margaret waved her hands dismissively. 'Yes, of course you did. That's not what I meant. I know that Perry is extremely dangerous – I'm not an idiot. But since we discovered he can find hosts, he's run loose. He could have taken off anytime he wanted to, but he hasn't. And yet you keep him isolated from everyone.'

'You're goddamn right I keep him isolated,' Dew said. 'That's what you do with a psycho. Forget it, Margaret. You're not going in there.'

'The action is over,' she said quietly. 'There's nothing but bodies in that house, so now it's my call.'

'Whoa, Nellie,' Amos said. 'I hear a glass ceiling shattering somewhere.'

'I'm not kidding,' Margaret said. 'This is now an analysis situation, which means that *you*' – she pointed at Dew – 'and *you*' – she pointed at Clarence – 'have to do what *I* say. Am I right?'

The two men said nothing.

Amos leaned forward. 'I'm afraid that's what Murray ordered, gents.' He pointed to his head. 'Photographic memory and all. Not as cool as carrying a gun, but being smart does have its uses.'

Dew threw up his hands. 'You know what? Fuck this. I have to go contact Colonel Ogden. Making sure nothing happens to Margaret is your job, Otto. Good fucking luck.'

Dew got out of the truck, slamming the door behind him as hard as he could.

'This is bullshit,' Clarence said.

'I'm going to the back to get body bags,' Margaret said. 'Amos, you come help me. Clarence, if you're so worried about my safety, get in there and tell Perry to stay put. Feel free to threaten him, because that's what you men do and it seems to work so well. But put on your hood *and* gloves before you go in!'

Margaret crossed in front of Amos to go out the sleeper cabin's passenger-side door. Like Dew, she slammed it shut behind her.

Clarence sat in silence, shaking his head.

Amos unsuccessfully tried to choke back laughter.

'Something funny?' Clarence asked.

'*Put on your hood and gloves,*' Amos said. 'If you weren't so pissed already, I'd probably make fun of you.'

'Now is not the time, Amos.'

'I said I *would* make fun of you. I'm not actually making fun of you. Big difference. Man, I can only imagine what that woman is like in the sack.'

'In the bedroom I'm in charge,' Otto said sullenly. 'Unfortunately, that seems to be the *only* place I'm in charge.'

'You're whipped.'

'I don't see you backing her down.'

'Everyone knows *I'm* whipped,' Amos said. 'My wife, my daughters, Margaret – not exactly a news flash. But you, Mister Alpha Male? You go ahead and carry the illusion that someday you'll be able to change the situation.'

'Fuck you, midget. And help me with these gloves.'

Amos held the gloves so Otto could slide his hands inside. Amos made sure the connecting rings snapped home, then ran sticky tape around them.

'Hey,' Amos said. 'Twenty bucks says Dawsey kills you.'

'You're on.'

'I'll take it out of your locker if he does,' Amos said. 'Wouldn't look right me rifling through the pockets of a corpse.'

'Whatever. If you win, I guess I won't really be worried about appearances.'

Both men fitted slim earpiece wires around their right ears. Each wire frame contained a small speaker that fit into the ear canal, a microphone and a transmitter that routed into the MargoMobile's communication center. The sets were on a predefined frequency, same as Dew and the other agents used. They let the scientific team communicate with one another as well as monitor any communication between Dew and his team.

Otto pulled on his black helmet. Amos helped him seal it, then ran a line of sticky tape around the metal collar. Otto held out his right hand, exposing the suit controls mounted in the inner wrist. Amos simply pressed the 'on' button, and the compressor mounted on Otto's belt started up with a nearly silent hum. His suit's heavy PVC fabric billowed up slightly, the result of higher pressure inside. Should the suit suffer a tear, air would flow outward, theoretically keeping any contagions or toxins away from his skin until the suit could be repaired and decontaminated.

'I'm off to make twenty bucks,' Clarence said.

'Been nice knowing ya,' Amos said. 'See you on the other side.'

Otto nodded, then opened the wide sleeper-compartment door and hopped down. The icy rain bounced off his black suit as he walked toward the house.

GETTIN' HIS DRINK ON

Perry finished his fifth beer. A blessed buzz started to work its way through his brain. He stood up and walked to the fridge. The door wouldn't open all the way. It was partially blocked by the body of the man who had shit all over himself. Perry put a foot on the man's hip and slid him to the right.

Inside the fridge he found another six-pack of Budwesier. Okay, so maybe the dead guy hadn't had any discipline, but at least he hadn't been one of those microbrew pussies.

Holding the fresh six-pack, Perry stepped over the body and sat back down behind the table just as another black-suited man came into the kitchen. This one carried only a pistol. Through the suit's clear visor, Perry saw the oh-so-serious face of Agent Otto.

'Hey, Clarence,' he said. 'You look like a fat ninja.'

'Thanks,' Otto said. 'That means so much coming from a source of wisdom like you.'

Perry opened the bottle and drank it in one pull. Six down. Five more and he'd be nice and hammered. Everyone has to have goals in life, right?

Otto slowly looked around the room, surveying the damage. 'Were you drunk when you killed these people?'

'They're not people,' Perry said. 'And no, I was not drunk, but I mean to correct that situation.' He opened the second bottle and drained half of it before putting it down.

'I guess so,' Otto said. 'Listen, man, you know you scare the crap out of me, right?'

Perry shrugged. That was the way of things. Didn't matter what he did, what he said, they looked at him like he was a monster. So why not live up to the billing?

'Margaret is coming in here,' Otto said.

'Sure she is,' Perry said. 'Look at all the new toys she has to play with. See this one?' He nudged the dead little boy with his foot. 'I call him Slinky.'

'Save me your psycho jokes,' Otto said. 'Just understand that when she's in this room, you make any sudden moves and I'll put you down.'

'Oh, come *on*, Clarence! A gun? Don't *be* that guy! How about you and I settle this the old-fashioned way?'

'Forget it.'

'What's the matter, Clarence? Massa Dew say you can't play with the white kids?'

Behind the helmet visor, he saw Clarence's eyes narrow.

'Go ahead, *boy*,' Perry said. 'Take a swing. I won't tell on you.'

Perry hoped he would do it. Otto was big enough to count as a challenge. Not much of a challenge, but something. It would feel good to smash in his face.

He had nothing against Otto, really. Except that Otto was fucking Dr. Montoya, which meant he was getting laid, which was something Perry figured *he'd* never do again. If that wasn't a good enough reason to hand out a beat-down, he didn't know what was.

'I'll pass,' Otto said. 'You can save all that macho bullshit. Only one way you and I are going to dance, and that's if a bullet takes the lead.'

'Oh, that's horrible,' Perry said. 'Did you write that shit yourself?'

Perry thought he saw Otto smile, just a little bit, but then the stone face slipped back into place.

Margaret came into the room carrying a double armful of green bags. She dropped them in a pile. In her black suit, she looked identical to Otto except that she was a foot shorter. Standing side by side, they looked like the adult and child versions of an alien from a bad sci-fi flick.

'Hey, Otto, your other massa is here,' Perry said. 'Wake up, white people. The Jew is using the black as muscle.'

'I'm not Jewish, Perry, I'm Hispanic,' Margaret said. 'And I've got *The Blues Brothers* on DVD, seen it about fifty times, so I know that line. Next are you going to tell me you hate Illinois Nazis?'

Good God. She knew *The Blues Brothers*?

'I also know you're not racist,' she said. 'So stop trying to push everyone's buttons. You're not good at it.'

Perry wondered if Clarence Otto really had any idea just how cool this chick was. He hated everyone in this fucked-up project, but he had to admit he hated Margaret a little less than the others. He tilted a fresh beer toward her.

'You want a beer, *chica*? I tried to offer your boy Toby one, but he told me the only good whitey was a dead whitey.'

Margaret sat down at the table, opposite the little body on the floor. She did it so casually it could have been a normal scene in any kitchen, save for her black biohazard suit and the corpses.

'No, Perry, *Clarence* didn't say that. And no, I don't want a beer, but thank you. You've got to stop this.'

'Stop drinking? Why, what a great idea. Sobriety has

done so much for me.' He finished the beer and grabbed another. The buzz was really kicking into gear now. He wanted it, needed it to take over so he could forget. If he got drunk enough, maybe he could sleep.

'Perry,' Margaret said, 'look around you. Look what you've done. You *killed* these people.'

'Why do you all keep saying they're *people*? They were the walking dead.'

'No they *weren't*, damn it. I saved you, didn't I?'

'And what a delightful experience that was.'

'I know it was painful,' she said.

Perry laughed. 'Yeah. *Painful*. By the way, you sure your last name isn't Mengele, not Montoya?'

'Oh, you can just kiss my ass, Perry,' Margaret said. 'I saved your life. Amos and I figured out how all by ourselves, because trust me, your disease wasn't exactly listed in Wikipedia. I know it hurt, but I saved your life – and you compare me to Josef Mengele? How about instead you just say *thank you for saving my life, Margaret*.'

'And you said I wasn't good at pushing buttons.'

It was funny how clearly you could see emotions through one of those visors. Margaret's eyes narrowed, and her upper lip wrinkled up just a bit. Frickin' adorable.

'Don't forget, Doc, I gave you quite a head start,' Perry said. 'I didn't have any triangles when you got to me, remember? And you can look around all you want, but you won't see any Chicken Scissors laying around. These people didn't even *try*.'

She looked away. Everyone did when he mentioned the scissors. She took a slow breath, then looked at him dead-on again.

'Perry, I learned so much from helping you recover. I can *save* these people. Why do you think Dew is trying so hard to bring them in alive?'

Perry looked at Margaret, looked into her brown eyes. She had saved his life, that was true. Most of the time he wished she hadn't.

It was so hard to believe there was a person as good as Margaret left in the world. It was also hard to believe there was a person this naive.

'You're kidding yourself, lady,' Perry said. 'You can't save them.'

'I can, Perry, and I will. We need your help, more than just finding the hosts. You still won't tell us anything about your experience. Do you know how frustrating it is when the one person who survived won't tell you the most basic information?'

Perry shook his head. 'I don't talk about that.'

'I've noticed,' Margaret said. 'Look, everyone understands it's traumatic. Believe me. You have to overcome this. I know you don't want to think about what happened with Bill, but—'

'*Don't* talk about him!' Before the words were even out of his mouth, Perry leaned toward her and banged the table hard with his fist. Margaret flinched, eyes wide in surprise and fear. Clarence's gun came up, leveled right at Perry's chest.

Perry quickly leaned back. Goddamit. He'd lost it. Scared Margaret. That was the last thing he wanted to do.

Margaret looked back at Clarence. 'Put that damn thing down.'

Clarence lowered the gun.

'My bad,' Perry said.

She put her gloved hand on his forearm. 'Don't worry about it. I'm sorry to bring up awful memories, but you've got to start doing the right thing.'

'The right thing?' He stood and set a fresh beer bottle on the table in front of her. A gift. She wouldn't drink it, but it's the thought that counts.

'You're a smart cupcake, Margo,' Perry said. 'But you don't know the right thing here. Trust me, the right thing is to let me help them.'

'Like you helped these people?'

Perry nodded. 'Exactly.'

He started to walk out, then stopped and turned to face her. 'And that suit, Margaret. That's the worst suit I ever saw. You buy a suit like that, I bet you get a free bowl of soup.'

'But it looks good on you,' Margaret said. '*Caddyshack*. I own that one, too.'

Perry smiled and gestured toward Otto, who looked horribly uncomfortable at the whole situation. 'Margie, you're too cool for Mister Funbags over there. Enjoy your new playmates.'

He walked out of the kitchen, hoping that one beer he'd left Margo wasn't the one that would have pushed him over the top.

He needed to sleep. Sleep, without hearing Bill's voice.

NOTHING IN THIS HAND

Dew waited in his car while Anthony Gitsham and Marcus Thompson connected the two semi trailers to make the MargoMobile fully operational. The two trailers weren't really trailers, they were flatbeds, each carrying a container that was eight feet wide by ten feet high by forty feet long. As standard-size cargo containers, the things could easily be transported by rail, by ship or even by air with a cargo helicopter. Once combined, the two containers made for a highly portable BSL-4 autopsy facility.

Painted blue and scuffed up a bit to make them look rusty and well used, they didn't rate a second glance on the highway. But it was only the outsides that looked beat up – the inside areas gleamed with the pristine whiteness of a high-tech hospital.

Three months ago there'd been no such thing as a mobile lab rated for BSL-4. That was as bad as it got – ebola, Marburg, superflu, shit like that. Some company had had the trailer on the drawing board. Margaret found out and insisted it was just the thing for the crazy, secret work of Project Tangram. Dew had agreed. So had Murray, who'd funded the rush job on a prototype and then ordered two more. At a this-week-only sale price of $25 million each.

Fuck it, Murray had said, *it's only taxpayers' money*.

The things you could do with a black budget. When

the trailers were delivered and the team checked them out, Amos had called them *the MargoMobile,* and the name just stuck.

Big dollars or no, Dew couldn't argue with Margaret – the trailer combo was a bargain at any price. The BSL-4 tents Margaret had used at various hospitals worked, but you needed to set them up, you had to deal with a concerned hospital staff, local media, et cetera. The MargoMobile solved that. You could take the full BSL-4 lab right to the bodies and do what had to be done. The thing even had a microwave incinerator, for fuck's sake – one-stop shopping from body acquisition to disposal.

The two trailers set up in parallel. From the rear, the right trailer, Trailer A, had normal cargo doors. Opening those up revealed two more doors – the cargo doors were just a front. The door on the left led into a small computer center, ten feet long by five feet wide. One thin desktop ran the length of the room. It supported three keyboard-and-mouse combinations that rested in front of three flat-panel monitors mounted on the walls. Add three office chairs and you were in business. Other equipment provided secure encrypted transmission to anyone on the trailer's frequency or could plug into a full NSA-caliber satellite uplink. Voice, video, data, whatever you needed. The communication equipment was originally meant to provide a secure connection to the CDC or the WHO, but it worked just as well for an old CIA spook.

The right-side door led into a claustrophobic, three-foot-wide airlock that ran ten feet into the trailer before it reached a second airtight door. That door opened into the eight-by-ten-foot decontamination center. In there, dozens of nozzles shot out a high-pressure combination of chlorine gas and concentrated liquid bleach. Lethal to anything from a microbe to a man. Once you got through decon, a final airtight door let into the main area: an eight-foot-wide, twenty-foot-long autopsy room. An area about the size of a typical living room to deal with the deadliest pathogens the world had to offer.

The left-hand trailer, Trailer B, held a narrow dressing room with lockers for the hazmat suits and gear. That room wasn't part of the airtight area – you had to walk into the dressing room, get suited up, then walk back outside and go through the Trailer A airlock to reach the autopsy room. Trailer B also held air compressors, refrigeration units, filters, generators, a nine-slot cadaver rack like you'd find in any morgue, and a clear-walled containment chamber designed for living hosts. That cell held two autopsy trolleys, side by side, with just enough room between them for someone to walk in, turn around and walk out. If they did have to use this cell, the host (or hosts) would likely be strapped down to the trolley: safety and secrecy, not comfort, were the rules of the day.

A collapsible covered walkway extended from Trailer B and connected directly into the autopsy room of Trailer A. That way they only needed one decontamination area to access the airtight areas of both trailers. Gitsh and Marcus were in the process of connecting the accordion-like walkway.

Dew liked those guys. Marcus was the kind you'd want by your side in a firefight. Gitsh not so much, but he always had a smile and a laugh, and on a long, isolated assignment that was just as important as being able to shoot straight. Dew checked his watch – the connection process usually took them ten minutes. Now it was eleven and counting. He'd give them some shit about that later.

Gitsh opened the door to the computer center. Dew

got out of his Lincoln, braving the rain once more to dart inside. He sat down at one of the computers, typed in his user name and password, then spread out the blood-smeared map on top of the keyboard. He grabbed the secure phone and punched in a memorized number. He still found it odd that he could dial Colonel Charlie Ogden in the middle of a field engagement and get him every time. The wonders of a high-tech army.

'Company X, this is Corporal Cope.'

'Dew Phillips. Get me Ogden.'

'Right away, sir.'

Dew waited. He held the phone with his right hand while the fingertips of his left traced an as-the-crow-flies line from South Bloomingville, Ohio, to Glidden, Wisconsin. About six hundred miles. Project Tangram had several V-22 Ospreys at their disposal. The Ospreys were perfect for their needs. They could take off and land anywhere, no runway required, courtesy of a helicopter engine on each wing. Once in the air, those engines slowly tilted forward, and the helicopter became a twin-turboprop plane. Seeing as each Osprey could carry up to twenty-four soldiers and do about three hundred miles an hour, they were invaluable for moving Ogden's troops from Point A to Point B. In a real logistical pinch, the Ospreys could even haul the MargoMobile trailers, one trailer per bird.

'Ogden here,' said the familiar voice. 'What have you got for me?'

'You first,' Dew said. 'Did you take out the construct?'

'Would I be talking to you if I hadn't?'

Dew shook his head. Charlie Ogden wasn't much for pleasantries.

'We've got something else,' Dew said. 'Punch in

Marinesco, Michigan, on whatever fancy map computer you've got there.'

Ogden barked an order to his staff.

'Got it,' Ogden said.

'We found another construct there.'

There was a brief pause. 'Okay, things make more sense now.'

'How long till you can be there, Charlie?'

'We've got our Ospreys close by. With midair refueling . . . maybe two and a half hours.'

'What about the two companies still at Fort Bragg?'

'I can send them now, but they don't have Ospreys and they're too far away for helicopters. We could get them on C-17s and drop them right in near the zone. Say thirty minutes to get wheels up, ninety minutes to fly and jump, fifteen minutes for them to gather and move in. Either way we're looking at two and a half hours best case, three hours more likely. You got pictures of this thing?'

'We're bringing satellites online now,' Dew said. 'We should have something any moment. I told the squints to send you pictures as soon as we get them.'

'Understood. Listen, I think South Bloomingville was a feint. Designed to draw our attention while they set up at Marinesco.'

'What are you saying, Charlie?' Dew asked. 'These little bastards are using high-level tactics?'

'They didn't defend themselves. When we closed in, they destroyed the construct, killing themselves in the process. And I think it was a prop.'

'A *prop*?'

'Yeah, like fake planes on a fake airstrip designed to fool satellite intel. It heated up like the other gates, but it was thinner. Just enough material to have the right shape and the right behaviors, not enough to be functional.'

Dew felt a helpless feeling spreading through his guts. 'So if this Marinesco gate is already hot,' Dew said, 'if you can't get there in time, then what?'

Ogden's voice dropped a little as he spoke to someone near him. 'Cope, order the FAC to this location.'

Dew heard a distant 'Yes sir.'

'Charlie,' Dew said, 'what the fuck are you doing?'

'I just deployed the FAC, the forward air controller. It's an F-22 Raptor fighter, fast as hell. It will acquire the target and transmit coordinates to the Strike Eagle squadron.'

'The F-15s? You're dropping fucking two-thousand-pound bombs on it? It's *Michigan,* not fucking Fallujah, Charlie. Why can't we use the Apaches like we did in Wahjamega and Mather?'

'Depends on if we can get them there in time,' Ogden said. 'If I send the Apaches now, it's a two-hour straight flight. The Eagles do Mach 2.5—they'll be there in twenty-five minutes.'

Dew's cell phone buzzed – he checked it to find a text message that was nothing but a sixteen-character code.

'I've got sat pictures, Charlie.'

'We just got them, too. Cope, up on the screen.'

Dew shoved the map aside and carefully typed in the code. A series of thumbnail images appeared, some in color, some in black and white. Dew clicked on the first black-and-white image, blowing it up to fill the screen. Most of the picture showed the black, irregular patterns of dense trees. The center of the image, however, showed a fuzzy white symbol that had come to represent the unknown terror of the infection.

White meant that the gate was already hot.

'I'm ordering a full strike,' Ogden said. 'Taking that damn thing out of the game.'

'Hold on, Charlie,' Dew said. 'The area *looks* pretty unpopulated, but we don't have any intel on the residents. Can we get some planes to make a pass? See if any people are around?'

'Phillips, I don't give a fuck if the gate is built right on top of a compound full of orphans and nuns. I'm taking it out.'

'Charlie, come on. You're talking about two-thousand-pound bombs on U.S. soil. We have to get approval from Murray on this.'

'No we don't,' Ogden said. 'I have authority from the president to make any necessary battlefield decisions up to Option Number Four. That one has to come from the big man himself. Other than that, it's my call.'

'But that order was from President Hutchins. Gutierrez probably doesn't even know about it.'

'I have my orders,' Ogden said. 'We have to strike immediately, and with force. Nice work uncovering this location, Dew. All I can say is thank God we've got Dawsey. He's the only thing keeping us in this game. Ogden out.'

Charlie broke the connection.

Dew put the handset back in its cradle.

Thank God we've got Dawsey. Imagine that. The kid was twelve doughnuts shy of a baker's dozen, and he was their ace in the hole. What would ol' Charlie have thought if he knew that Dew had almost shot Dawsey in the mouth with the .45? *Sorry, Charlie, our ace in the hole has a hole in his head.*

Dew rubbed his face with both hands, then picked up the handset again. The explosion caused by the Strike

Eagles' bomb run would be huge, probably even register on seismographs. Covering up such a thing would require spin, obfuscation and lies. And for something like that, there was no one in the world better than Murray Longworth.

YOU DROPPED A BOMB ON ME

The Situation Room buzzed with conversation. Images of the Marinesco gate lit up most of the flat-panel monitors.

To Murray there was something inherently defeating about that image. Via satellite, drone and surveillance planes, they had watched Ogden's men attack the gate in South Bloomingville. They had watched it catch fire, watched it burn and crumble, and yet here was a second gate that looked almost exactly the same.

Other monitors showed digital maps of Michigan; a green circle in the Upper Peninsula marking the gate, F-15 icons marking the position of Ogden's Strike Eagles. Those planes were just edging over Lake Michigan—they had already covered half the distance from South Bloomingville to Marinesco.

One large monitor showed nothing but a countdown: fifteen minutes, twenty-three seconds and counting. When that hit zero, the Strike Eagles would drop their payloads . . . unless the president called off the attack.

Gutierrez had given up on trying to look presidential. Small beads of sweat dotted his forehead. Despite appearances, though, he *hadn't* given in to the stress. He asked intelligent questions, he demanded intelligent answers and he had the Joint Chiefs jumping at his commands.

'Goddamit, gentlemen,' Gutierrez said. 'You can*not* tell me we have no other forces that can reach Marinesco and attack that gate in the next fifteen minutes.'

'That's exactly what we're telling you,' said General Hamilton Barnes. As Chairman of the Joint Chiefs, delivery of most military-related bad news fell to him, although Monty Cooper, the marines' top man, wasn't afraid to enter into the conversation uninvited.

'Mister President, sir,' Cooper said. 'We are in the middle of fighting two wars and a police action on foreign soil. Even if our troops were not badly depleted because of that, there is no way we could put a company-size element into play in Michigan's Upper Peninsula in less than an hour. The fastest-responding unit is the Division Ready Force, from the Eighty-second Airborne. First-response elements of the DRF can be anywhere in the world in eighteen hours, anywhere in the United States in probably seven, and you have no idea how fast that is in military terms. With all due respect, sir, we can't just wave a fucking magic wand and make troops appear.'

Barnes turned toward Cooper, obviously to lay down a fast rebuke.

'Save it, General Barnes,' Gutierrez said. 'It takes more than a little language to offend me. But don't do it a second time, General Cooper.'

'Sir,' Cooper said.

Gutierrez's eyes flicked up to the clock. Murray looked as well. Thirteen minutes, fifty-four seconds.

'How long until Company X reaches the gate?' Gutierrez asked.

'Their Ospreys just took off from South Bloomingville,' Barnes said. 'A little under two hours until they can attack. The Apaches are over an hour away.'

Gutierrez gave the table one quick, frustrated fist-pound.

'I don't understand,' Vanessa said. 'How can a colonel have the authority to launch a bombing attack like this? Doesn't he need to clear it with at least the Joint Chiefs?'

General Barnes answered. 'Ogden is the battlefield commander. He has the authority to use any elements at his disposal to achieve the objectives set before him. He doesn't need approval to deploy resources already under his command.'

'This is ridiculous,' Vanessa said. 'He doesn't need approval for anything?'

'President Hutchins set it up this way for a reason,' Murray said. 'In the time it's taken us to get the information and begin a discussion about what to do, the jets are already halfway to the target. Ogden can order Options One through Three without oversight. Only Option Number Four requires presidential approval.'

'And what, exactly, is Option Number Four?'

'The big whammy,' General Cooper said. 'Option Four is a tactical nuke.'

'A *nuke*?' Vanessa said. 'On American soil? Are you kidding me?'

'A *tactical* nuke, ma'am,' Murray said. 'We have three B61 warheads available. They're variable-yield warheads. We can dial the blast for anything from point-three megatons to one hundred and seventy.'

'Murray,' Gutierrez said, 'how could Hutchins even consider dropping a nuke?'

'We have to acknowledge the possibility that we won't see a construct in time,' Murray said. 'If that happens, it will open up and deliver that initial beachhead force. We don't know what kind of weaponry or technology we'll be dealing with at that point. We have to have this level of response in order to take out both the construct and the enemy force.'

'This is insane,' Vanessa said.

'It was approved by President Hutchins,' Murray said.

'*Hutchins* isn't the president anymore,' Vanessa said. 'John Gutierrez is.'

Murray nodded. 'And the orders of a former president stand until the current president gives new orders.'

Vanessa turned to face Gutierrez. 'So give a new order, Mister President,' she said. 'Call this whole thing off.'

Gutierrez sat back in his chair. 'These conventional bombs Ogden ordered, what kind of hardware are we talking about?'

General Luis Monroe, the air force's top man, spoke for the first time. 'The GBU-31, version three, is a two-thousand-pound bomb. It's a bunker-buster, biggest thing we've got short of a nuke. The blast will kill everything within a hundred and ten feet of the point of impact and will cause casualties at over a hundred yards. Total blast radius is about four thousand feet.'

'A *radius* of four thousand feet?' Vanessa said. 'But . . . that's a diameter of a mile and a half.'

Monroe nodded. 'They've worked very well in Iraq and Iran. If it was daylight, the smoke cloud would be visible from twenty miles. All the surrounding towns will feel the impact, probably think it's a minor tremor.'

'How the hell are we going to keep *that* secret?' Vanessa asked.

'I have a prepared cover story,' Murray said. 'This is a very rural area, remote, so it's feasible a terrorist cell set up a bomb-building facility. We learned about it, determined it was possible they were building a dirty bomb, so we sent in the F-15Es to take it out. A dirty bomb is a radiation threat, so we can lock down a large area while we investigate. Everyone wins – intelligence got the info, executive branch reacted definitively, military took out the terrorists.'

All eyes watched Murray. The Joint Chiefs weren't surprised; they'd seen him do things like this before. Donald Martin didn't look surprised, either. Working his way up to secretary of defense, he'd undoubtedly seen such lies. Gutierrez, Vanessa and Tom Maskill, however, looked astonished.

'Domestic or international terrorists?' Gutierrez asked.

Murray shrugged. 'Whichever you prefer, Mister President. I have an extensive background developed for a white supremacist group, if you want to go that route. Or we can go Al-Qaeda. Your call.'

Gutierrez rubbed his hands together slowly as he thought.

'Let's do the white supremacists,' he said. 'I can't have foreigners building a bomb on U.S. soil.'

'Yes, Mister President,' Murray said. 'I can make that work.'

'John,' Vanessa said, astonished. 'You've got to be kidding me. You're going to let those jets drop bombs *and* lie to the American people about it?'

All around the table, eyebrows raised at her use of the president's first name. She didn't seem to notice. Neither did Gutierrez.

'I just don't know what choice we have,' he said.

'We have the choice of telling the truth and trusting the people,' Vanessa said.

General Cooper laughed at her. 'Ma'am, with all due respect, where did you learn about the world, from a game of Candy Land? We're talking aliens and intergalactic gates, caused by an infection that starts as a goddamn skin rash. We tell the people about this and the country will disentegrate in total chaos.'

'I disagree,' Vanessa said. 'The people will come together for this.'

Cooper laughed again and started to say something back, but Murray interrupted.

'We need a *decision,*' he said. The screen behind the president changed from a static picture of the gate to a high-altitude cockpit-cam shot. The cool blacks and blues of a frozen Wisconsin forest raced by. A few spots glowed white as the plane passed over houses.

'The Strike Eagles will commence their bomb run in two minutes, Mister President,' Murray said. 'If you want to call this off, you have to say so right now.'

Gutierrez sat back in his chair and steepled his fingers together. He let out a heavy sigh and looked at the ceiling. Murray could sympathize. Carrying out an executive order that could result in civilian deaths was one thing; being the guy to *give* that order, that was another.

The main flat-panel monitor flared with a new light – the construct had just started to glow.

'Damn,' Gutierrez said. 'How long do we have, Murray?'

'Based on Wahjamega, maybe fifteen minutes. We're just not sure, Mister President.'

Gutierrez nodded. 'If we drop these bombs, how many people do you think could die? Off the record. Just give it to me straight.'

Murray shrugged. 'If we're lucky, none that aren't already infected. It's a very remote area, so if we're unlucky, ten at the very most.'

Gutierrez nodded. 'Proceed with the bombing. Get Tom a briefing paper that covers the high points of your cover story. Call a press conference for eight A.M. Donald, General Barnes, you'll be with me for that conference.' He turned in his chair to watch the bomb run.

Vanessa wasn't watching the screens. She was watching Murray. All the values Gutierrez had espoused while running for office had just taken a backseat to reality. In her idealistic mind, she probably blamed Murray for that. Too bad, so sad – the president was making the right choice for the country, and she'd just have to deal with it.

Within seconds the screen's cool blacks and blues revealed a white dot. That dot quickly grew in size. It was a little shaky, a little grainy, but there was no mistaking the construct's definitive fishbone shape.

A slash entered the screen from the top right. A split second later, the screen lit up in blinding white. That white quickly vanished, revealing a rising plume of smoke that started out hot-white but soon faded to a flickering light gray.

Everyone sat and silently watched. Donald finally broke the silence.

'I sure as hell hope they didn't build a third.'

AUTOPSY NUMBER ONE

Margaret watched Gitsh and Marcus push the sturdy autopsy trolley up the ramp and through the right-side door in the back of Trailer A. There was a lot of room in the body bag on that gurney, the little boy's body inside like a single pea in a pod made for three. She followed the trolley into the white airlock room, then shut the gas-tight outer door behind her. The three of them waited in the narrow airlock as the pressure inside equalized, which had to happen before the gas-tight inner door would open. Smooth white epoxy covered every surface, just as it did in all of the trailer's biohazard areas. The entire trailer, including the computer room, had a double seal – a continuous epoxy coat, then all wiring and ductwork, then a second epoxy wall. As in any BSL lab, the goal was to remove as many nooks, crannies and edges as possible.

Above the inner door, a light changed from red to green. Margaret opened the door, then followed the trolley into the decontamination chamber. Gitsh closed the inner door behind them. She stood back as the men worked controls that brought forth the high-powered spray of liquid bleach and chlorine gas from nozzles mounted on the walls, floor and ceiling. Gitsh and Marcus moved the body bag around, making sure the nozzles hit every last square inch.

Margaret spread her arms and turned slowly, letting the lethal spray cover her biohazard suit. She checked her heads-up display for breathable air – her suit tank had twenty minutes left. The decon chamber was really the only place they used the oxygen tanks. The rest of the time they connected the helmets to the trailers' air supply via built-in hoses or just relied on the filter system. The suit's filters could handle anything a half micron or larger, but chlorine gas would seep right through, burn the lungs and bring a painful death in a few short minutes.

After Marcus and Gitsh finished rinsing themselves in the chlorine spray, Margaret opened the final gas-tight door and stepped into the autopsy room. At eight feet wide by twenty feet long, this was the largest area in the MargoMobile.

Gitsh pushed the trolley all the way to the room's far end, where it locked in place at the front of an epoxy-coated sink. The two-foot-wide trolley left three feet of space on either side, plenty of room to work. He turned a knob at the foot of the trolley, raising the end one inch. The shallow angle ensured that any fluids would run down the ridges on the trolley's sides and spill into the sink, which drained into the waste-treatment system.

'Okay, guys, let's get connected,' Margaret said. Four curled yellow hoses hung from the ceiling. She reached up, pulled one down and handed it to Marcus. He connected the hose to the back of her helmet. She felt a quick hiss as pressurized air slid into her suit, making it puff up a little bit more. In her HUD the internal air-supply timer faded to a thin, ghostly illumination while the circular logo that marked an external oxygen supply glowed to life. The wireless communication icon also faded as the network connection light lit up.

'Let's get him out of the bag,' Margaret said.

After connecting their own helmets, Gitsham and Marcus unzipped the outer body bag and pulled it off. Marcus put it in a red disposal chute marked with a bright orange biohazard logo. They repeated the process for the second bag and put the child's body on the table.

Margaret couldn't suppress a shudder. His Milwaukee Bucks shirt had slid up around his armpits. Dawsey's kick had smashed at least eight of the boy's ribs, caving them inward like so much broken pottery. The child's spine was snapped on the right side of the eighth thoracic vertebra, bending him at nearly a ninety-degree angle to his right. A mask of pure rage had frozen on the boy's face, a wide-eyed, teeth-bared snarl that broadcast absolute hate even in death. She had seen faces like that too many times. The faces of the infected.

'Gitsh, get a sample in the microscope right away – I want to see the level of decomposition – then prepare the injections. Marcus, bring me the swab-test prototype.'

'Yes ma'am,' Marcus said.

'Recorder on,' Margaret said. A green light flashed in the upper right-hand corner of her HUD, signaling that everything she said and saw was being recorded in the control room.

'I'm online, Margaret,' Clarence said, his voice in her earpiece. 'I have the other bodies in the second trailer. Amos is checking out the baby, but he looks fine. Did you run the test prototype yet?'

'Hold tight, I'm doing it now.' She held out her hand and Marcus gave her a small white electronic device the size of two packs of cigarettes joined end to end. He then opened a thin foil packet and pulled out a four-inch plastic stick, the last half inch coated with damp fabric. She slid the fabric end along the boy's gum line and against the inside of his cheek.

The triangles harvested sugars common in the human body and used them to make cellulose, a material found only in plants. The cellulose formed a construction material that allowed the triangles to grow into hatchlings. Her theory was that some of the cellulose would leak into the bloodstream and eventually permeate bodily fluids, including saliva.

The prototype had few controls. The primary feature was a row of three square lights near the top: orange, green and red. She slid the plastic swab into a matching slot in the handheld device, and the orange light flashed, indicating a test in progress. The next indicator would be the green light, showing no trace of cellulose, or the red if the material was present in concentrations greater than one might find in a random grass stain.

The light flashed red.

'It works,' Margaret said. 'Clarence, the test *works*.'

'Fantastic,' he said. 'I'll let Murray know immediately. He can rush the testers into production. Great job, Margaret. That finally gives us what we need.'

'Thank you,' Margaret said. She had grown rather fond of Clarence's voice in her ear as she worked. He stayed in the computer control room, managing any requests she had, listening in to her and Amos theorizing as they cut up infected bodies.

Gitsh tapped her on the shoulder. 'The sample's up on the screen, Margo.'

She turned to look at the large flat-panel monitor mounted on the wall. She hadn't designed the trailer, but the monitor was her idea. Looking into microscopes was kind of annoying – routing them to a big plasma screen let everyone see what was going on.

The screen showed what she expected – the red, pink and white of highly magnified flesh and blood vessels, along with the gray of decomposing matter and the black of cells that were already long since destroyed by the apoptosis chain reaction. Only about 25 percent decomposed: the best sample she'd had yet. Even so, she didn't have long.

'Okay, boys,' Margaret said, turning back to the table. 'We need to work quickly.'

Anthony used scissors to cut away the boy's yellow pajama bottoms and the T-shirt, leaving his bent body naked on the table.

'Caucasian male, approximately six years old,' Margaret said. 'Severed spinal column, massive blunt-force trauma.'

Even before cutting into him, she could see that the boy's internal organs were smashed to hell.

'One triangle on the stomach,' Margaret said. 'Heavily damaged, lowest priority. One on the front upper-right thigh. Intact. Highest priority. Turn him over, please.'

The assistants flipped the little corpse. Now his broken body angled to Margaret's left instead of to her right.

'One on the lower back, just above the eighth thoracic. Completely destroyed. Lowest priority. No other triangles visible on the body. Flip him back and let's give him the injection series. Maximum dosage. I'll take the right thigh.'

They gently put the corpse on its broken back again. Marcus laid out six large syringes, each with a long needle sheathed in hard plastic. Margaret carefully unsheathed the first syringe and went to work in the area around the triangle.

As soon as the triangles died, they caused a chain reaction of apoptosis. Apoptosis is a normal part of human health: sometimes cells outlive their usefulness and become a drag on the body, so they self-destruct. The triangles did something to that chemical code, however, turned it into a cascading event that dissolved all the tissue of an adult male in less than two days.

Margaret had tackled that problem in working to save Perry's life. She'd performed immediate surgery on him to remove any trace of the dead triangles rotting inside his body. That hadn't stopped the apoptosis, but it slowed it, giving her enough time to find a solution.

Apoptosis is driven by proteins called *caspases,* also known as the 'executioner' proteins. Caspases exist in every cell in an inactive form, but when cells are damaged or old, the caspases activate and kill the cell. In a normal person, other proteins known as *inhibitor of apoptosis proteins,* or IAPs, shut down the process as soon as the intended cell dies. The triangles corrupted this normal process by neutralizing the IAPs' suppressive abilities, allowing the caspases to spread the deadly chain reaction to surrounding cells, which then released *their* caspases, which then destroyed *more* cells, and so on.

She'd fought this process by testing multiple drugs that inhibited caspases. The magic formula turned out to be a trial drug called WDE-4-11, which successfully shut down the apoptosis chain reaction. That saved human tissue, although the triangle corpses still decomposed within hours.

That meant she could operate on a live host, remove the triangles, then use WDE-4-11 to stop the apoptosis. Despite Perry's naive, violent beliefs, she *could* save them. When she did, however, saving the tissue was only one step – she also had to deal with the mental effects. For that she had a battery of mood-controlling drugs at her disposal, including drugs that had tackled the chemical imbalances in Perry's brain and returned him to a semblance of sanity.

Or so she'd thought at the time.

She focused her attention on cutting the triangle free from the dead boy's leg. The human tissue would keep, but the triangle would be black ooze in only a few hours, and she needed to move fast.

MEAN DRUNK

Dew parked the Lincoln in front of Perry's motel room. Fluffy snowflake clusters had replaced the rain and hail. As the saying went, if you don't like the weather in Wisconsin, just wait ten minutes. Dew had heard the same kinds of jokes about Michigan, Ohio and Indiana – and they were all true.

Perry sat in the passenger seat. He'd passed out with a beer in his left hand, his right still wrapped around a tattered six-pack that had only two bottles left. Dew didn't want to act as a chauffeur for this psycho piece of shit, but he wasn't about to put someone else at risk.

'Wake up,' Dew said.

Perry didn't move.

Dew put the Lincoln in reverse, backed up about five feet, put it in gear, then gunned it and jammed on the brakes. Perry's big body lurched forward against the seat belt.

His head snapped up, and he blinked in confusion.

'Home sweet home,' Dew said.

Perry turned and looked at him with drunken eyes. 'Thanks, Pops,' he said.

Dew said nothing. Perry stared and smiled for a few more seconds, seeming to wait for a response. He didn't get one. When he got out, the Lincoln rose up at least six inches. God*damn*, but that kid was big.

Dew shut off the car and got out. His room was right next to Dawsey's. Just like always.

'Dawsey, gonna stay in your room tonight, or are you going to find some more kids to kill?' Dew asked.

'I thought killing babies was your gig.'

Dew shook his head. A goddamn baby-killer reference. He'd walked right into it, sure, but even drunk, that kid really knew how to push his buttons.

'You know what?' Dew said. 'I'm too old and too tired for this. I'm going to bed. You go drink yourself into a coma. Just don't die on me, or I'll get into trouble.'

He walked to his room, keyed in, then shut and locked the door behind him, leaving Dawsey standing in the snow.

• • •

Perry nodded. *Don't die on me.* That's all he was to these people, an asset. A freak. He keyed into his room, shut the door, then fell on the bed. He dropped his beer. It spilled on the carpet. That was okay, he had two more. He rolled onto his back and stared at the ceiling. It was spinning pretty good. Without looking away from the ceiling, he felt for another bottle, found it and twisted off the top. He upended it. Most of the beer splashed on his face or landed on the bed, but some of it went into his mouth, so it wasn't all bad.

'I got some more, Bill,' Perry said. 'I killed those motherfuckers.'

Bill didn't answer. He never answered direct questions. He just piped up unexpectedly from time to time, told Perry to get a gun, to kill himself.

Bill. Why the fuck did Margo have to bring him up? Perry drank to *forget* Bill. Well, it didn't work. Nothing Perry ever did worked. Except when he wanted to hurt someone. To kill someone. That worked every time.

What the fuck was Dew's problem, anyway? Pretending to get all pissed about that family. Why didn't Dew and the others understand? Those people weren't human anymore. They were *weak*. They didn't have *discipline*. That meant they needed to die. If one of them, any of them, was even *trying* to cut out the triangles, then Perry would let them live. Maybe. But it didn't matter, because so far no one had fought.

No one but him.

Why? Why was he special? He knew why: because his drunken, fucked-up, wife- and child-beating father had toughened him up with a strap.

Perry set the beer bottle on the bed to the right side of his face. He tipped it – this time more made it into his mouth than onto the bed. His face was all wet and sticky.

He didn't feel a thing for the infected. Not a thing. That freakin' toddler had rushed him, for crying out loud. They weren't just infected, they were *stupid*.

That was the last thought to go through Perry's mind before he passed out for the second time that night.

THE BACKYARD OF CHUY RODRIGUEZ

Chuy Rodriguez lived at the corner of Hammerschmidt and Sarah streets in South Bend, Indiana. Chuy had a wife, Kiki, and two kids: John, sixteen, and Lola, fourteen.

In their backyard stood a sparsely leaved oak tree suffering from some kind of bark rot. The tree had another three years, maybe five, and Chuy was already dreading how barren his backyard would look when he had to cut it down.

Chuy's tree, however, wasn't really the point of concern. For that you had to look directly above the tree.

Some *forty miles* directly above it.

If you could look up there, even with a very high-powered telescope, you might not notice a little blur, like a tiny heat shimmer. That shimmer came from visible-light wavelengths hitting an object, sliding along its surface, then continuing on their way with almost their exact original trajectory.

This object wasn't *truly* invisible. Were it some massive thing taking up half the horizon, everyone would have spotted it by now.

Since it was just a bit bigger than a beer keg, however, no one noticed.

This object was inanimate. Cold. Calculating. It had no emotions. If it did, when it felt the Marinesco gate vanish in a ground-rending explosion, it probably would have said, *Awww FUCK, not again.*

The object's shape had once been quite smooth and polished, like a teardrop with a point on both ends instead of just one. But that had been at launch, before the long journey that brought it into a geostationary orbit above Chuy Rodriguez's diseased oak tree.

Space isn't really empty. It's got stuff in it. Stuff like dirt, rocks, ice, various bits and pieces – only those pieces are spread really, *really* far apart. If you travel far enough through that not-so-empty space, you're going to run into that stuff. Depending on how fast you're going, hitting even a teeny *speck* of dust can cause quite a bit of damage. The double-teardrop rock had been engineered to take that damage and keep on flying. The engineering worked, mostly, but the object's pitted and cracked exterior bore witness to a design adage true anywhere in the universe – you can't test for everything.

It had come so close to completing the mission. Once again, however, stopped before the gate could open . . . once again, stopped by the rogue host.

Stopped by the *sonofabitch*.

Its mission was simple in concept. Travel straight out from the home planet and search for signals that indicated sentient life. Space, as mentioned before, is big. Searching space for a suitable planet would require an investment far greater even than the economy-breaking project that had launched this object so long ago. There was one way, however, to narrow the search for planets that sustain life – find planets that already have it.

It did that by tracking broadcast signals.

Broadcast signals meant several things. First, they meant a planet that could support advanced biological life – predictable ranges of gravity, density, temperature, gases and liquids. Second, broadcasts meant a predictable range of resources – odds were, a planet of nothing but silica and sulfur could not create technology capable of sending signals into space. Finally, and perhaps most important, broadcasts indicated a large population capable of performing technically advanced tasks.

And that was important when you wanted slave labor to build your colonies for you.

Colonies, like exploration, are prohibitively expensive operations. Enslaving a native population provides a low-cost solution. It also helps cut off a potential interstellar rival.

If all went well, if the planet had suitable gravity and atmosphere, the object could get cracking. It would seed the planet with machines that could build a portal, a portal that connected two places so far apart that no living thing, nor the children of that living thing, nor the great-great-great-grandchildren of that living thing, could survive the trip by any other means. With the portal, however, such a trip took place instantly. Hundreds of light-years traversed in the blink of an eye.

This object, this *Orbital*, had arrived in Earth's solar system some twenty years ago after detecting multiple signals: radio, television, microwaves. It approached slowly, cautiously, because there was always the possibility sentient life was *too* advanced and would see it coming. So the Orbital watched for a few years. It analyzed, eventually reaching the conclusion it could move into a low, stationary orbit without being detected.

Once the Orbital drew to the operating range, it spent more years watching. While there were multiple shapes and forms in the signals, the dominant species was almost always present. Suffice it to say that thanks to repeated image analysis, the Orbital knew a human when it saw one.

After seven years the Orbital knew humanity's technological capabilities. It could identify major population centers and, more significantly, areas of little or no population. It could not understand any languages, but it didn't need to – it would accumulate language once the probes were successfully deployed.

The Orbital carried eighteen of the small, soda-can-size probes, each of which could cast over a billion tiny seeds adrift on the winds. Each seed contained two main elements. The first was the microscopic machinery needed to analyze potential hosts and hijack their biological processes. The second was a tiny, submicroscopic chunk of crystal. This chunk matched exactly with one in the center of every other seed and, more important, inside the Orbital. This irreplaceable, unreproducible chunk was the *template,* the device that reshaped the molecular structure of biomass so that it became the material needed to build a gate.

The first probe had been a total failure. Bad luck with the weather. The second probe actually produced several connections, but, unfortunately, they were all with nonsentient animals. When that happened, the seeds simply shut off – a half-formed triangle on a caged or penned domesticated animal could potentially alert humanity to the hovering threat. The seeds also needed sentient hosts to develop workers that could communicate and work together, could use tools and vehicles, could learn about the area and potential dangers.

It wasn't until the sixth probe that seeds latched onto a sentient being. Although those seeds died early, the

Orbital was able to gather some biofeedback. It analyzed the data, identified key problems, then modified the next batch accordingly.

The seventh probe proved closer still. More development, including successful creation of the biological material needed for worker construction. These were the strange red, blue and black fibers that would come to be associated with Morgellons disease.

Batches eight through ten were each more successful than the last, creating firm connections that flooded the Orbital with valuable biofeedback. It learned much about the structure of host-species DNA, refining the self-assembly process to a highly functional level. It gathered data about brain composition and chemical structure, enough to manipulate host behaviors, to steer them away from associating with noninfected hosts.

Batch eleven was a landmark achievement – access to the higher levels of a host's brain, including memory and language processing. The Orbital began to build a vocabulary of images, concepts and words. One host even found a suitable portal location. This host, Alida Garcia, died soon after, but the primary obstacles had been overcome.

That should have made batch twelve the one.

Batch twelve produced five hosts. A change in the language, from some Spanish to English. The Orbital's vocabulary grew. It understood more and more of the broadcast signals pouring off the planet. The workers incubated well and almost made it to the hatching phase before unexpected complications resulted in the deaths of the hosts – including Blaine Tanarive, Gary Leeland, Charlotte Wilson and Judy Washington. Martin Brewbaker's triangles activated a few days after the others, but he died just the same.

More data. More modifications.

Probability tables indicated that batch thirteen had an 82 percent chance of success. Multiple seeds implanted in eleven hosts for a total of seventy-two potential workers. Fifty-six of those actually hatched and made it to the location identified by Alida Garcia.

The workers started to build the gate. Success seemed inevitable.

But then the rogue host appeared. A host that fought back, that killed embryonic workers and brought the human military. The workers had a name for this host. They called it the *sonofabitch*.

The Orbital tried again. Aside from some minor biological upgrades, batch fourteen used the same strategy as batch thirteen. Probes went out, seeds landed, embryos germinated, workers hatched. Everything went fine, until the Orbital learned of yet another unanticipated fact.

The rogue host could still *hear*.

Structures grown in host brains acted like antennae, connecting embryos and hosts, allowing the Orbital to direct them, to guide them, helping them find each other so they could work together to reach the gate locations. The rogue host remained tapped into this communication grid.

It heard.

It found the Mather gate location.

It brought the military . . . again.

So *close*.

Successful worker design in itself wasn't enough to get the job done. The Orbital changed tactics.

Batch fifteen worked perfectly. It dispersed near Parkersburgh, West Virginia, and produced six hosts – all of which made it to the woods near South Bloomingville before hatching.

Batch sixteen fired only a few hours later, spreading over Glidden, Wisconsin.

Fifteen and sixteen hatched in record time, built their gates in record time. The Orbital activated the South Bloomingville gate as a decoy, drawing the human military.

The sonofabitch found *both* gates.

After all of these near hits, the Orbital had only two probes left. If those did not work, the entire mission was a failure.

It had to change strategy again.

The large explosion that destroyed the Marinesco gate demonstrated that humans could react quickly and with overwhelming force. Placing the gates in secluded areas had seemed like the best strategy at first, but it also allowed for massive ordnance without much risk to local populations.

The workers also needed protection. They were designed to hatch out of hosts and then *build*, not *fight*. They could kill, but were far outmatched by the human forces responding to each gate. The workers needed *defenders*, something to occupy the human forces, fight them long enough for workers to activate the gates.

Since defenders would not build the gate, they did not need the template. That was good. That opened a new strategy. Because the new defender design didn't need a template, it could do something that the template-carrying embryos could not – the new design could *reproduce*.

The Orbital began modifying the next batch of seeds.

DAY TWO

FUN WITH SNOWMOBILES

The Jewell family reunion was turning out to be a smashing success, and Donald Jewell couldn't have been happier.

Granted, there weren't that many Jewells left.

Ma and Pa Jewell had gone to that big snowmobile trail in the sky. Ma five years ago, Pa less than six months later. They left behind their three children: Mary, Bobby and Donald.

Mary Jewell-Slater now lived in London with her husband. She couldn't exactly fly overseas to see the family every Christmas. She called. That was enough.

Bobby Jewell now lived in Ma and Pa's house. He'd married his college sweetie, Candice, and promptly kicked out a bundle of joy named Chelsea, a curly blonde seven years old and worldly-wise.

Donald, the eldest member of clan Jewell, had divorced his bitch of a wife, Hannah, four years earlier. Hannah won custody of Betty, then twelve, now sixteen and hotter than a five-dollar pistol. Hannah moved from their home in Gaylord, Michigan, to Atlanta, taking Betty far away from her family. The divorce stipulated that Donald got Betty for every other holiday. So the first Christmas with Hannah, then Donald and so on. This was his second Christmas as a divorced father.

Donald – now living in Pittsburgh – talked to his daughter at least every other day on the phone. They also chatted on webcam, emailed and even wrote some old-fashioned letters. They were as tight as a father and daughter separated by seven hundred miles can be.

Mostly from a distance, he'd watched his daughter grow from a gangly twelve-year-old into a stunning teenager who could have graced the cover of practically any magazine. She looked exactly like her mother, which annoyed Donald, because that made him hate Hannah just a little bit less. He had thought he might be biased about his daughter's looks, but when he showed pictures of her to his co-workers, their lewd hoots confirmed his fears. Those hoots had also, unfortunately, generated a couple of fights. The same temper Hannah cited in the divorce papers hadn't gone away. His court-appointed psychologist called it 'impulse-control problems.' The shrink prescribed pills. Donald lied and said he took them. Everyone was happy.

His baby girl was growing up fast, and he didn't want her to lose touch with her family. Thus the family reunion. A flight for Betty from Atlanta to Pittsburgh, then an eight-hour drive from Pittsburgh to Gaylord. Did they dread the drive? Nope, they got to talk the whole way up. Donald learned more about hot music, hot clothes, school gossip and backstabbing friends than he cared to, and he loved every minute of it.

Once she was back in Gaylord, the Southern Girl faded away and the Northern Girl came back to life. Betty hadn't been on a snowmobile in two years, yet she hadn't lost a step. In a white snowsuit on a blue snowmobile, she raced across an open field, with her father only fifty feet behind her and closing. Even over the roaring Arctic Cat engines and the whipping wind, Donald could hear her laughter. Let's see Hannah compete with *this*. Bobby was at least a hundred yards back. He just didn't have the aggression of Donald and, apparently, Betty.

Betty shouted something. Donald thought it was *Try and catch me, old man*, but he couldn't be sure.

Bobby owned this whole area. Some places in the world, twenty acres was considered an 'estate.' Near Gaylord, Michigan, twenty acres was just called 'some land.' Mostly old cornfields, along with tall green pines, skeletal winter oaks and birch stands. Bobby lived smack in the middle of it all in total isolation – it took two minutes just to reach his house from the road.

Betty followed the trail into a left-hand bend that cut around a stand of pine trees. She slowed to start the turn, then gunned the engine, accelerating through the curve. She disappeared from sight for just a few seconds as Donald came around the curve behind her.

When he saw her again, he felt his nuts jump into his chest. Up ahead, the trail crossed a snow-covered road, and on that road was a brown and white Winnebago moving along at a good clip.

'Slow down, girl,' Donald hissed to himself. Betty couldn't hear him or read his mind, obviously, because she poured on the speed. Donald tried to catch up and cut her off, but she had her throttle wide open.

The Winnebago started honking, but didn't seem to slow. Betty apparently thought it would. Sick in his soul, Donald traced the two vehicles' trajectories – she wouldn't make it across in time.

Betty apparently saw the same thing. She locked up the brakes. The Cat's back end fishtailed to the right, kicking up a wave of powder in front of it. The sled lost most of its speed but still tipped. Betty hopped off as the sled flopped onto its side and kept moving. She actually landed on her feet and slid for a few yards before she fell hard. The Cat skidded along the path for another ten feet, coming to rest right at the edge of the road.

The Winnebago roared by, trailing a cloud of powder. The big vehicle slowed down, working toward a full stop on the snowy road.

Donald skidded to a halt and hopped off his sled. Betty was already sitting up. Sitting up and *laughing*.

'Betty, are you all right?'

She took off her helmet, black hair spilling out across the shoulders of her white snowsuit. She laughed again, then winced.

'Owww,' she said through a grimacing smile. 'Oh, Daddy, I think I hurt my boo-tay.'

He heard the Winnebago come to a stop and his brother's sled approaching. Donald didn't care about either; he was too angry.

'Betty Jean Jewell, what the *hell* were you doing?'

'Trying to beat you, of course,' Betty said. 'If I could have made it in front of that RV, you would have had to pull off, and I'd win.'

'You *idiot*. You could have been killed.'

Betty waved her hand dismissively. 'Oh, re-*lax*. You taught me how to dump a sled, Dad, I'm fine.'

'You're not going on a snowmobile again, and that's *that*.'

Betty's smile faded. 'Dad, seriously, I'm fine. I think you're getting a little fired up here.'

He was losing his temper again, the same temper that had fucked up his entire life. He took a deep breath and started to get a hold of it.

And he would have succeeded, were it not for the driver of the Winnebago.

'You stupid little brat!' the man screamed. 'What kind of a stupid fucking stunt was that?'

Donald looked up. The driver – a red-bearded fat man well past middle age – had gotten out of the Winnebago and walked over. He was only ten feet away. Donald's temper shifted targets in an instant, fueled by the language directed against his daughter.

'Don't you yell at her, Dale Junior, you're the one tearing up the road.'

'I was going the speed limit, dipshit.'

'Daddy, please,' Betty said.

Donny didn't hear her – he was already too far gone. 'Dipshit? *I'm* a dipshit? You ever heard of a fucking brake pedal?'

Somewhere in the back of his head, Donald heard his brother's snowmobile slow and stop.

The man pointed to the road. 'You *see* the snow-covered pavement there, genius? You think you can stop a *motor home* on a dime on *that*?'

'Maybe you should take some driving lessons then, you prick. You could have killed my daughter.'

'*I* could have killed *her*?'

'That's what I said, numb-nuts.'

'Donny, Mark, stop it!' Bobby yelled, but neither man was paying attention.

'Well,' the man said, 'if *you're* her father, maybe running her over wouldn't be so bad for the gene pool.'

That tore it. Donald threw down his helmet and stormed forward.

And found himself looking down the barrel of a gun.

'Daddy!' Betty screamed.

'Just hold your horses, pal,' the bearded man said. 'I don't really care for a fistfight today.'

'Oh, wow,' Bobby said. 'Uh, Mark, could you put that down?'

The man looked to his right but kept the gun leveled at Donald. 'You know this douchebag, Bobby?'

Donald didn't move.

'Uh . . . yeah,' Bobby said. 'This is my brother, Donny. Uh . . . Donny, this is my neighbor, Mark Jenkins.'

'Pleased to meet you,' Donald said. He kept himself very still while he said it.

The bearded man looked from Bobby to Donald, then back to Bobby again.

'Oh,' the man said, and lowered the gun. 'Well, sorry about that, then.'

A huge breath slid out of Donald's lungs.

'Bobby, sorry about drawing on your brother, but he was coming at me.' He clicked the safety on and slid the pistol somewhere in his ample back waistband. They all stood there in silence for a moment.

'This is just a bit uncomfortable,' Betty said.

'So, Mark,' Bobby said. 'How was your hunting trip?'

'Pulled an oh-fer,' Mark said. 'Got all new rifles, and the deer just didn't show up. This might not be a good time for small talk, though, Bobby. How about you and the family come over for dinner? Next week.'

'Will do, Mark,' Bobby said. 'Be seein' ya.'

Mark nodded, turned and walked back to his Winnebago. The Jewells watched him get in and drive off.

'That gun legal?' Donald asked.

Bobby shrugged. 'Probably. You know as well as I do you don't ask around here. He moved in last year. Has a bit of a thing for Candice.'

'No shit?'

'No shit,' Bobby said. 'He's fairly open about it. Normally that would chap my ass, but he can look all he wants. I don't really make a big deal of it, for reasons I'm sure you can now appreciate.'

'Yeah,' Donald said. 'I think I see where you're coming from.'

'*Gawd*, Daddy,' Betty said. 'You can be *such* an asshole. Can you please pick up my sled so I can go back to Uncle Bobby's house and die of embarrassment?'

Donald did just that. She hopped on, then raced off down the trail. The Jewell brothers watched her go.

'She can really drive that thing,' Bobby said.

Donald nodded.

'Donny, I'm going to throw out a wild guess here. You haven't been taking your meds, right?'

Donald shook his head.

'I figured as much,' Bobby said. 'What I love about you is your consistency – you never learn. Come on, Candice is working on a big lunch, and my daughter the Blond Tornado wants to watch the Pistons with her *Unkie Donny*. Think you can manage that without trying to beat somebody up?'

'I can give it the old college try.'

They got on the sleds and headed back down the trail. Donald felt like a complete idiot, losing his temper like that in front of his daughter. What if the guy hadn't been Bobby's neighbor? What if he'd just been some jackass with a gun? Then Donald, and his daughter, could have been in real danger. Maybe he'd start taking those meds as soon as he got back to the house.

MOTEL-ROOM COFFEE

Dew sat in his motel room sipping a cup of motel-room coffee. He remembered when it was all fancy to have one of those little single-cup coffee machines in your room. Now they were everywhere, and they all skimped on the vitals – who the hell made coffee with only one creamer and one sugar?

Shitty as the coffee was, he needed that caffeine kick for this conversation. He held the coffee in one hand, his old bricklike secure satellite phone in the other.

'It was a bloodbath, Murray,' Dew said.

'You screwed the pooch this time, Top,' Murray said, using the shorthand for *top sergeant*, Dew's rank back when they served together. Dew hated that phrase, and Murray knew it.

'You've put me up against it,' Murray said. 'The new chief of staff is going to have my balls on a platter for this. I told them Dawsey was under control.'

'Yeah, well, that was a pretty stupid thing to do, L.T.' Murray's old wartime shorthand for *lieutenant* annoyed him just as much as *Top* annoyed Dew.

'It's not all bad,' Dew said. 'At least Margaret has that test for the hosts. That's a big step.'

'True, that will help some,' Murray said. 'I don't know if it'll be enough – Vanessa Colburn has it in for me.'

'Something else might help, too,' Dew said. 'After I sent my report, the guys found the daughter, Sara McMillian, in a shallow grave in the backyard. Killed by a hammer blow to the head. So it's not like Dawsey was butchering innocents here.'

'Nice,' Murray said. 'How's the baby and the oldest son?'

'Baby is fine. No infection. Oldest son, Tad, he's physically okay. Psychologically . . . well, turns out the father made Tad dig the grave for the sister.'

'You're shitting me.'

'I shit you not,' Dew said. 'That's what the boy said. And he's probably telling the truth, because his hands are all blistered. It's pretty hard to dig through frozen ground. Hence the *shallow* part of the shallow grave.'

'Jesus. Well, I guess I can say Dawsey actually saved Tad while I'm at it. Less psycho, more brave hero.'

'Murray, listen. I'm thinking maybe it's time we put Dawsey away.'

A pause. 'Define *put him away*.'

'Not *that* kind,' Dew said. 'A sanitarium or something. A supermax. Whatever.'

'Come on, Dew,' Murray said. 'You know we can't do that.'

'He attacked two agents.'

'Baumgartner has a broken nose and Milner has a black eye, for fuck's sake,' Murray said. 'They've probably got worse in a pickup basketball game.'

'Doesn't matter. Assaulting an agent is a federal offense.'

'Oh, are you going to start obeying the letter of the law all the sudden? Let's make that happen, Top. Maybe you and I can share a cell and have some quality time together before they give us the chair.'

Dew said nothing.

'That's what I thought,' Murray said. 'You know what? The kid's no different from us. He just doesn't have a badge.'

That one hit home. Was Dew actually like Perry? Willing to do whatever it took to get the job done? No, they weren't alike for one key reason Dew didn't want to admit – he'd killed a lot more people than Dawsey had.

'He wrecked that car,' Dew said. 'He wants another one.'

'So get him another one. It's only taxpayer money. Enough bitching about this kid already. Dew, we need a live host.'

'Why the fuck do you think I'm bitching *about* him? How am I supposed to get a live host when Dawsey is running around killing them like a fucking wild animal?'

Murray was silent for a second. 'What the hell happened to you?'

'Oh, Christ,' Dew said. 'Are you firing up a rah-rah speech?'

'Just shut the fuck up and listen,' Murray said. 'And that's an order. Your job used to be getting men to follow you, because if they didn't, they'd wind up dead, and you probably along with them. This isn't any different. Find a way to get the job done. Do it in the parameters set before you. I don't want to hear about your obstacles or any kind of pressure you're under.'

'How about you see this shit firsthand and *then* you talk to me about pressure?' Dew said. 'I'll switch places with you in a heartbeat.'

'Vanessa Colburn would eat you alive,' Murray said. 'You wouldn't last five minutes here, just like I wouldn't last five minutes there. What the fuck is wrong with you?

You get your partner killed and you think you're excused from finding a way to get the job done?'

Dew took a slow breath. 'You'd best be real careful how you choose your words from here on out, L.T.'

'Oh, can the tough-guy drama,' Murray said. 'Malcolm is dead, Dew. Deal with it. You want payback, right?'

'You're goddamn right I do.' That was exactly what he wanted. More than anything else, save for a magic potion that would bring Malcolm back from the dead.

'Well, you're the one that can make it happen,' Murray said. 'You sure as hell aren't on this job because of your good looks or your physical prowess. You're old, you've got a gut, and you have a bad hip. You have only two things that make you worth a squirt of piss – you shoot when you're told to shoot, and you figure things out. Get Dawsey to play ball, and get . . . me . . . a . . . live . . . *host.*'

Murray broke the connection.

Maybe he was an asshole, but that didn't shake a nagging feeling that he was right.

'That's why they give you the tough jobs, old boy,' Dew said to the empty room. 'Because you can figure things out.'

So how the hell was he going to get through to Scary Perry Dawsey?

THE MOST IMPORTANT
MEAL OF THE DAY

Sometimes having a black budget was fun.

Bob's Breakfast Shack wasn't a shack at all. It was actually part of the motel – a nice little greasy spoon with twenty tables, four of which were kind of off in their own room. For the small price of five Ben Franklin portraits, Dew's people had the room to themselves.

Fuck it. It was only taxpayer money.

You could spend just so much time in the MargoMobile's computer area. Buying out the diner's back room let them talk openly. Dew sat at a table with Clarence Otto, Amos Braun and Margaret Montoya. Gitsh, Marcus, the black-eyed Milner and the nose-braced Baumgartner sat at another. Marcus was quietly whistling the melody from the Animals' 'House of the Rising Sun.'

Dew had sent the other men home last night after they secured the scene. They were local talent, which he used for muscle when he needed it – the tactic gave him just-in-case firepower yet cut down on people who knew the whole story.

Amos had the menu open in front of him. He could barely see over the top. Dew considered making a crack about a child seat, but he assumed Amos had heard that one a million times. They didn't get to do this often, maybe two or three days a week. Dew not only looked forward to it, he found time to make it happen. The whole situation had grown so dark, so desperate, that they needed a release. Breakfast meetings provided a rare chance to do something *normal,* to laugh and joke, even if it was gallows humor most of the time.

'Okay, Margaret,' Dew said. 'Give me the rundown on last night's autopsies.'

She looked up from her menu. 'What, here?'

'Yep, right here,' Dew said. 'I'm pretty sure the Russkies haven't bugged Bob's Breakfast Shack.'

'Russkies?' Otto said. 'Doesn't that phrase show your age?'

'Actually, my uneducated friend,' Amos said, '*Russkies* is accurate, since we now have a country called *Russia. Commies* would be inaccurate, since it's the USSR that's no longer around.'

Otto frowned, then smiled. 'Say, little white man, don't you owe me twenty bucks?'

'Aw, crap,' Amos said. 'That's right.' He fished out his wallet and handed over a well-folded twenty.

'What's that for?' Margaret asked.

Otto pocketed the twenty. 'He bet that Dawsey would kill me last night.'

Margaret took in a gasp of astonishment. 'Amos! You didn't!'

'I paid him, didn't I?'

She shook her head and scowled at both men. 'Seriously. That's not something to joke about.'

'If I don't laugh, I'll cry,' Otto said. 'Or something like that. I won twenty bucks – what else matters?'

The waitress came to take their orders. They sat in silence until she'd worked the room and left.

'Okay,' Dew said. 'Let's get back on task here. First of all, Margo, congrats on developing that triangle test.'

Otto and Amos both applauded lightly.

Margaret blushed. 'Oh, it's a team effort.'

Amos laughed. 'Give it a rest, Miss Modesty. It was all your idea, and it works.'

'What else did you find from the corpses?' Dew asked.

'Nothing completely new,' Margaret said. 'Although we refined a lot of our knowledge. Amos and I got great pictures of the parasite's nerve interface, the best yet. Same thing for the circulatory tap. I think we've pretty much documented how the thing interacts with those systems, although the disturbing part is still the brain interaction. These parasites clearly know more about the inner workings of our brains than we do.'

'What about the vector?' Dew said.

She shook her head. 'Still nothing. So much of that comes from interviewing disease victims, finding out what they ate, drank, where they went, who they touched, things like that. The only person who *can* talk about it *won't* talk about it.'

'Goddamn Dawsey,' Dew said. 'What about the number of hosts this time? There were three of them, and we had those three old ladies that Perry torched. Any significance to that number?'

'Probably not,' Amos said. 'There've been cases with just one host, like Perry, or with two and even three. What's more significant here is that this was one family, living under one roof, so they probably ate the same food, traveled in the same patterns. The three old ladies all lived at the same retirement home. They took walks together every day. That shows that whatever the vector is, it can hit some or all of the people in a specific area.'

'Could they have given it to each other?' Dew asked. 'One gets infected, gives it to the rest?'

Margaret shook her head. 'All the McMillians' triangles were at the same stage of development, which indicates they all contracted the disease at the same time. Add to that three people under the same roof who did *not* have triangles. As far as we can tell, it's not contagious.'

'Which brings up an interesting point,' Amos said. 'The gate was finished, right? Built by hatchlings that had already hatched. So if all the McMillians were at the same stage of development, they must have caught it *after* the other hosts. Why were they behind the times, so to speak?'

'They were obviously infected later,' Margaret said. 'Whatever it is, something they touched, something they ate, the infected members of the family were exposed at the same time. That still doesn't give us clues toward the vector. Amos, did Tad say anything?'

Amos shook his head. 'Turns out he's been grounded for a while. The parents left him alone at the house a few times. They could have picked it up shopping, running errands.'

'The follow-up FBI team will interview him,' Dew said. 'And maybe they can get something when they run the background checks on the McMillians.'

Margaret reached across the table and grabbed Dew's hand. 'Dew, that's all well and good, but we already *have* someone who was infected. If Perry would open up, provide us an overview of his behavior in the days leading up to his infection, that would give us something to work with. Can you talk to him again?'

Dew rolled his eyes. 'What the fuck is this, International Pile On Phillips Day? I just had this conversation with Murray, thank you very much.'

'Right,' Margaret said. 'And what did fearless leader say?'

'He said I have to find a way to reach Dawsey. Sound familiar?'

Margaret leaned forward, both elbows on the table. She pointed her fork at Dew. 'You've threatened Perry, and that hasn't worked. You've tried tricking him, following him so you could knock him out before he killed the hosts, and *that* hasn't worked. Have you tried just being nice to him?'

'Be *nice* to him?' Dew said, his voice rising. He pointed at Milner and Baumgartner. 'Look at their faces, Margo, and then tell me we should be nice to Dawsey.'

Margaret tilted her head to the right. 'And what were those men going to do when they caught up with Perry, Dew?'

Dew didn't say anything.

'Well? Come on, out with it.'

Dew ground his teeth. 'They had orders to Taser him.'

'Then what?'

Dew looked away. 'Then put him in handcuffs and inject him with a knockout drug.'

Margaret just nodded and smiled. This woman was too smart for her own good.

'*You've* been nice to him,' Dew said, surprising himself by how petulant he sounded. 'Look how far that's gotten us.'

'Dew, I'm female. Maybe this is a news flash to you, but Perry's opinion of women in general isn't all that high. I spent a lot of time with him when he was recovering. I can be nice all day, and he'll be nice back, but he doesn't *listen* to me.'

'That's sexist,' Dew said. 'I'm rather appalled.'

Margaret nodded. 'And we don't have several months of sensitivity training to get through to him. If we're going to reach him now, a man needs to connect with him.'

'So what the fuck do you want from me, Montoya?' Dew said. 'You want me to whip up a game of poker? You want me to take a warm shower with him and hold his hand until the wee hours of the morning?'

'No,' she said. 'And stop quoting Clint Eastwood movies. How about you start simple – did you ask him to join us for breakfast?'

Dew just blinked. It hadn't even crossed his mind.

'Huh,' Otto said. 'I never thought of that.'

'I'd rather you didn't,' Amos said. 'I'm not sitting at a table with that guy. He might mistake me for a breakfast burrito.'

'Maybe a half stack of mini-pancakes, you mean,' Otto said.

'I want my menu back,' Amos said. 'Maybe I'll order some *Black* Forest ham and flush it down the crapper.'

'Oh, Amos,' Otto said, smiling as if he'd just had the most helpful idea in the history of man. 'Are you upset because you can't see over the table? Should I ask the waitress for a child's seat?'

'Like I haven't heard that one a million times.'

Dew reached out and squeezed Margaret's elbow, then stood.

'Where you going?' Amos asked.

'To see if Perry wants to join us for breakfast,' Dew said. 'Margaret's got to be wrong about something sooner or later, so let's find out.'

'He won't come,' Amos said.

'I bet he will,' Otto said. 'Dew here can be very persuasive.'

'Twenty bucks says Dawsey doesn't even leave the room,' Amos said.

Otto nodded. 'You're on.'

Margaret shook her head. 'Is there anything you two won't bet on?'

'I'm sure there's something,' Otto said.

'Twenty bucks says there isn't,' Amos said.

Margaret shook her head some more.

Otto smiled at Dew. 'Well, go on and bring him here so I can win another twenty.'

Dew turned and walked out of the restaurant.

WAKEY-WAKEY, HANDS OFF SNAKEY

Bang-bang-bang.

A pounding at the door.

Each bang matching the pounding in his head.

Perry's eyes fluttered open. Could it hurt to blink? Yes, it could.

Bang-bang-bang.

'Go away,' Perry said. Whispered was more like it.

Bang-bang-bang.

'Go away!' Perry screamed, and instantly regretted it. His hands shot to his head, palms covering his eyes. Why was his face all sticky? The bed reeked of stale beer.

'Get up, Dawsey. Time for breakfast.'

Dew Motherfucking Phillips. At his door at the crack of dawn. Perry sat up and looked at the glowing red clock on the nightstand.

8:45 A.M.

Okay, so it wasn't the crack of dawn. It was still too damned early to be out of bed.

'Rise and shine, big boy!' Dew yelled. 'Let's go! Everyone is waiting for you, and my food is getting cold.'

God*damn* did his head hurt.

'Dew, go away,' Perry said. 'I'm not kidding.'

Dew wanted to parade him around at breakfast so they could all have a good laugh at the freak's expense? No way. Perry didn't know what their game was, but he wasn't playing.

'Come on, kid, I can smell the beer all the way out here. You bathe in the stuff?'

Perry stood and walked to the bathroom. He put the plastic ice bucket in the sink, then turned on the cold water.

'Hold on,' Perry said. 'Let me get dressed.'

'That's the spirit,' Dew said. 'And if you smell like the rest of your room, you might want to take a shower. A quick one, though. I don't have all day.'

Perry turned on the shower's hot water and let it run. He grabbed the now-full ice bucket out of the sink and walked to the front door.

'Hey, Dew?'

'Yeah?'

'Hey, is it cold outside?'

'It's the dead of winter in northern Wisconsin,' Dew said. 'It's friggin' freezing.'

In one smooth motion, Perry opened the door and sloshed the ice-bucket water into Dew's chest. He had a brief glimpse of Dew flinching before the water soaked him, then the old man's eyes going wide with cold and surprise. Perry shut the door and locked it.

'I'll pass on breakfast,' Perry said. 'Rain check?'

Bang-bang-bang.

'Open the fucking door, you *fuck*.'

Perry started to lie down again, then remembered that his bed was soaked with beer. He pulled the blankets off and tossed them on the floor.

'You better go change,' Perry said. 'Like you said, it's friggin' freezing.'

Bang-bang-bang.

'Kid, I am going to beat your ass.'

Perry laughed, but that hurt even more than talking. He pulled off the sheets and tossed them on top of the blankets, leaving a naked mattress. It had a few beer-wet spots, but it would do. He'd passed out in his clothes – they were beer-soaked as well, so he took them off and lay down. The running shower helped drown out Dew's shouts a little. Perry just closed his eyes and waited. If Dew didn't go away soon, his clothes would freeze on him, and he'd catch pneumonia and die.

Either way, Perry won.

A wave of nausea hit him. He slid his head over the side of the bed and threw up on the floor. As if his head didn't hurt enough already – was a hangover vomit not one of the worst pains in the world? And Perry Dawsey *knew* pain. He dragged his face back, using the corner of the mattress to wipe the puke away from his mouth.

The banging stopped, and he quickly fell asleep.

ROOM SERVICE

A knock at Dew's door.

He was still shivering as he buttoned up a dry shirt. He should have hopped into the shower to warm up, but there just wasn't time – too much work to do.

'Who is it?'

'Margaret. I brought your food.'

Dew hadn't eaten yet. He'd been so pissed he hadn't really noticed how hungry he was. He stuffed his shirt into his pants, buttoned and zipped, then opened the door.

Margaret stood there in the morning light. She looked good, as always, dark eyes staring back with that combination of kindness and an ever-present haunted look, the result of seeing too many horrors in too short a time. But what *really* made her attractive was the Styrofoam food container she held in her left hand and the steaming Styrofoam cup she held in her right.

'Double cream, double sugar,' she said. 'That's how you like it, right?'

'You're an angel, lady,' Dew said. He took the container. 'You want to come in?'

Margaret nodded and walked into the room. She looked around, eyes lingering on the suitcase placed neatly in the closet, at the shoes lined up next to the suitcase, and the wet shirt, sport coat and pants hanging on the clothes rack, each on its own hanger.

'What happened to you?' she said.

'I took your advice, that's what happened.' Dew sat down and opened the container. Plastic utensils were in there, rolled up in a paper napkin. He pulled out the fork and shoveled eggs into his mouth.

She sat on the bed next to the nightstand. She looked at Dew's array of weapons laid out there – the .45, the .38, the Ka-Bar knife, the switchblade, the collapsible baton – then casually scooted farther down the bed, away from them.

'So you were nice to Perry,' she said. 'And then what, you went for a swim?'

'He opened the door and doused me,' Dew said as he chewed.

'You're kidding.'

Dew shook his head. 'Ice bucket, I think.'

'Looks like Amos won his twenty bucks back.'

'Those guys bet a lot?'

Margaret nodded. 'They'll bet on anything. That same twenty-dollar bill has traded hands at least a dozen times. Must be some guy bonding strategy.'

'It's called having fun,' Dew said. 'Guys don't have *bonding strategies*, they just do stuff.'

'Like douse someone with water?'

'That's not doing stuff,' Dew said. 'That's being a fucking asshole. Pardon my French. His room smelled like a frat house. I think he's hungover. Bad.'

Dew stabbed the fork until it filled with the last of the eggs. 'Kid is a fucking alkie,' he said just before he stuffed the eggs into his mouth.

'He hasn't had enough time to become an alkie, Dew. It's only been six weeks since he cut those things out of himself, you know.'

Dew swallowed half the eggs, then picked up a sausage and crammed the whole thing into his mouth.

'Wow, eat much?' Margaret said. 'You'd be a classy dinner date.'

'I do sorta *reek* of class,' Dew said as he chewed. 'It's all in the breeding. We ran a full background check on Dawsey, you know. Kid used cash for everything except the bar, but trust me, his credit-card bills showed he spent *plenty* at those bars.'

Margaret rolled her eyes, an expression Dew found simultaneously dismissive and alluring.

'He's in his *twenties*, for God's sake,' she said. 'Did *you* spend any time in bars when you were in your twenties?'

'Of course not,' Dew said. 'I was busy building churches and helping the poor.'

'Oh, now I can see your halo,' Margaret said. 'I missed it earlier. Bad lighting in here.'

'Okay, so you've got a point. But you know what? Your calm, doctory logic kind of gets on my nerves. Do you always have to be right?'

'*Doctory?* I rather like that word. I don't *have* to always be right, Dew, that's just how it works out.'

He took a big drink of coffee. It scalded his mouth a little, but he didn't care – he felt the heat going into his chest.

'Well, Doc, I'm afraid you're *not* always right. I tried it your way and got water thrown in my face.'

'So try again.'

'Why the hell should I?'

'You mean besides the fact that we need a live host to figure out what the heck is going on?'

'Yeah,' Dew said. 'Besides that.'

'How about having compassion, Dew? How about being understanding? Perry's been through hell. He lost his best friend.'

'Yeah? So *what*? So did I.'

'And did you beat your best friend to death? Did you nail his hands up with steak knives and write *discipline* on the wall in his blood?'

In his entire life, he'd never been around anyone who made him feel as stupid as Margaret Montoya did. At least not without punching them in the mouth.

Dew grabbed his shoes and started putting them on. 'No,' he said. 'I didn't do any of that.'

'Right. So maybe, just *maybe*, Perry is trying to deal with some things that you can't understand.'

'That shit only floats for so long,' Dew said. 'I'm starting to think he's nothing more than a glorified bully, and the only way to get through to a bully is to give him a whuppin'.'

Margaret smiled. It wasn't the kind of smile that said, *I bet you'd be a fun roll in the hay,* because Dew knew what those smiles looked like on a woman. At least he *used* to know what those looked like. He didn't get them anymore. This was another kind of smile, the kind a young woman gives to an old man when the old man says something silly.

'Dew, I know you're very good at what you do, but just keep some perspective, okay?'

He grabbed his dry coat off the hanger and put it on. 'Perspective? What the fuck is that supposed to mean?'

Margaret shrugged. Her smile grew a little wider, a little more condescending. 'Well, look at *you* and . . . look at *him*. You're not going to beat any sense into him, and shooting him won't work. You already tried that.'

Dew quickly put the weapons in their various holsters and hiding spots. 'Doc, you stick to the sciencey and doctory stuff and leave the rest to me, okay?'

She smiled that smile again, then shrugged. 'Whatever you say. So what do we do next?'

'We have to finish up some things here. Then I think we're heading closer to Chicago.'

So far there was no pattern to the location of the four gates. Chicago seemed as central as the next spot, within quick striking distance of Wisconsin, Michigan, Indiana and Ohio.

'How about you make sure the MargoMobile is battened down, Doc,' Dew said. 'I want us out of here before the local media stops writing about a white supremacist group getting bombed in Marinesco and decides there might actually be another story afoot.'

He opened the door for her and gestured outside. Margaret walked out, and Dew followed.

DEEEEE-TROIT BASKET-BALLLL!

'Unkie Donny, you sit *here*,' Chelsea said. She patted the center cushion of the couch. It was Daddy's spot, but Unkie Donny was a guest. She got to sit in Daddy's lap all the time. She didn't see Unkie Donny anymore, hardly ever. Not since he moved to Pittsburgh. She didn't get to see Betty, either. That was worse.

Betty was so pretty. She had pierced ears. Daddy wouldn't let Chelsea pierce her ears. *Maybe in a few years,* Daddy would say. A year was such a long time. A *few* years? Chelsea couldn't imagine that a few years would ever come. She'd *never* get her ears pierced, *never* be as pretty as Betty.

Unkie Donny sat down on the middle cushion. 'Right here, honey?'

'Yes,' Chelsea said. 'Right here. And to sit here you have to pay the toll.'

'The toll? What's this going to cost me?'

'Smoochies!' Chelsea said.

Unkie Donny lifted her clear up off the ground. 'Ready?'

She nodded. They both puckered up and made a *mmmmm* noise as they slowly brought their lips together, then made an exaggerated kissing sound as the *mmmmm* turned into a loud *ahhhh*. Unkie Donnie sat her on the cushion to his left. Chelsea immediately crawled into his lap.

Betty smiled and sat down on the cushion to their right.

'O-M-G, that was so cute I could just keel over,' Betty said. She leaned toward Chelsea. 'And where's *my* smoochies?'

Mmmmm-ahhhh.

Daddy sat on the cushion to the left. He clicked the remote control. The TV changed from a cartoon to show men in white pajamas shooting the basketball.

Chelsea clapped, then leaned back on Unkie Donny's chest.

He gave her shoulders a little shake. 'Honey, do you know what time it is?'

She checked her Mickey Mouse watch. The big hand was on the eleven, the little hand was on the one, so that . . . was . . .

'Not *that* kind of time,' Unkie Donny said. 'The *game*, Chelsea. It's time for . . .'

Chelsea took a deep breath, sat up, then screamed in unison with Unkie Donny, '*Deeeee*-troit basket-ballll!'

She rested against his chest. 'Unkie Donny, who is your favorite Piston of all time?'

'Hmmm,' he said. 'Well, I've been watching them for a lotta years, honey. I'd have to say Bill Laimbeer or Chauncey Billups. Who's yours?'

'I like Peyton Manning!'

'Wrong sport, baby-girl,' Unkie Donny said.

'Oh,' Chelsea said. 'Then I like Chaunney Billups.'

'Chauncey, baby-girl,' Unkie Donny said.

'*Chaun-see*,' she said, trying the word on for size. 'I was going to name my puppy Fluffy, but now I'll name him Chauncey. Then you can come and play with Chauncey, Unkie Donny.'

'Sounds like a plan,' Unkie Donny said.

Daddy sighed. 'We're not getting a puppy, Chelsea. Don't start trying to get other people to campaign for you like you always do.'

'But *Daddy,* I *want* a puppy!'

'Chelsea, we're not going to talk about this now.'

Chelsea crossed her arms. 'You're not the boss of me.'

Mommy came out of the kitchen so fast that Chelsea flinched. Mommy had her heavy wooden mixing spoon in her hand. The *spanky-spoon*. It was still clumped with mashed potatoes.

'Little lady, if you say that one more time, you're going to get it.' Mommy shook the spoon as she talked, flinging little bits of mashed potatoes.

'But *Mom . . .*'

'Not another *word,*' Mommy said.

Chelsea pouted and fell back against Unkie Donny's chest.

Mommy nodded once, blond hair bouncing, then turned and strode back into the kitchen just as fast as she'd come in.

'Chelsea is in a bit of a willful stage,' Daddy said to Unkie Donny. 'Usually when she doesn't get what she wants, she throws a tantrum. Seems she's on her best behavior because you and Betty are here.'

'Be careful,' Unkie Donny said. 'Sometimes they don't grow out of the tantrum phase.'

Betty smacked Unkie Donny on the shoulder. 'Knock it off, geezer.'

Unkie Donny laughed, and Chelsea forgot all about the puppy. She watched the men in the pajamas for a second, then grabbed Betty's hand. 'Who's *your* favorite player, Betty?'

Betty reached up and stroked her cousin's hair. 'Oh, I don't know, dolly. I don't pay that much attention to basketball. If you want to talk about clothes or flowers, I'm your girl.'

The way Betty stroked her hair, it was *so nice.*

'I like dandelions,' Chelsea said.

'Oh, those are pretty,' Betty said. 'Do you like the yellow kind or the white kind better?'

'I like the white kind,' Chelsea said. 'I like the way they float and fly.'

Betty agreed with her. Betty always agreed with her, which was *very* nice. Chelsea had Daddy on her left, Betty on her right, and she was sitting on Unkie Donny's lap. This was just so *awesome.*

She watched the men take off the white pajamas. She thought this was the funniest part of basketball. If she took off her pajamas in front of people, she'd get in trouble. She wanted more ice cream. She'd already had one bar, and that was supposed to be it, but Mommy wasn't in the room.

'Daddy, can I have an ice cream bar?'

'Don't you mean *another* ice cream bar, Chelsea? It's not even noon, and I know for a fact you had one already.'

'Why can't I have more? I like it.'

'Chelsea!' Mommy shouted from the kitchen. 'Do I need to come in there?'

'No,' Chelsea said quickly. 'I'll stop.'

She sighed and fell back against Unkie Donny's chest again. It just wasn't *fair*. She watched the men walk onto the court to start the game.

HELP IS ON THE WAY

Forty miles above Chuy Rodriguez's backyard, the Orbital finished a probability analysis.

The results showed an 86 percent chance of success. Well above the required 75 percent specified in its parameters.

It began to modify the seeds of batch seventeen. It also broadcast a message to the remaining hatchlings, the ones that hadn't been able to make it to Marinesco or South Bloomingville in time, the ones that were hidden away. It sent the message to the triangles still growing in hosts, from seeds that had blown around for days before making a lucky landing.

The message said, *Stay hidden, stay quiet.*
Help is on the way.

VOICES

Perry Dawsey suddenly sat up in his bed. Steam floated near the ceiling. Every glass surface in the room was beaded with water, even the alarm clock that read 4:17 P.M. He still had a hangover, although it wasn't as bad. Hunger hit him like a wave. Maybe that breakfast place Dew wanted to eat at was close by.

But it wasn't the hangover that had woken him. It wasn't the hunger.

It was the *voices*.

Not the same voices he usually heard. *Sort* of like that, yet different. It danced away from his ability to define it, like having a word right at the edge of your thoughts and not being able to lock it down.

Something had changed. Something big. But it was also something small. Did that even make sense? No, and yet there it was.

He didn't understand specific words, didn't even know if the message contained words at all. More like an urge without emotion. The urge made him want to hide, to be quiet, to stay away from anyone.

Hide . . . and *wait*.

Perry stood up. The room was a disaster. Beer-soaked blankets in a little mountain on the floor, beer-soaked clothes next to the bed. Oh, for fuck's sake – he'd thrown up on his jeans. The place reeked.

He walked to his duffel bag and rummaged through it. Shit, all these clothes were dirty. He'd have to get some of Dew's people to wash them. Perry did the sniff test and found the least offensive T-shirt, sweatshirt, underwear and jeans. The only score was one pair of clean athletic socks. He carried the clothes into the steam-filled bathroom.

First a shower, then he'd track down Dew.

SIR DICKSICKLE

The probe wasn't made of solid material. Not permanently solid, anyway. The whole thing was a collection of tiny particles, each smaller than a grain of sand. A special locking shape combined with a static charge made the individual particles act like a solid sheet of material. It was even airtight. Depending on where the bonds were applied to each particle, any shape could be made. This included moving parts like ailerons, containers to hold fuel and nozzles to direct the force created by igniting that fuel. These parts combined to drive the soda-can-size probe through the upper atmosphere and into a thick cloud layer. High winds pulled the probe first in one direction, then the next. It rode with the wind, using the engines more for guidance than for directed flight.

At 6,250 feet the probe passed through the cloud layer. It identified a target zone and shot northwest. To the Orbital and the probe, one place was the same as the next. On human maps, however, this place had a name.

It was called Gaylord.

At 1,500 feet the probe completed its final instruction. It sent a charge through every particle that turned off the static bonds.

The probe didn't explode. It disintegrated, changing from a solid machine one second to a cloud of grains the next, grains that would spread as they fell and never draw an ounce of attention. The disintegration also released the seeds.

Over a billion of them.

A light southwesterly wind dispersed the seeds like a trail of thin smoke. Each breathy gust spread them farther, some sailing off on a lone journey, some driven in clusters like translucent contrails or intangible ghost-snakes.

The seeds spread.

The seeds fell.

The vast majority of them would land on ground, water or snow. They would sit there until the elements damaged their delicate internal machinery and they simply became lumps of inanimate matter. A few might get lucky and sit around long enough to wind up on a host, but the odds were against them. Of course, that was kind of the point in releasing a *billion* seeds at a time – even with shit odds, a few were still going to land in a suitable place.

One of the expanding, ethereal seed trails drifted near a house on the outskirts of Gaylord, close to Highway 32. This house was the home of the Jewell family.

The Jewells had had their fill of snowmobiles and basketball, it seemed. Bobby, Candice, Chelsea, Donald and Betty were hard at work on the winter ritual of building a snowman.

Donald even made Bobby promise not to give the snowman a boner, something Bobby had done since they were kids. He always sculpted a prodigious member and called the snowman 'Sir Dicksickle.' Funny? Hell yes. But hardly appropriate now that Betty was sixteen. Besides, Chelsea was well into the age where Bobby would have to start acting like a grown man rather than a kid trapped in an adult's body.

The strand of seeds rose and fell on the light breeze. Dipping to the ground, half of them hit the snow and stuck, doomed to a frigid end. The other half caught the wind coming off the snow and cruised along almost horizontally with the ground.

Donald finished rolling up the snowman head and had Betty help him lift it. It was packed pretty tight, but you never knew if these things would hold when they came off the ground. Besides, Betty was being 'too cool' to wear mittens, so having her pick up a big block of ice and snow seemed rather fitting. Bobby wore only a T-shirt and jeans, which didn't really help show Betty the need for proper winter clothing. They'd probably both catch a cold, and Donald would have the last laugh. The only problem with that was that Chelsea wanted to be like her cousin and had also tossed her gloves aside. If Chelsea caught a cold, Donald would be pretty pissed at Betty.

They successfully set the head on top as Chelsea danced in place, hands clutching a big orange carrot. Her puffy baby-blue snowsuit made her look quite chubby. The carrot was the final stroke in the annual snowman masterpiece (who, sadly, would be Sir Dicksickle only in spirit this year), so naturally the honor fell to the youngest.

Just as Bobby reached down to pick up Chelsea and lift her so she could place the snowman's carrot nose, the invisible cloud of microscopic seeds whipped through the Jewell family.

They missed Candice entirely.

Bobby's T-shirt proved to be a disastrous choice – he caught seven on his left arm.

Donald was turned just so and inhaled three of them into his nose. Two more landed on his left hand.

Betty's hat and thick black hair acted as a defense of sorts, trapping the seeds in the wool or amid her hair-sprayed locks. The wind whipped around her head, however, and four landed on her left cheek. One fell off as soon as it hit, but she would still have to deal with the three that stuck fast. If she *had* been wearing gloves, she would have at least avoided the one that stuck on her left hand.

Little Chelsea had the worst luck of all. She made a hole in the snowman's head with her left thumb, then jammed the carrot in with her right hand. As she twisted the carrot, driving it deeper, setting it in real good so it wouldn't fall off, *fifteen* seeds landed on her clammy, exposed skin, sticking fast to the backs of her hands, her palms and her fingers.

Still laughing, the family finished the snowman and applauded. Chelsea made everyone give her smoochies. *Mmmmm-ahhhh! Mmmmm-ahhhh!* Then they all went inside.

LAYIN' DOWN THE LAW

Room 207 had become the de facto ops center for the Glidden/Marinesco installment of Project Tangram. A little extra money and hotel management magically made the bed disappear, replacing it with a wooden table and chairs from the restaurant. Add a smaller table for a row of four briefcases that opened up to be computer/phone stations, and you had an instant office. At the moment the office contained Dew, Baumgartner, Milner and Amos. They were handling various cleanup aspects of the McMillian situation. Amos was only there for the free doughnuts, but that was to be expected.

The really sensitive communications still took place in the MargoMobile, but there was only so much room in there. Dew wanted to finish debriefing everyone, make sure he hadn't missed anything. He also had to keep tabs on local law enforcement and the media.

Local police were almost always a snap. Despite jurisdictional squabbles, cops were all in the game for pretty much the same reason, and it wasn't to get rich. If you told city cops, county cops or even state police that there was some shit going down, shit you couldn't actually talk about, but it was *real* serious and that it was *over*, people were *safe* . . . well, ninety-nine times out of a hundred they'd let it go. And for that one-in-a-hundred liberal prick who wouldn't let something slide? He always had superiors who would play ball, put pressure on the guy to let things lie. Sometimes not even that worked. In those cases Dew would give a last warning, a final face-to-face chat. He'd tell the guy that his whole life was about to turn into a steaming pile of donkey shit, that his reputation was about to be trashed, and if push came to shove he'd be facing some trumped-up charge that would end his career in law enforcement.

If *that* didn't work, Dew pitched it to Murray and washed his hands of the whole situation. Murray Longworth made problems go away. Sucked balls for the guy with the burr under his saddle, but every war has collateral damage.

This time, however, Dew wasn't having any problems. Reports of domestic terrorists, army troops, gunfire and a ground-shaking bomb in Marinesco gobbled up attention. Not that people weren't interested in the sad story of Thad McMillian Sr. going nuts and killing his wife, his daughter and his little boy. A tragedy, that's what it was. A shame he was running a meth lab in that house, a real shame, but it explained the sightings of men in hazmat suits carrying guns, and it explained the two big semi trucks parked in the McMillians' driveway. It also explained the absence of Tad Jr. and the baby. Witness-protection plan. Just for a short time as the feds in town worked through the meth-lab case. The boys were safe, although no one could say when or if they'd be back in town. Seems their grandmother (on the wife's side) lived in Washington State, and the boys were eventually going to go live with her. The local media bought the story hook, line and sinker. METHED-OUT FATHER MURDERS FAMILY would be in area headlines for another few days, sure. Glidden was so small it didn't even have its own newspaper. Soon it would all die down.

This was America. People got killed. Such is life. What time is the game on?

So Dew Phillips was in as good a mood as could be expected for a man trying to deal with a bizarre parasitical invasion. He had helped shut down the fourth gate. He had dry clothes. He was warm again. The media and local police were playing ball. He had a full belly, and room service kept bringing pots of coffee and boxes of doughnuts from Bob's Breakfast Shack.

Everything was going great guns, right up to the moment when the door opened and Perry Dawsey stepped inside.

Four heads turned to stare at him. Milner's hand went to the grip of his pistol and stayed there. Baumgartner's hands locked down on the back of a wooden chair. Amos backed up against a wall, a chocolate doughnut with nuts still hanging in his mouth.

'Dew, I need to talk to you,' Perry said. 'Right now.'

'So talk.'

'Get these faggots out of here,' Perry said.

'I'd be happy to vacate the premises,' Amos said. 'If you'd be so kind as to remove your substantial bulk from the doorway, I'll be gone forthwith.'

Perry stepped aside. Amos shot out of the room like a world-class sprinter coming off the blocks.

'Kid,' Dew said. 'If you've got something to say, just say it. These guys are part of the team.'

'They're fucking peons,' Perry said. 'Don't make me beat their asses again, old man.'

Dew Phillips nodded. Yes, that was just about enough of this shit. It most certainly was.

'Milner, Baumgartner,' Dew said. 'Take a walk.'

Baumgartner seemed uncertain and looked at Dew. Milner kept staring at Perry and kept his hand on the gun. He wasn't taking his eyes off the big man for even a second.

'Sir,' Baumgartner said, 'I think we should stay here.' His metal nose brace glinted in the hotel room's light. Between the brace and the mustache, he couldn't possibly look any dumber.

'I said take a walk,' Dew said.

'Sir,' Baum said. 'Uh . . . you being alone with Dawsey, maybe it's not—'

'Take a motherfucking *walk*, boys,' Dew said. 'Get out. I want to have a private discussion with Citizen Dawsey.'

Baumgartner let go of the chair. He walked out, patting Milner on the back as he did. Milner managed to follow Baum out the door without taking his eyes off Dawsey and without taking his hand off the gun.

Perry shut the door. 'Listen, Dew, something's up.'

'We'll get to that in a second,' Dew said. 'First I've got a pesky little agenda item that we need to address.'

'Dew, you don't understand.'

'Is there a new gate?'

Perry thought for a second, then shook his head.

'Are you hearing new voices?'

Perry thought again. 'Kind of. Yeah, voices, but they aren't saying any words.'

'No words,' Dew said. 'So you're *sure* they're not talking about a gate, then?'

Perry nodded.

'Good,' Dew said. 'Then we'll table the discussion for a few minutes and address my topic of conversation.'

'But Dew, I—'

'Shut your fucking mouth, you little shithead.'

Perry stared for a second, then smiled. 'Oh, I see,' he said. 'Are we going to have a lecture about my behavior?'

'That's right,' Dew said. 'I don't give a fuck how loony tunes you are, Dawsey. I'm sick of your shit. You're going to start playing ball, you got me?'

Perry leaned forward and put his hands on the wooden table. It was the only thing that stood between the two men.

'I call you when I need you,' Perry said. 'I can't roll out a bunch of army assholes with guns and helicopters. You can. Other than that, your services aren't required, so just keep being a good little bitch and go where I tell you to go.'

Dew felt his temper slip into the bad place. Somewhere in the back of his head, he wondered if he'd come out of this alive.

'Say,' Perry said. 'I didn't see a new Mustang parked in front of my room. What's the holdup?'

'You're just a little bastard trapped in a big boy's body,' Dew said.

'There's not a fucking thing you can do about it.'

'*Boo-hoo-hoo,*' Dew said. 'So you had a rough time, and now the world owes you a lollipop?'

'You're goddamned right the world owes me a lollipop. At least my government does. Where the fuck was my government when I was going through hell, huh? Where the fuck were you when those things were eating me up from the inside?'

'You survived,' Dew said.

'I'm the *only one* who survived,' Perry said. 'Because I fought. Because I've got discipline. You've *got* to have discipline.'

Dew laughed. 'You want discipline? I'd like to give you some discipline.'

Perry smiled. 'You want to shoot me? Shoot me. It's

the only way you can put me down. You ain't jack shit without that gun, old man.'

Dew had him. A fight was a foregone conclusion at this point. He just had to keep pushing buttons, get Dawsey out of control. Put him in a rage.

'You mean this gun?' Dew pulled his old .45 from his shoulder holster. He ejected the magazine, cocked back the slide and held up the gun to show there was no bullet in the chamber. He set the gun between them on the table. He held up the magazine with his right hand and used his thumb to flick out the first bullet. Then the second. He stared straight into Perry's eyes as he emptied all seven rounds. He held the final bullet, then tossed the magazine away and bounced the bullet up and down in his palm.

'So now I don't have a gun,' Dew said. 'What do you have to say now, *boy*?'

'Right,' Perry said. 'Like that's the only piece you've got.'

Dew gave an exaggerated nod. The kid was smarter than he looked. Dew pulled up his right pant leg and drew his Taurus Model 85 .38 revolver from his ankle holster. He emptied the five-round cylinder and dropped the gun on the floor. From his left leg, he took a steel telescoping baton and tossed it across the room into a wastebasket. As soon as he did, he wished he'd kept it. A flick of the wrist would expand the baton from six inches to sixteen inches – instant steel billy club. The cat was out of the bag, though; he couldn't exactly go back and get it. Dew then reached to the small of his back and extracted his Ka-Bar from its horizontal sheath. Finally he slid his hands into his crotch and removed a black switchblade. The switchblade and the Ka-Bar followed the baton into the wastebasket.

'What the fuck, old man? You going to war or something?'

'Every day, kid, every day. Now, unless you're going to give me a body-cavity search for the frag grenade I carry up my poop-chute, you're gonna have to take my word for it that I'm disarmed. So are we gonna do this, or are you just gonna sit there wankin' your crank?'

'Are you *serious*, old man? Look at you. Gut hanging out. I see you sometimes limping and shit. I hit you half as hard as I can, I'll probably kill you.'

'I'm not your little butt-buddy Bill,' Dew said quietly.

Perry's eyes widened, a combination of rage and shame.

'You're a big man, Dawsey,' Dew said. 'Killing someone who weighed all of a buck-fifty soaking wet.'

'Don't you talk about him,' Dawsey said in a quiet voice that sent goose bumps up Dew's back.

Dew smiled his best asshole smile. 'What's the matter, pussy? You don't want to take a swing at me? Maybe I can find a midget around here somewhere. Maybe a baby, or a fat woman, or an eighty-year-old grandmother. But that won't work, because those people wouldn't be your friends. They wouldn't be your *best* friend. Someone who trusted you, who tried to help you.'

Dawsey's hands curled up into cinder-block-size fists. 'It wasn't my fault,' he said in that same quiet voice. 'I . . . I wasn't in control.'

'Sure you weren't,' Dew said. 'It's called *accountability*, boy. If you actually had any *discipline*, your little faggot friend would still be alive.'

Perry reached down with his left hand, across his body, and grabbed the right corner of the table. He lifted and threw in one motion, effortlessly flipping the table to his left. It smashed into the wall, legs breaking on impact. The empty .45 bounced across the carpet.

Dew waited.

A snarling Perry Dawsey raised his right fist. Huge muscles rippling, he stepped forward to throw a haymaker.

And just when Perry took that step, Dew flicked the bullet at Perry's face.

The bullet bounced off Perry's forehead. He blinked and flinched, an automatic reaction caused by something flying at his face. He turned his head just a little, his fist hung in the air, and he took an instinctive shuffle-step to maintain his balance as momentum pulled him forward.

Dew opened his right hand, making the space between his thumb and pointer finger as wide as possible. He stepped into the oncoming monster, snapping forward with his horizontal open hand. The crook of his thumb smashed into Dawsey's throat. Dew held back a little – any harder and he would have broken Dawsey's windpipe, making him suffocate to death. He wanted to hurt the guy, not kill him.

Not yet, anyway.

Dawsey's hands shot to his neck, and his eyes scrunched tightly shut. He made a single noise, part-cough, part-gag.

Then Dew Phillips thumbed him in the left eye.

Perry flinched away again, turning his head to the left to protect the eye, left hand coming up to cover it, right hand staying clutched at his throat. He couldn't breathe. He couldn't see.

Dew stepped forward to kick Dawsey in the knee, but the big man flailed his fist in a wild arc that caught Dew's right shoulder. The force spun Dew all the way around, and he fell hard, knocking over the table full of open briefcases. Dew felt the sting of a cut on his right temple, and only a second later a bit of blood came trickling down.

Dew had been in hundreds of fights, and he'd *never* been hit that hard.

He scrambled to his feet. He tried to move his right arm but couldn't – it was numb and unresponsive.

Dawsey was still coughing, still trying to draw a breath, still keeping his watering left eye turned away, still swinging wildly and blindly back and forth with his right hand. Dew skirted the wall to the broken table. With his left hand, he picked up a table leg by the thinner end. The leg's thick top made it look like a polished wooden mace.

Dew stepped forward and swung it low. The thick wood slammed into Dawsey's right knee. Dawsey cried out, his throat capable of producing only a hoarse whisper. He dropped, left knee and right hand holding his weight.

'You want discipline?' Dew said. 'I'll give you discipline.'

Dew swung the table leg in a big arc and brought it down on Perry's head. The skin split open instantly, blood spilling out of a two-inch-long gash that stained his blond hair. Despite the cut, Dawsey barely flinched. His right lid fluttered open a bit, but his left stayed pinched shut. From his half-crouch, he lunged forward, both hands reaching out.

Dew Phillips calmly scooted backward and jabbed the table leg into Perry's mouth, splitting his lip on impact.

Perry fell flat on his face, then put his hands down and tried to rise.

'You're going to play ball,' Dew said. He brought the table leg around in another vicious arc, the club end whistling through the air before it landed on Dawsey's back with a meaty thud. Dawsey let out another choking hiss and fell on his face again.

'You're going to do it because it's the right thing to do.' Dew whipped the table leg in a low swing that hit Perry's right side, crunching into the younger man's ribs. Perry rolled to his left, curling up into a near-fetal ball. He still couldn't see, squinting eyes betraying his blindness. Blood covered his head, poured from his mouth. His knees curled up to his chest, and his hands stuck out in front of him, trying to ward off the attack.

Dew swung again, as hard as he could this time. The club head hit Dawsey's right thigh. Dawsey managed to push a deep scream out through his choking throat.

'I don't want any more shit out of you,' Dew said. He swung the leg and hit the thigh again, knowing that it would hurt far worse the second time. 'Are you going to stop being such a prick?'

'Stop!' Perry shouted. 'Please!'

'You begging for your life, Dawsey? Like your friend Bill did? Like those triangle hosts did?'

'I was *helping* them!' His voice sounded like he'd gargled broken glass.

Dew jabbed the leg straight forward, hitting Dawsey in the forehead. The wood-on-wood sound accompanied another cut, this one longer than the first and bleeding even worse.

'*Helping* them? You psycho fuck, maybe I should just beat you to death right here!'

'No!' Still on his side, knees up to his chest, Perry waved his hands blindly.

Dew raised the table leg for another shot to Dawsey's ribs. He wanted to make this boy *hurt*.

Perry's voice was half-scream, half-cry. 'Don't hit me any more, Daddy! *Please!*'

Dew stared for a few seconds, the table leg suspended in the air.

'Puh . . . please, Daddy,' Dawsey stammered. 'No more.'

Dew lowered the table leg to his side, then dropped it on the floor. He still couldn't move his right arm. The bloody, giant-size man lay crying on the floor, big body shaking with sobs.

'I'll get someone in here to clean you up,' Dew said. 'Then go back to your room. I'll come talk to you there. We've got work to do.'

Dew walked out of the room.

BITCHES GET STITCHES

Clarence leaned his head into the communications trailer. Margaret smiled at him. She couldn't help it. She had thought him handsome the first moment she saw him. Now, after three months on this assignment and more than a few nights in his bed, she found him gorgeous. She was falling for him. No, she had *already* fallen for him. She didn't know if it would be a temporary romance, if when this insanity ended they simply would go their separate ways. Maybe their attraction was just an outlet, a way to deal with the death that surrounded them on a daily basis.

Maybe he was with her because she was the only woman on the project. That thought had crossed her mind more than a few times. She was older, twenty pounds overweight, and while she still got plenty of attention from men, it wasn't as much as she used to get. Was she already in love with him? She pushed the thoughts away – if she let it go that far and he didn't love her in return . . .

'Doc,' Clarence said, 'Dew says you need to go to the office.'

'I'm a little busy,' she said. 'Tell him if he wants to see me, he can come to the trailer. Then I'll get rid of him, and you can give me a nice shoulder rub.'

Clarence shook his head. 'Uh, no can do, Doc. You need to get to the office, and bring a first-aid kit. Seems Dew and Perry had it out.'

'Oh, no. Do we need an ambulance?'

'You're going to have to see this for yourself,' he said. 'Don't worry, I'll go with you.'

Margaret looked through the comm room's cabinets. There was a first-aid kit in here somewhere. . . . She found it, grabbed the white plastic box by its built-in handle and ran out of the trailer toward Room 207.

In a way, Clarence had made her question her life choices, even as she rode a rocket-train of career success and quite literally stood in the path of a potential global catastrophe. She was *the man*, for lack of a better term, something she always longed to be, but thanks to her feelings for him it was starting to ring empty. When this was over, if they separated, what did she have to look forward to? Her sparse apartment in Cincinnati? A place she really used only for sleep, because she worked all the time?

'You don't need to be afraid,' he said as they reached the room. 'I'll be right here with you.' He opened the door for her.

'Afraid? Why would I be afraid of Dew Phil—'

Her voice broke off when she saw Perry Dawsey curled up in a fetal position, bleeding like a stuck pig.

'Like I told you,' Clarence said, 'I'll be right here.'

She couldn't believe it. Dew Phillips had beat up Perry Dawsey? *Beat up* wasn't really the term for it. *Thrashed him to within an inch of his life*. Yeah, that was more accurate.

'Clarence, leave us alone.'

His head whipped around, looking from Perry to her.

'Are you crazy? He's down, he's not dead.'

'I know.'

'He could snap at any second, Margo,' Clarence said. 'I'm staying right here.'

She took his hand and led him out of the room, then pulled his head down so she could whisper in his ear.

'Honey, I know you want to protect me, but he's not going to hurt me.'

'He's a *killer*, Margaret,' Clarence whispered back.

'You're going to have to trust my judgment,' she said. 'I've taken care of him for five weeks, and I'm telling you he's not going to hurt me.'

'Fine, then I'll stay to watch and see how wrong I am.'

'He just got the crap kicked out of him,' Margaret said. 'I'm not a guy, but I think that makes you guys feel a little ashamed? Am I right?'

Clarence stared at her, then nodded.

'So maybe having a woman in there, instead of another man, won't be as bad, because he won't think I'll be wondering if *I* can beat him up, too?'

'Well, that's not exactly how I'd think of it,' he said. 'But yeah, I'd be embarrassed if there was another guy watching me get stitched up. A non-doctor guy, of course. Doctors aren't embarrassing in a situation like this.'

'Guy logic?'

'Guy logic,' he said. 'Listen, can't we at least get Amos to take care of him?'

She smiled at him. 'If you can talk Amos Braun into being in a room alone with Perry Dawsey, I'll give you twenty bucks.'

'I'm not taking that bet.'

'Clarence, I'm a professional. I love the fact that you want to protect me, but this conversation is over, okay? Stand out here if you're worried. If he tries anything, I'll scream for help.'

'That only works if you can make a noise before he breaks your neck.'

She sighed, then slapped him once on the chest and walked into Room 207. She shut the door behind her.

'Perry? It's Margaret.'

He opened his right eye. His left was swollen shut.

'Hey,' he said.

'I'm going to fix you up, okay?'

'Just leave me be.'

'No can do. I'm a doctor. You're bleeding. That's the math.'

Perry looked at her with his one good eye, then slowly sat up. He scooted until he rested his back against the wall.

'Fine,' he said. 'Just till you stop the bleeding.'

She knelt and opened the first-aid kit. She pressed gauze bandages against the cut on top of his head. 'Hold that there, please.'

Perry did.

She put another one on the forehead cut. Blood instantly soaked it.

'Okay, Perry. Tell me what hurts.'

'My ego. I just got my ass kicked by the poster boy for the AARP.'

'Maybe you're lucky,' Margaret said.

'Well, buy me a fucking Lotto ticket. How do you figure I'm *lucky*?'

'Dew's told me a couple of stories over the past three months. He's killed a lot of people, Perry. I know you're big and strong and athletic. You know how to *fight* – Dew Phillips knows how to kill or be killed.'

'Ha,' Perry said. 'He didn't do either. Does that mean I won?'

Margaret laughed. 'See? You're cracking jokes. You can't be hurt that bad.'

'Guess again.'

She tossed the bloody gauze aside, then poured some peroxide on the cut.

'Does that hurt?' she asked.

'Compared to getting hit with a table leg? Might as well be a sensual massage.'

'Good, then just think of this part as your happy ending.'

She proceeded to stitch up his cuts. Six stitches on the forehead, five on the top of the head, and three more on his lip.

'How bad is the eye?' Perry said. 'Is it ruined?'

She pulled open his upper and lower eyelids and flicked a penlight at the pupil. The eye was already filled with blood, but the pupil contracted with each flash.

'You're going to have a hell of a shiner, but I think you'll be okay.'

She made him take off his shirt. Her eyes lingered on the gnarled, fist-size scar on his right collarbone, then inadvertently flicked to the similar one on his left forearm. She'd treated him for weeks and knew of his other horrible scars: on his left thigh, the center of his back and his right gluteus, along with a smaller one on his left shin.

Margaret checked his ribs and found they weren't broken. He refused to remove his pants, so she had to take his word for it that the thigh was okay. She finished by checking his knee, sliding up the pant leg and using her fingertips to probe the area. It was swollen, but she didn't feel anything broken, so she dug her fingers in a little deeper to check for ligament damage.

'Does it hurt when I do this?'

'Yes,' Perry said.

'Describe the pain.'

'Is *goddamn near excruciating* a standard medical term?'

She stopped. 'If I was hurting you that bad, why didn't you say something?'

He shrugged. 'Me and pain go way back.'

'Well, you and your *old buddy pain* are going to be spending some quality time together while you heal up from this. Can you make it back to your room?'

Perry struggled to his feet. Margaret tried to assist, but he was so heavy she felt like a little girl pretending to help rather than making any actual difference. She found a bottle of ibuprofen in the first-aid kit.

'Take four of these and just go to sleep, okay? I'll come and check on you later.'

He took the bottle and hobbled to the door. He opened it, then turned back.

'Tell Dew I need to see him,' Perry said. 'Tell him it's important, and that . . . and that I won't give him any more trouble.'

'Can it wait until tomorrow morning? I want you asleep.'

Perry thought for a second, then nodded. He held up the bottle, gave it a single shake as kind of a salute, then limped toward his room.

She did want him asleep, but she also didn't want to risk a second round of fighting. Perry acted different, *defeated*, but Dew probably hadn't calmed down yet, and any number of insignificant words might set the two men off again.

The only reason Perry Dawsey was still alive was that Dew Phillips wanted him to be.

Margaret needed to make sure Dew didn't change his mind.

THAT CAN'T BE GOOD

As the Jewell family slept, the changes began.

The new seed strain behaved much like the one that had infected Perry Dawsey. At first, anyway. *Demodex folliculorum* – tiny mites that live on every human being on the planet – found the seeds. Since the seeds looked and smelled like the pieces of dead skin that made up *Demodex*'s only food, the mites ate them. Protein-digesting enzymes in the microscopic arachnids' stomachs hammered away at the seed coats, breaking them down, allowing oxygen to penetrate and germination to occur.

And also like Perry's infection, this round began in many microscopic piles of bug shit.

Each activated seed pushed a filament into the skin, penetrating all the way down to the subcutaneous layers. At the bottom of the filament, receptor cells measured specific chemical levels and density, identifying the perfect spot for second-stage growth.

Unlike Perry's strain and those that came before it, these filaments released one of two chemicals into the bloodstream:

Chemical A if it was a hatchling seed, similar to the ones that infected Perry Dawsey and Martin Brewbaker.

Chemical B if it was the new strain.

The chemicals filtered through the host's circulatory system. After a short time, the filament measured the levels of both A and B. This produced a simple majority decision: if there was more Chemical A, the hatchling seeds continued their growth and the new strain seeds shut down. If there was more Chemical B, the inverse occurred.

As it turned out, Bobby Jewell was the only one with more standard hatchling seeds. Five of his seven infections, in fact, were the same thing that had infected Perry.

Betty, Donald and Chelsea Jewell would have the honor of incubating the new strain.

From this point the two strains followed almost identical growth patterns. Second-stage roots reached out to draw material from the subcutaneous environment: proteins, oxygen, amino acids and, especially, sugars. Both strains harnessed the host's natural biological processes to create new microorganisms. There were the *reader-balls* – cilia-covered, sawtoothed, free-moving things designed to tear open cells and examine the DNA inside, analyzing the host's biological blueprint like a computer reading lines of software code. There were the *builders* – they created the flexible cellulose framework that in the original strain would become triangles. There were the *herders* – microorganisms that swam out into the body to find stem cells, cut them free and drag them back to that framework where the reader-balls would slice into them and modify the DNA.

The new strain added to this list. It modified stem cells to produce tiny, free-floating strands of a strong, flexible micro–muscle fiber. These fibers would self-assemble, binding together in specific, collective patterns. While Bobby

Jewell's body dealt with the activities of reader-balls, builders and herders, his daughter, brother and niece would have to deal with the newest microorganism.

Chelsea, Donald and Betty would feel the effects of the *crawlers*.

DAY THREE

CRAWL

Perry Dawsey's seeds had come from batch thirteen. His triangles hatched in seven days. Due to constant design improvements, the seeds of batch seventeen needed only five.

Five days is an engineering marvel of self-organization, a testament to some seriously advanced technology. Consider it an upgrade to the old strain.

For the *new* strain, however, five days seemed like an eternity. Whereas Perry's structures had to build many complex parts, the new structures produced only one thing.

Microscopic strands of modified human muscle.

Hacked muscle.

Each strand contained muscle cells, of course, but also tiny neurotransmitter secretors and a complex crystalline set of molecules capable of both sending and receiving rudimentary signals.

A hacked strand by itself was worthless. It could wiggle . . . and that's about it. It could also send and receive 'I am here' signals, which was key because the strands weren't designed to work by themselves.

The 'I am here' signals drew them together, almost like the last individual bits of cereal floating on top of your milk. The bits just float there, until they get close, and then surface tension yanks them together. When a strand detected an 'I am here' signal from another strand, it wiggled toward it. The wiggling strands reached out to each other, touched and intertwined. Now their signal was twice as strong, drawing more strands, and so on.

A normal human muscle cell by itself is useless. Many cells working in unison, however, produce complex movement. The hacked strands followed a similar logic – the whole proved greater than the sum of the parts. When the hacked-strand collections reached a certain size, about five hundred microns wide, the 'I am here' signal shut off.

A micron is one one-*millionth* of a meter. Five hundred microns is five ten-thousandths of a meter, or about two-*hundredths* of an inch. Damn small, but you can still see something like that with the naked eye.

If you could have looked inside the bodies of Chelsea Jewell, Donald Jewell and Betty Jewell, you would have seen something rather disturbing, something that looked very much like a human nerve cell. On one end, a long, thin axon. On the other end, branching dendrites spreading out like the tributaries of a river.

But in a regular nerve cell, the dendrites don't latch onto other nerve cells, muscle cells and membranes, and they certainly don't reach out and *pull*.

Regular nerve cells, you see, don't *crawl*.

The crawlers implemented a very simple navigation system: cause pain. This was a practical strategy, not a sadistic one: the human body is wired to give pain messages the highest priority. The crawlers' stretching dendrites reached out, locked onto axons, then released a chemical that mimicked normal pain signals. Some nerves ignored this message – those were the *efferent neurons*, the ones that carried signals from the brain to the rest of the body. Also called *motor neurons,* they let the brain do its thing, controlling muscle reactions and bodily functions. The nerves that did *not* ignore these messages of pain, but instead replicated them and passed them on to the brain, those were the *afferent nerves.*

Once the crawlers identified afferent chains, they grabbed, and pulled, and crawled. Every three or four nerves, they released the pain signal again, measured the results and kept moving.

Eventually their crawling would lead them to the brain.

UNKIE DONNY DEPARTS

Fluffy snow blew lightly in all directions, flying into Chelsea's eyes and tickling her nose.

She didn't feel good. She felt kind of hot, achy, and she had some little bumps on her hands. Those hurt a bit, but didn't itch or anything. She held her daddy's hand as Unkie Donny and Betty got into Unkie Donny's car. Betty blew her nose into a pink Kleenex, then put her head back on the car seat and closed her eyes. She didn't feel good, either.

Unkie Donny shut the driver's door and rolled down the window. He coughed hard, a rattling sound in his chest, then stuck his hand out of the window toward Daddy. Unkie Donny's breath billowed out as he talked.

'Little brother, thanks for having us,' he said to Daddy. 'And thanks for the gift that keeps on giving.'

'Oh, put a sock in it,' Daddy said. 'You imported the creeping crud from Pittsburgh. I'm not shaking a hand you just coughed in.'

Unkie Donny's eyes narrowed. 'What the hell is that supposed to mean?' Chelsea took a step back. Unkie Donny suddenly looked kind of scary.

'I'm just teasing,' Daddy said. 'Relax, big brother.'

Unkie Donny stared for a few seconds, and then his face softened. He blinked a bunch, like he was waking up or something.

'Sorry, man,' he said. 'I . . . I guess I really took that the wrong way.'

'Meds?' Daddy said.

Unkie Donny nodded. 'Took them. Honest.'

'Cool,' Daddy said. 'We'll come down to Pittsburgh sometime soon.'

Unkie Donny's eyes narrowed again, then opened again. He shook his head the way a puppy would.

Mommy stepped forward and leaned in the window to give Unkie Donny an awkward hug. 'Drive safe,' she said. 'This storm is supposed to turn into freezing rain. The roads are full of downstaters, and the traffic is going to be terrible. Watch out for the drunks.'

She backed out of the window. Unkie Donny smiled and nodded. Mommy went around the other side of the car to say good-bye to Betty. Unkie Donny looked right at Chelsea. He held out his hand.

'Come here, dolly,' he said. 'Say good-bye to me.'

Chelsea shrank back. Why did Unkie Donny want to touch her? Was he going to do something to her?

'Honey,' Daddy said, 'go say good-bye to your uncle.'

Unkie Donny smiled. Chelsea blinked a few times. It was Unkie Donny – why would she be afraid of him? He loved her. Chelsea let go of her daddy's hand and ran up to the car door. She stood on her tiptoes and kissed Unkie Donny on the cheek.

'Bye-bye, Unkie Donny.'

'You be a good girl, okay?'

Chelsea nodded. He seemed . . . different. So did Daddy. So did Cousin Betty. The only one who didn't seem different was Mommy. Why was that? Maybe Chelsea didn't need to fear Unkie Donny at all – maybe she needed to fear Mommy. Mommy might get the spanky-spoon.

Chelsea leaned in and whispered in Unkie Donny's ear. 'When we come see you, can you take me to get my ears pierced?'

Unkie Donny laughed, then touched her cheek. 'I'm afraid that's up to your dad.'

Chelsea loved the way Unkie Donny smiled at her. Just like Daddy did. Unkie Donny was a lot like Daddy. Chelsea wished he would come by more often. He knew a lot about the Deeeee-troit basket-ballll.

Unkie Donny's face wrinkled up. He gently pushed Chelsea away, then coughed so hard his head almost hit the steering wheel. He coughed again, then leaned back and laughed a little. He waved his hand at his face, like he was trying to cool off.

'I'm going to get you for giving this to us,' Unkie Donny said to Daddy. 'I hope we get home before it really kicks in; I've got a feeling this is going to be a humdinger.'

'If you get sick, just be safe and get a hotel,' Mommy said. 'Don't be a stubborn bastard like your brother.'

'Candice, come on,' Daddy said.

Chelsea knew that Daddy was pointing at her, even though she couldn't see him do it. He did that when Mommy used the bad language.

'Aw, crap, sorry,' Mommy said. 'Okay, guys, you get going – and *drive safe!*'

Unkie Donny rolled up the window and backed out of the drive. As he drove away, Chelsea poked at the little bumps on her hands.

Mommy knelt down in front of her. 'Honey, are you okay?'

What did Mommy mean by that? Maybe she meant . . . nothing. Chelsea did feel really hot. Mommy was just trying to take care of her. Chelsea shook her head.

'Okay, baby,' Mommy said. 'Let's get you out of this cold air and back to bed.'

'Me too,' Daddy said. 'I feel wrecked. Let's hit the sack.'

The Jewell family walked inside the house.

MALE BONDING STRATEGIES

Dew Phillips knocked on Perry's door.

'Come on in.'

Dew did so and shut the door behind him. Perry Dawsey looked like hell. A red and black scalp line ran through his blond hair. Another such line ran down his forehead in an angle from above his left eye almost down to the bridge of his nose. His lips were horribly swollen. The left eye was pure red dotted with a blue iris.

Dawsey was sitting on his bare mattress, elbows resting on his thighs, head hung low. He held a half-empty bottle of Wild Turkey American Spirit.

'Where the fuck did you get that bottle?'

'You get your per diem, I get mine,' Perry said. 'Had another bottle in the trunk of the 'Stang, but it broke.'

Dew casually pressed his right arm against his right side, feeling the comforting bulge of the .45 under his jacket. He'd gotten lucky fighting Dawsey, and he wasn't about to push that luck – if Dawsey attacked, Dew was going to shoot him.

'How you feeling?' Dew asked.

Perry raised his head. The blond hair hung in his face.

'I feel like someone hit me in the head with a table leg,' Perry said. 'And the mouth. And back. And thigh. And look at you – I can tell by that little Band-Aid that I really fucked up your world.'

Dew's hand went to the small Band-Aid on his forehead. The cut from hitting the table hadn't even required a stitch.

'If it's any consolation,' Dew said, 'I can still barely move my arm.'

'Why, do you have arthritis? I didn't even land a punch.'

'You grazed me,' Dew said. 'That's all it took. Look, I'm not going to lie to you – my patience is at its end. You hurt any more of my men, I'm going to shoot you. If you come at *me* again, I'm going to shoot you. In the leg if I have time, in the face if I don't. We need you real bad, but I'm not about to take one for the team, if you catch my drift.'

'I'll . . . I'll behave,' Perry said. 'You whipped me fair and square.'

Dew marveled at the phrase. It sounded like something Dew would have said in *his* childhood after a fight. But that had been over fifty years ago. Kids today weren't like that: they didn't trade punches, then shake hands and call it good. Nowadays they talked shit and found a gun. Dew felt a surprise spike of admiration for Perry.

'I'd hardly call beating you with a table leg fair,' Dew said.

Perry shrugged. 'I outweigh you by like sixty pounds. If I'd got my hands on you, I think I would have killed you. Besides, it doesn't matter *how* you win, as long as you win.'

Silence filled the room for a few moments.

'So,' Dew said, 'you're not looking for a rematch?'

Perry stared at the wall for a few seconds, then spoke slowly, thoughtfully. 'Not very many people can take me out. There's you, and . . . there was one other person that's ever done that. I don't want a rematch. I'll play ball.'

Dew nodded. He let himself hope that maybe he'd finally gotten through. 'Okay, kid. Let's start from the top. You told me that something had changed. What changed?'

'The voice.'

'The voice. You said they hadn't said any words yet. Can you hear any now?'

Perry shook his head. 'No. If I'm close enough to an infected, I can hear words, but when I'm far away, it's more like a sensation. Images, emotions, stuff like that. Sometimes I can get a grip on it, sometimes it's like a half-whisper in a crowded room. The more infected there are in one place, the stronger the sensation. You can only pick out little bits and pieces, maybe enough to get the gist of a conversation, you know what I mean?'

Dew nodded.

'Now there's the same bits and pieces, but there's a different . . . intensity. I don't know how to describe it. Sort of feels like . . . like you were down by twenty-one at the end of the half but you adjusted your blitzing strategy, you shut them down, and your offense scored twice to cut it to seven, and there's three minutes left, and you're *so excited,* because if you get just *one more stop,* your offense can tie it up or even win it. And that's hard to do, right? But you feel like it's destiny, it's going to happen for sure. You've got the momentum. You think you've got them figured out, and the win is . . . is . . .'

'Inevitable?' Dew asked.

Perry snapped his fingers, pointed at Dew and smiled. The smile looked ghastly on his stitched, swollen lips.

'That's it,' Perry said. 'It's inevitable. That's what it feels like.'

'So this voice of God says, or feels like, it's . . . uh, mounting a fourth-quarter comeback?'

Perry nodded. 'Yeah, that's pretty close.'

'So what happens next?'

'I don't know,' Perry said. 'Maybe it actually *is* the voice of God, and if we get to heaven, he's going to kick us in the Jimmy and send us packing.'

'There ain't no heaven,' Dew said. 'And there ain't no God. 'Cause if there is some all-powerful deity, he sure is one mean fucker. He likes to let good people die and bad people live. And, apparently, he likes to infect former football stars with things that eat them up from the inside.'

'I'll drink to that,' Perry said, and took a long swig of Wild Turkey.

'We're in a bit of a pickle here, boy,' Dew said. 'Maybe you should stop drinking.'

'Maybe you should *start*,' Perry said. 'I killed my best friend, cut off my own junk, and I'm some kind of psychic call-in line for these things. And *you*? Dude, you're dropping bombs on *America*. You're in charge of fighting honest-to-God *aliens*. Ask me, that's a pretty good reason for a snort or three.'

Perry held out the bottle. Dew looked at the nasty scar on Perry's left forearm. War scars, that's what Perry had.

Dew accepted the bottle. The kid was right. Dew took a long swig. The bourbon tang was a welcome sensation, a friendly memory of distant times when he could just have a drink and relax. He knocked back another long pull, then handed the bottle to Perry.

Perry drank. 'You got something you got to do?'

'I'm doing it,' Dew said. 'Margaret asked that we stay here a little longer, give you a chance to rest. So until we leave, getting you to be more cooperative is kind of my main job.'

Perry looked at the chair. Dew wasn't sure, but he thought the kid turned a little red. Like he was embarrassed or something.

'You, uh . . .,' Perry said. 'You want to . . . sit down and . . . shoot the shit?'

Perry offered the bottle again. Dew took it, sat down and had another long swig.

UNKIE DONNY HAS
HAD BETTER DAYS

Donald Jewell, or 'Unkie Donny,' as Chelsea liked to call him, did not feel good. Perhaps it was more accurate to say that he felt like a tainted can of boiled elephant ass.

The fever had picked up steam. It came nicely packaged with an overall ache, as well as annoying shooting pains in his left arm. Far worse was that Betty seemed just as sick. She was slumped in the passenger seat, head against the window, eyes closed. And she was sweating.

But that wasn't the worst of it.

Someone was *following* him.

He couldn't be sure who it was; there were so many cars on the highway. But he'd seen cars behind him, the same cars, several times. Who was it? What did they want?

He'd been on the road for over two hours. He had at least six to go, more like eight or nine if the weather didn't let up. Freezing rain made driving a royal bitch. All the traffic on I-75 moved along at forty-five miles an hour. At least up north, people knew how to drive in winter: it was a safe bet that the cars in the ditch belonged to downstaters or people from Ohio.

He was hot, he was sleepy, the conditions were crap – not a good combination when his whole life sat in the passenger seat next to him.

Who was following him? *Who?*

Donald pulled off the highway into a rest stop near Bay City. He exited slowly, seeing which cars behind him did the same. None did. They must have known he was onto them.

Or maybe he was acting crazy. . . . No one was following him. That was just nuts.

He pulled up to the rest stop building and parked gently, so as not to wake his daughter. Cars packed the lot. Some were still running, tailpipes trailing exhaust, windshield wipers fighting the constant battle against icy clumps. Other drivers had thrown in the towel, shutting off the engines and letting the freezing rain cover their cars in a thin, bumpy sheet of ice.

Since he was here, maybe he could just get some sleep. He shouldn't be driving when he felt like this. What if he fell asleep at the wheel?

He quietly opened the door and headed to the trunk, shoulders hunched against the frigid, driving rain. He stopped halfway, face scrunching in pain and head twitching to the left until his ear touched his shoulder. Another shooting pain, this one a real doozy. It faded slowly. By the time it was gone, Donald's jacket was nearly soaked. He cursed his brother for making him sick, then opened the trunk and pulled out a sleeping bag.

Darting back into the car, he removed his wet coat before spreading half of the sleeping bag on his daughter. He spread the other half on himself, coughed, blew his nose, cursed his brother one more time, then laid his head against the headrest.

Just an hour or two, a quick nap while the storm blew over and the snowplows cleared the highways, and then they'd be back on the road.

Inside Donny's body, things were rapidly shifting from Fucking Bad to Even Fucking Worse.

The problem began with his telomeres. What is a telomere? Picture the little plastic bits on the end of your shoelaces. Imagine each time you tie your shoes, you have to clip off a little bit of that plastic part to get it to go through the lace holes. After you've done this enough times, the plastic tip is gone and the shoelace starts to unravel. Once the laces unravel enough, it's impossible to tie your shoes, and you walk around looking like a goober.

Telomeres are the DNA equivalent of those plastic shoelace bits. When your cells divide via mitosis, the chromosomes of those cells also divide. One set of chromosomes divides to become two half-sets. Your body duplicates each half-set, and one cell becomes two daughter cells.

Simple enough, but there's a catch.

When your chromosomes split, it's like a zipper splitting into two parts. Enzymes flood the newly divided chromosome and fill in the missing zipper halves, one little zipper tooth at a time. Problem is, the zipper teeth can't reach all the way to the end – there has to be a little cap there, and that cap is the last bit of the repetitive telomere. On the next cell division, that last bit of telomere is discarded just like the snipped bit of the plastic shoelace.

If cells with shortened telomeres continue to divide, bad stuff can happen. The cell might enter into apoptosis (the natural kind, not the triangle-induced chain-reaction kind). Worse, damage to a critical gene might make the cell cancerous. This can happen in skin cells, muscle cells, lung cells . . . and even stem cells.

When a stem cell splits into two daughter cells, it uses a process called *differentiation* to make one daughter cell another stem cell, while the other becomes any number of good things – muscle, bone, nerve cells, whatever. Stem cells are just funky that way. But as they divide, they suffer the same telomere reduction as any other cell.

As you get older and cells continue to divide, those telomeres shorten and problems become more likely. We have a simple word for this phenomenon: *aging*. Cells with telomeres that are too short stop dividing and stop replenishing themselves. This is why your skin gets thin when you age, because the cells stop replicating as effectively – they have used up their telomeres during your preceeding years of life.

Or to think of it in simpler terms, a copy of a copy of a copy can get pretty messed up.

Triangles used many stem cells to make their cellulose framework and become full-blown hatchlings. Sometimes old stem-cell lines produced bad shit: defective cells, even cancerous cells. When that happened, the reader-balls and herders and builders identified bad stem cells and simply removed them.

The stem cells producing crawler strands, on the other hand, worked as solo operatives. They were in a *hurry*. Herders focused on finding and converting more stem cells, not doing quality control.

Donald, being the oldest of the three infected Jewells, had more shortened telomeres than Betty, and far more than Chelsea. Most of his modified stem cells produced defective muscle strands. Some of these strands were dead on arrival, just floating bits. Others lived long enough to send and receive the 'I am here' signal and join up with other strands. Still others made it to full crawler size and began their mission along the nerves, although this effort alone was usually enough to make them shut down after a little bit of distance.

And when they shut down, the rot began.

Slowly at first, a low-level exponential reaction. But as the number of dead strands grew, so did the level of rot-inducing chemicals.

Each modified muscle strand carried both the apoptosis catalyst and a strong counterchemical that blocked the catalyst. If there were more living strands than dead strands, the apoptosis couldn't gain a foothold. But when there were more *dead* strands than *living* strands, that balance tipped the other way.

Throughout Donny's body that balance was tipping fast. Tiny areas of cell death expanded and multiplied. Particularly in his left hand, the apoptosis compounded on itself and started to spiral out of control.

While he slept, Donny Jewell began to dissolve from the inside out.

THE LITTLE BLUE BOOK

Zero casualties. Well, one if you counted Private Domkus tripping on a branch and spraining his ankle, but other than that, nothing. So if it was his most successful hatchling encounter yet, why did Colonel Charlie Ogden feel so anxious?

Air transport had pulled all of Whiskey and X-Ray companies out of Marinesco and taken them back to Fort Bragg. North Carolina wasn't exactly a central location for the missions, but it wasn't that far, only a forty-five-minute flight to Detroit on a C-17 Globemaster transport jet.

Fort Bragg was a big base. Big enough to sequester an entire battalion for five weeks and counting. Aside from missions, the men hadn't left the base or had any contact with people outside the unit save for CIA-screened letters, or CIA-monitored phone calls to immediate family only. Ogden was no exception – he hadn't seen his wife in over a month. It sucked, but that was war.

Fort Bragg also housed the USASOC, the United States Army Special Operations Command. Unconventional warfare, special reconnaissance, antiterrorism – all kinds of aircraft, coming and going at all hours. No one asked where they went, no one asked why they went. That was life 24/7 for the USASOC, and it provided ideal cover for Project Tangram operations.

Throw in all the aircraft available at the adjacent Pope Air Force Base, including plenty of those C-17s, and you had a perfect mix – built-in secrecy, endless options for transport. The DOMREC came and went; no one wondered why.

Ogden sat alone in his quarters, performing his nightly ritual. It consisted of three things:

A letter to his wife.

The Bible.

The Little Blue Book.

He kept the letter short. He was tired and had to get some sleep. *I love you, I miss you terribly, I don't know when I can come home, but I pray it will be soon.* The usual stuff, repetitive only because it was sincere and he had to express it to her every day. Fold, insert, but don't seal – tomorrow some CIA shithead would read it and make sure he wasn't writing home about the hatchlings.

The Bible was just the New Testament, actually. Most of the gold lettering on the faux-red-leather cover had flaked off. Half of the back cover had torn off somewhere in the Mideast. Just random damage, not sacrilege.

Every night he read passages from the New Testament, then moved on to the Little Blue Book. Sometimes he'd skim the Bible passages, skip around, read some sentences and not others, but he didn't do that with the Little Blue Book. With that one he read every single word.

Every single name.

He opened it and started reading.

Lewis Aucoin, 22.

He never wrote down rank. Death was death. You didn't get a better death because you had a better rank, right?

Parker Cichetti, 27.

He remembered Parker. Good guy. Could juggle.

Damon Gonzalez, 20.

He'd never met Damon. Not even once.

He continued down the list of names, giving each one a moment of remembrance, a flicker of light in the terrestrial world just in case the afterlife was dark and silent. Sometimes he wondered if the souls of the dead could experience heaven only when someone remembered their name. Once you were forgotten, you were truly gone forever. Guys like Einstein, Patton, Caesar . . . every day people read about them in history books, saw their names in movies and TV – they spent an eternity in heaven. Guys like Damon? Probably would wink out of existence shortly after Ogden himself passed on.

He didn't know where he'd picked up that strange belief, but it was always at the back of his head, driving him, pushing him to greater and greater achievements. He had to make a name for himself. He'd never thought the name could be as grand as that of a Churchill or a Schwarzkopf, but now he knew better.

He'd been given a once-in-a-lifetime task, and if he succeeded, victory would land him in the history books forever.

Was God testing him with this task? That was definitely possible. God worked in mysterious ways, true, but twenty years in the military had shown Ogden more of man's inhumanity to man than he cared to remember. Sometimes God just put the players on the field and let them have at it.

Before all this began, he thought he'd spend four or five more years at lieutenant colonel, *maybe* make colonel near the tail end of his career, then retire as such. He wasn't that great at playing the political game. He knew tactics and strategy. He knew how to win battles and minimize casualties. That's what the army *should* base promotion on, but it doesn't always work that way.

How things had changed in the past five weeks. He was a full bird colonel. He talked directly with the Joint Chiefs, had their total confidence. He had a black budget, a blank check for resources, for transport, for air support.

A command like this should have gone to a more senior guy, but President Hutchins had been obsessed with secrecy, limiting those in the know. Ogden had simply drawn the lucky card for the first mission, and now he got to keep playing it.

He'd fulfill the mission to destroy any gate he found, and he'd do it while adding as few names to the Little Blue Book as possible. Thirty-seven names was enough, but he knew there would be more.

Many more.

He put the book and the Bible away, then lay down to get his usual four hours of sleep. At least he didn't have to finish the night by writing condolence letters to mothers, fathers and wives. In the morning he'd start planning again, figuring out how to prepare for an enemy no one had ever fought, an enemy guaranteed to change tactics.

Whatever happened, Colonel Charlie Ogden would be ready.

GAYLORD GOES TO BED

The Jewell family won the honor of having the most infected, but they weren't the only residents of Gaylord sleeping away fevers, exhaustion and paranoia.

Bobby and Chelsea Jewell were already in bed. Donald and Betty slept fitfully at a rest stop on I-75 outside of Bay City, Michigan.

Sam Collins was damn old, damn tired and, although he was convinced that someone would probably break in and kill him, he just locked all the doors and went to sleep in his bed.

Wallace Beckett wasn't quite so brave. He couldn't stop scratching at his cheek and lower neck. He hid in his pantry, blocked the door with a stepladder, then went to sleep right on the floor. His son, Beck (yes, the lad was saddled with the unfortunate name of Beck Beckett), was so hot he took off all his clothes and went to sleep naked in an empty bathtub. Nicole Beckett, wife of Wallace, mother of Beck, was off seeing her grandmother in Topinabee. Unfortunately for her, she'd be home the next morning.

Ryan Roznowski was also itchy as all get-out. He *hated* being itchy, a phobia carried over from the time he'd been a kid and gotten poison ivy on his 'nads. His mom had always told him to stop touching himself so much, but did he listen? That incident meant Ryan always stocked a healthy supply of calamine lotion. He doused his four itchy spots, then promptly hid behind the lumber pile in his garage and went to sleep.

Bernadette Smith suddenly had a sneaking suspicion her kids were talking about her behind her back. She sent her son and daughters to their rooms, told them not to come out or make a noise. If they did, they'd get the paddle again. Her husband, Shawn, argued with her about paddling the kids, but she told him to shut the fuck up or she wouldn't let him go to bowling league. In fact, Shawn, why don't you just go to the store and get me some tampons, and when you get back, don't you *dare* wake me up or let the kids out of their rooms. Do you hear me, Shawn? Shawn did hear her. She didn't use the paddle on him, but she could control him just the same.

Chris 'Cheffie' Jones was a little more off-kilter than the others. Cheffie had hardwood floors covered with a big roll-up carpet. For reasons known only to him, he crawled under said carpet. Confident that this made him effectively invisible, Cheffie went to sleep.

The Orbital had estimated fifteen to twenty infections. Ten was below those projections, but still within acceptable parameters for success. And it broke down evenly, five with the triangle strain, five with the new strain. That part, at least, was on par with the statistical projections.

All of these hosts slept.

The only question was . . . how many would wake up?

DON'T CALL DR. CHENG

Margaret, Amos and Clarence sat in the MargoMobile's computer room, waiting for a scheduled all-hands call with Murray Longworth. Right on time his face appeared on the center flat-panel screen. Murray was watching them on a similar monitor back in Washington.

'Where's Dew?' he asked.

'Talking to Perry.'

'Can't you guys talk on the road?' Murray said. 'I want you out of there.'

Clarence leaned forward. 'Perry had a little accident. Margaret wants to let him rest a bit more before we head out.'

'An accident?' Murray said. 'What kind of accident?'

'He fell down some stairs,' Clarence said. 'Then bumped into a doorway. He's happy to cooperate with us now.'

Murray smiled thinly. 'I guess the good news just keeps on rolling in. We finished the first batch of your testers, Margaret. Ten thousand are being distributed to police, paramedics and hospitals all over the Midwest.'

'Wow,' Margaret said. 'How did you get them made so fast?'

'Money, how else?' Murray said. 'We'll have another fifty thousand ready by late tomorrow.'

'Fantastic,' Margaret said. 'But we're still at square one when it comes to the vector.'

'You know we've got people on that, Doctor,' Murray said. 'Some of the most brilliant minds the nation has to offer.'

'Such as?'

'You're not cleared for that information,' Murray said. He sounded annoyed, and Margaret couldn't really blame him – she'd lost count of the number of times they'd had this conversation. She prayed President Gutierrez would loosen the noose of secrecy around this project, but so far Hutchins's policies were still in force.

'Fine,' Margaret said. 'I'm not cleared. Let me ask this another way. Do these brilliant minds know *exactly* what they are looking for? Do they have the whole story?'

'You just keep feeding us whatever biological information you discover,' Murray said. 'We have to keep this compartmentalized.'

Margaret rolled her eyes. 'Murray, we had to drop a *bomb* this time. Your compartmentalization isn't working.'

'Look, I'm not a complete idiot,' Murray said. 'Doctor Cheng is using the full resources of the CDC to find a vector.'

'Right,' Margaret said. 'And how can he do that if he can't say what the disease is?'

'He's using flesh-eating bacteria as a cover story, entering in additional symptoms like blue triangles, skin necrosis, paranoia, et cetera. He's using all the CDC's disease-tracking databases looking for such symptoms, and he's also working with data that FBI investigators have collected on each of the hosts and the hosts' families.'

Margaret sat back. Actually, modifying the symptoms of flesh-eating bacteria to include the triangle symptoms was a brilliant idea. Everyone in the medical profession took necrotizing fasciitis very seriously and would pay close attention to any updates and requests for information.

'Okay, I can see that strategy,' Margaret said. 'So what angles is Cheng pursuing?'

'Everything from mechanical and biological vectors to doomsday cults intentionally targeting specific victims,' Murray said. 'He's focusing on the rural nature of the constructs, hoping for a correlation to deer or other animals that flourish in remote areas.'

'The Bambi vector,' Amos said. 'Well, that's just plain brilliant. I'm so glad one of the nation's *most brilliant minds* is on this.'

Margaret gently put a hand on Amos's arm to silence him. 'Murray,' she said, 'deer are not the vector, and this isn't a doomsday cult. Cheng is grasping at straws. We need access to the same data he has.'

Murray smiled. 'Margaret, Doctor Cheng's track record is impeccable, and he's been working on Morgellons for years. He also has CDC's computer system, the most advanced disease-tracking database on the planet. What makes you think you can do any better from a damn autopsy trailer?'

'The three people in this room already know *everything*,' Margaret said. 'If there's a connection to be made, we're the ones most likely to make it. Hey, if you're happy with your *Option Number Four* fighters flying around America, then by all means keep the status quo – just make sure we're *very* far away from the *eighteen-million-degree* fireball, okay?'

Murray considered this for a moment. 'All right, fine, I'll give you access.'

'What about signals intelligence?' Clarence asked. 'Ogden thinks there has to be a satellite involved. Anything on that?'

Murray shook his head. 'Nothing. The NSA still isn't detecting any kind of signal. NASA is looking for indications of anything weird in orbit, but so far nada.'

'It could be a stealth satellite,' Clarence said.

'They're telling me the physics doesn't add up,' Murray said. 'It's way beyond me.'

'The enemy is doing things with biotechnology that we can't even *fathom* yet, let alone replicate,' Margaret said. 'Maybe hiding something from NASA isn't as hard as we'd like to think.'

'Maybe,' Murray said. 'You'll get your access, but *do not* contact Cheng directly, understood? Apparently he's not fond of you, Margaret.'

'I can't imagine why,' Margaret said.

Murray broke the connection.

'That's great we have the data,' Amos said. 'But seriously, Margo, the CDC has that software, one of the world's most powerful supercomputers to run it and systems analysts to tweak it. I know the three of us are a clever bunch of monkeys, but what do we have that they don't?'

'That's simple,' Margaret said. 'We have a newly cooperative Perry Dawsey.'

THE YOUTH OF A NATION

A child's cells haven't divided as many times as an adult's. Hence children's telomeres have suffered less damage, mutation and shortening. They're just plain healthier.

So when the reader-balls converted Chelsea's stem cells into hacked-muscle factories, most of those factories produced exactly what they were supposed to produce: healthy, modified muscle fibers.

The fibers sought each other out, then turned into crawlers that slinked up her nerves.

Pains shot up the little girl's body, making her twitch in her sleep, making her whimper, making tears leak from her closed eyes. Like the rest of the newly infected, she slept through the pain.

Unhindered by bad production or spreading apoptosis, her crawlers made excellent time. The army of slowly moving microorganisms followed the afferent nerves from her hands to her arms, her shoulders, and soon found themselves sliding inside her backbone and into the spinal column.

The journey to this spot hadn't been easy. Nerves run through and/or around muscles, veins, bones, tendons, ligaments and cartilage. The crawlers forced their way through these dense areas like explorers fighting through thick jungle underbrush. Reaching the spinal column, however, was like stepping out of that jungle onto the smooth asphalt of a superhighway.

The crawlers poured into her spinal column by the thousands.

From there it was a hop, a skip and a jump into Chelsea Jewell's brain.

DRUNKEN CONVERSATION

Dew hadn't been this drunk in a long, long time.

The last time had been with Malcolm, his partner. Malcolm, who had been killed by a hatchet to the stomach courtesy of Martin Brewbaker. One of the infected. And now, Dew was getting drunk with another of Brewbaker's kind.

But Dawsey wasn't infected anymore.

'I'll tell you something, hoss,' Dew said. 'I'll tell you. I have met a lot of tough bastards in my day. I have to say, in some ways, you might be the toughest.'

Perry smiled his split-lip smile and raised the bottle in salute. There was only a swig or two left.

'Thanks, Mister Phillips,' Perry said, then tipped back the bottle. He left a little bit, perhaps half a shot's worth, and offered the bottle to Dew. Dew took it and drained it.

'For all the good it does me,' Perry said. His smile faded, and it had been fake to begin with. He looked haunted. Dew had seen expressions like that before, many years ago. He'd seen them on the kids in his platoon. Not all the kids, and not all the time. Usually after losing a friend, or hunkering down against a mortar attack that lasted for days, or killing a little boy who was holding a hand grenade and running right at their buddies, or the first time they put a knife into a man's belly and held a hand over his mouth while he died.

'So I'm *tough*,' Perry said. 'Whoop-de-fuckin'-doo. What did being *tough* get me? My cock is ruined, man. They sewed it back on, but they don't know if I'll ever get a boner again. They said I might be impotent for the rest of my life. For sure I can never have kids.'

'So you don't get to have kids, so what? I'll never have a son.'

'You have a daughter,' Perry said.

Dew nodded. 'True, and I love her to death. You've got me there. But you know what? She hates fishing. Wouldn't go even one time just to try it. She saw fish on TV and thought they *looked* slimy. I never went fishing with my kid. Won't be able to do it with grandkids, either, because she's not having children. My line gets snuffed out just like yours.'

'Why won't she have kids?'

'She's a dyke.'

'No shit?'

'No shit,' Dew said. 'I don't see her and her *partner* kicking out a passel of little ones, if you know what I'm sayin'. And I love her for who she is, by the fucking way, so if you use the word *dyke* again, I'm going to kick you right in the nuts.'

'I didn't say dyke, Mister Phillips. You did.'

'I did?'

'Yeah.

'Oh,' Dew said. 'Well, then stop calling me Mister Phillips, goddamit.'

'Yes sir.'

'And can that *sir* shit. I work for a living. You call me Dew. But not *Dewie*. I hate that.'

'Okay, Dew,' Perry said. His voice sounded deeper than normal. Elbows on his thighs, his head hung low again, uneven hair drooping down like a blond curtain hiding the stage of his face.

Dew realized he'd just threatened to kick Perry in the nuts. Probably not the most sensitive thing to say to someone who had taken a pair of poultry shears to Big Jim and the Twins. Dew took a deep breath – he'd have to remember to think before he talked.

'You know what, hoss?' Dew said.

Perry managed to shrug without lifting his head.

'I'm kind of sick of your whining.'

This time Perry looked up. Not all the way, but enough for the blue eyes to stare out from behind the blond curtain.

'Whining?' Perry said in a hiss. 'How about you cut off *your* junk, get shot twice, then go through two weeks of an experimental treatment that feels like little men made of fire walking around under your skin and pissing flames on all the important stuff, stuff like your brain. And while you're visiting my slice of paradise, bring in a team of specialists to sew your Jimmy back on, *minus* your nuts, of course, 'cause they had tentacles growing through them, and *then* listen to the motherfucking specialists tell you your cock has maybe a ten percent chance of ever functioning again. How about you do that, *Dew,* and tell me I'm whining.'

'You pooooor fucking baby.'

Perry's eyes showed another emotion – shame. Or maybe it was just pain. The pain of hearing someone you respect tell you you're worthless.

'Look, hoss, that sucks,' Dew said. 'But the thing is, you need to quit feeling sorry for yourself.'

'I think I've got a golden ticket to feel sorry for myself,' Perry said. 'I think I pass "go" and collect two hundred bucks on the way, because if *I* don't have the right to feel sorry for myself, who the fuck *would*?'

'How about Marty Hernandez?'

Perry's eyes narrowed in confusion. 'Who the hell is that?'

'A kid I served with back in 'Nam.'

'Oh, come on,' Perry said. 'War stories?'

'Yes, war stories. Just listen, okay?'

Dew let it hang in the air. Perry gave that narrow-eyed look again, but nodded.

'We were on patrol in the foothills of Binh Thuan. We came under fire, caught off guard. Couple guys went down right away. Marty and I jumped off the trail into a nice little depression that gave some cover, only Marty took a round just as he jumped. Hit his leg below the knee, man. *Severed* it, except for a little string of meat and skin. So he starts screaming. I get to the edge and return fire, because they might have been right behind us, you know?'

Perry nodded as if he knew.

'Marty is in real bad shape. But I can't help him, because I've got Charlie coming at us. I can see them charging, so I'm shooting. Marty is bleeding all over; he has leaves and sticks and shit stuck to the stump of his leg. He stops screaming. I'm still firing. I know I killed two, maybe a third, then Marty, he says real calm, *Dew, let's get out of here*. I sneak a look at him. He'd used his knife to finish the job on the leg, and he's holding his foot and leg to his chest like it's a fucking baby. Bullets are hitting all around me, so I turn back and start firing again. Then you know what Marty does?'

Perry shook his head.

'He starts talking to me about the Raiders.'

'Get the fuck out of here,' Perry said. 'The Oakland Raiders?'

Dew nodded. 'Yeah, he loved them. Had that logo with the shield and the swords tattooed on his shoulder, man. Bad tat, too. Another guy in the platoon did the work, but that doesn't matter, right?'

'Right.'

'Right. So he's in shock, he's sitting there, holding his leg like you'd hold a baby, and he says, *They gotta get Flores back.* You know about Tom Flores?'

'Sure, he won two Super Bowls as a coach.'

'He was a quarterback first.'

'No shit?'

'No shit.'

Perry was leaning forward now, his eyes wide with interest.

Dew continued. 'Quarterback. First hispanic QB in the league, so of course Alvarez, *El Mexicano*, he thinks Flores is fucking God in a helmet and pads. The Raiders traded Flores to Buffalo, and Alvarez was pissed. He says, *Dew, they gotta get Flores back.* He's sitting there holding his severed leg, and he's talking goddamn football.'

'So what did you say?'

'I didn't say anything. I'm killing gooks left and right and I'm thinking, God help me for thinking it, but I'm thinking, if he can hold his leg, he can hold a gun, and why isn't he laying down fire? Anyway, our line forms up on the right and left and we held, and then our F-O called in artillery.'

'F-O?'

'Forward observer.'

'Oh.'

'So the artillery comes in, practically right on top of us. I'm still shooting. Marty starts talking again, but he has to yell to be heard over the artillery. So he's yelling, *I just got this goddamn tat and they trade Flores to Buffalo. I'm not getting a Buffalo Bills tattoo, Dew. I'm just not.* Artillery stops, Charlie is gone, so I decide to get the unit the hell out of there. I turn to help Marty, and he's dead.'

'But you said he was just talking all normal and stuff.'

Dew nodded. 'He was. We could have been in my living room watching *Monday Night Football*. He was just dead, laying there with his foot and leg in his arms like it was a teddy bear.'

Dew stayed quiet for a moment, wondering if Perry would get it.

'I don't get it,' Perry said.

Maybe Perry knew computers, but he had the common sense of a goat.

'How old are you?' Dew asked.

'Twenty-seven,' Perry said.

'Marty Alvarez was nineteen and three days. He'll never have kids, either. He never even saw his *twenties*, man. Your life is fucked up, I'll give you that, but you've already had a decade more than Marty ever had. And he went out way more peaceful than most, hoss. I watched guys go out trying to stuff their guts back into their bellies. I watched guys crying and begging when someone stabbed them in the chest with a bayonet, over and over. So your life is fucked up? So fucking *what*? At least you're *alive*. You play the hand you're dealt. You can either be a man, or not.'

Dew stood up. It took two tries. Perry didn't say anything. Dew swayed a bit as he looked down at the big man.

'Kid, I got to know something.'

'Okay,' Perry said.

'When you knocked out Baum and Milner, you didn't take their guns. Why?'

'I didn't need them.'

'Bullshit,' Dew said. 'You were going in there to kill those infected people. As far as you knew, they were dues-paying members of the NRA. Maybe you wouldn't mind getting killed, but I know your kind – the game was on, and you wanted to stop a gate from opening up. You didn't want to *lose*. Am I right?'

Perry looked at the floor, blond hair hanging. 'I want to stop them more than anything,' he said quietly. 'They've taken so much from me, but I . . . at least I can still win. If they can't do what they were sent to do, junk or no junk, well then, guess what? I win. Fuck them, *I win.*'

Dew nodded. 'I know what you're saying. I want to stop these little fuckers like you have no idea. But you didn't take the gun, which means you left a way for them to beat you. *Why?*'

Perry sat still and quiet. Dew just waited. Sometimes you get more done with silence than with all the words in the world.

'You're going to think I'm crazy,' Perry said.

'I already think you're more batshit than a padded room full of Charlie Mansons. So out with it.'

'I . . . I still hear Bill.'

Dew hadn't expected that. This was one messed-up camper.

'You mean, like you heard your dad? Back when you were infected?'

Perry nodded. 'Yeah, kind of like that. Bill keeps telling me to shoot myself.'

'Shoot yourself.'

'Uh-huh. So I don't want to pick up a gun, 'cause . . . 'cause maybe I want to listen to him.'

'If you really want to kill yourself, you don't need a gun.'

Perry looked up. 'Yeah, but the other ways, they take at least a little preparation. Some time to think. Maybe you come to your senses. But a gun? You go from thinking about it to pointing it, pulling the trigger in what, like two seconds?'

Dew nodded. He'd planned on doing just that if he found strange, itchy lumps on his own skin. Wasn't eating a bullet better than enduring Perry's ordeal?

'Yeah,' Dew said. 'Two seconds, if even that.'

'So that's why I didn't touch their guns.'

He was no psychologist, but even so drunk he could barely stand, Dew Phillips still had all the common sense his mama had given him. Perry had suicidal thoughts but was cognizant enough to stay away from something that could instantly make those thoughts a reality.

'Dawsey, have you ever shot a gun?'

Perry shook his head.

'Get some sleep. Your life is what it is. Tomorrow we're going to stop letting you feel sorry for yourself.'

THIS IS YOUR BRAIN ON CRAWLERS

Chelsea Jewell woke up. She wiped a mist of sweat from her face, then got out of bed. She grabbed her pillow and dragged the comforter off the mattress.

Mommy might come in when she slept. She might come in and punish her. Chelsea had to hide.

She opened the closet's folding doors and pulled out all of her shoes. She put those under the bed, then lugged her pillow and blanket inside. She shut the closet door, then lay down, head on the pillow, body on top of the comforter, and fell asleep even before she could cover up.

Inside Chelsea's head 1,715 crawlers were waiting at the base of her skull. As a unit, they released enkephalins and endomorphins into the blood pouring through her brain. These powerful natural opiates spread through her brain, locking onto opioid receptors and stopping them from receiving any information – in particular, messages of pain.

Which, considering what was about to happen, might have been the only humane thing the crawlers would ever do.

The crawlers surged upward, expanding through her frontal lobe like a gas. Once dispersed, they *un*bundled, turning back into individual hacked muscle fibers ready to rebind in new ways with entirely new functions.

The 'I am here' signals began again, but this time the fibers latched onto each other end to end, forming long strands. These strands crossed over each other on all axes, X and Y and Z and everything in between, creating a ropy mesh that ran through her frontal lobe, her parietal lobe, her hippocampus and, in particular, her orbifrontal lobe. In many places fibers formed dendritelike fingers that connected to Chelsea's brain cells on one end and to the mesh on the other.

In just a few hours, 1,715 crawlers morphed into a neural net lacing through the parts of Chelsea's brain that controlled higher functions. Functions like memory. Thought. Reason. Abstraction. Emotion.

Finally, the remaining fibers wiggled and converged at the center of Chelsea's brain. If you could have seen in there, you would have sworn they were attacking each other, ripping each other to pieces. But the fibers weren't alive, and they weren't individuals; they were part of a larger function. They weren't tearing each other apart; they were rearranging, rebuilding . . . melding.

When they finished, they formed a ball some one thousand microns in diameter. Tendrils reached out from this ball, connecting with the neural net of converted crawlers. Once those connections were made, the ball did what it was designed to do.

It sent a signal.

REACH OUT AND TOUCH SOMEONE

The Orbital had monitored early biofeedback from the new strain. Based on initially high levels of apoptosis, the Orbital had logically assumed that this batch of crawler-building seeds was a total failure. The growing workers would once again have to fend for themselves, try to avoid the sonofabitch as they built a gate.

The Orbital was already working on creating a second crawler-building batch with a modified code. This would be the last chance, the eighteenth and final probe.

When it received the signal, however, it abandoned the modified code. It focused all processing power on the new situation.

This signal, this lone signal, meant potential success. It provided a direct point of entry. And if the Orbital could communicate clearly enough, gather enough information, send enough reprogramming code back down the signal chain, then that lone signal meant a *vector*.

The Orbital sent a signal of its own and started gathering information.

SENIOR PICTURES

'Daddy, wake up.'

Donald's mind swam in a sea of subdued pain. His body burned. Every inch seemed to be deep-fried, and his left hand felt even worse than that.

'Daddy, *wake up!*'

He didn't want to wake up. When he was asleep, he didn't have to feel it.

'Daddy, mah face! *Mah face!*'

The voice finally hit home, as did the hysterical urgency of Betty's words. She was mispronouncing things, as if she had food in her mouth. He blinked awake, hissing in a sharp breath as the pain continued to wash over his body. A cough caught the tail end of that breath, then ripped out, dragging barbed wire through his lungs, his throat, smashing his eyes shut as liquid burned his mouth. He'd coughed so hard he'd thrown up.

'*Daddy! Omahgod!*'

Donald pulled his right hand out from under the sleeping bag, put it on the steering wheel and eased himself back. The steering wheel felt hot and wet from his vomit. He didn't want to move his other hand – it burned too much – so he left it under the blanket. He opened his eyes.

And found that it wasn't vomit at all.

Blood covered the steering wheel. Blood, and bits of something black.

'Daddy, are you okay? You're coughing up blood!'

Donald blinked, trying to get his bearings. He hurt so bad. His body burned. His daughter screaming right in his fucking ear. He had to calm her down. Donald turned to look at her and flinched when he saw her face. Three oozing black sores clung to her left cheek. For a second, he thought how nothing could be worse to a teenage girl than something messed up on her face. Only for a second, though, because through the haze Donny realized that this wasn't some monster pimple – there was something very wrong with his baby girl. He had to get her to a hospital. He had to get *both* of them to a hospital.

'Baby, I . . .' Another coughing spasm built up in his chest. *No, not again, it hurts too much.*

The cough hit, and he covered his mouth with both hands. As he did, his left hand felt like he'd punched jagged glass. Blood sprayed between his fingers, all over the steering wheel and even into the windshield.

'Omahgod Daddy your hand *yourhandyourhand*!'

Betty was in full-bore hysterics now, her syllables running together without punctuation, broken up only by the level of her screams.

Donald lifted his left hand. It looked as if he'd dipped it in acid. The wet, shriveled, blackened fingers stuck out lifelessly. Most of the flesh was gone. He could see bare bone in some places. At least he guessed it was bare bone, because even that was black and pitted.

Donald Jewell screamed. He reached across himself with his right hand and grabbed for the door handle. He bumped his left hand as he did.

His pinkie and ring fingers fell off in a clump, right into his lap.

'*Omahgodomahgod!*'

He ignored the missing fingers, the blowtorch sensation. What else could he do? He ignored them and yanked the door open and scrambled out of the car. His blackened fingers fell off his lap and bounced on the icy pavement. The rain had stopped. Donny ran straight for the nearest snowbank, now a shriveled thing all crusted with ice. Crying, screaming, he kicked at it with his foot to break the crust, then jammed his blackened hand through the hole and into the snow. His hand *burned*. He had to cool it off, but the snow didn't make it any better.

Another cough hit, this one deep, from way inside his stomach. Hot blood gushed into his mouth. He tasted chunks of something rotten, chunks that burned his tongue. The whole mess spilled onto the icy white snowbank, covering it with bright red and wet black. Donny Jewell fell over on his side. Pain overwhelmed him, jabbing into his body from every possible angle.

He just wanted to go to sleep again.

The next cough yanked him into a fetal position. More red and black sprayed out of his mouth. Something inside *broke*. He knew it, not from increased pain, but when his stomach muscles seemed to suddenly relax, like he'd been curled up by a rubber band that had just snapped.

He could still hear his daughter screaming.

The last thought he had was a hope that her face would clear up in time for senior pictures.

CHEFFIE

Cheffie Jones awoke to find himself under the living-room carpet.

He had two infections. One on his left collarbone, one just under his Adam's apple. The skin between them had blackened and sagged, the necrosis spreading toward his face, down his chest and deeper into his throat.

Before he died, Cheffie had just enough time to flip the carpet back and wonder why he hurt so bad. While he'd slept, the apoptosis had weakened his carotid artery, which gave way at that exact moment. Just one tiny hole at first, enough for blood to squirt out into the blackened sludge surrounding it. He was in so much pain he didn't even notice the difference. The first pinhole became a second, then a third, and then blood pressure against the thin artery wall ripped open a hole the size of a pencil eraser.

Blood sprayed all through his throat. A few thin jets pushed out through the black rot, but most of it just shot around inside his body. He gurgled as he breathed it in. Blood filled alveoli and soon reduced the ability of his lungs to draw oxygen.

He couldn't scream, because his vocal cords had dissolved right before his carotid gave way. He managed to stumble to the front door and open it; then he fell. He tried to crawl, but it wasn't very effective – Cheffie hadn't been in good shape to start with, and without oxygen his muscles shut down right quick. He got to his knees, struggled to get one hand out the front door, then fell again.

Cheffie Jones stopped moving. He had drowned in his own blood.

The apoptosis chain reaction continued.

THE SONOFABITCH

The Orbital rearranged the probability tables and ran scenario after scenario. The child's mind had produced a clear signal. She might be strong enough to carry out the new strategy's next phase. And if she wasn't strong enough, the *other* child might be. He wasn't as well developed as Chelsea, but he was coming along fast. Both of them together would provide all the ground-based brain power the Orbital needed to direct the protectors.

Unless, of course, the sonofabitch found them, as he had found the rest.

Biofeedback from the new strain showed the Orbital that cultivating muscle fibers from each host was too risky. Too much potential of harvesting damaged stem cells.

A problem with a simple solution – the children would become the vector. The children had successfully developed modified muscle fibers, fibers that could split on their own, reproduce. Introduce those fibers into new hosts, and the infection would spread.

That solved one problem – creating protectors – but a second, equally significant problem remained: how to stop the sonofabitch. The Orbital hadn't been built for situations like this. The creators hadn't programmed specific instructions on how to handle a host-turned-hunter.

Killing him was the obvious strategy, but that hadn't worked yet. Hosts from each of the last three batches had tried and failed. Not only failed, they had died in the process, removing their potential hatchlings from the build phase. Sonofabitch was human, he *could* die, but targeting him was too risky.

The simulations rolled on, and one strategy continued to show the highest probability of success – just keep the sonofabitch away.

Could the Orbital block just one host from the communication mesh? Yes, it decided it could. It would be difficult, taking up much of the Orbital's ability to process communication for the rest. The female child host could be modified. She could act as the central communication bridge, freeing up enough of the Orbital's processing power to locate and block the sonofabitch.

If he couldn't hear, he couldn't find the new gate.

DAY FOUR

BIG SAMMY'S BAR

Margaret hadn't given the computer-room chairs a second thought until Perry sat in one. He'd opted to stand at first, but his little grimaces made it obvious his knees were killing him. Margaret pulled the *I am your doctor* trump card and ordered him to sit. Put an ironing board in front of him with a plate of turkey on top, and he would have looked like a grown-up forced to sit in one of the kiddie chairs at Thanksgiving.

She sat in the chair to Perry's right, Dew in the chair to his left. Clarence stood behind Margaret, his body radiating tension. Everyone noticed Clarence's vibe except Clarence himself.

Amos, of course, was nowhere to be seen.

'I really don't like to talk about this,' Perry said.

Dew grabbed Perry's left shoulder and gave it a supportive shake. 'All the more reason to get this done quick and get it done right,' he said. 'Besides, what else are you gonna do with your time? Go lift some weights?'

Perry nodded. 'Push-ups and sit-ups, actually.'

'I think you're studly enough for the moment,' Margaret said. 'We have access to a lot of data about the individual triangle hosts. I'm hoping that adding details of your experience can help us locate the source of the infection.'

Perry shrugged. 'I'll do what I can.'

Margaret tapped at the keyboard, calling up a map on the flat-panel monitor in front of him.

'This is a map of the homes of the seven known triangle hosts from the Ann Arbor area,' she said.

She moved the mouse and hit a selection on the screen. Seven house icons appeared on the map.

Perry saw that two icons, one stacked on the other, sat over his apartment complex between Ann Arbor and Ypsilanti. Those two formed the point of a triangle, with the second point almost in downtown Ann Arbor, and the third point south of Ann Arbor in Pittsfield.

The other three house icons looked more random: one in Whittaker, about five miles south and a little east of Perry's apartment complex, then two very close together in the farmland just south of Ford Lake and Rawsonville.

'What's the pattern?' Perry asked.

'There isn't one,' Margaret said. 'These are just the home addresses of the victims. We can also add work or school addresses.' She clicked the mouse again, and seven blue dots appeared. 'We can also add any known locations of the hosts for the two weeks prior to the day you started itching, but the map gets kind of crazy if we do that.

'The problem is, we can't find any correlation in these locations. We still have no idea exactly *when* or *where* people were infected. We need to use your memory of the days before you started itching, and compare that to the information we have. Hopefully, we can make a connection that points us to the time and source of infection.'

Perry nodded.

'Okay,' Margaret said. 'For starters, you and Patricia DuMond both lived in the same apartment complex.'

'Who is Patricia DuMond?' Perry asked.

'I believe you called her *Fatty Patty*,' Margaret said.

Perry had fled his own apartment shortly after killing his friend Bill, just before the police arrived. He'd had only moments to hide and nowhere to run. Fatty Patty lived one building over – her triangles had called to Perry, promising refuge. He'd turned out to be a less-than-pleasant guest, even roughed her up a little. He hadn't killed her, she'd died when her triangles ripped out of her body, but he sure as hell hadn't done anything to help her. Patty's ordeal was a major reason Perry killed every host he found – dying at his hands, no matter how brutal, was far, *far* better than death from a hatching.

'Oh,' Perry said quietly. 'Yeah, her. Okay.'

'So that's two hosts living in the same apartment complex,' Margaret said. 'But *only* two. If the vector was in the complex, or went *through* the complex, we would assume there would be more hosts.'

'Unless you were banging her,' Dew said. 'Which means you could have been infected at the same time.'

Perry shook his head. 'Hate to admit it, but I hadn't been laid in weeks. I might have seen her around from time to time, but I'm not sure. The apartment complex was pretty big. I can say for certain I never spoke to her, though.'

'She worked in Royal Oak, you worked in Ann Arbor,' Margaret said. 'So you traveled in opposite directions for work.'

Margaret tapped the keyboard, and two of the blue dots started pulsing, one on the location of American Computer Solutions, where Perry had worked as a support rep.

'We're trying to figure out where you and Patty might have crossed paths,' Margaret said. 'We know roughly where she was in the days before the Monday you started itching, because this database has her cell-phone records and credit-card receipts.'

'Is that legal?' Perry asked.

Dew laughed. 'Don't worry about it, kid.'

'I wondered the same thing,' Margaret said. 'But stopping this thing from killing people takes priority, wouldn't you say?'

'The right of the people to be secure in their persons, houses, papers and effects, against unreasonable searches and seizures, shall not be violated,' Perry said. 'The Fourth Amendment; you guys ever heard of it?'

Margaret stared at the big, beat-up man crammed into the tiny chair. He only *looked* like a dumb jock. Dew was equally speechless.

'Don't be so shocked,' Perry said. 'I went to college, remember?'

'Tell you what, college boy,' Dew said. 'You find the history book that talks about Thomas Jefferson having blue triangles growing on his nut-sack, then you can quote the founding fathers all you want.'

Perry leaned back in the chair and sighed. 'All right, fine, whatever. Let's get on with it.'

Margaret continued. 'Your records aren't as detailed as Patricia's. The only person you seemed to call was Bill Miller. We show you made ATM withdrawals every week in the same amount, from a machine near your apartment, but you have almost no credit-card purchases.'

'I only use credit cards at the bar,' Perry said. 'When I've had a few, I tip too much on each round. With the credit card I only tip once and I don't overspend on my drinks. I use cash for everything else. That's how I stayed on budget. When my weekly cash ran out, I stopped spending.'

Margaret nodded, feeling a flutter of hope. If Perry had shopped somewhere and come into contact with another triangle host, Cheng might have missed it simply because Perry had used cash.

'Since we don't know what causes the infection, we don't know the length of the gestation period,' Margaret said. 'Maybe the vector hit you the day before, the week before or the month before, so let's take it one day at a time. You told us you started itching on a Monday, so try and remember – what did you do that Sunday?'

Perry touched the stitches on his lip as he thought. 'Me and Bill probably watched football all day.'

'Where?'

Perry shrugged. 'Probably just my apartment.'

'Naw, we know you were at a bar that night,' Dew said. His finger traced a line on his flat-panel screen. 'Here we go. Where is Big Sammy's Bar?'

'Westland,' Perry said. 'Just about halfway between Ann Arbor and Detroit. Big screens, lots of hot girls.'

'That Sunday night you spent forty-six dollars even,' Dew said. 'It's on your credit-card history.'

Perry thought for a second, then nodded. 'Yeah, sure. I do that with the tip, put in the right amount of change so it comes out even. Bill and I went to Big Sammy's to watch the Lions play the Colts. The late game. They lost.'

'There's a surprise,' Dew said.

'Come on,' Perry said. 'Cut 'em some slack. They only lost by two touchdowns that time.'

'Then what happened?' Margaret said. 'Game ended, what did you do?'

As he thought, Perry moved his finger from his stitched lip to his black eye. 'I went home. I think I was a little drunk, so I was driving real careful. No, wait, I got hungry so I stopped at a store to grab some munchies.'

'Where did you stop?'

Perry shrugged. 'Man, I can't say. That was like six weeks ago, and I was drunk.'

Dew leaned closer to the flat-panel. 'Could it have been the Meijer grocery store, in Belleville?'

'Could be,' Perry said. 'That's on the way home.'

Margaret stood and walked over to stand behind Dew. 'Why?' she said. 'What's significant about that particular store?'

Dew pointed to another line. His fingertip left a little smudge on the screen.

'Credit-card history shows Patricia DuMond bought over a hundred bucks' worth of groceries at Meijer in Belleville,' Dew said. 'At ten thirty-one P.M.'

Margaret sat back down in her chair and started pounding on the keys, excitement bleeding through to her fingertips. 'That might give us something.'

Now Dew got up from his chair and stood behind Margaret. 'So the vector is a grocery store?'

Margaret shook her head. 'No, it's probably not the store itself, or the food it sold. Otherwise we'd have certainly traced other hosts back to it. But for the first time, we may have two hosts in the same location at the same *time*.'

She typed a few keys, and the icon denoting Perry and Patricia's infection slid west to hover over the Meijer store. The icon's new location instantly created a visual curve, one that started in Whittaker, then moved gradually northeast through the two house icons near Rawsonville, then sharper east toward the Meijer in Belleville.

Perry had been there around 10:30 P.M. So had Patricia.

If the hosts that lived in Rawsonville had been home at that time, which was likely . . .

'Clarence,' Margaret said, 'can this thing call up historical weather patterns?'

'Probably,' he said. 'Let me drive.'

Margaret stood and Clarence sat down.

Perry leaned over to watch Clarence's hunt-and-peck typing. 'You need a hand with that, champ?'

Clarence kept his eyes on the keyboard and the screen in front of him. 'I think I can swing it, *chief,* but thanks for being such a helper.'

'So it's not the grocery store,' Dew said. 'You think maybe something blowing through the air, right? Something airborne?'

'*Airborne* is a term for one host passing the disease to another through sneezes, coughs or even breath,' Margaret said. 'Look at the range on this curve. We're talking *miles* here, not feet. The more accurate term is *wind-borne,* where wind is the mechanical vector driving the spore.'

'But wouldn't Cheng have checked weather patterns?' Dew asked.

'Of course,' Margaret said. 'But the wind can change direction from minute to minute. We now potentially have an exact time of infection. Cheng never had that. Perry, what did you do after you got your food?'

'Ate it on the way home,' Perry said. 'Got home, got undressed and went right to bed. I had work the next day.'

'The vector must have been on your hands,' Margaret said. 'Or maybe on your clothes, and when you got undressed you spread it around. You must have touched . . . uh . . . some private places.'

'A guy scratching his balls in the privacy of his own home,' Dew said. 'Imagine that.'

'Okay,' Clarence said. 'I have historical weather. What do you want, Margo?'

'Give us wind direction at ten thirty P.M. on that Sunday,' she said. 'Focus in on Belleville if you can.'

Otto tapped away. Blue arrows appeared, pointing mostly east and a little bit north. A green line of text at the bottom read .5 MPH, 260 DEGREES.

'That doesn't work,' Dew said. 'The wind direction doesn't line up the Rawsonville hosts with the store.'

'Clarence,' Margaret said, 'show me a time-lapse projection of wind patterns from ten P.M. to ten thirty P.M.'

Otto looked at the keys for a second but didn't type. 'Uh . . . I don't think this computer can do that.'

'Jesus H,' Perry said. 'Give me that.'

He grabbed the keyboard and pulled it onto his lap. His big fingers flew across the keys. Data fields popped up on the screen and filled with strings of text faster than Margaret could even read them.

'You people remind me of the idiots I used to support at my job,' Perry said. 'It's like you've never read a software manual in your life. This is basic stuff, guys.'

He hit one last key, and the blue arrows on the screen changed. Instead of a west-to-east orientation, they started pointing north, then curved northeast, and finally wound up pointing due east.

Perry clacked a few more keys. The blue arrows vanished save for one – an arrow that started at the Whittaker house's icon, curved to the right to cross over both the Rawsonville icons, and then farther to the right to cross over Meijer's.

'Holy shit,' Dew said. 'That's it. It's fucking airborne.'

'Wind-borne,' Margaret said.

'Wind-borne, right,' Dew said. 'So what about the other hosts that are outside of this pattern?'

'Could be a number of things,' Margaret said. 'They could have passed through the wind curve at just the right time, could have been another . . . I don't know . . . another *gust* that carried the spores to other areas. This curve doesn't account for everyone, but it accounts for half of them. It's statistically significant, no question.'

Clarence turned in his chair to face her. 'But what does this really tell us? I mean, wind can blow all over.'

Perry spoke before Margaret could. 'It gives us a projection based on wind speed and the distance between infection points. From there we can potentially extrapolate a vector path and possibly even a range for potential release-point locations. Combine this data with hosts from the other infection locations, maybe you can reduce the search area for the release point. What Margaret is saying is that Colonel Ogden was right, it's a satellite. This weather analysis might tell us where to look for it.'

Margaret smiled and nodded at Perry. He winked at her.

'College?' Dew said.

Perry nodded. 'College.'

'Perry,' Margaret said, 'can we do that here?'

Perry shook his head. 'That takes way more computational power. You have simple wind-direction history, sure, but you need to extrapolate that against the distance between infection points, air temperature, humidity . . . and probably a bunch of other shit I don't even know. It's a whole different ball game from what I just showed you.'

'Let's kick this back to Murray,' Clarence said. 'See if he can put it in front of some of his *most brilliant minds the nation has to offer.*'

'Fuck yes he can,' Dew said. 'He'll have the National Weather Service and climatologists and God knows what on this faster than you can hum "Oh! Susanna." '

Clarence kept staring at Perry. 'I might have been wrong about the dumb-jock stereotype,' he said. 'You're pretty goddamn smart.'

Perry didn't look away from his monitor. 'Naw, you were right about the stereotype. It just doesn't apply to football. You have to be smart to be good at football, because it's complicated.'

He turned and smiled at Clarence. 'The dumb jocks play basketball.'

Perry turned back to face the monitor.

Clarence shook his head, and Margaret just laughed.

CHELSEA IN CHARGE

Chelsea Jewell slowly woke. Her head hurt real bad. She wanted her mommy.

No, that wasn't right. She had to watch out for Mommy. Mommy might want to hurt her. Chelsea wanted her daddy. Daddy was still okay.

And yet *that* wasn't right, either. She didn't *want* her daddy . . . she wanted to *protect* her daddy.

She wanted to protect what was *inside* of Daddy.

A r e   y o u   a w a k e ?

She looked around the room. Where had that voice come from? She couldn't see anybody.

A r e   y o u   a w a k e ?

'Yeah,' Chelsea said. 'Where are you?'

I   a m   v e r y   f a r   a w a y .

'Oh,' Chelsea said. 'Then why can I hear you?'

B e c a u s e   y o u   a r e   s p e c i a l .   Y o u   a r e   t h e   o n l y   o n e   t h e r e   w h o   c a n   h e a r   m e .

'Mommy and Daddy can't hear you?'

N o t   y e t .

'My daddy is sick,' Chelsea said. 'So am I. I feel a little better now, but my head hurts real bad, and now my tongue feels all thick and stuff. Mommy scares me real bad. I think she wants to hurt me.'

**You don't need to be
afraid of your mommy.**

'Are you sure?'

Yes.

Chelsea felt the fear of her mother vanish as if a breeze
had blown it away.

**Your daddy is not sick.
He's very important.**

Chelsea saw visions of something triangular, something
that resembled one of her yellow wooden blocks, the one
that looked like a little pyramid, except in her vision it
was black and moved on strange legs. It was beautiful. It
was *special*. Just like Mommy always called her *special*.

'Daddy has pretty dollies inside of him,' Chelsea said.
'Is that why he's important?'

**That's right. Daddy has
dollies inside of him.**

Mommy called Chelsea special, and Mommy had
always protected Chelsea.

And now Chelsea would protect Daddy. Daddy, and
the dollies.

The closet door opened, spilling light inside.

'Honey,' Mommy said, 'what the heck are you doing
in here?'

Chelsea blinked as her eyes adjusted to the light. She
waited for the fear, but it didn't come. The voice said she
didn't need to be afraid, and she wasn't.

'Sleeping,' Chelsea said.

'But why in the closet?'

Chelsea shrugged. 'I dunno.'

'That's what your father said. I found him sleeping
behind the couch, of all things. Are you guys playing some
joke on me?'

Chelsea shook her head.

'Riiiight,' Mommy said. 'You both hide somewhere to sleep, and it's not a joke on me? We'll just see about that. But enough playing around. How are you feeling?'

'No so good,' Chelsea said.

Mommy picked Chelsea up and laid her back down on the bed. She put her hand on Chelsea's forehead. Mommy's hand felt cool and nice.

'You're not as hot as you were,' she said. 'Do you feel worse or better than before?'

'A little better,' Chelsea said.

Mommy's brow wrinkled up, and her eyes narrowed.

'Honey, open your mouth,' she said. 'Stick out your tongue.'

Chelsea did. Mommy got that worried look on her face.

'Honey, you've got blue spots on your tongue. Does your tongue hurt?'

'A little,' Chelsea said.

'Stick it out again. I've never seen that before. I don't like it. I think tomorrow we're all going to the doctor.'

Chelsea felt a shiver ripple across her skin. The *doctor*. The doctor that always hurt her with needles and stuff. The voice was wrong – she *should* be afraid of Mommy.

'But I don't like the doctor,' Chelsea said.

'And I don't care if you like him or not, young lady, you're going. You and your father both. He's itching like crazy, and he's getting these orange welts on his skin.'

'Daddy has dollies inside of him,' Chelsea said. 'My special friend said so.'

'Oh, you have a special friend now? How *nice*, honey. What's his name?'

Chelsea thought for a second, but she didn't know his name. She shrugged. 'I dunno.'

'Well, you can't have a special friend and not give him a name,' Mommy said. She gently pushed Chelsea back down in the bed and started tucking the covers around her. 'What would you like to call him?'

'How about . . . Chauncey?' Chelsea asked.

Mommy smiled. 'Ahhh, Chauncey, like Uncle Donald's favorite basketball player?'

Chelsea nodded. 'Yeah. And his name sounds like mine. Chelsea and Chauncey.'

'Well, that's a fine name,' Mommy said. She stroked Chelsea's hair, and that felt really nice. 'You get some more sleep, okay?'

'I'm not that tired anymore,' Chelsea said. 'I want to get up.'

'Just lie here for a little bit longer, honey. Then you can get up if you want, but stay here and play with your toys, okay? I don't want you running around. I'll check on you later, and we'll see the doctor tomorrow.'

Mommy leaned down and kissed her forehead, then left the room and shut the door behind her. Chelsea sat in the darkness, wondering if Chauncey would talk to her again.

He did.

You must not go to the doctor. You have to stop her.

Chelsea whispered so Mommy wouldn't hear her. 'How can I stop her, Chauncey? Mommy's in charge. I have to do what she says.'

She's not in charge of you.

'She's not?'

No. You're in charge of her.

'I am?'

You are.

'Well . . . she's still lots bigger than me. What if she *makes* me go to the doctor's?'

You can stop her tonight. After she goes to sleep.

A picture flashed in Chelsea's thoughts.

Yes, she could do that to Mommy.

THE SHOOTER

Dew could only take so much hemming and hawing.

His Colt M1911 .45-caliber pistol lay on the shooter's table. It was loaded, hammer back, safety engaged. Perry Dawsey stood there, in ear protectors and goggles, staring down at the weapon.

'Look, Dew, this is cool and all, but I just don't want to shoot, okay?'

'Pick up the gun, kid,' Dew said. 'I have a mean piss of a hangover thanks to you, and I'm really not in the mood for this. You're embarrassing me in front of an entire shooting range.'

The range was empty, of course. Dew had rented the whole thing.

Perry stared down at the .45. 'But what if I pick it up and . . . you know . . . I get the urge to shoot *you*.'

Dew pulled up his pant leg and drew his .38. 'I'll stand behind you, with this aimed at your back. If you even turn around funny, I'll kill you. Does that make you feel better?'

'A little,' Perry said. Dew would have laughed if the kid hadn't looked so damn serious.

Perry kept staring at the .45.

Dew sighed. 'Now what?'

'What if I . . . what if I listen to Bill?'

'What if you kill yourself, you mean?'

Perry nodded.

'Look kid, you gotta grab this thing by the balls.'

'That's not funny.'

'Shit, sorry,' Dew said. 'Just a figure of speech. Listen. Ronald Reagan, the greatest president that ever lived, he had a quote that sums this up nicely: *If it takes a bloodbath, let's get it over with.* So if you're going to kill yourself, let's stop fucking around and get it done.'

'You're one of those sensitive hippie types, I see.'

'I have a flower garden at home,' Dew said. 'And I'm wicked good with a crochet hook. Seriously, you can't go through life afraid of this shit. Stop being a fucking pussy and pick up the goddamn gun already.'

Perry slowly reached for the .45, then drew his hand back.

'If you shoot yourself in the head, that only hurts for a second,' Dew said. 'If I shoot you in the foot, it's going to hurt for a long time. So pick it up or say good-bye to a little piggy.'

Perry reached out again and picked up the .45. His hand shook violently at first, so badly that Dew wondered if the gun might actually go off. He was playing a dangerous game here. Dew kept the .38 pointed at Perry's back, just in case.

'Just breathe easy,' Dew said. 'Point the gun and squeeze the trigger slow. You should be a little surprised when it goes off. And remember, after you shoot, remove the magazine and lock the slide to the rear. That will eject a round, so don't be surprised by that. Inspect the chamber and magazine, then lay it on the table and move your hands away. Just like you did when we practiced.'

'Yeah, but then the gun wasn't loaded.'

'Just do it like I told you, and you'll be safe, okay?'

'Okay,' Perry said.

Dawsey pointed the .45 down the range and let out a breath. The pistol looked like a toy in his big hand. Dew would have given Perry the .38, but he wasn't sure if the kid's finger could fit through the trigger guard.

Dew waited, then *bang*, the gun fired. A little smoke curled up from the barrel as both men looked down the firing range. The target was at thirty feet. Perry had hit the center ring, just to the left of the *X*.

'Nice shot,' Dew said.

'I thought this thing was supposed to have a kick.'

'Remove the magazine, lock the slide to the rear . . . ,' Dew said, letting his voice trail off.

Perry nodded quickly and energetically. He carefully followed all of Dew's instructions, then set the weapon on the table in front of him. He raised both hands slowly off the gun to show he wasn't holding it. He looked . . . relieved. Like all the pressure was off, like he'd just lost his virginity.

'Okay,' Dew said. 'So you didn't feel the gun jump in your hand?'

Perry shook his head.

'When I shoot it, I can feel it kick, but it's not so bad,' Dew said. 'Strong as you are I shouldn't be surprised you can't feel it at all.'

'Uh . . . Dew?' Perry had a look on his face like he was afraid to ask a question. For fuck's sake – he had cut monsters out of his own body, had taken two bullets and kept on fighting, and he was afraid to ask a question.

He doesn't want to look stupid, Dew thought. *He doesn't want to look stupid in front of* YOU.

'Spit it out,' Dew said. 'You can ask me whatever.'

'Um . . . squeezing real slow is cool and all, I guess, but if I have to use this for real, don't I want to fire faster than that?'

Dew smiled. 'Sure, that's a logical thing to ask. Not that you'll have to use one of these for real, but just in case, reload the magazine and fire off the whole thing, fast as you can, okay? We'll look at the target and you can compare accuracy. Then we'll talk about how to fire in different situations. Sometimes you want one accurate shot, sometimes you want to lay down as much lead as you can as fast as you can. Okay?'

Perry smiled and nodded. A *real* smile for a change.

Still looked hideous with the stitches, but at least it was genuine.

Dew took three steps back. He casually pointed the .38 at the floor, but he wasn't about to put it back in the holster. Not yet.

Perry loaded two more bullets into the magazine, inserted it, then thumbed the slide release so it clicked home. He pointed the weapon and fired off seven shots in less than two seconds. It sounded like a machine gun. Dew watched the kid's hand move, or rather he watched it *not* move. It might as well have been chiseled out of granite and bolted to the wall.

Perry ejected the magazine, checked the chamber, set the gun and the magazine down, then raised both hands off it again in seeming slow motion. Dew stared downrange. He couldn't believe his eyes. He flipped the switch that brought the target back to the firing station for a closer look.

Perry had put all six shots in the center ring. The center *X* wasn't even there anymore, just a big hole with ragged paper edges.

Perry smiled and looked down at Dew. 'That's pretty good, right?'

'Kid, are you fucking with me? Are you *sure* you've never shot before?'

The big man shook his head. 'No sir. Dad wouldn't let me touch any of the guns. But, I mean, it's only hand-eye coordination stuff, right? Like a video game. I've always been good at anything like that.'

Dew stared at the target. It made sense. Dawsey had been an elite athlete. Would have gone first round in the NFL draft, probably first overall, had it not been for the knee injury that ended his career. He was so strong he didn't even feel the .45 kick – he could just point the barrel accurately and keep it perfectly still while he emptied the clip.

Dew suddenly wondered if teaching Perry to shoot was such a good idea after all. If Perry could kill people with his bare hands, imagine what he could do with a weapon and plenty of ammo.

UGLY BETTY

Betty Jewell's body faced a dire situation. Half-formed crawlers disintegrated, spreading apoptotic death. She was guilty of nothing more than being just old enough for her telomeres to shorten and suffer the minor damage that faces us all. Her telomeric breakdown wasn't as bad as her father's, of course, as he had been twenty-six years her senior.

Had she been younger, maybe as little as five years younger, it would have gone better for her.

Of course, 'better' meant that more crawlers would have already reached her brain. Her brain-mesh was thin, emaciated – it needed additional crawlers to fully complete the change and send the signal. More struggled to reach her brain, either dragging half-rotted bodies along her nerves or trying to move past the dissolving corpses of crawlers that had already shut down. These survivors reached out their pseudodendrites, grabbing, pulling, sending their pain signals to gauge the response.

If Betty died, the crawlers' mission failed, so they fought the rot with counterchemicals designed to neutralize the chain reaction. Her original infection spots were already a lost cause – there was too much apoptosis there to stop the process. The crawlers sent some of their number to stay at the edges, secreting the neutralizing chemical, trying to localize the damage and stop it from spreading.

Inside these perimeters the rot dissolved flesh and scored bone.

That meant bad news for Betty Jewell's face.

The crawlers didn't consider the face a priority. Eyes to see, yes, mouth to breathe, of course. Those were important, as were her hands.

Hands could use tools.

Hands could use *weapons*.

The crawlers used their collective logic to split into several groups. Some moved to the hands to try and save them, some moved to the brain to try and achieve the critical mass needed for the neural net, some to the eyes and ears and mouth to protect sensory input. A Betty who could not see, hear or talk could not defend, and that wasn't a very useful Betty at all.

INTERFERENCE

Chatter.

That really was the best name for it. Perry heard chatter again. Coming from the south. South and . . . east? Yes, the east.

Somewhere out there, triangles were waking up.

So far he'd heard only snippets of thoughts, just a few syllables. The triangles didn't know *how* to talk yet. They had to learn that from their hosts' memories.

How many were out there? Perry couldn't tell. He could never tell for sure.

He'd picked up a few wisps that morning. Like smelling something in your apartment, something you smelled only if you turned a certain way, and then it was gone. And you *know* that smell, because you've smelled it before. You just can't remember what it is. It was that kind of familiarity.

Familiar, yet different. There was something else in those wisps. Something *less* random. More powerful, maybe?

Perry knocked on the door to Room 207. Dew answered.

'Hey Perry,' he said, and smiled, almost as if Dew were happy to see him. 'Come on in.'

Perry followed him into the room. Baum and Milner were there, as was Amos, who had a bagel in one hand, a stack of papers in the other and a laptop sitting on his legs. Baum and Milner stiffened. Amos's eyes immediately shot to the door. As soon as Perry moved into the room, Amos dropped the bagel, shut the computer and ran out.

'Damn, that little guy is twitchy,' Dew said.

'Yeah,' Milner said. 'Can't imagine why.'

Perry stared at the smaller man. 'Milner, I'm standing right here if you've got something on your mind.'

Baum laughed. 'You sure you want some? You look a little roughed up from your last go-around.'

'Baum, shut the fuck up,' Dew said. 'If you think you can take Dawsey, I'll be happy to move all this stuff out of the way and you two can have at it.'

Baum stared at Perry and said nothing.

Perry couldn't believe what he was hearing. Was Dew sticking up for him? Well, not *sticking up*, exactly, but calling Baum out to back up his mouth.

'Well?' Dew said to Baum.

Baum shook his head. 'I'm good.'

'Then keep your pie-hole shut,' Dew said. 'Milner, you too. Now, Perry, what have you got for us?'

'I'm hearing chatter,' Perry said quietly.

All three men perked up.

'Where?' Dew asked.

Perry shrugged. 'Not sure yet. Southeast is as close as I can get.'

'Michigan again?' Dew asked. 'Maybe Ohio?'

Perry shrugged once more.

'So why haven't you gone after it?' Milner asked. 'Got in your fancy car and headed out.'

'Because he and I have come to an understanding,' Dew said. 'Perry's part of the team now.'

Milner laughed. Dew shot him a *you're already on thin ice* glare, and Milner's smile faded.

'What's it sound like?' Baum asked, his disdain for Perry suddenly gone. 'Can you pick out any names? Places?'

Perry shook his head. 'Not yet, but it's getting stronger.'

'Just have a seat, kid,' Dew said. 'And relax, it will come like before. We'll get everyone loaded up and head in that general direction.'

Perry limped to a chair and sat.

And right then, the chatter . . . changed.

'Something's wrong,' Perry said. 'It's getting . . . quieter all of a sudden.'

'Concentrate,' Dew said. 'Maybe you have to focus?'

'Doesn't work like that,' Perry said. 'It's always on. I don't have any control over it. It's fading. I can't hear the chatter. What I hear now sounds . . . well, it sounds kind of gray.'

He looked at Dew. 'It's gone. I can't hear them anymore.'

DR. DAN COSTS AMOS TWENTY BUCKS

The V-22 Osprey helicopter passed over the highway at a high altitude, then turned 180 degrees. It dropped closer to the ground and came in for a landing in the parking lot, putting the rest-stop building between it and the road.

As the chopper set down, Margaret saw the familiar sight of two nondescript semi trailers parked in parallel. They had a different paint job from the ones she'd left behind in Glidden – brown and dented, another flavor of faux-shabby industrial. Aside from the plastic extension connecting the two trailers, no one would have given them a second glance.

'I wonder if they got last year's model,' Amos said. 'The MargoMobile lot must be jumping this time of year.'

The trip here had been a whirlwind. Once word came down that two bodies had tested positive for cellulose, Dew kicked the operation into high gear. Margaret, Amos, Clarence, Gitsh and Marcus were in the air within fifteen minutes. Murray ordered radio silence for the trip – he wasn't taking any chances. An hour and a half later, their Osprey was touching down at this rest area in Bay City, Michigan.

Margaret hadn't known there were more MargoMobiles. Even with his inner circle, Murray still had secrets inside of secrets. In fact, now she wondered just how many MargoMobiles existed. Certainly made sense to use multiple units – driving the first set from Glidden would have taken ten hours. Even moving them using cargo helicopters would have cost valuable time. With multiple units and multiple crews, Murray could lock down infection sites much faster.

Margaret and her team hopped out and headed straight for the brown trailers. A man stood outside, wearing an air force uniform covered with a heavy blue jacket and a hat that flopped warm-looking flaps down over his ears. The man snapped a taut salute.

'Captain Daniel Chapman,' he said.

'I'm not military,' Margaret said. 'Neither is anyone else here.'

The salute vanished. 'Good. I hate saluting.' He stuck out his hand. 'Doctor Chapman. Call me Dan. Nice to meet you.'

Margaret returned the shake. 'Doctor Margaret Montoya. This is Doctor Amos Braun and Agent Clarence Otto.'

'Agent of what?' Dan asked as he shook the men's hands.

'Agent to the stars,' Clarence said with a smile. 'It's really not important, don't you think?'

Dan nodded and held up one hand, as if to say, *Sorry I asked, I should have known.*

He led them into the MargoMobile's computer room. It looked exactly the same as the one she'd left back in Glidden, save for air force logos on the flat-panels and a coffee-mug ring or two on the counter. Dan waited until Margaret sat, then stood behind her. Amos sat in the chair next to her, while Otto seemed to fade away into the background. How he could manage to do that in a five-by-ten-foot room, Margaret couldn't say, yet he did it just the same.

'We have two cases of infection,' Dan said. 'Donald Jewell, age forty-two, from Pittsburgh, and his daughter, Betty, age sixteen. Of course, I'm not allowed to know exactly *what* they're infected with. I just follow the procedures assigned to me. I'm happy to play along, but please don't feed me the company line about necrotizing fasciitis. If, however, you should choose to let me know what the hell is going on, I won't complain.'

'What if that knowledge means you'll be sequestered for months?' Amos asked. 'That, or shot because you know too much?'

'Then I might complain a little,' Dan said. 'But I've always been a bit of a whiner.' He pointed a small remote at the computer and clicked a button.

Up on the screen, the air force logo disappeared, replaced by a picture of a man lying on icy pavement. He was in front of the rest-stop building right outside the trailer. The man's clothes hung on his skeletal frame. A black skull stuck out from a loose collar, and something black had stained the pavement around him.

'This is Donald Jewell,' Dan said. 'Security-camera recordings show he pulled in to this rest area yesterday at approximately thirteen hundred hours. There was a pretty solid storm at the time, freezing rain, so no one reported seeing him get out of his car. Not sure how long the body sat there before someone came across it. Best guess, ten minutes. The guy who found the body called 9-1-1. State troopers were on the scene within fifteen minutes.'

'Did they touch anything?' Margaret asked.

'Trooper Michael Adams used surgical gloves to check for a pulse,' Dan said. 'Finding none, he removed the gloves, left them on the spot, and had no further contact with the body. The daughter was still in the car. She refused to let Adams in. He saw sores on her face, so he called for an ambulance. She wouldn't allow paramedics inside the car, either. At that time, the paramedics performed the swab test on the corpse. My team was stationed in Detroit, so the CDC called us. We were actually the ones to remove the girl from the car.'

'How long have you been in charge of this rig?' Amos asked.

'Three weeks,' Chapman said. 'We haven't had much to do, to tell you the truth.' He put his shoulders back, puffed up his chest and spoke in a deep voice. 'Just play with the equipment and wait for a call. If you don't get that call, it's good news. If you get it, just be ready to do whatever it takes.'

Margaret had to stifle a laugh. Dan was doing a dead-on impression of Murray Longworth.

'That's uncanny,' Amos said.

'Thanks,' Dan said. 'You should hear my Gutierrez; it slays. Anyway, after the paramedics called the CDC, Trooper Adams and his partner evacuated the rest area and shut it down. They followed all the instructions, line by line. Sharp guys; they were pretty impressive. They took pictures.'

He reached over Margaret's shoulder and clicked the computer keyboard. A series of shots flashed on the wall monitors, showing Donald Jewell's initial stage of decomposition, then gradually shifting to his current state.

'Wow,' Clarence said. 'Those guys saw a lot. Any worry about them talking?'

Dan threw his shoulders back and puffed up his chest again. 'It's taken care of. They understand the gravity of the situation and the importance of secrecy.'

'Seriously,' Amos said. 'That's creeping me out.'

'I'd laugh,' Clarence said, 'only I'm sure Murray has a camera in here somewhere and he's watching.'

Dan started nervously looking around the room. 'Oh man, for real?'

Margaret reached back and tugged Dan's sleeve. 'Relax, he's kidding.' At least she hoped he was kidding.

'Run the pictures again,' she said.

Dan did.

'How often did they take these?'

'Every fifteen minutes,' Dan said. 'Just like your instructions specify.'

Amos and Margaret exchanged a glance.

'What is it?' Clarence asked.

'This guy decomposed more rapidly than anyone we've encountered,' Amos said. 'Twice as fast as before, maybe even faster.'

Clarence grimaced. 'How about the others? We have names and addresses of everyone who was here at the time or came after?'

Dan nodded. 'The troopers got everyone's ID, license plates, registrations, the works.'

'Clarence,' Margaret said, 'we need to have Murray get agents to every one of those people and run the swab test.'

'Yes ma'am.' Clarence moved to the third computer chair and grabbed the phone.

'But Margo,' Amos said, 'it's not contagious.'

'Not from host to host,' Margaret said. 'But the McMillians were infected later, remember? Whatever the vector is, it might be persistent, lying on clothes or hair. And looking at these pictures, the disease *has* mutated, at least to some extent – as far as we know, now it *could* be contagious.'

Amos nodded. 'Better safe than sorry, I suppose.'

'Everyone followed precise biohazard procedures,' Dan said. 'We treated it like it was a strain of ebola that could do a stutter-step, fake you out, then jump in your pants if you weren't careful. Mister Jewell's remains are in the Trailer B body locker. Each piece of clothing is in a separate biohazard container, in case you want them.'

Otto put the phone on his shoulder and looked back at Amos. 'Twenty bucks says Doctor Dan put each sock in a separate bag.'

'You're on,' Amos said.

Dan smiled. 'I even labeled the sock bags *left* and *right*. Sorry, Doctor Braun.'

'Call me Amos, you incredibly diligent and overwhelmingly anal-retentive young man.' Amos pulled the folded twenty from his pants pocket and handed it over to Otto without looking away from the screen.

The young doctor impressed Margaret. 'For someone who has no idea what's really going on, you did a hell of a job, Dan,' she said. 'Looks like we're ready to rock. Let me see pictures of the girl's remains.'

Dan seemed surprised. 'Didn't you get the reports on your way in?'

Margaret shook her head. 'No, radio silence the whole way. Why? What's with the daughter's corpse?'

'She's not a corpse, she's alive,' Dan said. 'She's in the containment chamber.'

ARE YOU THERE, GOD? IT'S ME, CHELSEA

A conversation was taking place.

One half of this conversation hovered forty miles above the Earth, straight up from the diseased oak tree in Chuy Rodriguez's backyard.

The other half sat on the floor of Chelsea's bedroom. On her left rested a pile of Barbies, Bratz and other dolls. On her right sat a similar but smaller pile. As she talked, she would pick up a doll from the pile on the left, take off all its clothes, hold the doll in her lap, then draw on it with a blue Sharpie.

She drew little triangles.

They were *very* pretty.

She finished with a doll, put it on the pile on the right, then grabbed another with her left hand.

'Chauncey, do you like ice cream Crunch bars?'

I have never had one. I could not eat them.

'Oh,' Chelsea said. 'Then what do you eat?'

The Orbital directed some processing power to answering this. Being inanimate, it had endless patience for her questions, which was fortunate, because the questions indeed seemed endless. Most often it simply didn't know the answer. It had accumulated a good bit of knowledge from the triangles' interfacing with dozens of human hosts, but it still took time to make associations between language and fact.

I eat gravity.

'Oh,' Chelsea said. 'Is it good?'

The Orbital worked to associate her use of the word *good. Good* meant many things to humans. It could mean a self-profession of capability. It could mean the socially acceptable course of action. It could mean a field goal. The Orbital searched to compare it with food consumption. Many stored host images came up, things like barbecued chicken, chocolate, cake, mashed potatoes. That is what she meant. Without the gravity processors, the Orbital would plummet to the Earth, so it applied the correct definition and answered.

Yes, it is very good.

'Oh,' Chelsea said. 'Chauncey, who is your favorite Detroit Piston?'

I do not know.

'Oh,' Chelsea said. 'Chauncey, are you God?'

The Orbital accessed images. An elderly human with a big white beard. A younger human with long hair and a short brown beard. Glowing heads. Love. Hatred. Divine intervention into human lives. Punishment. Wrath. Destruction. The Orbital cross-referenced these images against cataloged emotional responses, and determined that this was something it could potentially use to motivate hosts.

Why do you think I am God?

'You know, because you can talk in my head and stuff. People can't do that, mostly.'

What do you think of God, Chelsea?

Chelsea sang. '*Jesus loves me, this I know, for the Bible*

tells me so. We go to church most Sundays, except during football season sometimes we don't. I love God because God loves me.'

The Orbital called up more images. He examined the signals coming from Chelsea's brain as she talked of God and Jesus. Yes, this was a powerful motivator.

Chelsea, if God told you to do something bad, would you do it?

Chelsea stopped drawing on her Barbie. She looked at the wall, just kind of staring out, tilting her head to the right as she thought.

'Daddy says sometimes God tests us, but God loves us and he wouldn't ask us to do anything bad. So if *God* asked me to do something, then it *couldn't* be bad, so I would do it.'

Yes.

'Yes what?'

Yes, I am God.

'Oh,' Chelsea said. 'Okay. Can I still call you Chauncey?'

Yes.

Chelsea picked up her doll and started drawing blue triangles.

'Chauncey, do you like Snickers or Twix better?'

The Orbital continued to answer questions.

The door to her room opened slowly, and Mommy peeked her head inside.

'Chelsea, baby, how are you feeling?'

'Okay,' Chelsea said. She picked up another doll and took off its clothes.

'Chelsea, what are you doing in here?'

'Just drawing triangles on my dolls and talking to Chauncey.'

'Ohhh,' Mommy said. 'Your special friend Chauncey?'

'Uh-huh,' Chelsea said. She drew a blue triangle on this doll's forehead. *Very* pretty.

'What are you talking to him about?'

'Oh, you know,' Chelsea said. 'Flowers, and my pink dress, and what's the best cartoons, and basketball and gravity and ice cream and God and dollies and—'

'Okay, honey,' Mommy said, cutting Chelsea off. Mommy was laughing a little. Chelsea didn't know what was so funny.

'You keep talking to Chauncey,' Mommy said. 'Are you drawing on all your dolls? Is that a permanent marker? Don't ruin them, honey.'

'I'm not ruining them, Mommy,' Chelsea said. She picked up a blonde Barbie with blue triangles on her arms, legs and face. She held it up so Mommy could see. 'They're not ruined. I'm making them better. I'm making them *pretty.*'

'Okay, honey,' Mommy said. 'You come get me if you need anything, okay?'

'Okay, Mommy.'

Mommy closed the door. Chelsea set the Barbie on the right-hand pile, then grabbed another doll from the pile on the left.

TEEN ANGST

Margaret refused to cry.

She had a job to do. But looking at the flat-panel monitor, looking at that poor girl's *face* . . .

'Let me *go*!' the girl screamed. She pulled weakly against her restraints, but she wasn't going anywhere. Even if she got out of the restraints, she couldn't escape the tiny containment chamber's clear, reinforced walls.

Cameras mounted outside her chamber provided an excellent view. White epoxy walls blazed under the ceiling's embedded neon lights. Leather cuffs held Betty Jewell's wrists and ankles tight to the autopsy trolley. A disposable roll of thin foam on top of the cart gave it a little bit of padding, but it was still a steel cart and wasn't designed with comfort in mind. She wore a blue hospital gown spotted with purple where her oozing sores leaked blood.

'We injected her with the WDE-4-11 formula,' Dan said. 'That slowed the apoptosis reaction, but she's still breaking down, particularly around her facial lesions.'

'We have to operate immediately,' Amos said. 'We have to get rid of that compromised tissue, see if we can stop the chain reaction entirely.'

Margaret turned to Dan. 'Has she given any indication of when she started showing symptoms? What has she said so far?'

'She just won't talk to us,' he said. 'She believes we're

here to kill her. She keeps asking for her father, but I think she knows her father is dead. She's asking for her mother, too.'

'Did you contact the mother?' Margaret asked.

Dan shook his head. 'We haven't tried.'

Amos turned on him. 'What the hell do you mean, you *haven't tried?* The girl just lost her father. She needs her family.'

'I have orders to keep any infected victims in isolation,' Dan said. 'No contact of any kind until I've relinquished custody, which I'm doing now to you, Doctor Montoya.'

'Well, fine,' Margaret said. 'We've got custody now. Clarence, please call the girl's mother.'

'No,' Clarence said.

Margaret stared at him, dumbfounded. Dan she could understand, he was military, but Clarence? 'We are calling this girl's family, and *right now.*'

'I'm afraid we can't do that, Doc,' Clarence said.

'But she doesn't have triangles,' Margaret said. 'She's got something, sure, but nothing is going to hatch out of her. She's not a threat.'

Clarence shook his head. 'You know we can't say that for sure, Margaret. How many times have you told me that the disease might shift, might become contagious? You said it's mutated, right?'

Margaret didn't know what to say – he was using her own words against her.

Amos jabbed a finger at the monitor. 'That is an *American citizen* in that *cage.* Yes, *cage.* She's got *rights,* goddamit.'

Clarence again shook his head. 'Not right now she doesn't. We contact the mother and the next thing you know, the press is all over it.'

'The *press*?' Amos shouted. 'You're worried about the *press*? Listen up, you goose-stepping assho—'

'Amos, stop,' Margaret said. 'He's right. She could be contagious.'

Amos looked at her like she was crazy. 'Well, sure she could be contagious,' he said. 'That's why we have her in a fucking BSL-4 containment cell. It doesn't change the fact that she's a scared teenage girl. She needs her family. We can bring in the mother, keep her under surveillance or whatever.'

'He's right about the media, too,' Margaret said.

'Margaret, what the hell is wrong with you?' Amos said. 'You're a *doctor*. Remember the phrase *primum non nocere*?'

Margaret swallowed. The phrase was Latin for *first, do no harm*. It wasn't actually part of the Hippocratic Oath, but the words were still drilled into every med student's head.

'Yes, I remember,' she said. 'I also remember another Latin phrase, the one we found painted in Kiet Nguyen's bedroom. The house with all the dead kids. *E pluribus unum*. You remember that?'

Amos said nothing. He looked away.

'What's that mean, Amos? Say it.'

'It means "out of one, many,"' he said quietly.

'So we follow the orders,' Margaret said. 'We don't call the girl's family. Get suited up. We're going to go in there and talk to her.'

Fully suited, Margaret and Amos walked into the autopsy room. An airtight door led into the collapsible walkway that connected Trailer B. Margaret watched the light above that door turn from red to green. Amos pulled up on the latch and swung the door outward to reveal a four-foot-long corridor and a matching door on the other side. They had to close their door to open the other, both because it was an airlock and because there wasn't enough room in the corridor to open both.

When it came time to move the MargoMobile, built-in nozzles would douse the walkway's interior with the chlorine/bleach. Gitsh and Marcus would then fold the walkway into its bracket inside Trailer B, shut the seamless outer door, and the MargoMobile would make like Willie Nelson – on the road again.

She stepped into the walkway. Amos shut the door behind her. Above the door to Trailer B, the light turned from red to green. Amos opened that door, and they stepped through. Only four feet away sat Betty's containment cell.

The girl lifted her head to see them, and Margaret's heart nearly broke in two.

Three giant black sores soiled the left side of her face. One centered on her cheekbone, one on her jaw where it met the neck, and one up on her temple. The last one undercut dark hair that must have been beautiful once. Now, wet strands clung to her face, her forehead and the table around her.

The decomposing black spots on her face were by far the worst, but they weren't the only trouble areas. At least two dozen dime-size circles spotted her body. Her hands looked terrible; half the skin there was wrinkled, black and oozing, her fingers like a modern-art sculpture made from wet raisins. Several IV needles ran into veins on her feet – two of the few unblemished areas left on her body.

The girl shook with sobs. Even though she'd been strapped down for something like sixteen hours, she had no shortage of tears.

Margaret and Amos walked up to the clear glass cell. A flat-panel touch-screen controller mounted on the door served as a wireless interface for all systems in the containment cell. It could even be used to trigger a last-ditch emergency sterilization. All someone had to do was type in #-5-4-5-5, and every inch of both trailers would fill with the deadly chlorine/bleach combination.

Margaret hit a button to turn on the intercom system – they would be able to hear Betty on their earpieces, and their voices would be pumped into speakers inside the cell.

'Hello, Betty,' Margaret said.

Betty stopped whimpering for a second, just long enough to draw in a huge, ragged lungful of air.

'Let me go!'

'We can't,' Margaret said. 'You're very ill.'

'*No fucking shit* I'm ill, you fucking *assholes*! Did you do this to me? *Please*, get my dad. Get my mom. *Please*!'

'Your father is dead,' Amos said.

Margaret quickly pressed a button on the touch screen to turn off the intercom.

'Amos, what are you doing?'

'Telling her the truth.'

Margaret wanted to smack him right in the mouth. 'Amos, we need to get this girl to talk, not put her further into hysterics.'

'Margaret, I've got a teenage daughter,' he said. 'You do not. So shut the fuck up.'

He had a cold look on his face, an expression Margaret hadn't seen on him before. Amos was personalizing this, projecting Betty's situation onto his own child. He reached for the button and turned on the chamber's speakers. 'It's true, Betty,' Amos said. 'Your father is dead. I'm very sorry.'

Margaret realized that Betty wasn't screaming anymore. The girl still had tears streaming down her ruined face, but there was also a hard lucidity in those eyes.

'Daddy's . . . dead? You *killed* him?'

'He died in the parking lot before anyone could get to him,' Amos said. 'Before anyone could help him.'

A single sob hit her body like a big cough, and then she lay still.

'But I've been here for like hours,' Betty said, fighting back sobs. 'Why didn't anyone just fucking *tell* me?'

'Because they didn't think you could handle it,' Amos said. 'They treated you like a child. I'm sorry about that, but Doctor Montoya and I are in charge now. My name is Doctor Amos Braun.'

'What's . . . what's happening to me?'

'You are very sick,' Amos said. 'You have whatever killed your father. We don't know why it's developing more slowly in you.'

'Why are you doing this to me?'

'We're trying to save you,' Amos said. 'We need to ask some important questions first. Where were you and your father coming from?'

'Just let me go,' Betty said in a low voice. 'I'm not one of the ones you want, I swear. Don't kill me, *please* don't kill me.'

'Betty, we're not trying to ki—'

'*I will fucking slash your throat, you needle-dick motherfucker!*' She yanked at her restraints so hard the heavy trolley wobbled. '*Lemmegolemmegolemmego!*'

'Amos, we need to put her under,' Margaret said. 'She's paranoid.'

Amos ignored Margaret. His face showed anguish, his deep need to see Betty calm down and cooperate. Was it

Betty Jewell he saw in there or his own daughter – rotting, terrified and strapped to an autopsy trolley?

'Where were you coming from?' he asked. 'We need to know where you were.'

Betty stared at them, wide eyes full of hate and terror. She screamed, one long, ragged note. She stopped only to draw a deep breath, then hit the ragged note again.

'Please,' Amos said. 'Stop this. We're trying to help you.'

'Amos, that's enough,' Margaret said. She reached to the control panel and hit a button, sending fifty milligrams of propofol through one of the IV needles taped to Betty's feet. Amos put both of his gloved hands on the glass. He and Margaret silently watched as Betty's screams slowed, faded and stopped.

'She's out,' Margaret said.

'Then let's get her wheeled into Trailer A,' Amos said. 'I want to operate immediately.'

MIXED MESSAGES

The neural net stretched through Betty's frontal lobe, but it was still very thin. *Too* thin to send the signal. It needed more connections.

For hours Betty's crawlers had fought the dissolving chain reaction, struggling to reach her brain. The WDE-4-11 injection turned out to be a lifeline for the crawlers – combined with their own apoptosis antidote secretions, it stalled the chain reaction before it grew so bad that they couldn't even move.

As Margaret and Amos wheeled Betty through the collapsible walkway and into the autopsy room, some of the muscle fibers coalesced at the center of her brain, tore themselves to bits and formed a ball. Where Chelsea's ball of fibers was a thousand microns wide, Betty's was closer to six hundred, just over half the size.

It was enough to send a weak signal.

And enough to receive a response.

That response signal wasn't for the crawlers. It was meant for the host.

The remaining crawlers stopped producing the apoptosis antidote and started flooding Betty's brain with neurotransmitters.

They had to wake her up, wake her up so she could receive the signal.

CHEFFIE'S OPEN DOOR

Neither snow, nor rain, nor heat, nor gloom of night stays these couriers from the swift completion of their appointed rounds.

The phrase is attributed to Herodotus and refers to the courier service of the ancient Persian Empire. Many people incorrectly think this is the motto of the United States Postal Service. The phrase *is* inscribed over the James A. Farley post office in New York City, but it's not an official slogan.

Official or not, John Burkle figured it was a pretty dead-nuts on-target description for driving a white postal truck in weather fifteen goddamn degrees below freezing, complemented by goddamn thirty-mile-per-hour winds that were blowing thin sheets of snow right across the goddamn back roads. Who drives in this weather?

Postal workers. That's who.

He drove the truck's right wheel into a frozen rut in front of the Franklin place. Yesterday this had been a mud puddle filled with chunks of brown ice. That was because it had been fifty degrees for two straight days. If you don't like the weather in Michigan . . .

John stuffed the Franklins' mail into their metal mailbox, then drove to the next house. Houses were pretty spaced out around here, at least a couple of acres apart. The next house belonged to Cheffie Jones. Cheffie had always been a little off. Hit in the head in an industrial accident or something. Pretty much kept to himself. Plenty of time to buy shit on eBay, though – John put four small boxes into Cheffie's supersize mailbox. Sometimes Cheffie came out to get his mail and say hello. John looked toward the house, but didn't see any movement. He started to drive on, then stopped short and looked back.

Was the front door open?

It was. He was a good hundred feet away, and it was a little hard to see, but it looked as if something covered in snow was blocking the door.

Fifteen below zero, and the front door was open.

John put the postal van in park. He reached into his bag and pulled out his Taser. Could be a burglar in there. Did Cheffie have a dog? John couldn't remember. He had a schedule to keep, but he didn't feel right ignoring an open door in weather like this. He cautiously approached the house.

'Cheffie?' he called. Out here you really didn't want to approach a house quietly. People took gun rights seriously in northern Michigan. You made a lot of noise and let them know you were coming, so as not to be mistaken for a robber if the home owner was sober, or for a deer if he was exceedingly drunk.

The door was open about eight inches. Underneath a light coating of snow, something long and thin and black blocked the door. John walked up on the porch for a closer look.

It was a hand.

A black, skeletal hand.

Despite a thick layer of blue post-office winter wear, John Burkle sprinted back to the van in near-Olympic-qualifying time.

BETTY JEWELL'S FACE

Betty Jewell picked the worst possible time in the history of mankind to wake up.

Eyes still closed, she wondered how many flavors of pain there were. Baskin-Robbins didn't have shit on her.

Stay still.

She didn't know where those words came from. Not her ears. With her ears she heard the clinking of instruments and the muffled voices of a man and a woman. Those voices were connected with one of the new flavors.

They were cutting into her *face*, for fuck's sake. Agony, pure hell, but was it any worse than the fire rippling through her entire body? Shit, did it even *matter* which was worse? Either one was enough to make her put a gun in her mouth and pull the trigger if it meant the pain would stop.

Betty, you have to save your soul.

Her soul? Couldn't she just save her face? You don't need a soul for senior pictures.

Oh, *gawd,* did it hurt. So much *pain.*

Kill them, Betty. Kill the people who are hurting you. Then all your pain will go away.

That voice. So beautiful. Was it the voice of God? If

not, how else could she hear it? But really, it didn't matter who was speaking, because the voice promised her that the pain would stop.

For that, Betty would do anything.

Her right cheek rested on a hard pillow. They had put her on her right side, left arm still behind her in the cuff. The man and the woman hovered over her, fucking with her face, her once-beautiful face. She felt them cutting.

Which one was hurting her this bad? Dr. Braun? That Mexican bitch? It didn't matter, they were in it together. They would *pay* together.

She slowly opened just her right eye. She saw nothing but blue. They had covered her face with a napkin or something. It felt as though the napkin also covered her left eye. Could she open it? She decided not to – she had an advantage only as long as they thought she was out. Whatever the napkin was, it didn't quite reach to the table. If she looked down the table with only her right eye, she could see just under the napkin all the way down her right arm, all the way down to the leather cuff that held her fast.

She moved her left foot very slowly – they had uncuffed her feet to turn her on her side.

With all her weight on her right shoulder, she couldn't pull her right hand without making her whole body lurch. But she could pull the left hand if she did it very, *very* slowly.

Just a little bit at a time, real slow, a steady, gradual increase of pressure.

'This doesn't make sense,' the man said. The rubber suit muffled his voice, but she could make out his words. He sounded very close, like he was leaning down right over the top of her covered face.

'She doesn't have triangles,' the man said. 'She doesn't have the colored fibers of Morgellons. So what's causing this excessive cell death?'

Betty kept pulling. It hurt. A new flavor added to the dessert bar. She felt a tearing sensation. Without a sound, she kept pulling, kept applying constant pressure. Skin slowly sloughed off her hand, allowing her to pull the hand through the cuff, like sliding off a bloody black glove. She felt chunks of ruined skin bunching up on the cuff's far side. She knew she should have been horrified, but it was too late for that.

God helps those who help themselves.

She needed to *act*.

Without her skin, things would be slippery. She'd have to get it exactly right.

'Margaret, look at this!' the man said. 'I . . . oh my God, I see something. There's something *moving* in here, something really tiny. Put the magnifiers on, look.'

He took the Lord's name in vain. Sinner. Betty heard the *zip-zip* of a rubber suit as the woman moved to stand next to the man.

'What the hell is that, Amos?' The woman's voice. Also right in front of her, also hovering right over her face. 'It looks like . . . it looks like a nerve cell.'

'This is amazing,' the man said. 'You can see it moving. It's hard to tell with all the damage, but I think it's following the V3 nerve toward the brain.'

Betty felt her left hand slide all the way inside the cuff. She didn't pull it out, not yet, but now she could anytime she chose.

'Cut it out of there,' the woman said. 'Maybe these things are what's causing the rot. If we can get them out, maybe we can stabilize her.'

'Sample tray, please,' the man said. 'Crawling organelle isolated and removed. Examining. Object tears into smaller pieces. . . . Margaret, *look*! These pieces look sort of like . . . muscle fibers. They're . . . they're moving on their own.'

'Get another one out of her face,' the woman said. 'Let's get some side-by-side video of these.'

Betty waited. She waited until she felt the scalpel slide in again, waited until she was sure she felt it hit her cheekbone.

She waited for that, so she knew *exactly* where it was.

Keeping her head and body as still as she could, Betty Jewell slid her hand out of the cuff.

Margaret watched Amos's deft, delicate technique as he cut away the rotting flesh, searching for another crawling nerve.

The high-powered magnifying goggles mounted in front of her visor showed Betty's open wound with amazing detail, a super-closeup landscape of blood vessels, muscle, veins, bone and black rot. And amid all that, something moving. So *tiny*. Dendrite-like arms seemed to stretch out like an amoeba's pseudopods. The arms contracted, pulling the body forward, the tail dragging behind.

Just like the camera mounted in Margaret's helmet, the magnifying goggles would record their own feed. Judging by the rapid rate of rot, watching that video might be the only way she could study these things because they wouldn't be around for long.

And neither would Betty, unless they could do something drastic.

'This isn't like Dawsey at all,' Margaret said. 'Unless

this is some larval stage, something that was already over before we examined him.'

'You've got me,' Amos said. 'Wait, here's another one. Look at that, crawling along the afferent nerve. Let me get it out of there.'

Margaret watched closely. Amos's scalpel danced around a second patch of black rot, cutting it out in a neat circle.

Then a flash of red. A blur, something that looked huge through the high-magnification glasses. That sudden movement, like it was flying at her face, made Margaret rear back.

She heard a snap and a gurgling sound.

Margaret whipped her right hand up and under the magnifying goggles, knocking them off her head.

Betty Jewell sat up.

Not all the way up – her right hand remained locked in the cuff, but her bloody, skinless left hand waved free, holding a scalpel.

Amos's gloved hands clutched frantically at his suit-covered throat, grabbing, trying to claw through the black PVC. Blood sprayed against the inside of his visor. Drips of it leaked down the black suit's outer surface, leaked from the small hole in his suit.

He took a half step back. Betty lunged forward again with the scalpel, her restrained right arm making the movement awkward and off balance. The scalpel's tip sliced through his suit, just above his left pectoral.

Betty gathered her strength for another strike.

Margaret grabbed Amos's shoulders and yanked him away from the trolley. She pulled far too hard for the confined space – they smashed into the trailer wall and fell to the floor. Amos landed on top. He kicked and kept grabbing at his throat, gloved fingers trying to reach inside the hole and tear it open, but the blood-slick PVC fabric wouldn't give him purchase.

'Amos! Get off me!' Margaret pushed and pulled at the small man, trying to free her legs.

She looked up to see Betty slide her knees underneath her body. The girl rose up, kneeling on the autopsy trolley, right arm still trapped by the cuff. She leaned toward the cuff, then crossed her skinless left hand over the inside of her right elbow.

'Oh, God . . . ,' Margaret hissed.

Betty yanked backward, twisting to the right, throwing all her weight against the cuff.

Her right hand slid free. Chunks of sloughed skin fell to the floor with a wet slap. Momentum carried her over the trolley's left side. She hit the white floor, droplets of blood splattering across the autopsy chamber.

Amos's movements slowed.

Margaret managed to kick her legs free. She pushed Amos off, then stood, her back against the trailer wall.

Betty leaned her right shoulder against the sink and pushed herself up with wobbling legs. Blood streaked her blue gown, the only clothing on an otherwise-naked body. The right side of her face was mostly cut away, black-and-white cheekbone blazing under red smears, bits of jellyish rot still clinging to what little skin remained.

Margaret just stared. She couldn't move a muscle. She wanted to run, to scream, but she couldn't even draw a breath.

Blood dripped from Betty's skinless fingers. She still held the scalpel in her left hand, cradled it more than gripped it, trying to keep the stainless steel steady against exposed, blood-slick muscles.

Betty smiled. Only with the left half of her face, of course, because the muscles on the right side were mostly gone.

'You *bish*,' she slurred. 'Lesh shee how you like it.'

She shuffled forward, trying to keep her balance, bare feet leaving bloody streaks on the white floor.

The autopsy trolley was the only thing separating her from Margaret. Betty reached down with her right hand and rolled it out of the way. She pulled her hand back, but her right pointer finger stayed behind, stuck to the trolley in a red and black mess of rotted meat and jutting bone.

Betty half-smiled again.

She stood only three feet away.

She took a small shuffle-step forward.

Margaret still couldn't will her muscles to move, not even a bit. Her breath returned in a sucking gasp, then shot out in a ragged scream that sounded impossibly loud inside her suit helmet.

But not so loud that she didn't hear the gunshot.

The right side of Betty's head, the undamaged side, exploded outward in a fist-size hole that sprayed blood, brains and bone on the back wall and into the sink. She dropped like a cloth puppet.

'Margaret!'

Clarence's voice, muffled.

'Margaret, are you okay? Did she cut you?'

She turned to his voice. He wore his black biohazard suit. Gitsh and Marcus, also wearing suits, were right behind him. Clarence's gloved hand held a pistol, still smoking. He knelt by her side, the gun pointed down and away from her.

Gitsh's gloved right hand held a knife, much larger than Betty's scalpel. He cut away at Amos's suit, slicing it open at the chest and neck. Blood sloshed out of the cut suit as if someone had wrung out a soaked towel. It splattered on the floor and on Gitsh's feet as he reached in to apply pressure. Marcus grabbed Amos's legs.

'Clarence, get him on the table,' Marcus said. 'His jugular is cut. Gitsh, keep pressure there. Margaret, get his helmet off!'

The men lifted Amos and set him on the already bloody trolley.

Margaret found herself standing, pulling off Amos's helmet. Gitsh's gloved hands stayed pressed down on Amos's neck. Blood covered Amos's face, matted his hair, pooled in his eyes.

His wide-open eyes.

She looked at Gitsh's gloves. There was no blood oozing up from beneath the fingers.

Amos. Margaret's thoughts snapped back into place.

'Do exactly what I say,' she ordered. 'Remove your hands on a count of three, then be ready to reapply pressure as soon as I say *go*. One . . . two . . . *three.*'

Gitsh pulled his hands back a few inches, where they hovered, ready to be put back into use.

No blood flowed.

The scalpel had punched in just to the right of Amos's windpipe, then slid outward, slicing open the whole right side of his neck.

She couldn't check his pulse without taking off her gloves, but she didn't need to.

Amos Braun was dead.

SMOOCHIES!

Chelsea turned the knob ever so slowly. It didn't make a sound. Neither did the door when she opened it. She crept into her parents' room. Daddy was snoring. He always snored. Sometimes Mommy would go sleep on the couch, but not tonight. She must have been tired.

When Daddy snored, his mouth was always wide open. He looked silly. Mommy slept with her mouth closed.

Chelsea would have to fix that.

She tiptoed up to the bed, her pajama feet barely a whisper on the carpeting. Mommy wanted to make her go to the doctor? The doctor who poked her with stuff? The doctor who had the *needles*? Well, now Chelsea was in charge. Chauncey had said so. And Mommy wasn't going to make her do anything anymore.

Chelsea stood at the edge of the bed, looking down at Mommy. Mommy had such a pretty face.

Chelsea reached out with her finger and thumb and slowly, tenderly, pinched Mommy's nose shut. Not enough to hurt her, just enough to stop the air from going in. There were a few seconds where nothing happened, then Mommy's mouth opened and she took in a sharp breath. Chelsea let go of Mommy's nose and dropped to the floor, lying flat against the edge of the bed. If Mommy woke up, she'd have to look over the edge to see Chelsea down there.

Chelsea waited, but Mommy didn't seem to move. It was so hard not to giggle.

Chelsea slowly got to her knees, then to her feet, real quiet, like it was slow motion in the movies. Her head rose up until her eyes peeked over the edge of the bed.

Mommy's mouth was still open.

Her eyes were still closed.

She was breathing real slow.

Mommy was asleep.

M a k e   h e r   o b e y .

Chelsea nodded. She moved her head forward slowly. Chelsea waited three more seconds to see if Mommy would wake up.

One-one-thousand . . . *two*-one-thousand . . . *three*-one-thousand . . .

Ready or not, Mommy, here I come.

Chelsea put her lips over Mommy's lips. Her tongue caressed Mommy's tongue. There was a fizzing sound and a feeling like putting a bunch of Pop Rocks in your mouth. Chelsea fell to the floor again, this time rolling under the bed, trying *so hard* not to giggle.

'Eaungh,' Mommy said. Chelsea felt the bed move as Mommy awoke and sat up fast. She made a noise that was like coughing and spitting at the same time. The bed twitched with Mommy's sharp movements.

'Unh!' Mommy said. 'My mouf!'

'Hon?' Daddy said in a sleepy voice. 'Hon-bun . . . you okay?'

'No, my mouf is on fiah!'

'Did you just eat something?'

'No, ah wah sleepin'!'

Even with a burning mouth, Mommy could still do

that thing with her voice where she made it sound like Daddy was really stupid.

'Just relax. You must have had a bile burp or something. A little acid came up.'

'Unh!' Mommy said. 'Un-huh.'

'Go rinse out with mouthwash,' Daddy said. 'Take a Rolaids.'

Chelsea felt the bed move again. She kept herself very still. Mommy's feet hit the floor, than she walked to the bathroom. The bathroom light came on for a second before the door shut behind her, leaving just an illuminated outline of the door.

Chelsea felt the bed thump again. Then, only two seconds later, Daddy snored. Wow, was he *good* at that! She bit down on her hand to choke back some major giggles. Daddy sounded so *funny*!

Chelsea Jewell slid out from under the bed and quietly ran to the bedroom door. She eased out into the hallway, carefully shutting the door behind her, and in seconds was back in her own bed.

'I did it, Chauncey!' she whispered. 'I did it!'

She will not make you go to the doctor now. Tomorrow, you will be in charge.

' For real?'

You don't have to speak out loud to talk to me. If you think really hard, I can hear you.

Chelsea squealed and hid her face in her pillow. Chauncey *was* special.

'For *real?*'

Try it. Tell me your favorite color.

Chelsea controlled her giggles and tried to think hard, whatever that meant. She liked pink. But blue was real nice, too, and she had those light-blue socks with the brown stripes that Daddy bought her on his last trip, and then—

Focus. Your mind is full of thoughts. Concentrate.

Chelsea took a deep breath. She closed her eyes and *thought*.

Pink.

She opened her eyes and looked at the ceiling. Could Chauncey *really* hear her thoughts? If he could, then he *had* to be God.

'That's a lucky guess, Chauncey.'

Then pick your favorite number.

She nodded and closed her eyes. When she thought of the number, she smiled to herself, then concentrated really hard.

Number one.

Chelsea threw her face into the pillow and squealed with delight.

It will get easier the more you do it. Now go to sleep. Tomorrow is an important day.

Good night, Chauncey, Chelsea thought, as loud as she could. She rolled over and closed her eyes.

It was so cool to have a special friend.

DAY FIVE

THE INVASION

Like most jobs, being the president's go-to, behind-the-scenes man had pros and cons. Black budgets? *Pro.* Watching the most powerful people in Washington do whatever you told them to do? *Pro.* Meetings in the Oval Office where you were the center of attention? *Pro.*

That same meeting at 3:00 A.M. to deliver bad news? That would be a *con.* A *big* con.

'I'm afraid there are new incidents,' Murray said.

The president in his pajamas. Vanessa fully dressed, hair pulled back tight as ever. Maybe, like Murray, she hadn't even been to bed yet. Or maybe she was a vampire and didn't need to sleep at all. He wouldn't have ruled that out.

'With that weather analysis?' Gutierrez asked. 'Did Montoya's idea find this mystery satellite?'

'Not yet, Mister President,' Murray said. 'We're still getting NASA to pull their heads out of their asses and focus all their energies on it, if you'll pardon my French, sir.'

'Even in an emergency, bureaucracy is what it is,' Gutierrez said. 'Keep me informed on that. So, let's hear about this new development.'

Murray cleared his throat and stepped into the breach. 'Two people infected with the rot were found at a rest stop near Bay City, Michigan. They did *not* have triangles.

Donald Jewell of Pittsburgh and his teenage daughter, Betty. The father died on the spot. The daughter was being kept in one of the portable labs for observation. We flew Doctor Montoya's team there, they performed the examination, and in the process the girl became violent and killed Doctor Amos Braun.'

'*What?*' Gutierrez said. 'How? How did it happen?'

'She took his scalpel and stabbed him in the throat, sir. The girl then tried to attack Doctor Montoya. Agent Clarence Otto shot and killed the girl.'

'How is Montoya?' Gutierrez asked. 'Is she okay? Was anyone else hurt?'

'No sir,' Murray said. 'Doctor Braun was the only casualty.'

Gutierrez slumped into his chair. Vanessa seemed to pick up on this and leaned forward.

'And why wasn't Otto in the room?' she asked.

Murray felt his face flush red, just a bit. 'Montoya and Braun were doing emergency surgery on the girl. Agent Otto was in the computer room monitoring the situation.'

'But he wasn't *inside* the room where they were operating?'

'No.'

She raised her eyebrows. 'And how, exactly, does that happen in a case where all types of people turn into murderers?'

Murray said nothing. If he'd insisted on proper procedure, Otto would have been inside the room and Amos would probably still be alive. The trailer was cramped and extra bodies got in the way, but that was no excuse to ignore safety.

Vanessa had him dead to rights.

'You said *incidents*, plural,' Vanessa said. 'What else?'

'We have a body in Gaylord, Michigan,' Murray said. 'Male, Caucasian, found alone in his house. Corpse was black and rotted. Paramedics performed the swab test and got a positive result.'

Gutierrez sat forward again. 'When did this happen?'

'About eight hours ago.'

'Eight *hours*?' Gutierrez said. 'Don't you have an alert system in place for things like this?'

'Yes, Mister President. The paramedics called the hospital, and it seems one of the local doctors wanted to evaluate the body himself. That delayed a call to the CDC, and when that call was made, it took a little while for the information to reach Doctor Cheng.'

'Cheng,' Vanessa said. 'He's the only one outside of Dew Phillips's team that knows everything about this situation, is that right?'

'Yes ma'am,' Murray said.

Vanessa nodded. 'So it's safe to say that your high level of secrecy is responsible for this delay? If we had a nationwide alert out, we'd have heard about this Gaylord corpse much sooner, correct?'

She had his balls, and she was squeezing.

'That's possible, ma'am, but we have more pressing issues at the moment. I ran Donald Jewell's cell-phone and credit-card records. A few days ago, he made multiple calls to a Bobby Jewell in Gaylord. Turns out that's his brother. We also obtained all of Betty Jewell's cell-phone text messages from the past week. Messages from yesterday described her feeling ill and said that her father and cousin Chelsea Jewell were feeling the same.'

'Wait one second,' Vanessa said. 'You read this girl's private text messages?'

'Yes ma'am,' Murray said. 'All cell-phone text messages are recorded in the databases of the phone companies. Every text message ever sent, I'm told, is still stored somewhere. We acquired Betty's text history.'

'"Acquired,"' Vanessa said. 'Which is war-against-terrorism lingo for *illegally obtained.*'

'With all due respect, Miss Colburn,' Murray said without even a shred of respect in his voice, 'I think we have more important things to worry about right now.'

'I agree,' Gutierrez said. 'What else did you get out of the texts, Murray?'

'We think Chelsea has the same strain as Betty and Donald. We don't know much, but this strain does *not* show triangle growth. It's something new. However, Betty's texts said Bobby Jewell had some small welts on his arm, and that he was itching. We think that means first-stage triangle growths. This is a chance for us to get the infection at its earliest stage, sir. I'd recommended sending Dew Phillips and his team immediately.'

'Dew's *team*,' Vanessa said. 'By that you mean Perry Dawsey. No way. We're not going through that again.'

Murray's stomach churned. He needed a Tums and pronto – he'd sent Dew to Gaylord right before he'd walked into the Oval Office.

'We have to send Perry, sir,' Murray said. 'Dawsey is the only one who can detect the hosts.'

Vanessa smiled. He hated that smile. Really . . . fucking . . . *hated* it.

'But you already know where the Jewells live,' Vanessa said. 'And you didn't get that information from Perry Dawsey, correct?'

He had walked right into that one. So fucking obvious he hadn't even realized it.

'Yes ma'am, but they could behave like other infected hosts and run, so we need Dawsey.'

'I see,' Vanessa said. 'Well, I would think that if Dawsey had detected this Gaylord infection, you would have already said so. So am I right in assuming he did *not* detect this one?'

'That's correct,' Murray said. 'He feels that . . . uh . . . his ability to detect the hosts is being jammed by some unknown force.'

'So he did *not* detect it this time,' Vanessa said. 'Which means if the Jewells *do* run, there's no knowing whether Perry can track them at all.'

Murray's face felt very hot. 'I would say that's correct, ma'am. But we also don't know if this jamming will continue, or if he can hear them should he get closer. He's the only detection asset we have. We need to send him now.'

'What we *need* to do,' Vanessa said, 'is make sure we help the Jewells before it's too late. After we have them, then bring in Dawsey – under heavy guard – to communicate with the triangles. He can still do that, right, Murray?'

'Yes,' Murray said, although he really didn't know the answer.

'Then we agree that it's a bad idea to send Dawsey in first.'

Murray shook his head. 'That's not what I said.'

'Come on, Murray,' she said. 'Your tangled web of secrets just isn't working. We need to stop fucking around.'

'I hardly think Amos Braun was *fucking around* when he died in the line of duty, Miss Colburn.' The words shot out of his mouth before he could control them.

'Of course that's not what she meant,' Gutierrez said coolly. 'Right, Vanessa?'

She glared at Murray. The eyes sent a clear message: *You just embarrassed me in front of the president, and I won't forget it.*

'Of course,' she said. 'My apologies, Murray.'

Gutierrez nodded once, as if the apology ended the incident for good.

Vanessa turned to face Gutierrez. 'What I meant to say, John, was that we need to step this up a level. We need to send in Ogden.'

Again with calling the president by his first name.

'And have Ogden do what?' Murray asked. 'Blockade the town? Go door-to-door and administer Margaret's test?'

'Exactly,' she said. 'That's *exactly* what we have to do.'

President Gutierrez looked at her for quite a long time, his fingers tapping a pattern on the desk. He turned and looked at Murray. 'Won't it be impossible to control secrecy if we do that?'

Murray looked at the president, then at Vanessa. Her eyes were cold and emotionless once again. He didn't like her, but he respected that kind of bold move. She wanted to send in the troops? Lock down an entire town? Vanessa Colburn did not fuck around.

'Actually, sir,' Murray said, 'I agree with Miss Colburn. And I believe we can preserve secrecy. Doctor Cheng has been using a story about flesh-eating bacteria as cover for his research. Say a plane is flying over Gaylord with research material for the flesh-eating bacteria, the plane goes off the radar . . . well, that could inadvertently expose civilians. The local population is at risk, which gets us total cooperation of area law enforcement. We use local cops as our spokespeople; the residents will listen to them. We have enough tests to check all the residents we can find. Testing is an easy sell when we tell people they could rot and die horribly if they have the bacteria and go untreated.

'We evacuate the town, test everyone on the way out, then go door-to-door to see who's left behind. We either get the infected coming out of town or get them in their homes. As soon as we secure the town, we let everyone back in. Two days at the most.'

Gutierrez raised his eyebrows in surprise. 'You rattled that off like you've invaded a town before.'

Murray nodded. 'There have been instances. If you're willing to sign the secrecy-assurance documents, I can share any story you'd like to hear. I have thirty years' worth.'

Gutierrez tapped the desktop some more before he spoke. 'How long will it take Ogden's men to deploy to Gaylord?'

'Otsego Airport is right in the town proper,' Murray said. 'Ogden and his men can land in C-17s, complete with Humvees, and we'll have Ospreys and Apaches in support. He'll probably be on the ground in Gaylord three or four hours from the time I make the call. But sir, I still *strongly* suggest putting Dawsey in play. If he can sniff out the hosts, it could shorten the process. Ogden's men can make sure he stays under control.'

Gutierrez turned to Vanessa. She nodded.

'Do it, Murray,' Gutierrez said. 'Get Tom Maskill an overview of the bacteria-story details, and we'll coordinate. But I want Dawsey and Phillips to sit tight until Ogden arrives. And I'm not kidding, Murray – they better sit down and get some coffee and not do a *damn thing*. I am going to check up on that, and if I find out that my orders have been ignored, you're finished.'

Murray needed to get the hell out of the Oval Office and call Dew before Perry could do anything stupid.

'Yes sir,' Murray said. 'If you'll excuse me, I have to implement this right away.'

Gutierrez nodded. Murray almost ran out of the room.

WAKE UP, MOMMY

Chelsea stood at the foot of her parents' bed eating a Crunch Bar Eskimo Pie. It was only 8:00 A.M., and this was her *third* Crunch.

Mommy and Daddy didn't get to make the rules anymore.

Try to wake them up. But don't use words.

'For real?'

Speak to me with your thoughts.

Sorry, Chelsea thought.

My connection is going to be the strongest with you. You will help me talk to the rest. Now try to wake them up.

Chelsea took a bite of ice cream, swallowed it, then concentrated.

Wake up, sleepyheads.

Nothing happened.

Try again. Don't be nice, Chelsea. You know how when you get angry, when you scream, your voice gets louder?

Yes.

**Thoughts work the same
way. Have your parents
ever done anything to
make you angry?**

Chelsea's smile faded away. Why shouldn't she have all the ice cream she wanted? Why wouldn't Daddy let her get her ears pierced? And why couldn't she get a puppy? She *wanted* a puppy. That just wasn't *fair*. Maybe Daddy needed protection, but he also need to stop being *bad*.

Chelsea focused again.

Wake up, Daddy . . . or I'm going to spank you.

Daddy sat up fast, fully awake. He just stared at Chelsea. She had never seen Daddy's face look like that before. His mouth was open and his eyes were all wide.

'Did you say something, honey?'

He absently scratched at his left arm. A big orange scabby thing came off in his hand. Without taking his eyes from his daughter, he tossed the scabby thing away and started scratching again.

I told you to wake up or I would spank you.

Daddy stopped scratching. His right hand just sort of hung on his left shoulder, frozen in half-scratch.

'That's what I thought,' he said in a quiet voice.

Chelsea turned to stare at Mommy. *Wake up, Mommy.*

Mommy lifted her head, then set it back down, rolled over and groaned.

'Oh, I'm so hot,' she said. 'Bob, tell Chelsea to stop screaming and go back to bed. She made me so goddamn sick.'

Daddy kept staring. 'Uh, Candy? Uh . . . you better wake up.'

'I'm not kidding, Bob,' Mommy said in her *Daddy Is So Stupid* voice.

Chelsea dropped the ice cream stick on the floor.

Mommy, you get out of bed or I'll make Daddy spank you.

Mommy sat up slowly and pulled the blankets right under her chin. She stared at her daughter, face full of confusion.

'Chelsea,' Mommy whispered, 'am I hearing you . . . in my . . . my *head*?'

'Get up, Candy,' Daddy said. 'Please. She's making me want to . . . to punish you.'

Mommy looked at Daddy and started to cry. She wasn't getting up. Chelsea had *told* her to get up.

Daddy, Mommy is being a bad girl.

Mommy shook her head. Daddy got out of bed and walked out of the bedroom. Chelsea stared at Mommy as they listened to Daddy walk downstairs, open a drawer in the kitchen, then walk back up. When he came into the bedroom, he was holding Mommy's heavy spanky-spoon in his shaking hand.

Mommy, this is going to hurt Daddy more than it hurts you.

Mommy just kept shaking her head and crying until Daddy really got going. Then she started to scream.

THE NEED FOR SPEED

Colonel Charlie Ogden looked over Corporal Cope's shoulder. They both stared at a computer screen showing a map of Gaylord, Michigan.

'Lot of roads in and out of that town, Colonel,' Cope said.

'Noted,' Ogden said. 'What's the population?'

'Over thirty-five hundred, sir. That's a lot of people to manage with one company.'

'I'm thinking the same thing,' Ogden said. 'But we have state and local police helping. How long a flight for the C-17s?'

'About an hour, sir,' Cope said. 'Plus an hour to load up and another to fly. We could have X Company offloaded and ready to deploy in under three hours.'

'Call the pilots and the platoon leaders,' Ogden said. 'They don't pay us to have our bags packed for nothing. We scramble now. I want to be offloaded in two and a half, not three.'

'Yes sir.'

Cope left the desk and started making calls. Ogden sat down and studied the map. The airport was right in town. The hatchlings had made that mistake in Wahjamega as well, building a gate so close to a landing strip that Ogden had landed his troops only a couple of miles away from the target.

Cope was right – there were a lot of roads. First glance showed about twenty ways out of town, not counting the highways I-75 and M-32. No real choke points. Ogden could have the police handle the highways, keep a lower profile that way, but he wasn't going to put a couple of cops on each back road. The infected were just too dangerous for that. He'd need to put a roadblock on each small road, stationed with at least four men.

The smaller roads were mostly paved rural routes through farmland, although there were a lot of vehicle-capable dirt trails that wound through wooded areas. And then the woods themselves, where people could just walk out and avoid the roads altogether. His men would be spread fairly thin to cover it all.

'Cope,' Ogden said.

'Sir?'

'Call Captain Lodge and activate Whiskey Company. We need them for this. We'll leave Yankee and Zulu companies at Fort Bragg. Best to have a reserve that can react fast, in case we're tied up in Gaylord, don't you think?'

'Are you asking my opinion, sir?'

'No,' Ogden said. 'It's a rhetorical question.'

'In that case I agree with whatever you say, Colonel.'

'That's what I like about you, Cope, you're so opinionated. Now make the calls.'

'Yes sir.'

Ogden would have felt better using all four companies, but it was just too much to move a full battalion into a small town. Plus, it was prudent to leave two companies of the DOMREC free to react, in case a gate popped up somewhere else. The DOMREC was the only unit that could deploy and be combat-ready anywhere in the

Midwest inside three hours. The next-fastest response time would come from the Division Ready Force. The DRF's mission was to put lead elements anywhere in the world within eighteen hours of an alert. If DRF had to deploy in the continental United States, that would probably cut it down to seven or eight hours, but no way in hell could they be ready to fight in three hours.

When it came to that kind of speed, there was Charlie Ogden's unit and no one else.

HOW TO DEAL WITH THE DEATH OF A FRIEND

Clarence Otto sat in the modified sleeper cabin of the MargoMobile, Margaret on his lap, her forehead in the crook of his neck and her legs supported by his arm. Her tears and snot dripped onto his jacket. If he noticed, he didn't seem to care.

She couldn't stop crying. She wanted to, tried to, but she couldn't. She'd cried all night until she'd fallen asleep on the computer-room floor, then started again as soon as she woke.

They were driving north to Gaylord. Driving to more death. To more horror.

She was still wearing her scrubs, the same ones she'd slept in, the same ones she'd been wearing under the hazmat suit when Betty Jewell killed Amos Braun.

Killed her *friend*.

A friend she would never, ever see again. She just wanted him back. Why couldn't he just *come back*?

'I'm so sorry, Margo,' Clarence said as he gently petted her hair. He kept saying that. Maybe he didn't know what else to say. It didn't matter *what* he said, really. She was grateful just for the sound of his voice.

She should have been the one to call Amos's wife. She'd never met the woman, but still, Margaret should have done it. She'd taken the coward's way out, though – Dew sent a couple of FBI agents to deliver the news.

'I need to get up,' she said. 'I have to watch the video from my helmet-cam. Maybe I missed something, maybe I already forgot something when . . .' Her voice trailed off.

'There's plenty of time to work later,' Clarence said. 'You need a rest. Besides, we're driving. It's not safe for you to be in the trailer when this thing is rolling along.'

He kept petting her hair.

The cold lump in her chest wouldn't go away.

'If only . . . I could have . . . gotten his helmet off sooner,' she said quietly, her sobs breaking up her sentence.

'You know that's not true,' Clarence whispered. 'She cut his artery. There was nothing you could have done.'

'But I . . . was in charge. It's . . . it's my fault.'

She felt Clarence shaking his head, his chin rubbing softly against her hair.

'You're smarter than that, Margo. I know you're going to try and blame yourself, because that's the kind of person you are. You want to take everything on your shoulders. But blaming yourself for his death is stupid, and you know it. That girl had enough drugs in her to knock out an elephant. She had shown no signs of violent behavior. Hell, her hands were *strapped down.* No one could have seen it coming. In fact, if it's anyone's fault, it's *mine,* because I'm responsible for protecting you both. I wasn't even in the room.'

'But we told you to stay out of our way,' Margaret said. 'Too cramped in there with an extra body. If . . . if you hadn't been in the computer room, watching it on the monitor . . .'

'I can override any order you give me if I think your safety is at risk. I could have stayed in the autopsy room. If I had, Amos would still be alive.'

Margaret sat up and looked at him. 'Don't do that, Clarence. It's not your fault!'

'I know. And it's not *yours,* either.'

Another sob grabbed her body, grabbed it and shook it. Amos was *dead.* Who was going to look after his daughters? Had the FBI agents delivered the news yet? Would his family ever know the truth, or was Murray already dealing another cover story? Amos Braun deserved a posthumous Presidential Medal of Freedom – his family would get a lie about a lab accident and an insurance payout.

'We can look for blame all day,' Clarence said. 'That's not going to bring him back. All it's going to do is take our focus away from the job at hand. More people are going to die, Margo, you can bet on that. More good people like my boy Amos. It sucks to say, but we can grieve him all we want once we beat this fucking thing. You want to place blame? Place it where it belongs. Place it on this infection. That's what killed Amos, not me, and not you.'

Another set of sobs hit, but this time she finally forced them into submission. Clarence was right. This disease had taken Amos, taken all the others. If she could stop it, if she could *kill* it, that was the greatest tribute she could pay to her friend.

'You know what's funny?' Clarence said.

'What?'

'I finished up twenty bucks ahead. He'd be so pissed if he knew I won.'

Margaret couldn't believe Clarence could joke at a time

like this. Then she thought of Amos's face when he took the twenty from Otto, or the scowl when he had to hand it over. For some reason she pictured him looking down on both of them, pointing and laughing.

And despite the pain, she laughed a little herself.

MR. BURKLE THE POSTMAN

John Burkle was a bit behind. Neither rain, nor sleet, nor the gloom of night, but notice how no one ever listed *nor horribly rotted blackened corpses* as one of the things that could keep you from your appointed rounds.

John had called 9-1-1, then waited for the ambulance and cops to arrive. He couldn't say for sure if it had been Cheffie in that house. Cheffie was the only one who lived there, but that black . . . *thing* . . . could have been anyone. The paramedics had even given John some test for flesh-eating bacteria, which – thank God – turned out to be negative. He'd gone home after that, a bit shaken up by the whole ordeal, which meant that today he had a double load of mail to deliver.

He stuffed shopper coupons and magazines into the mailbox, shut it, drove back onto the road and checked his next batch.

The Jewells.

It was insane to think that flesh-eating bacteria had hit Gaylord of all places. Nothing happened in Gaylord, which was exactly why John Burkle loved it so much.

He pulled up to the Jewells' mailbox and put in two days' worth of mail. He started to drive away, then stopped when he saw Bobby Jewell walking down his long, tree-lined driveway. Bobby was carrying his little daughter, Chelsea, who was waving a letter. What a doll that one was. All those blonde curls. If she turned out to be half the looker her mother was, the girl was going to break some hearts when she got into high school.

'Hey there, Chelsea,' John called. 'Got some mail for me?'

'Yes sir, Mister Postman!'

About ten feet from the truck, Bobby set Chelsea down. She ran forward, holding the letter up as if it were an object of great importance. Little kids were such a hoot – something as mundane as mailing a letter could carry newness and excitement.

'Here you go, Mister Postman!'

John took the letter with affected importance. 'Well, thank you very much, young lady.'

Chelsea actually curtsied. John just wanted to eat her up.

'You're welcome, Mister Postman. My daddy wants to show you something.'

'Oh?' John looked up. Bobby had closed the distance and just stood there. John knew Bobby from summer softball league, but damn, the guy didn't look good at all. Sunken eyes, pale skin. Looked like he'd lost at least fifteen pounds.

'Hi, John,' Bobby said. 'I got to show you the damnedest thing.'

'What's that?'

Bobby unzipped his coat, reached in and pulled out a rusty red monkey wrench. 'This thing is stuck like you wouldn't believe.'

John looked at the wrench, then looked at Bobby. Why the hell would Bobby show him a stuck monkey wrench? John's internal alarm went off – what if Bobby looked like crap because he had that flesh-eating shit?

'Uh . . . Bobby, I don't have time right now.'

'Why's that, Mister Postman?' Chelsea said.

John automatically looked down at the girl. Even as he did, he knew that it was a mistake. By the time he looked up, the monkey wrench was a rusty red blur. He flinched just before the wrench smashed him on the left side of his jaw. He slid to the right, falling off his seat and into the van. He tried to get to his feet, but they were tangled in the gas and break pedals. Time became a dreamy, slow-moving sludge. He knew that the wrench was coming again, the moment before that metallic hit dragged on forever.

His Taser.

His hands searched for his bag, for the weapon that could save him, but it was too late.

The slow-motion sensation evaporated when he felt a blast on his left ear. His head exploded with concussive pain. The van seemed to spin around him. He tried to get up again, but his arms and legs felt so weak. Then he felt weight bearing down on him; he felt strong, callused hands on forehead and jaw, forcing his mouth open.

He felt a small, hot, wet tongue slide into his mouth.

And then he felt the burning . . .

APPLEBEE'S

Perry Dawsey had never thought normality could seem so surreal.

Or so goddamn *uncomfortable*.

He sat in an Applebee's in Gaylord, Michigan, waiting for his burger to arrive. Kitsch lined the walls. Some Top 40 shit played on the sound system. There were tables filled with fat men, fat women and fat kids. Dew sat to Perry's left. Perry sat across from Claude Baumgartner. Baum had lost the metal brace, but his nose was still a mess. Jens Milner, whose eye remained quite black, sat on Perry's right, across from Dew.

Add in Perry's nasty facial cuts and they looked like a foursome back from a fight club – a fight club that Dew had clearly won, since all he had was a little Band-Aid on his head.

Baum and Milner just sat there, staring at Perry, not saying a word.

This was another of Dew's brilliant ideas. Sure! Why the hell not? Let's sit down for lunch with a couple of guys I fucked up before I walked into a house and slaughtered a family. Why, a lunch like this is so damn normal it should be in a fucking Applebee's commercial.

'I don't get it,' Baum said. 'Why don't we just go to the Jewells' house?' Baum's right hand hovered near his left lapel, next to his tit. Sometimes it rested on the table, sometimes Baum pretended to scratch his chest, and sometimes the hand just hung there in midair. His hand seemed to orbit around the pistol in his shoulder holster. Perry didn't mind so much. He kept his own hand on the table's edge – if Baum made a move, he'd jam the table into the fucker's chest and drive him right to his back.

Baum kept staring at Perry, staring with that *attitude*. It was hard enough to keep things under control without some motherfucker calling you out with his eyes. Perry wanted to smash his face in, but Dew expected more of him. So Perry would hold it in. For now, anyway.

'We can't go near the house,' Dew said. 'Murray's orders.'

Milner huffed. 'That's to keep Mister Happy here from killing the family, and you know it. We've got the address. Baum and I can go.'

Like Baum, Milner just kept staring. Didn't anyone teach these CIA guys any manners?

'No way,' Dew said. 'We can't go near it until Ogden arrives and sends some boys with us. Believe me, Murray was *really* specific. Seems the new chief of staff has it in for him. If we show our faces at the Jewell house before Ogden arrives, Murray is screwed. And if Murray is screwed, he'll make sure everyone at this table is even *more* screwed. Trust me on that. So we might as well get some grub while we wait. And incidentally, Baum, if you don't get that hand away from your gun, I'm going to shove it up your ass.'

'The gun or the hand?' Baum asked without taking his eyes off Perry.

'Both,' Dew said. 'But I'll surprise you with the order of entry. And quit staring. Jesus. You'd think you two had never sat down to eat with a guy that kicked your ass before.'

'Sure,' Milner said. 'All the time. It's like a regular outing with my buddies back home.'

Perry smiled at him and held up one hand, waving his fingers toward his palm. *Come on,* the gesture said, *let's go.*

'Knock it off, Dawsey,' Dew said. 'All three of you, just can the shit. Perry is here because he wants to work with us, ain't that right?'

Perry nodded.

'As for you two' – Dew looked at Baum and Jens in turn – 'stop being pussies. This is too important for you guys to be all bitchy because he got the drop on you.'

Dew stared at Baum. 'Well?'

Baum kept looking at Perry for a few more seconds, then let out a sigh and shrugged his shoulders. 'Fuck it,' he said. 'He's not the first prick to break my nose.'

Dew slid his stare over to Milner. 'How about you?'

Milner finally tore his glare away from Perry to return Dew's stare. 'Your boy here is bad news, Dew,' he said quietly. 'You could track this guy just by following the trail of corpses. He *murders* people.'

'They're not people,' Perry said. Why couldn't anyone understand that?

'Save it,' Milner said. 'He's a fucking psycho, Dew, and I'm not eating with him.'

Jens stood up and dropped his napkin on his plate.

'Sit your ass down, Milner,' Dew said.

'You got a problem with it?' Milner said. 'Then fire me. Otherwise, I'll be in the car.'

He turned and walked out of Applebee's.

Perry looked down at his plate. Was Milner right? Was

he just a psycho? No. Those people were not *people* at all. They were *infected*. They had to die. *All* the infected had to die.

'Don't sweat it, Perry,' Dew said. 'He'll come around.'

Maybe he would, maybe he wouldn't. Perry didn't give a shit what two peons thought. But . . . maybe he should. Dew seemed to think their opinion was important.

If Dew thought it mattered, well then, it mattered.

OATMEAL

Chelsea squirted the lighter fluid all over the kitchen. Daddy was crumpling up newspapers into big balls. He crumpled, then Mommy squirted them with her can of lighter fluid and put them into the kitchen cupboards.

Family time was really fun.

'Daddy, are you *sure* there aren't any guns in Mister Burkle's truck?'

Daddy nodded. Chelsea wondered if Daddy knew what he was talking about. Mr. Burkle would be awake in a few hours, and then Chelsea could ask him personally.

'Daddy, why don't *we* have any guns?'

'Why do you want guns, honey?' Daddy said. 'Are . . . are you going to shoot me?'

Chelsea sighed. Now she understood why sometimes Mommy used the *you're so stupid* voice on Daddy. Of *course* she wasn't going to shoot him. Why would she shoot someone who had the dollies?

'Well, Daddy, Chauncey says we need guns. So go buy some.'

'We can't just go *buy* them, honey,' Mommy said. 'There's, like, a waiting period or something, right Bobby?'

Daddy nodded.

Chelsea frowned. 'Well, you two need to find guns. If you don't, you're going to have to punish each other.'

Daddy shook his head. 'Chelsea, baby . . . I don't want

to hit your mom with the spoon again. Don't make me do that.'

'Please,' Mommy said. 'No more. And we need to figure out where we're going to go. Chelsea honey, are you *sure* we have to set the house on fire?'

'*Mommy,*' Chelsea said. 'If you ask me that just one more time, you get the spanky-spoon for sure!'

'I'm sorry,' Mommy said in a fast whisper. 'I'm sorry, honey, I won't ask again.'

'Not another word!' Chelsea said.

Daddy crumpled the newspapers faster.

Chelsea squirted a bunch of the smelly fluid under the fridge. Would the fridge burn? She wished she could stay and watch, but Chauncey said they needed to leave.

Daddy snapped his fingers. 'Mark Jenkins! He's got guns. Pistols and hunting rifles – he's got everything.'

'So go get them,' Chelsea said.

'Honey,' Mommy said quietly, 'he's not going to just give them to us. We have to figure out how to take them.'

Chelsea thought on this for a minute. She sensed that Mommy didn't really need the spoon anymore. Mommy was *different* from Daddy. Mommy was a protector, like Chelsea. Which meant that Mommy could . . .

'Mommy, stick out your tongue.'

Mommy did. Chelsea looked close – Mommy had dozens of pretty little blue triangles on her tongue. Information flooded Cheslea's brain. Each of those triangles held thousands of little crawlers, ready to shoot out, shoot into someone else. That's how Chelsea had given God's love to Mommy – and now Mommy was ready to give it to other people.

'Mommy, can you give Mister Jenkins smoochies? Like I gave to you?'

Daddy smiled. 'That would work. He's got the hots for you, Candy.'

Mommy glared at Daddy. It was the *you're so stupid* glare that usually went with the *you're so stupid* voice.

'Well?' Chelsea said. 'Can you do it, Mommy?'

'I . . . I guess I could.' Mommy sounded sad and excited all at the same time. She had sad eyes when she looked at Daddy, but Chelsea could feel her excitement at the thought of spreading God's love.

Mommy cleared her throat. 'How long will it take after I give him smoochies?'

'He'll get sleepy pretty quick,' Chelsea said. 'You may have to be with him for an hour, but then Chauncey says he will feel sick and want to go to sleep, just like Mister Burkle the Postman. Can you do that, Mommy? Can you get Mister Jenkins to play for an hour after smoochies?'

'Yes honey,' Mommy said. 'I think I know a way to get Mister Jenkins to play for an hour, then go to sleep.'

'Well get going, slowpoke! I'll stay here and watch Daddy.'

Mommy looked at Daddy. 'I guess this is how it has to be.'

He nodded. Now *he* looked sad.

Mommy got her coat and left the house.

Things were changing for Chelsea, changing fast. She had no frame of reference to truly understand what was happening to her, what was happening around her. The Orbital knew this, and put it to use. Her simplicity and lack of experience made her a powerful tool. Chelsea was *moldable*.

The Orbital had to prepare her for the worst-case scenario: its own destruction. Every day the probability of an attack increased. Should something happen to the Orbital, it had to ensure that Chelsea could still complete the objective. The Orbital could change her brain, make the fibers reproduce, fill in spaces between brain cells and increase her computing power and intelligence. It could make her a focal point of communication. But all the processing power and communication ability wouldn't help if she couldn't think for herself.

The Orbital had to turn Chelsea Jewell into a *leader*.

Chelsea sat on her bed, thinking. The kitchen was too smelly. So was the living room. Daddy had used a whole can of gasoline in there, said it would burn real nice.

Chelsea, the bad guys may come for you soon.

'Oh,' Chelsea said. 'That's why we're burning the house, right? So they won't find us?'

Yes, but they will also come for the others.

'Others? What others, Chauncey?'

The others like you, like Daddy.

Chelsea hopped off her bed. She wanted to dance. There were other people like her? How exciting! She started to spin in circles.

'Where are they, Chauncey? How do I find them?'

You need to make them come to you. You have the power to find them with your mind.

'Can I talk to them like I talk to you?'

Not the same way, not yet, but you can send simple

**messages. We will start by
you talking to me with your
mind, not your mouth.**

Chelsea stopped spinning and closed her eyes. *Yes, Chauncey.*

**Good. Now reach out. Use
your thoughts, reach out
and find them.**

Chelsea *thought*. She reached out. What a funny feeling! She felt her consciousness expanding, spreading. She sensed Mommy first. Then Mr. Burkle the Postman, although it was harder to sense him. He wasn't as strong as Mommy. Chelsea sensed Daddy next – actually, she sensed the dollies inside Daddy. Oh, how fun! They were growing so *fast*!

**Keep trying. More, find
more. You must become
stronger.**

Chelsea took a deep breath and let it out slowly. She pushed. It felt . . . slippery. Her mind reached out, and made contact! *Several* contacts.

Ryan Roznowski. He had dollies, although he suspected that his wife was going to call the police soon. Chelsea couldn't let that happen.

Mr. Beckett had dollies, too. And Old Sam Collins. And a woman named Bernadette Smith.

And . . .

And . . .

Beck Beckett, Mr. Beckett's son. Beck felt *different*. Not like Daddy or Mr. Beckett. Chelsea knew Beck from school, even though he was a grade ahead. Thoughts of Beck made Chelsea angry, and she didn't know why.

I have found five, Chauncey. What do I do now?

T e l l   t h e m   t o   c o m e   t o
w h e r e   y o u   a r e .   T e l l   t h e m
t o   b r i n g   g u n s .

Chelsea nodded. She did what Chauncey asked. But why was Beck coming if he didn't have dollies? What good was he?

Chauncey? Beck Beckett isn't like Daddy. Touching him feels like touching Mommy, but I didn't give Beck smoochies.

T h a t   i s   b e c a u s e   h e
r e c e i v e d   G o d ' s   l o v e
d i r e c t l y   f r o m   m e ,   j u s t   l i k e
y o u   d i d .   T h e   d o l l i e s   a r e
v e r y ,   v e r y   i m p o r t a n t ,   b u t
p e o p l e   l i k e   y o u   a n d   B e c k
w i l l   p r o t e c t   t h e m .

Chelsea suddenly felt mad. Did Chauncey like Beck more than her? Would Beck be Chauncey's favorite?

Are you talking to him?

Y e s ,   b u t   i t   i s   t a k i n g   h i m
l o n g e r   t o   d e v e l o p .

Chauncey was *Chelsea's* special friend, *not* Beck Butthead Beckett's. Her anger grew.

What do we do now?

Y o u   h a v e   t o   s t a r t   l e a r n i n g
t o   t h i n k   f o r   y o u r s e l f ,
C h e l s e a .   L e t   m e   s h o w   y o u
a   n e w   p r e t t y   p i c t u r e .

Chelsea waited. Her mind still felt funny, like it was in many places at one time. Slippery? Was that the right word? No, more like . . . mushy. Like lumpy oatmeal. Ah, the lumps were the people she connected with.

An image exploded in Chelsea's thoughts. A *gorgeous* image. Unlike anything she'd ever known. Like four lit-up hula hoops buried halfway in the ground, a big one at the end, three smaller ones behind it. And pointing away from the smallest hula hoop, two big logs. The dollies would make this.

Oh, Chauncey. It's the prettiest thing I've ever seen. What is it?

When Mommy and Daddy take you to church, do they tell you about heaven?

Oh, yes! The preacher talks about God, and heaven and Jesus and how Jesus loves us no matter what.

This image you see, Chelsea, is a door to heaven.

She felt joy in her chest. *Really? This is really a door to heaven?*

You will protect the dollies so they can build it. When they open it, Chelsea, angels will come through.

Angels? Really? Will they have wings?

They are not nice angels, Chelsea. They are angels of vengeance.

What's ven-jance mean?

They are coming to punish people who have been bad. Do you like bad people, Chelsea?

She shook her head. She most certainly did *not* like bad people.

**C h e l s e a ,   I   w i l l   n o t   a l w a y s
b e   h e r e   t o   h e l p   y o u .**

Chauncey, you can't leave! You're my special friend!

**I ' m   n o t   l e a v i n g   y e t ,   b u t
m a y b e   s o o n .   S o   y o u   n e e d
t o   t h i n k   f o r   y o u r s e l f .   I f
y o u   m u s t   h e l p   t h e   d o l l i e s
b u i l d   t h i s   g a t e   t o   h e a v e n ,
h o w   c a n   y o u   m a k e   t h a t
h a p p e n   f a s t e r ?**

Chelsea thought. This was like school. She had to help the dollies build the gate to heaven. Only a special girl could do such a thing, but Jesus loved her, the Bible said so. She could do it. But how to make it build faster. Well, she needed . . .

We need more dollies! And more chosen people to protect them!

**T h a t ' s   r i g h t ,   C h e l s e a .   A n d
h o w   c o u l d   y o u   f i n d   m o r e
d o l l i e s ?**

The answer came quicker this time.

I need to search farther.

Chelsea pushed her thoughts. The oatmeal spread. She sensed dollies, out in many, *many* places. They were too far apart to come together, and she needed many to build the gate. She needed . . . she needed at least thirty-three dollies.

Chauncey hadn't told her that number, and yet she knew it. How? She searched her thoughts. The number seemed to come from the dollies. Was that what Chauncey meant by thinking for herself?

She could do this on her own. She could make Chauncey proud.

Chelsea pushed further. More hits, more dollies . . . and something else . . .

. . . something dark . . .

. . . something . . . *mean*.

Her breath came faster. She couldn't move. It was like a dream, one of the nightmares when the boogeyman came for her and she ran and then she fell and she couldn't get up and the boogeyman was coming and he had that sharp knife and he was going to stab it in her back but it couldn't be a dream she was awake this *thing* this *monster* this *giant monster* was going to *get* her.

'No!' She meant to scream the word, but it came out a hoarse whisper so quiet she could barely hear it herself. 'No no nonono!'

C h e l s e a ,   s t o p ,   d o   n o t   c o n n e c t   t o   h i m .

'The boogeyman,' she hissed. 'Chauncey, the boogeyman is *real*.'

C h e l s e a ,   s t o p !

The connection broke. Chelsea blinked, then sucked in a big breath. Her whole body shook. Her pants were hot and wet.

She'd peed herself.

D o   n o t   c o n n e c t   w i t h   t h a t   o n e .   H e   i s   t h e   d e s t r o y e r .   H e   w a n t s   t o   s t o p   u s ,   C h e l s e a .   H e   w a n t s   t o   h u r t   y o u .   Y o u   m u s t   r e m e m b e r   w h a t   t h a t   o n e   f e e l s   l i k e ,   r e c o g n i z e   i t ,   a n d   n e v e r   c o n n e c t   w i t h   h i m   a g a i n .

She nodded. She knew the destroyer was evil. She'd *felt* it.

Chelsea got off her bed and looked down. Her pants were soaked with pee-pee. She felt her face flush red. She'd *wet* herself. She was a big girl, and that wasn't supposed to happen anymore. She'd peed herself because of the boogeyman.

The fear hadn't left, but Chelsea Jewell started to feel the first embers of other emotions.

The embers of rage.

The embers of *hate*.

Perry sat very still. He waited for the feeling to return.

It did not.

A tear in the grayness, brief but painfully intense, like listening to quiet static on headphones only to be shocked by an unexpected blast of screeching feedback so loud it made your ears ring for days.

But it wasn't noise, and he hadn't heard with his ears. It was an emotion – fear. Pure terror, rich and undistilled by logic or rationality. He'd felt it in his soul. He still felt an echo of that fear. So *pure*. He hadn't experienced anything like that since . . . since he was a little boy.

A little boy so afraid of the shadows under the bed that he couldn't move, couldn't look, sure that whatever was under there would grab him and pull him down forever and ever.

But now he wasn't *afraid* of the thing under the bed.

He *was* the thing under the bed.

BY ANY MEANS NECESSARY

Corporal Cope drove Charlie Ogden's Humvee out the back of the C-17 Globemaster and into the winter night. It didn't have to go far. Just off the end of the runway, a black Lincoln waited. Four men stood outside it. Even from a distance, there was no mistaking the size of Perry Dawsey.

Ogden tapped Cope on the shoulder and pointed to the Lincoln. Seconds later, Ogden hopped out in front of Dew, Perry and two other men Ogden didn't know.

'Colonel,' Dew said, shaking hands. Dawsey didn't offer his hand, and if he had, Ogden probably wouldn't have shaken it. The other two men just stood there, respectfully silent.

'A damn shame about Amos,' Ogden said. 'Please convey my condolences to Margaret.'

'I will,' Dew said.

'Status report?'

'No problems so far,' Dew said. 'State troopers have shut down all off-ramps to Gaylord from highways I-75 and 32. They have a dozen troopers at each on-ramp administering the swab test. Traffic is backing up a bit, but it's not that bad.'

'Any positive tests?'

Dew shook his head. 'So far, so good. The cops have

people waiting to go over area maps with you, suggest the best places for roadblocks.'

'What about reports of violence?' Ogden asked. 'Any of these bastards fighting?'

Dew again shook his head. 'Nothing reported. Gaylord police can't believe how smoothly it's going, but I guess the small-town rumor mill has been spreading stories of the body the postman found. Tack on the news coverage talking about what necrotizing fasciitis can do and people are only too happy to cooperate, get the test and get the hell out of Dodge.'

Ogden nodded. He'd come to expect smooth sailing out of a Murray Longworth cover story. The slimy bastard knew his shit.

'I understand that you need men,' Ogden said. 'How many and for what?'

'Eight should cover it,' Dew said. 'Those bodies they found in Bay City? The guy's name was Donald Jewell. He was probably here visiting his brother, Bobby Jewell, age thirty-three. We have to go bring Bobby in.'

'Bobby have family in the house?'

'Wife Candice, also thirty-three, daughter Chelsea, seven. That's it.'

'Stay right here,' Ogden said. 'I'll send a full squad, nine men instead of eight. Acceptable?'

Dew nodded.

Ogden walked closer to Dew and talked quietly so that only Dew could hear.

'Murray said we need to watch out for Dawsey going apeshit,' Ogden said. 'My men have orders to stop him from doing anything stupid. I'll load them up with Tasers, but if push comes to shove they *will* take Dawsey down by any means possible.'

'You going to shoot him, Colonel?'

'If I have to,' Ogden said. 'So make sure it doesn't come to that.'

BECK BECKETT, THIRD-GRADER

Chelsea watched the last car drive down her long, winding dirt driveway. She watched that car very carefully, just as she had the last three. She pushed her thoughts out, wondering if this car might bring the boogeyman.

She could tell that the boogeyman was *very* close, maybe even in Gaylord. And he would kill her . . . unless she could kill him first.

Chelsea *hated* the boogeyman.

She let out a long, slow breath as she connected – he wasn't in that car. The car stopped behind the others. Two people got out, a man and a boy.

It was a good thing she'd called everyone here. Mr. Beckett had a blue triangle on his cheek. Another one peeked out from beneath his collar, just the point visible past the neckline of his sweater.

Beck Beckett looked fine.

He was a third-grader at South Maple Elementary, the same place where Chelsea was a second-grader. Beck was older. People might listen to him.

She couldn't have that.

Daddy went out and shook hands with Mr. Beckett, then led him into the house. Beck followed along. The front door led into the kitchen, where Daddy and the Becketts joined Old Sam Collins, Ryan Roznowski and Ryan's wife, Marie.

Marie was dead, but that was okay.

Mr. Beckett waved his hand in front of his face. 'Whoa,' he said. 'Someone leave the stove on?'

'Hello, Mister Beckett,' Chelsea said. 'Welcome.'

Mr. Beckett stopped waving his hand when he saw her. 'Hello, Chelsea. It's an honor.' The change in his voice was so funny. Grown-ups used to talk to her like a kid. Now they sounded like *they* were the kids, and *she* was the grown-up.

'Thank you, Mister Beckett. Sorry about the smell. We had to get some things ready for God.'

Why are you using your mouth?

She looked at Beck. He was smiling at her. It wasn't a nice smile, either.

You think you're so smart, Chelsea thought back. *You better realize God loves me the most.*

Beck nodded. *For now.*

'We have to get out of Gaylord,' Chelsea said. 'Daddy thinks they will come for us.'

'That's just stupid,' Beck said. 'How would they know to come to your house?'

The adults seemed to freeze in place, as if they were afraid to breathe. They all had wide eyes.

'Don't you call me stupid,' Chelsea said. 'You're in *my* house.'

'It's not your house,' Beck said. 'It's *God's* house. We should stay right here until the hatching.'

'We're leaving,' Chelsea said. 'You do what you're told.'

Beck Beckett was going to get *such* a spanking.

Mr. Beckett took a step forward. 'Maybe . . . maybe we should listen to Beck, Chelsea. He is older, after all.'

Mr. Beckett would have to be spanked, too. That was okay. She'd planned for that all along, but it made her feel better to know that Mr. Beckett *deserved* it.

'Mister Beckett is a *spy*,' Chelsea hissed. 'So is Beck.'

Mr. Beckett's face blanched. 'No! No, Chelsea, we're not spies.'

'Shut up, Dad,' Beck said.

Mr. Beckett looked at his son, then took a step back.

Beck smiled again. 'God doesn't want us to argue, little Chelsea,' he said. 'We're not spies, and we're going to stay here.'

Chelsea smiled her sweetest smile. 'You want to stay here? Okay, Beck. You can stay as long as you like.'

She took a quick, deep breath, then thought as hard as she could. *Get them!*

It was Beck's turn to widen his eyes. Chelsea knew why. She was much, *much* stronger than he was. He hadn't realized how much stronger, and now it was too late.

Daddy stepped up and kneed Mr. Beckett where it counts. Mr. Beckett let out a painful groaning noise and fell to the floor. Old Sam Collins ran up and kicked Mr. Beckett in the face over and over again as Daddy pulled a knife out of the knife drawer and fell on Mr. Beckett.

Kick, stab, kick, stab, kick, stab.

Mr. Beckett screamed, but that was okay.

Beck shook his head, as if he didn't want to believe what he was seeing. He turned to run, but Mr. Roznowski tackled him from behind.

Chelsea heard Beck's mental scream. *Stop it! God, save me!*

C h e l s e a , w h a t a r e y o u
d o i n g ?

Mr. Roznowski held Beck's head on the linoleum floor and started kneeing him in the face. It made a weird crunching sound.

He was dangerous, Chauncey.

We need him. Stop this right now.

'You're not the boss of me, Chauncey,' Chelsea said.

Beck still kicked a little after the third knee in his face. He twitched after the fourth. He stopped altogether after the fifth. Mr. Roznowski stood up. Beck's face looked very funny.

Then Daddy stood, covered in Mr. Beckett's blood. Old Sam Collins was limping. Looked like he'd hurt his foot kicking Mr. Beckett in the face.

Chelsea, I am God, you must obey me.

She shook her head. *I'm a big girl now, Chauncey. Beck was dangerous. It's for the best. Someday, you'll understand.*

That was a lie, of course. Beck wasn't dangerous, but Chauncey might have loved Beck more than her. Chauncey was *Chelsea's* special friend. With Beck gone it would stay that way forever and ever.

'Okay, everybody,' Chelsea said. 'Time to go play at Mister Jenkins's house. Someone make two trips so we can get rid of Mister Beckett's car. Mommy, you can take me in a snowmobile. Daddy, you clean up here and then come over on a snowmobile, too, okay?'

'Yes, Chelsea,' Daddy said.

Chelsea, Mr. Roznowski and Old Sam Collins got their coats and walked out the front door, while Daddy got the box of matches.

BETTY'S AUTOPSY

Betty Jewell's autopsy was a disaster.

Margaret could barely think after Amos's horrifying death, let alone focus on the job. By the time she'd dragged herself into the biohazard suit and started working on Betty, the girl's body had mostly dissolved.

Margaret approached the trolley, Clarence beside her in his suit. Gitsh, Marcus and Dr. Dan stood next to Betty's blackened corpse. It made for tight quarters, but Clarence refused to leave her side. Gitsh and Marcus had done an amazing job cleaning up. The autopsy room looked spotless. The trolley carried a steady, slow, thick stream of black goo down the runners and into the white sink.

Margaret wanted a look at those crawling things. They were the key to everything now, but she'd waited too long. Any crawlers in Betty's body had already dissolved. Even the samples that Amos had taken were now nothing but chunky black liquid.

She'd let her grief get in the way of her work.

Margaret felt weak. She put a hand on the autopsy trolley to steady herself – when she looked at the table, her mind's eye saw Betty Jewell's skinless hands stabbing the scalpel at Amos. When Margaret looked down, she saw Amos clawing at the throat of his biohazard suit, unable to get his hands at the cut, unable to stop the blood from sheeting the inside of his visor. When she saw the drainage sink, she saw Betty's brains splattering against the white epoxy and dripping toward the drain.

Clarence's hand on her shoulder. 'Margo, you okay?'

She nodded. 'Yeah, I'm fine.'

A lie anyone could see through.

'Dan,' Margaret said, 'have you watched the video from my helmet? The video of the autopsy?'

'Yes ma'am,' Dr. Dan said. 'Several times.'

'And what did you see?'

'Something crawling in her face. Doctor Braun thought it was crawling along the V3 nerve toward the brain.'

'Do you agree?'

'It certainly looked that way,' Dan said.

Too bad they didn't have a brain to look at. No chance of that, thanks to Clarence's bullet and rapid decomposition. When that crawler reached the brain, then what?

Then it would come apart.

It would split up into those muscle fibers Amos saw, split apart . . . reorganize . . . come together again.

In a mesh. Just like in Perry Dawsey's brain.

'The crawlers,' Margaret said. 'They want to replicate what we've seen in Dawsey's CAT scans.'

Dr. Dan stared at her. 'That's a pretty big leap. We haven't seen anything like these crawlers before. I read your reports on the hosts found in Glidden; the father, mother and little boy. You had fresh bodies, yet they didn't have these crawling things.'

'It's something new, obviously,' Margaret said. 'I don't care if its a leap. It's *right*. These things infect a human body, maybe replicate somehow, then crawl toward the brain. If we can stop them from crawling, we just plain stop them.'

'It's got a structure,' Dan said. 'A shape. It can move. For that it needs a cytoskeleton.'

'The little things have skeletons?' Clarence asked.

'Cytoskeleton,' Dan said. 'It's like microscopic scaffolding that lets a cell hold a shape.'

'Without it, a cell would just be a membrane holding fluid,' Margaret said. 'Without a cytoskeleton to hold structure, it would be like a water balloon. Amos thought the crawlers looked like human muscle fibers. If these things are some kind of modified muscle cell, and we disrupted their cell structure, then the cells couldn't contract. They couldn't move. They couldn't *crawl.*'

'So you dissolve this cytoskeleton,' Clarence said, 'and that stops it? That's it?'

'It's not that easy,' Dan said. 'Our normal cells also have cytoskeletons. Anything that would kill the crawlers would also kill our cells.'

'But it's something,' Margaret said. 'A human body can regrow lost cells, eventually repair damage, but these crawlers are so small, just a few cells. If we disrupt their cytoskeleton, they might just die. At any rate, we can stop them before they reach the brain.'

'I can order a screen,' Dan said. 'We can get all the drugs that might work and have them ready when we get another host.'

'*If* we get another host,' Clarence said. 'Let's hope there aren't any more.'

'Oh grow up, Clarence,' Margaret said. 'You know goddamn well there will be more. There's *always* more.'

Silence filled the trailer. Margaret rewound the moment in her head, realized how nasty she had just sounded.

'Sorry,' she said.

Clarence shrugged. 'Don't sweat it, Doc. Can we test these cytoskeleton wreckers on Betty's remains?'

'There's nothing left,' Margaret said. 'We're too late for that. I'll tell you what we're going to do with this body. We're going to burn it.'

She stared at Betty's remains, the blackened, rotting, murderous remains.

'Uh, Margo,' Clarence said. 'Don't we want to . . . I don't know . . . study it?'

She turned on him. 'What, exactly, are we going to find? Huh? It's another blackened corpse, Clarence. Apoptosis chain reaction. Boom, dead, done. That's it. She has whatever the father had, so we'll run chemical analysis on *his* remains. We don't need this . . . this *thing*.'

She turned back to Gitsh and Marcus. They looked at her with pity in their eyes. They were saddened by Amos's death, she knew that, but they just didn't understand.

'Incinerate this bitch,' Margaret said. 'I don't want a single ounce of her left, you understand me?'

Gitsh and Marcus both nodded slowly.

She turned and walked out of the autopsy room.

BURN, BURN,
YES YA GONNA BURN (REDUX)

Even though most of the Jewell house was already gone, flames still shot into the dark sky. Flashing fire-truck lights added to the visuals, the mixed illumination coloring snowflakes that dropped straight down like slow-motion rain. In the dark isolation of the Jewell property, the place felt like an island of light surrounded by an infinite black ocean.

Hoses from the trucks poured water onto the burning house, turning the yard into a slushy mess filled with cinders and mud. A lead on a triangle case taking him to a house on fire? *Gosh*, Dew thought, *what a surprise*. If he'd come as soon as they reached Gaylord, he'd probably have the Jewells in custody right now. Instead, Dew had a feeling all he'd get would be more corpses for Margaret's collection.

Margaret. She was a mess. Amos had gone out hard. The longer she stayed in this business, in the secret land of the Murray Longworths and the Dew Phillipses, the more she'd understand shit like that was inevitable. He wondered if she'd block it out, or if someday in the future she'd be telling her own war stories.

Dew looked at Perry, who stood expressionless, watching the fire. What was going on in that big melon of his? Three days since they'd tussled, and Perry really seemed to have come around. Looked like Margaret was right again. Dew hoped it was a genuine change. As fucked up as it sounded, and it sounded damn fucked up, he was starting to like the kid.

Dew nudged Perry. 'You feel anything?'

Perry shook his head. 'Just that gray feeling. Something else is there, but I can't lock onto it.'

'How about that other feeling?' Dew asked. 'The one where they're mounting the fourth-quarter comeback?'

'Yeah,' Perry said. 'I still feel that. Only now it's stronger.'

A man wearing fireman's gear stomped through the slush toward them. 'You Dew Phillips?'

Dew nodded and offered his hand.

'Brandon Jastrowski. The police chief said I need to help you guys in any way.' Brandon looked at Perry, then offered his hand. 'And you are?'

Perry looked at Dew. Dew nodded.

'Perry Dawsey,' Perry said, shaking the offered hand.

'Dawsey? *Scary* Perry Dawsey?'

Perry nodded.

'Holy shit,' Brandon said. 'A real pleasure to meet you. Used to love watching you play. Oh how I hate Ohio State, am I right?'

Perry nodded again.

'And what was up with all that murder stuff in the news a few months back?'

'Mistaken identity,' Dew said. 'Perry's working for the government now. What's the deal with the house? Any bodies?'

'Unfortunately, there are,' Brandon said. 'Adult male, adult female and a child, maybe seven to ten years old. Probably Bobby and Candy Jewell – they owned the place – and their daughter, Chelsea.'

'Probably?'

'Bodies are in bad shape,' Brandon said. 'All three were in the kitchen, where the fire started. Definitely arson, no question. And some major foul play. The woman has a hole in her skull, likely a gunshot to the back of the head.'

'We need the bodies,' Dew said.

'Excuse me?'

'The bodies, we need them. Have your men get them out, put them in body bags, then leave them over there, under that little swing.' Dew pointed to a tree in the front yard. Two ropes hung down from a bare, snow-covered branch and ended in a little plank of snow-covered wood.

Brandon looked at the swing, then looked back at Dew. 'But . . . ah . . . we need to take bodies to the county morgue.'

'Not today,' Dew said. 'The morgue is coming to us, so to speak. Put the bodies in the bags, put the bags over there, do it as fast as you can. Understood?'

Brandon stared for a second, then nodded. He went back to the fire.

Dew pulled out his cell phone and dialed. Otto answered immediately.

'Otto, it's Dew. We're at the Jewell place. Whole family is dead, house fire, maybe some gunplay.'

'Perry go off again?'

'No, he had nothing to do with it.'

'Seriously?'

'Shut your pie-hole,' Dew said. 'Get your team moving, I want the MargoMobile here ASAP. It's time for Margaret to sack up and get back to work.'

THE MAP

Chelsea sat behind a glass door looking out over Mr. Jenkins's backyard. She'd pulled the curtain almost closed, leaving only a one-inch space to look through the glass. That was enough to see up the hill and watch the flames lick up from her house. It looked so small from this far away. She couldn't really make out individual people, but she knew they were there.

One person in particular.

The boogeyman.

Chelsea was very careful not to reach to him, not to connect. If he sensed her now, when he was this close . . .

'Chelsea,' Daddy called from Mr. Jenkins's living room, 'I think you need to see this.'

Chelsea carried her bowl of ice cream into the room and sat down next to Daddy. Mr. Jenkins didn't have ice cream bars, but double chocolate almond wasn't bad, either.

The TV was showing a commercial. Five people were in the living room: Ryan Roznowski, Daddy, Old Sam Collins, Mommy, Mr. Burkle the Postman and Mr. Jenkins.

Mr. Jenkins sat in a La-Z-Boy. He didn't look well, all sweaty and pale under his big red beard, but he was getting better fast. Chelsea could already sense his mind. Mommy's smoochies had worked. Chelsea knew that was very important – the ones Chelsea kissed could kiss others.

God's love could spread from person to person to person, until everyone in the world knew the joy.

Mommy was sitting on Mr. Jenkins's lap, petting his head with a wet washcloth.

It will be okay, Mr. Jenkins. You'll feel better very soon.

The man looked at her with sunken eyes. He smiled. 'Thank you. Thank you for the gift of God's love.'

'It's coming back on,' Daddy said. He pointed the remote at the TV and turned up the volume. The picture showed a pretty lady sitting behind a desk.

'Once again, the breaking news tonight is a transport plane that went off the radar somewhere in Otsego County,' the lady said. 'The plane was carrying samples of necrotizing fasciitis bacteria, the bacterium that causes flesh-eating disease, which may have been released in the crash and has already been potentially linked to one death. The National Guard has been called in, and state officials have ordered a temporary evacuation of Gaylord.'

The picture changed to show a big man in an immaculate blue uniform. Everyone in the living room stirred uncomfortably at the sight. Chelsea felt a similar reaction, her body recoiling from the uniform, from the gun on the man's hip. This was an enemy of God . . . this was another one of the devils.

Below the man were the words TROOPER MICHAEL ADAMS, MICHIGAN STATE POLICE SPOKESMAN. Below that was a phone number that started with 800.

'It's only a temporary evacuation,' said the tool of the devil. 'It's important we test everyone for exposure and do a sweep of the town. Then everyone can return. For those without transportation, or for those who can't travel on their own, we're providing a toll-free number for people to call. Very soon we'll be doing door-to-door checks, just to make sure we haven't missed anyone. The National Guard will be assisting with this.'

'Turn it off,' Chelsea said. Daddy fumbled with the remote, then turned off the TV. All eyes turned to Chelsea.

'They are coming for us,' she said. 'That's what they mean by "door-to-door." They want to find us and kill us. The National Guard, that means *soldiers*. They want to stop the gates of heaven.'

'I knew they were out to get us,' Daddy said. He was shaking with anger and excitement. 'Chelsea . . . *soldiers* . . . what are we going to *do*?'

Everyone in the living room nodded. Chelsea heard them all mumbling that terrifying word: *soldiers*.

'God sent the soldiers to us,' Chelsea said. 'You must trust in Him, it's all part of His plan. He sent us soldiers with lots of *guns*. Do you see? We need to show the soldiers how much God loves them.'

She pushed out images of men with guns standing around a gate. She felt the images flash in the minds of the others, and then something strange happened – for just a moment, their thoughts melded as one and the image took on startling clarity. Like it was *real*. As soon as it started, the moment was gone.

'What was that?' Mr. Burkle said. 'What the fuck just happened?'

'Bad word, Mister Burkle,' Chelsea said.

Mr. Burkle hung his head. 'I'm sorry, Chelsea.'

She didn't know what had just happened. She knew that she was the cause of it, though. Everyone thinking together, thinking the same thoughts, they had felt so . . . so . . . *smart*.

They all ate their ice cream and stared at Chelsea. They wanted to know what to do next. Chelsea closed her eyes and thought *hard*.

Chauncey, where do we build the gate?
You have to find a place.
Should we go into the woods?
**No, not this time. The
devil will use bombs on
you there. If you go to a
place with many people,
the devil will hesitate to
use bombs, and that could
get you a little more
time.**

Somewhere with lots of people. The dollies would probably like that a lot. Lots of people to play with when they got there. But Chelsea still had to hide everyone, or the devil would find them.

'Mister Jenkins, do you have a map?'

'Of course, honey,' he said. Mommy helped him out of the chair. He waddled to the kitchen.

Chelsea had to get everyone out of there. She was running away, not just from the devils but from the *boogeyman*. Running away wasn't as bad as peeing her pants, but it wasn't good, either. She was growing stronger, she knew that. Maybe someday soon she could face the boogeyman.

Face him, and *kill* him.

Mr. Jenkins came back with a folded paper map and walked to the dining-room table.

It was covered in guns – four hunting rifles with those big scope things, two shotguns and one pistol. Boxes of ammo filled in the spaces between the guns.

'Can you guys clear this off?' Mr. Jenkins said. 'Chelsea wants to see a map.'

Hands shot in to remove the guns and ammunition. Chelsea liked how fast everyone moved.

Mr. Jenkins spread the map out on the newly cleared table. Chelsea, Mr. Burkle, Mommy and Mr. Jenkins gathered around it.

Chelsea stared at it, but she didn't really know how to read a map.

Mommy stroked her hair. 'Do you know what you're looking for, honey?'

Chelsea nodded, then shook her head. 'How can you tell where there are lots of people?'

Mr. Burkle pointed to a yellow spot on the map. Chelsea saw the word FLINT in big black letters on top of the yellow.

'See the yellow?' Mr. Burkle said. 'The more yellow, the more people there are.'

Chelsea bent her head and stared at the map. Her blonde hair hung down and touched the paper. She put her finger on the map and raised her head, her face all smiles.

'This place has the most yellow! So that means it has the most people, right?'

Mr. Burkle looked, then nodded. 'Yes. There would be a lot of people there, all right.'

'This is where we're going.'

'So what now?' Mommy asked.

'Well,' Mr. Burkle said, 'we have to figure out how to show a soldier God's love, make sure no one finds out, *and* get out of town without getting killed.'

'And pick up more dolly daddies on the way,' Chelsea said. 'We need enough dollies to make the gate. Mister Jenkins, how many people will your big car hold?'

'The Winnebago?' Jenkins said. 'Hmm, probably ten more people, no problem. Will that be enough?'

Chelsea shrugged. It was getting easier to reach out, to find the others. She was in contact with three more dolly daddies. So many things to do – give a soldier smoochies, get past the other soldiers and get to the place with lots of people. How could they do it all?

She had an idea, an idea that Chauncey wouldn't like. Maybe she just wouldn't tell Chauncey. She wasn't sure if the idea would work, though – she needed some help to figure it out.

What she needed was more brain power.

Like a few minutes ago, when they all had that feeling . . .

'Everyone, think with me,' Chelsea said. She closed her eyes. Even though she couldn't see, she felt the others close their eyes, one by one. Their thoughts melded together, and they started to plan.

DAY SIX

INBRED TRAILER-TRASH HICKS WATCHING SPRINGER

Three more cars to go. She could fool them. She *had* to fool them. They wanted to kill her whole family but Bernadette wouldn't let that happen.

She had to stay calm, keep the kids calm. William was in the passenger seat, all buckled in. He was scared, she knew, but he was being quiet. Sally and Christine were in the backseat. They were being so good, just perfect little angels. She'd tucked a blanket around them so they wouldn't get cold.

Two more cars to go. She pulled her Saab up one car length.

Shawn was still back home. The cheating bastard. Let him stay there, let him have the whole house to himself. He'd fucked around on her, she just *knew* it. Maybe with that little whore secretary at his construction office. He hired a girl who dyed her hair jet-black and wore all that eye makeup to be a *secretary*? Bernadette didn't know what a *goth* was and didn't want to know. Probably just another term for *slut*, which is what the little whore most likely was.

She *knew* he'd cheated, because the voices told her so.

One more car to go. She pulled up again. She rolled down her window. Cold winter air poured in.

The soldiers were everywhere. Soldiers and cops. They

wanted to *kill* her, she just knew it. She didn't want to go near them, but the voices had told her to go this way, told her she could get past the checkpoint, onto the highway and away from Gaylord.

The soldiers had some kind of test. Maybe it was like a Breathalyzer. She'd passed those before. The voices told her she could pass it, and she believed them.

After all, if you can't believe the voices in your own head, who *can* you believe?

'Mom, where are we going?'

'We're leaving, William,' she said. 'Now, I told you to be quiet. Are you going to talk again?'

William's eyes grew wide and he shook his head violently. No, he wasn't going to talk again. If he did, she'd just have to deal with him.

The pickup truck ahead of her pulled forward. A state trooper stood in front of her car. He waved her closer. She inched up slowly until he snapped his palm out, signaling her to stop.

She stopped.

Another state trooper leaned down and looked in her open window. He had one hand on her door, the other hand on his gun. Peeking out under that ridiculous cop hat – where did they get these meatheads, anyway?

'Good afternoon, ma'am,' he said. 'We've set up this roadblock to do a quick test for a bacteria that may be in the area. Are you familiar with the situation?'

'Of course I'm familiar with the *situation*. You think I don't watch the news? You think I'm some inbred trailer-trash hick that watches the Springer show? I know all about the *situation*, and we're fine, we don't have the bacteria. We'll just drive through, then you can get on with it.'

The trooper looked less than pleased that Bernadette would not be taking the stupid test, but those were the breaks. Fuck him.

'I'm afraid we do need to test you, ma'am,' the trooper said. 'It will only take a second. We also need to test your children, but let's get you first.' He held up a narrow foil envelope. He was wearing surgical gloves. 'Please open this packet, ma'am, then pull out the swab inside, run it inside your cheek and along your gum line, then hand it back to me stick-first.'

'I'm sorry, Officer, but are you *deaf*? I just told you we don't need to be tested. Let's remember that *my* taxes pay *your* salary. Now, unless you want me to take your badge number and make your life a living hell, get your partner out of the way. We're in a *hurry*.'

The trooper stared at her for a second. Then he looked at William. Then he looked into the backseat. His brow furrowed beneath the brim of his hat. His eyes widened. He suddenly stood up and took a step back.

His hand stayed on the grip of his gun. 'Ma'am, step out of the car, right now.'

He knew. That fucking cop *knew*.

Bernadette pushed the gas pedal to the floor. Her Saab shot forward. The state trooper in front of her car dove out of the way. The on-ramp to I-75 was only a few hundred feet from here – she could make it. There was a state police car parked across the on-ramp. Maybe there was enough room on the shoulder to get around it.

She heard a popping sound, like cap guns.

Her car lurched to the left. Bernadette turned the steering wheel hard to the right, trying to recover. More popping sounds. The car pulled violently to the right and skidded. It hit the snowbank and stopped suddenly, throwing her forward.

The tires. They'd shot out the tires, like this was a fucking TV show like *Frankie Anvil* or something. Did they not understand that the voice *told her* she could go past?

Bernadette opened the door, grabbed her purse and got out of the Saab.

'Down on the ground!' a trooper shouted. More shouts, all of them saying the same thing. 'Down on the ground, now!'

They had guns pointed at her. Blue jackets and round hats everywhere, in all directions. They were going to *kill* her.

Bernadette reached into her purse and pulled out the butcher knife. That would show them. It had worked on her daughters, made them shut up, and it had sure as hell taught Shawn an important lesson about not fucking around on his wife. It worked on them, it would work on the troopers.

She rushed at the trooper who had been leaning into her car.

Everything blurred, her body twitched and trembled, she dropped the knife and fell to the cold, slushy pavement. Such *agony*. The pain stopped as suddenly as it started, leaving an echo effect rolling through her body. She shook her head and tried to stand, but suddenly there were hands all over her. She felt her face pushed into the wet pavement, something heavy on her spine. Her hands were pulled behind her back, and she felt handcuffs snap into place.

ROADBLOCK

About six miles east of the I-75 on-ramp, Private First Class Dustin Climer looked to the sky and watched a Black Hawk helicopter head west. For the past thirty minutes, the helicopter had been cruising around slowly, watching the roads below. Something was up. Dustin wondered if they'd got one.

'Dustin?' Neil Illing called out. 'The swab?'

'Sorry,' Dustin said, then slid the swab into the white detector. He'd been holding both, swab and detector, but the helicopter's sudden movement had distracted him. After just a couple of seconds, the detector let out two short beeps and the green square lit up, indicating a negative result.

'She's fine,' he said to Neil.

Neil bent down just a bit to look in the car window.

'You're all set, ma'am,' Neil said.

The woman let out a huge sigh of relief. Dustin wasn't sure if her relief came from a negative result on the flesh-eating-bacteria test, or because the four heavily armed men surrounding her car finally seemed to relax.

'When can I come back home?' the woman asked. 'This is just so crazy.'

Neil nodded. 'Yes ma'am. You should be able to come back tomorrow, or the next day at the latest. Just watch the news.'

'Thank you, Officer.'

Neil laughed. 'I'm a soldier, not a cop, ma'am.'

The woman gave an exaggerated nod, as if to say, *Yes, of course*. Neil smiled again and stood back from the car. The woman put it in gear and drove past the checkpoint, continuing down the snow-covered dirt road.

Dustin and Neil stood there in the early-morning cold, waiting for the next car. Joel Brauer was at the side of the road, manning the M249 machine gun, so he had to endure the cold as well. James Eager, the fourth member of their team, slid back into their Hummer's heated interior. He only had to come out when a car drove up, which meant Dustin was damn jealous of him at that moment. Fifteen more minutes, and then he and Neil would switch positions with James and Joel.

With the helicopter gone, they could hear the faint sound of snowmobiles again. Local boys whipping through the woods, probably.

James opened the door and leaned out. 'They got one,' he called. 'Triangle host trying to get on the I-75 on-ramp. Cope said to stay sharp. They're sending the backup units to reinforce the on-ramp in case there's more, so we're on our own for a bit.'

'Got it,' Dustin said.

James slid back inside the heated Hummer, and Dustin hated him a little more.

'This is kind of trippy,' Neil said.

'What is?' Dustin said. 'Fighting little monsters and shit?'

'Well, sure, but what I mean is, even though we're fighting little monsters and shit, we're still pulling checkpoint duty. I mean, I'm staying sharp and all, but this is boring, you know? We've seen three cars in the past two hours.'

Dustin shrugged. 'What are you gonna do? We have to check everyone. They just got one, didn't you hear James?'

'Yeah, yeah, I heard,' Neil said. 'It's just . . . I mean, five days ago we shot the bejesus out of that construct thing, and now here we are checking IDs and swabbing civvies. Five days ago we're shooting friggin' electric bullets at monsters, and today our primary weapons are *these.*'

Neil pulled a zip-tie out of his pocket and waved the long, thin piece of plastic. The plastic restraints let them detain large numbers of people, if necessary, and were much lighter than handcuffs.

'I might beat a hatchling to death with this,' Neil said, whipping the zip-tie like a flacid sword.

'Oh relax,' Dustin said. 'Colonel Ogden isn't telling you not to defend yourself. If we're in danger, we shoot.'

Neil spun 180 degrees and landed in an overly dramatic, wide-legged stance. He pulled out another zip-tie and waved one in each hand like nunchucks.

'I don't know,' he said. 'I bet I can stop *bullets* with these bitches.'

Joel was cracking up. The laughter made Neil ham it up some more.

Dustin shook his head. Fucking idiots. These were the morons he got to work with?

The sound of the snowmobiles seemed to draw closer for a bit, then stopped. Climer and Neil looked to the trees but couldn't spot the sleds.

'Joyride?' Neil asked.

'Maybe,' Dustin said. 'Doesn't sound like they're trying to slip past the roadblocks. If they were, we wouldn't have heard them all morning. They would have just gone through in the woods.'

'How the fuck can people be joyriding at a time like this?'

Dustin shrugged. 'You can't reach everyone, I guess. Although that one dude turning all black and shit, that has people falling all over themselves to get this test. Fuck, man, I should charge five bucks a head.'

The sound of another vehicle drew Dustin's attention. A U.S. Postal Service van drove toward the checkpoint, pristine white near the top, spackled with thick arcs of frozen brown slush down on the bottom, particularly behind the tires.

'Mail must go through,' Dustin said. 'You want to run the detector this time?'

'Sure,' Neil said. 'Something different. Gimme.'

Dustin handed over the plastic detector.

James Eager got out of the Hummer and moved to the other side of the road, giving him and Joel converging fields of fire toward the front of the postal van.

Dustin stepped into the middle of the road. He held up his left hand in a *stop* gesture. His right hand rested on the grip of his sidearm. The van gently slowed and stopped.

He walked around the driver's side. The driver opened the sliding door.

'Good afternoon, sir,' Dustin said. 'May I have your name and identification, please?'

'John Burkle,' the man said. He handed over his driver's license. Dustin took it, moved one step back and examined it, then looked up again. The picture definitely matched the man, but John Burkle had a big bruise on the left side of his jaw, and under his hat some gauze was wrapped around his head, holding a big, puffy bandage on his left ear.

'You look like you've had a rough time, sir.'

'Dogs,' Burkle said. 'One chased me yesterday; I slipped on some ice and hit a tree. Pathetic, right?'

'That's unfortunate, sir.'

'Well anyway, I already got swabbed,' Burkle said. 'I was the guy that found that body.'

Dustin nodded. 'Who swabbed you?'

'The paramedics did. I was so freaked out I went to the hospital and insisted they do it again. I tell you what, you couldn't pay me enough to do your job.'

'I appreciate that, sir,' Dustin said. 'However, if you don't mind, I have to swab everyone who goes through this checkpoint.'

The postman shrugged. 'No problem, it's painless. You need me to get out?'

'That's okay, sir, please stay where you are.' He handed John back his license, which the man took. Dustin then offered the foil packet with his left hand. 'Please open this, pull out the swab inside, run it inside your cheek and along your gum line, then hand it back to me stick-first.'

John reached for the foil packet. Just as he was about to grab it, his hand shot forward and gripped Dustin's left wrist. Dustin yanked back reflexively, causing John to stumble out of the van. Dustin reached over with his right hand and grabbed John's wrist. He was about to wrench it free and twist the arm down to put John on his face when he saw something in the postman's other hand.

It took only a fraction of a second to realize it was a Taser, another fraction to feel fifty thousand volts hit his left hand and course through his body. He jerked convulsively, brain on hold, body doing its own thing. From the far side of the road, past the van, Dustin heard gunshots, the long reports of a hunting rifle echoing through the woods.

Dustin Climer found himself on the ground. He heard automatic weapons firing, the sharp cracks of an M4, the stuttering bark of the M249. Then the echo of more hunting rifles, this time from behind him, on the other side of the road.

The M249 stopped.

He tried to move, but could not. 'We're under fire, we're under fire!' He heard Neil scream, then two more rifle shots.

The M4 fire stopped.

'Climer . . .' Neil's voice. 'Oh fuck, man, help me . . .'

Dustin shook his head, tried to get to his knees. He heard movement in the van, then feet hitting the road.

A gunshot – no echo this time, it was so close. Something hit the back of his left shoulder. His left arm gave out. He found himself facedown again.

He'd been shot. Holy shit, he'd been *shot*.

'No!' Neil said. 'No, please!'

Another rifle shot. This one only ten feet away.

Neil said no more.

Snowmobile engines, getting closer. Another sound, a vehicle approaching, larger than a car or the mail truck.

Noise, pain, movement – it all overwhelmed his senses.

Dustin was flipped onto his back. Hands covered his eyes, hands held his arms, a whirlwind of confusion and pain. He started to kick, but a fist in his stomach ended the struggle, curling him up into a fetal position. Hands on his face, holding his jaw open, something wet in his mouth, *burning* in his mouth.

Hands pushing him away.

The bigger vehicle's noise fading.

His body screaming for air, his shoulder just plain *screaming*.

A crackling sound, a whooshing sound.

Heat. *Real* heat, nearly scorching the side of his face.

A mini-eternity without oxygen, then a half-gasp that let in just a little, and finally a deep, ragged breath.

'I'm gonna kill you, soldier boy.'

Dustin sucked in air. He rolled to his hands and knees, then pulled his sidearm. His right hand filled with the knurled handle, the cold feeling of power, of protection.

'You better pull that trigger, soldier, or I'm gonna shoot ya like I shot your friends.'

Dustin pushed himself to one knee, right hand holding the pistol, left hand dangling uselessly, dripping blood onto the frozen dirt road.

To his right, flames billowed out of the postal van, fat orange tongues licking the air and spewing forth roiling black smoke.

In front of him, a man standing, holding a hunting rifle. It wasn't the man who had been driving the van. He pointed the rifle at Dustin.

'Gonna *kill you,* soldier bo—'

Dustin's first shot hit the man dead center in the chest. Two small feathers drifted away from his down coat. The man took one step back, then looked at his chest.

Past the man, far past, Dustin could see the rear end of a white and brown RV driving along the road.

The man looked up. He smiled and started to say something right before two more shots hit him in the chest. Still holding the hunting rifle in both hands, the man sagged and fell to his back.

Dustin struggled to stand. He felt weak, cold, but turned and looked for Neil. Neil lay on his back in a puddle of dark red. Someone had shot him in the face, blowing his brains all over the road. Looked like he'd also been hit in the leg, a fist-size blood spot above his right knee.

Dustin turned. He had to check on the others. He stepped forward, his right hand keeping the shaking gun pointed at the fallen man. The man's eyes were wide open, a snarl locked on his face. Dead as fuck. Just like Neil. Tit for tat, you infected motherfucker.

Dustin stumbled again, barely catching himself as his foot slid on the snowy road. Oh man, getting shot fucking *hurt*.

He kept moving, checking his squadmates. Joel was slumped facedown over the M249. Not moving. The man with the hunting rifle probably took him out first. On the other side of the road, James was also down, helmet sitting upside down about three feet away from him.

The ground came up and smacked Dustin Climer right in the face. Oh man, oh *man* . . . he'd fallen. He forced his eyes open. So fucking *cold*. No sound but the wind. Then a soft humming, growing louder, growing closer. He knew that sound. A V-22. No, a couple of 'em. Climer put his gun hand on the ground and tried to push up, but his palm weakly slid across the snow-covered dirt road.

Finally he passed out.

IMPROPER EQUIPMENT

If this kept up, they'd need another MargoMobile just to store the bodies.

The live triangle host was on the way. Dew and Ogden had decided to leave the MargoMobile at the Jewell house and transport the host instead of parking the trailers next to a highway on-ramp and off-ramp. Made sense, as the Jewell house was far more rural and somewhat isolated.

The host would go into the containment cell in Trailer B.

The cadaver cabinet was filling up as well. In there they already had the liquefied remains of Donald Jewell, the pitted black skeleton of Cheffie Jones, the burned corpse of Bobby Jewell and the corpse of his wife, Candice. Their daughter would join them as soon as Margaret finished the last of the preliminary autopsies.

Once again a biohazard-suited Margaret stood in Trailer A's autopsy room, looking at a big body bag filled with a small body. Gitsh was with her. Clarence had suited up and checked each body for himself, making *damn sure* they were all dead before taking up his usual position in the computer room.

She needed to make this fast. Bernadette Smith would be here soon, and that would require all of Margaret's attention. Also on the way was the body of Ryan Roznowski, the triangle host who had killed those soldiers at the roadblock. He was a low priority – she needed to clear her schedule for Bernadette.

'Gitsh, get Chelsea out of the bags and let's get cracking. We need to do this fast. Marcus, you there?'

'Yes ma'am,' she heard Marcus's voice say in her earpiece. 'At the cadaver locker, making sure Bobby Jewell's remains are properly stowed.'

'Okay, finish up and hurry back. We need to get the girl done before the live host arrives.'

She'd already completed preliminary autopsies on Candice and Bobby Jewell. Candice had died from a gunshot to the back of the head, well before the fire scorched her body. Bobby had multiple knife scores on his ribs – Margaret couldn't say for sure yet, not with such a rush job, but odds were he'd also died before the fire burned him.

Gitsh removed the girl's small corpse and put it on the table. Burn victims and charred flesh. Always such a joy. The human body doesn't actually burn up in a house fire. To cremate a body, you need fifteen hundred degrees Fahrenheit for two hours or more. House fires usually hit about five hundred degrees. While some *could* burn as hot as two thousand degrees, at that temperature the flames usually consumed all available fuel material within a half hour or so. Bobby Jewell's body had been blackened and charred, but preserved enough for Margaret to find one scorched triangle on his cheek, another at the base of his neck.

She'd been on the case long enough to know the story: Bobby Jewell had contracted the triangles, and as a result he'd killed his family. Then he'd set a fire and committed suicide by stabbing himself repeatedly. Sounded crazy, but she'd seen worse – at least Bobby hadn't chopped off his own legs with a hatchet. The bullet hole in the back of the wife's skull fit the murder-suicide profile. Margaret was sure the girl's cause of death would support it as well.

Gitsh folded up the body bag and put it in the incinerator chute.

Margaret stared at the girl's body. It was curled up in the fetal position, legs and arms flexed, fists tucked beneath the chin. That didn't mean the person had burned alive and curled up from the pain – dehydration from fire causes muscles, even dead muscles, to contract, pulling bodies into this posture.

The fetal position wasn't what held Margaret's attention, however. What really caught her eye was the size of the body.

She looked at the wall-mounted flat-panel, part of which showed stats on Chelsea.

'Clarence, this is supposed to be a seven-year-old girl?'

'Checking,' Clarence said in her earpiece. 'Yeah, Chelsea Jewell, seven years, four months, ten days.'

'How tall is she on the medical records?'

'Ummm . . . three feet, six inches.'

'This body is bigger than that,' Margaret said. 'And the hips are wrong. Gitsh, roll the body onto its back.'

Clarence's voice in her ear again. 'You don't think it's Chelsea Jewell?'

Gitsh moved the body.

Margaret took a good look, then shook her head. 'Not unless Chelsea Jewell was more like four-foot-two and had a penis. Get Dew on the line, right now.'

IF IFS AND BUTS WERE CANDY AND NUTS

'How is Private Climer, Doc?' Ogden asked.

'He'll be fine,' Doc Harper said. 'He was lucky the bullet didn't hit the bone. Took out a chunk of muscle, though. Colonel, I have to request again that we transfer him out of our area and to the base hospital.'

'Request denied, again,' Ogden said. 'Unless it's a life-and-death situation, he's not leaving our area until I talk to him. And you just said he'll be fine, so it's *not* life and death, correct?'

'But sir,' Doc Harper said, 'you can pick up the phone and have a replacement for him sent from one of the companies at Fort Bragg here in . . . what, three hours?'

'I don't need a replacement for him. I need to find out what happened. There's no way one redneck should have taken out four soldiers.'

'Colonel, we just pulled a .308-caliber bullet out of that boy's shoulder,' Doc said. 'Three hours ago he was facedown on a dirt road bleeding all over the place.'

Ogden checked his watch. 'It's sixteen hundred right now. I want him talking by seventeen hundred, got it?'

'He's my patient, sir,' Doc said. 'As soon as he wakes up, he's yours, but I'm within my rights to say that I will not bring him out of it early.'

Ogden sighed. Couldn't have Doc Harper bitching about putting wounded troops at unnecessary risk, not when that general's star was so close. He'd have to ship Doc Harper out soon, though, get someone else in here who followed orders no matter what they were.

'Who's with Climer?' Ogden asked.

'Brad Merriman,' Doc Harper said. 'The guy they call "Nurse Brad."'

Ogden nodded. He knew Nurse Brad. Good kid. Medic first class, but somewhere along the line the boys started ripping on him for being a 'male nurse,' and the nickname stuck.

'You and Merriman both sit with Climer,' Ogden said. 'If one of you has to take a crap, the other is staring at Climer to see if he wakes up. And when he does wake up, you call me immediately, you understand?'

Doc Harper nodded and saluted, then turned and walked out.

Charlie didn't like being such a hard-ass, but he needed answers. Three of his soldiers killed. The only known enemy unit a thirty-one-year-old civilian named Ryan Roznowski who had stolen a mail truck and tried to run the roadblock. The postman assigned to that truck was missing and presumed dead.

Roznowski had four triangles. He also had a wife, who was nowhere to be found, and a house that showed signs of a struggle, including blood on the living-room floor. Charlie knew that triangle hosts were dangerous, sure, killers, no question, but a guy with a hunting rifle setting a postal van on fire, then taking out four trained soldiers? It just didn't add up.

But it wasn't all bad news. They had finally succeeded in capturing a live host. Mission accomplished. That's what made the general's star a lock, just as long as he didn't fuck anything up.

But that star would come at a price – more names in his Little Blue Book.

Neil Illing.

James Eager.

Joel Brauer.

If he'd been able to put a full squad at each checkpoint, nine men instead of four or five, those boys might still be alive. Maybe he should have brought the other two companies. No, his plan was solid; it allowed for the maximum situational flexibility under the circumstances. *If* they'd had more time, *if* he'd had more men . . .

If ifs and buts were candy and nuts, what a wonderful Christmas it would be.

He'd write the families later that night. The best part of the job, really, telling some proud mom that her son had died while serving his country.

'Corporal Cope! Get in here!'

Cope was in the tent before Ogden even finished the second sentence. He must have been waiting right outside, just in case he was needed. You didn't get guys like Cope all that often.

'Sir?'

'Where the hell are my updates on the air search?'

'Nothing so far,' Cope said. 'All recon flights came up negative. Satellite squints say the same thing. Doesn't look like there's a construct within at least fifty miles.'

Damn it. It had to be out there. Bernadette Smith had tried to escape. So had Ryan Roznowski. How many infected *had* slipped out, either between the roadblocks or before Ogden arrived? No maps this time: none in

Smith's car or at her house. Same for Roznowski, and the Jewell place was a cinder. No clues.

If they were going to find the gate's location, once again it was all up to Perry Dawsey.

APB ON CLAN JEWELL

Dew Phillips sat in the MargoMobile's computer room. He and Perry had the room to themselves. Gitsh, Marcus, Margaret and Clarence were all in the Trailer B containment cell, locking down a feisty Bernadette Smith.

Dew wanted to hit a certain chief of staff, then rub her face in broken glass and finish up with a nice saltwater spritz on the fresh cuts.

'Dew, you okay?' Perry asked. 'You've got veins pulsing in the top of your big bald head.'

'I'm not okay,' Dew said. 'Fuck, we had them.'

Vanessa Colburn was the reason the Jewells had escaped. If she'd just let Murray do his thing, Dew would have that family in custody right now.

'We almost had who?' Perry said.

'The Jewells. Those bodies we found in the fire? *Not* the Jewell family. We don't know who the woman is. The man was Wallace Beckett. Identified from dental records. They're guessing the dead kid is his son, Beck. They searched the Beckett house, found Nicole Beckett chopped up and stuffed into a laundry hamper.'

'But Margaret said the man had triangles.'

'That's what's fucked up,' Dew said. 'Wallace Beckett *did* have triangles. The Jewell family was a man, a woman and a kid. We found the bodies of a man, a woman and a kid, and the man had triangles. Sounds familiar, right? Man gets triangles, goes gonzo, whacks his family.'

'Wait a minute,' Perry said. 'You're saying the Jewells killed three people, *including* a host, so we would think it was a nice neat package while they skipped town?'

'Try to keep up, college boy,' Dew said. 'Clan Jewell pulled the switcheroo on us. We didn't even bother to search the fucking area.'

'Then who is the woman?'

Dew shrugged. 'Who knows? It's not Candice Jewell, though. They know that from dental records, too. So we have three bodies, none of which belong to the Jewells. The Jewells, who are nowhere to be found. If they took off right when they started the fire, we're talking a fifteen-hour head start. They could be fucking anywhere.'

'What if they didn't leave right away?' Perry said. 'Maybe they're still in Gaylord.'

Dew scratched his chin. 'Maybe. Or maybe they were part of that attack on the roadblock.'

'Which had another triangle victim.'

Dew flipped through the paperwork. 'Yeah, Ryan Roznowski. He killed three soldiers and wounded Private Dustin Climer. Climer returned fire, killing Roznowski.'

'What the fuck,' Perry said. 'Was this Roznowski, like, a Special Forces Rambo guy, or what?'

'A plumber,' Dew said. 'Roznowski is married, but the FBI can't find his wife. That's not a cause for alarm in itself, because this whole town just bugged out, but there are signs of a struggle at the Roznowski house, blood on the living-room carpet, so do your college-boy math.'

'Roznowski's wife is the burned woman in the Jewell house?'

'Probably,' Dew said. 'We'll see if they identify her, but that all adds up. Roznowski kills or hurts his wife, then brings her over to the Jewells' house.'

'And the Becketts either go there or are brought there.'

'Nicole Beckett was murdered,' Dew said. 'So maybe someone kills her and kidnaps Wallace and his son, but I'm thinking that maybe Wallace killed her, then went to the Jewell house on his own, just like Roznowski.'

'Went on his own,' Perry said. 'Or maybe was called. Summoned.'

'Like the triangles put you and Fatty Patty together?'

Perry shrugged. 'Maybe. So what do we do now?'

'We get some pictures of the Jewell family, for starters, and put out an APB on them. Hell, we'll use the media again, say the Jewells are carrying the flesh-eating bacteria.'

Perry nodded. 'Okay, that will work, but what about their cars?'

'All the cars registered to the Jewells burned up in their garage.'

'So they took someone else's car?'

Dew nodded. 'Probably. They had three snowmobiles registered, two of those are gone. If they stashed them in the woods somewhere, we won't find them for weeks. So maybe they did take someone else's car, but this whole town just evacuated – we have no way of knowing what cars should be here and what cars were taken by the evacuees. We can search neighboring houses for signs of a struggle, though, maybe get lucky and find a body. But if we don't find one, there's no way to connect them to a specific vehicle.

'Bottom line? The Jewells got out. All we can do now is circulate their pictures and hope they fuck up.'

THE TOWER OF POWER

Performance far beyond projections.

The Orbital measured the growing abilities of Chelsea Jewell. Not only was her communication ability developing faster than expected, it showed signs of immense power – eventually more powerful than even that of the Orbital.

Reasons for this remained unclear. The crawlers in her skull continued to divide and grow, adding length to the dense mesh that melded with her brain. The denser the mesh, the more processing power, and yet there was something more. Triangles could interface with a human brain, use it for their purposes, but Chelsea was human to begin with. No need for informational conversion or translation. Her thoughts were a native tongue. All she needed was a connection, which the crawlers provided.

How strong might she become? The Orbital did not know. What mattered was that her development was ahead of schedule. She would handle most of the communication, the organization, allowing the Orbital to focus on blocking the sonofabitch.

STRANGE THINGS ARE AFOOT . . .

Mio, Michigan, is a tiny town about thirty-five miles southeast of Gaylord. Mr. Jenkins's Winnebago stopped at a gas station in Mio to fill up and to pick up a passenger by the name of Artie LaFrinere.

Artie had heard Chelsea's call, but since he was outside the checkpoints, he drove to Mio, ditched the car, then walked to the gas station and waited. To be precise, he waited *near* the gas station, because Artie LaFrinere didn't look so hot.

Four days ago Artie had gone tobogganing with his friends. He lost control of the toboggan, slid into the woods and plowed into a drift. Artie's friends laughed at him as he wiped snow out from under his jacket and the crack of his ass. Unfortunately for Artie, that snowdrift had been a landing pad for a big gust full of seeds, which – of course – wound up all over his belly, his back and yes, the crack of his ass. Artie didn't know it, but he was now a world record holder with his *thirteen* triangles. He coughed up blood every fifteen minutes or so. He didn't talk much. Everyone understood. They welcomed him into the Winnebago and made him as comfortable as possible.

Artie was actually the second passenger: they'd picked up Harlan Gaines on Country Road 491 just outside of Lewiston. He and his four triangles were getting along just fine. With Mr. LaFrinere's thirteen, plus Mr. Gaines's four, Daddy's five and Old Sam Collins's three, Chelsea had twenty-nine dollies in the Winnebago.

Only four to go! Math was one of her favorite classes.

Chelsea sensed one more dolly daddy out there, a man named Danny Korves, trying to make his way to meet up with the Winnebago. She also sensed something even more exciting – free-moving dollies that had already hatched weeks ago, sneaking across the countryside, trying to reach her. She told them where to go, but since they could only travel at night and they had far to run, she doubted if they could make it in time. Everything would come down to Mr. Korves. Chelsea pushed out to him and told him that he had to reach her no matter what the cost.

She just might have enough dollies to build that gate, and that made her happy. Another thing that made her happy was that Mr. Jenkins had bought all the Nestlé Crunch Eskimo Pies the Circle-K gas station had in its little freezer. The Winnebago was still in the parking lot. Everyone sat in the back, enjoying that yummy ice cream on a stick.

Mommy and Daddy only got one bar each.

'We can't stay here for long, Chelsea,' Mr. Jenkins said. 'Pretty soon they'll find out that the bodies in the house aren't you and your parents.'

'What are you talking about?' Mommy said. 'Won't they burn up?'

Mr. Jenkins shook his head. 'House fires don't get hot enough for that. When they find out the bodies aren't yours, the cops might start looking for you guys. You'll be wanted for murder, probably. Depending on how bad they want you, they'll run vehicle registrations for all your neighbors, figuring maybe you stole a car or took a hostage.

Cops might be looking for this Winnebago before too long.'

'Is that for sure?' Mommy asked.

Mr. Jenkins shrugged. 'You guys left three bodies in a burned-out house. Not like it's an unpaid parking ticket.'

'How long do we have?' Mommy asked.

Mr. Jenkins shrugged again. 'I couldn't say. But I can say we should get the 'Bago off the road as soon as we can.' He rattled the map, his finger tracing their route. 'We're on Highway 33 right now. We can take that to Highway 75, which will get us there after dark.'

Chelsea crawled under the map and into Mr. Jenkins's lap. They looked at it together. She pushed the route out with her mind, telling the remaining dollies and Mr. Korves to meet them along the way, or at the end.

'Mister Jenkins, if we go that way, will we see any more soldiers?'

'I don't know,' he said. 'I hope not. They scare me. I know we had a good plan, honey, but I think we also got lucky.'

Chelsea nodded. 'Me too. But if we do see them, we'll just deal with them, so they *better not* try to stop us.'

STAREDOWN

This time Clarence Otto was by her side. He had a gun on a nylon cord hanging around his neck, because a holster really didn't work with the biohazard suit.

When Margaret looked into the containment cell, she almost wished she had a gun herself.

Inside those clear walls, another woman was strapped to the autopsy trolley. Naked. She had a blue triangle on her left breast, one on her right forearm and one on her right hip.

Almost three months of work, all the insanity, all the violence, and this was the first time Margaret had seen a live triangle. After seeing so many dead ones, she had thought she knew what to expect – black eyes staring, blinking.

But she'd never thought about them staring at *her*. Their blinking made it so bizarre. It made them look . . . real. She wished Amos could have been here to see it. A live triangle meant they were that much closer to stopping this nightmare.

The woman was unconscious. She had enough meds in her to make sure she stayed that way. At least Margaret hoped. Betty should have stayed under, too, and look how well that had turned out.

Margaret looked at the touch-panel display mounted on the door. Bernadette Smith. Age twenty-eight. Mother of three. Well, not anymore. Now she was a mother of one and a widow – she'd killed her husband and slit the throats of her two daughters, one age five, one age three, before bundling the dead girls into the backseat of her Saab.

What would this woman be like after they removed the triangles? Perry still carried the guilt of murdering his best friend. How would this woman live with the knowledge she'd killed her husband, her own *children*?

And that was *if* they could remove the triangles at all. Margaret had seen the X-rays. The ones on the hip and the forearm would be tricky but doable. In each case the triangle's barbed tail was wrapped around bone and arteries, but during surgery Margaret could repair a damaged artery.

The one on Bernadette's chest . . . that was another matter.

The tail of that one was wrapped around Bernadette's *heart*. The X-ray showed dozens of those wicked hooks, like sharp rose thorns, pressing up against it. One wrong pull and they'd cut multiple holes. If that happened, even with Bernadette on the operating table and Dr. Dan at her side, Margaret didn't know if they could save her.

The heart monitor began to beat faster. Margaret punched buttons on the display, calling up the woman's EKG. Pulse rate increasing.

'Shit,' Margaret said. 'She's waking up.'

'I thought you knocked her out for a couple of hours.' Otto said.

'I did. The triangles are countering the anesthesia somehow. Daniel?'

'Yes ma'am.'

'Call Dew,' she said. 'Tell him to bring Dawsey. The patient is waking up. We're going to have to knock her out again and operate right away. If Dew wants to ask these things some questions, he'd better do it fast, because in thirty minutes I'm going to save this woman's life and kill these little bastards in the process.'

DUSTIN GETS RELIGION

Dustin Climer woke up on a cot. His shoulder hurt. His head felt like it was going to explode. A fever washed through his body, and every nerve throbbed with shooting pains. He rubbed his eyes and sat up. The infirmary tent, and he was the only one there.

His training kicked in, and his hands found his weapon. The empty M4 carbine was leaning against a small metal cabinet of drawers at the side of his cot. Just having the M4 in his hands made Dustin relax a bit.

The tent's soft plastic windows showed darkness outside. He'd been attacked in the morning, so he'd been out for what, eight hours? His clothes and shoes were folded up under a metal rack next to the bed. Something about his jacket bothered him. The shoulder patch . . .

Images flashed through his mind. A little girl. A blonde, perfect, *angelic* little girl. Had he ever seen anything so gorgeous? He had. When he'd been out, he'd had visions of something black, something triangular.

The hatchlings.

Beautiful?

Yes, *beyond* beautiful. Perfection. Utterly divine.

Shame washed over him. He looked down at his jacket again, at the shoulder patch depicting a lightning bolt hitting an upside-down roach. And even worse, the three small black triangle patches sewn beneath it. One of those patches was just black. One had a glossy white *X* embroidered on it.

One had *two X*'s.

Oh, sweet God . . . what had he done? He'd *destroyed* them. *Three* of them.

Are you awake?

His head snapped up. A voice. A little girl's voice. But he wasn't hearing it – it was in his head. He put his hands on his face and lay back down on the bed. He was a sinner. He had destroyed perfection, and now he would have to pay.

Wake up, sleepyhead.

'I'm awake,' he said. 'Your man tried to kill me, and now I understand why. I'm ready to pay the price.'

You don't have to pay a price, silly. You didn't know. And he wasn't trying to kill you. He sacrificed himself so that you were a hero – you killed the man who killed the other soldiers. He only shot you so no one would question why you were tired and wanted to sleep. He died so that you could see my pretty dollies. Do you see now? Do you understand?

'Yes,' Dustin whispered. 'Yes, I see them. I . . . I killed them.'

That's okay. You didn't know, so it wasn't your fault.

'No, I didn't know. I didn't know how *beautiful* they were.'

You can make up for it.

'How?' He sat up again. 'How can I? I'll do anything!'

You need to make others see, the voice said. *You are the protector. You need to make them all see, especially your leader.*

'Colonel Ogden?'

Yes. You need to give him smoochies and let him see the pretty dollies.

More images flashed in Climer's brain. Images of Chelsea watching her mother sleep. Images of Chelsea's tongue.

You know what you need to do?

Dustin nodded. 'Yes.'

Then hurry, but be careful. Don't get caught. You are a protector now. You and the others must join us, because we want to open the gates to heaven.

The tent curtain opened, and two men came in. Doc Harper and Nurse Brad.

'Well, look who's up,' Doc Harper said. 'You jabbering to yourself in here?'

The men walked over to the cot.

Dustin shrugged. 'I guess so, Doc.'

'Well I'm not surprised,' Doc Harper said. He slid a stool next to Dustin's bed and sat. 'You're probably a better conversationalist than Brad here.'

'Ha-ha-ha,' Brad said. 'Keep it up and I'll stop letting you win at chess.'

Doc Harper picked up Dustin's wrist and checked his watch. 'Brad, you couldn't beat me in chess if I played with my queen shoved up my rectum.' Doc released Dustin's wrist, then pulled a penlight out of his breast pocket and started flicking it in Dustin's eye.

'Just stare straight ahead, Private,' Doc Harper said. 'Everything looks okay. How's your head?'

'Hurts a bit,' Dustin said.

Harper nodded as he switched to the other eye.

'Describe the pain on a scale of one to ten,' Doc Harper said.

'Um, maybe a three.'

'Doesn't sound like a major problem,' Doc Harper said. 'Well, since you're alert, the colonel wants to see you

ASAP. I'll let him know you're ready to talk. Brad, grab some Tylenol packets. Four should do the trick.'

Brad knelt down to open a drawer of the cabinet next to Dustin's cot.

Dustin grabbed the back of Doc Harper's neck and head-butted him in the nose. Before Harper even slid off the stool, Dustin picked up his M4 with both hands.

Brad turned his head to see what was happening, just in time to catch an M4 stock right in the mouth. He sagged to his left butt cheek, mouth bleeding, staring out with eyes that didn't really focus on anything. Dustin hit him again. Brad fell to his back, arm resting awkwardly against the open medicine drawer.

Dustin looked down at the two men. Doc Harper blinked like mad. Tears poured from his eyes, and blood gushed from the bridge of his broken nose. He tried to back away, a reverse crab-walk, but he couldn't seem to send enough strength to his feet. The heels of his shoes pushed weakly at the floor.

Dustin pulled his zip-ties from his pants pocket.

'Does that hurt, Doc?' Dustin said. 'Let me kiss it and make it all better.'

Chelsea let her mind spread farther and farther. This was *so* cool. Better than all her best toys combined. She'd *felt* Dustin hit those men, like she had been there, like she had hit them herself.

She liked it. It was really fun.

Every time she spread her mind, the feeling got stronger, the connections got stronger. Each host, each dolly, each converted person – they all felt a little different. Kind of like how vanilla ice cream tastes one way and chocolate another way. That was it; each had its own *taste*.

Dustin was a long ways away, but she could still connect with him. She could connect with Bernadette Smith, too, with each of the three dollies growing in her body.

Those three tasted like anger. Anger and fear.

Sending Bernadette to the highway worked, but Chelsea had thought the soldiers would shoot the woman. Chelsea even had Bernadette kill her daughters and bring the knife. But the devils captured Bernadette, and that was bad.

Bernadette's dollies were growing so *fast*! Maybe soon they would come out to play, come out to build. Chelsea sensed needles poking into them, so many needles. Just like the doctor had always stuck needles into her. Poking, prodding, testing. Dollies didn't feel pain like she did, though. The needles were really just kind of annoying to them.

So why were they so scared and angry? None of the other dollies tasted like that. Chelsea concentrated on those three dollies, listened to their thoughts, and she found the answer.

The sonofabitch.

The *boogeyman*.

They were staring *right at* the boogeyman! Of course they were angry, of course they were afraid. Chelsea felt a stab of that same fear, a stab of that same anger. Chauncey had told her not to connect to the boogeyman, but that was before. She was stronger now. The dollies were so close to the boogeyman, maybe only a few feet away. She could connect through them and *talk* to him.

The boogeyman made Chelsea afraid. That wasn't fair. Now it was *his* turn to be scared.

FACING HIS PAST

Perry Dawsey had never been claustrophobic. Then again, he'd never been crammed into a full-body suit obviously not made for someone his size, then walked into a friggin' semi trailer so jam-packed with stuff he had to turn sideways to walk through these pitiful excuses for aisles.

But claustrophobia was the least of his concerns. The naked woman in the clear glass containment cell took up most of his attention.

Her, and what was on her. *In* her.

Tight restraints held her wrists, ankles and waist. She was crying. Perry felt shame wash over him, shame at how he'd treated Fatty Patty. He'd screamed at Patty. He'd hit her. *Cut* her. Watched her die, hoping that in the process he could learn something that might help him save himself. He hadn't even been a man then.

Milner was right.

Perry was a monster.

The woman in the chamber pulled weakly against the leather straps.

'Those restraints tight?' Dew asked Margaret.

'Goddamn right they are,' Margaret said. 'I put those on myself. Any tighter and she'd lose circulation.'

Margaret's voice sounded colder than before. Colder and *harder*, as though maybe cutting off that woman's circulation wouldn't be the worst thing in the world after all. That wasn't the voice she'd used when she was helping him recover, or sewing up the cuts Dew had given him. Then she'd sounded like she cared, like she really wanted to help. Now? Now she had a touch of disgust in her voice. Maybe even a slight helping of hate.

'Please,' the woman sobbed. 'Please, let me go. I swear, I won't tell anyone.'

'Try to relax, Bernadette,' Margaret said. 'We want to help you.'

'*LIAR*!' the woman screamed. 'You're the *POLICE*! *You want to cut me up!*'

She couldn't move anything but her head, so move it she did, thrashing it around as if she were being electrocuted. Her sweaty brown hair flew in all directions. Her face carried an expression of wide-eyed terror one second, psychotic fury the next, then back again.

The triangles stared out. With their black eyes, they could have been looking anywhere, but Perry knew they were looking right at him.

S o n o f a b i t c h . You will die. Your death will be worse than the rest.

Perry took a half step back. That sensation of grayness remained, but whatever was jamming him, it didn't work this close to a triangle. He hadn't expected that – he'd hoped to come in, not hear a thing, then get the fuck out.

Perry didn't realize he was shaking until he felt a hand on his shoulder.

'Take it easy, Perry,' Dew said. 'They can't get to you.'

'I gotta get out of here, Dew. I gotta get out.'

Dew's voice stayed low. Low and calm. 'What you gotta do is focus. We need to talk to these things. We need the location of the next gate, and you're the only one who can get it.'

'But Dew—'

'Listen to me,' Dew said. 'Sometimes we have to do things we don't want to. You can't bring Bill back, but this is your chance to make it right. You *have* to take it.'

Dew was right. Dew had fought, had sacrificed. He wasn't asking Perry to do anything he wouldn't do himself.

'Can they hear me in there?' Perry asked.

Margaret nodded. 'There are speakers in the cell. The microphone in your earpiece picks up your voice. They can hear you just fine.'

Perry nodded inside the helmet. Now he was grateful for the suit, because if he pissed himself no one would see. He cleared his throat. For some reason he remembered the punch line to an old joke: *It's sure not gonna suck itself.*

No more waiting.

'I'm supposed to talk to you,' he said. 'Figure out what you want.'

W e w a n t to kill you. You are the destroyer.

Full sentences. Punctuation. Soon they would tear free from the woman's body.

'Where is the next gate?'

Nothing.

'You want to . . . open up the door, I know that. What's going to come through?'

A y y y n n n g e l l l s .

Angels. Coming through the gate. Perry had never heard that from his own triangles, and there was something profoundly disturbing about it.

The angels are coming. People build for them, just like we do. We're going to make your life a living hell, and that's what you deserve, you cheating bastard.

They seemed different, different from his own triangles, the ones he had called the Magnificent Seven. Different from Fatty Patty's triangles and hatchlings. These three sounded feminine, but caustic, angry. Perry wondered what Bernadette Smith's personality had been like before the infections. Something told Perry there was one word for it – *bitch*.

'What did they say?' Dew asked.

'Hard to tell,' Perry said. 'I think whatever is coming through wants to make us build things.'

'Build things?' Dew said. He spoke louder, as if that would help him be heard inside the containment cell. 'What are we going to build for you?'

You'll do what you're told or you'll get the paddle.

'They're not going to say what it is,' Perry said. 'I can tell. So much hate, derision coming off them . . . I think they want to make us slaves.'

'Oh fuck that,' Dew said. 'The Jewells. Ask them where the Jewells are, see if you get any vibes.'

Kill him. Get the gun, kill kill kill.

Perry stared at them, waiting to feel the rush of violent desire.

But he didn't feel anything.

He'd beaten them. Dew was right, he *could* do this.

'Where is the Jewell family?' Perry said, his voice growing a little stronger with each word. 'Bobby Jewell, Candice Jewell, Chelsea Jewell. Where are they?'

Perry locked onto their jet-black eyes. Nothing.

And then he heard a voice. Not the triangles, something new.

Something cold.

I think you should leave the Jewell family alone.

A little girl's voice. Clear, *human,* but in his head.

You're scared, aren't you? You should be scared.

'You're scared, too,' Perry said. 'I can feel it.'

Dew nudged Perry's shoulder. 'What are they saying, kid?'

Kill that man.

'Nothing,' Perry said. 'They're not saying anything.'

I can make you do it. I'm in charge. People have to do what I say.

An intense rage swept through Perry. Oh, God, there it was, that heated lust to *hurt.* The hatchlings couldn't stir that up in him anymore, but this girl could, and far more powerfully than he'd ever felt before.

Only this time he felt it for Dew Phillips.

Kill him.

Kill him.

'I gotta get out of here,' Perry said. 'I can't be in here.'

'Kid, come on,' Dew said. 'Don't chicken out now. We have to find the Jewells, or at least see if the triangle-whatever will negotiate or something.'

What's the matter, scaredy-cat? Are you afraid?

Perry shook his head. 'No. I got to go. Margaret, whatever you're going to do, you need to do it quick. They're going to hatch soon.'

'How do you know?' Margaret asked.

'They're using complete sentences,' Perry said. 'Pauses, like they're talking with punctuation. They didn't do that with me until near the end. You've got a day, maybe half a day before they hatch.'

Margaret looked at Bernadette, then back to Perry. 'You're sure about that?'

'Perry, talk to them,' Dew said.

I feel your fear. I'm going to get you . . .

Perry put his hands to his ears, a subconscious effort to block out the voices. His gloved hands hit his helmeted head before he remembered he couldn't actually *hear* the voices with his ears at all.

'Leave me alone!'

'Okay, kid,' Dew said. 'Just take it easy.'

'Don't worry, Perry,' Margaret said. 'We're going to operate on her right now. We'll get rid of them.'

Perry had to turn his whole body so he could look at Margaret. She seemed so small, a tiny face swimming inside that big helmet, like a guppy in a fishbowl. Was she really that naive?

'You know what?' Perry said. 'I never thanked you for saving my life.'

He turned and opened the airlock door. The light changed from green to red. He walked out. Dew followed, shutting the door behind them both.

Margaret stared at the red/green light above the airlock door for a few seconds, irrationally worried it wouldn't change from red back to green, that she wouldn't be able to open the door again and that Bernadette might tear free from the trolley at any moment. When it finally turned back to green, Margaret realized she'd been holding her breath.

'Margo, you okay?' Clarence asked.

'Fine,' she said.

'Man,' Clarence said. 'That guy is soooo messed up.'

'Yes, he is,' Margaret said. 'It's got to be hard to see triangles again. So disturbing to see them for anyone . . . I can't imagine what it's like for Perry. Despite that, aside from what he just had to endure, I think he's making progress. It was nice of him to finally thank me for saving him.'

'That's not what he said. He said he *never* thanked you. I don't think he wanted to live.'

She started to correct Clarence but stopped herself. Maybe he was right. Perry Dawsey's life wasn't exactly a bed of roses.

'It doesn't matter, because I *did* save him.' She jerked her thumb toward Bernadette. 'And I'm going to save her, too. Now, please help me prep this woman for surgery. If Perry's right, we don't have much time.'

'We need to go back to the control room first,' Clarence said. 'We need to talk to Murray.'

'Why the hell do we need to talk to Murray? We need to get moving, hon. Every second counts.'

'Please, Margaret,' Clarence said. 'This is already complicated enough. We have to make sure the president is informed. Doctor Dan needs to suit up, anyway. He can prep the patient while we tell Murray what's going on. Okay?'

She didn't have time for this. But then again, keeping the wheels greased was part of the program. Gutierrez wanted to pretend he was in control? She could play that game, but only for so long.

'I'll talk to him,' she said. 'But you've got fifteen minutes, hon. Then I'm operating no matter what. We're going to need all hands for this. We might have to work as two separate teams simultaneously, Dan and Marcus on the heart, Gitsh and I on the hip.'

'Sure,' Clarence said quietly. 'I'll get everyone ready. You get back to the control room, okay?'

Margaret nodded. She squeezed his gloved hand, then opened the airlock door and walked out.

'**Perry, wait up.**' Dew tried to run after him, but the biohazard suit combined with his aching hip and popping knees made that practically impossible.

Perry kept walking. Even though he had a limp of his own, his long strides quickly carried him into the darkness of the Jewell family's expansive property.

Dew stopped and put his hand on his hips. He was too old for this crap. 'Perry! *Come on.*'

Perry stopped and turned.

'Stay there for a second,' Dew said. 'Better yet, come back here.'

Perry glared at Dew, then walked, big steps bringing him back just as fast as they'd taken him away.

'What was that all about?' Dew asked. 'Those things are behind glass, and they haven't even hatched yet. I know they're freaky, but come on, you have to be stronger than that.'

'It's not them,' Perry said. 'It's . . . something else.'

'What?'

'I think Chelsea Jewell was talking to me. Talking to me through the triangles.'

Dew longed for the days when he could hear something like that and say, *You're fucking crazy*. But Perry Dawsey wasn't crazy. This was just another facet in his waking nightmare.

'What makes you think it was Chelsea?'

'I'm taking a guess,' Perry said. 'It was a little girl's voice. Chelsea and her family got out, she's a little girl, I'm making the connection.'

'You're a regular Columbo,' Dew said.

Perry stared, then smiled a strange smile. 'That's more of a compliment than you can know.'

There was probably a story behind that, but now wasn't the time. 'So you had Chelsea Jewell in your head. Tell me why that scares you so bad.'

Perry leaned back a little and stared up at the black winter night.

'Power,' Perry said. 'It wasn't like when the triangles talk to me. This is something different. I don't know, Dew, not all of these things have easy definitions, but she wanted . . . never mind what she wanted. She's got power, Dew. Big-time. Whatever she is, it's nothing I've felt before.'

'What about her parents? You get anything from them?'

Perry shook his head. 'No, just her. We need to find her. Deal with her. Before she gets stronger.'

'We're working on that, kid. We've got an APB out on Clan Jewell. Every cop in ten states has their pictures. Now, come on, we have to get the gate location. We have no maps this time – it's Bernadette Smith or bust. Let's get back in the trailer and ask some more questions.'

'I'm not going back in,' Perry said.

'Don't be a pussy,' Dew said.

Perry's eyes widened, and the corners of his mouth turned up in a slight smile. He pointed a finger at Dew. 'Don't. Push. Me.'

Perry turned and walked into the darkness.

Dew let him go. There was a time to lead, a time to follow and a time to get the fuck out of the way.

He'd seen that look on Perry's face once before –
when the kid had been coming right at him, smiling,
wide-eyed, naked and covered in blood, hopping on
one foot with his severed cock flopping in his clenched
fist.

Yep, definitely the time to get the fuck out of the
way.

The Orbital couldn't understand it. It had given
Chelsea very specific instructions.

**Chelsea, I told you not to
talk to the destroyer.**

I know you did.

So she hadn't forgotten. She remembered the order,
yet she had disobeyed anyway.

**If you knew it was
forbidden, why did you do
it?**

I dunno.

The Orbital tried to process the response. Tried, and
failed.

**What do you mean, you do
not know?**

I dunno.

**Do not disobey me,
Chelsea. You will bring
the destroyer if you talk
to him. You must never,
ever connect to him again.**

*I already told you once, Chauncey. You're not the boss of
me.*

The Orbital felt the connection end. *Chelsea* had broken
it. The Orbital hadn't known that was possible.

Clearly, it had to make additional changes. Now it would have to divert yet another part of its processing to making sure Chelsea could not speak to the destroyer again.

She was already more powerful than projected, and that power would only increase as she connected to become more and more converted.

MURRAY AND VANESSA, BFF

The president of the United States of America sat in his Oval Office chair, holding a glass of sixty-year-old Macallan on the rocks. Vanessa Colburn sat in a chair near the desk. She didn't drink, Murray had heard. Except, maybe, for the blood of her victims. Or of random orphans. Or maybe a kitten.

The Macallan was an Inauguration Day gift from the Scottish ambassador. It was rumored to cost upwards of thirty thousand dollars a bottle. You didn't exactly give the president of the United States a bottle of Chivas Regal as a present. That glass alone was probably worth more than Murray made in a week. He would have loved to let Gutierrez savor the scotch, but now wasn't a time for slow sipping.

'Mister President, we need an answer,' Murray said. 'Doctor Montoya wants to operate on Bernadette Smith immediately.'

'So operate,' Vanessa said. 'Ogden's men got you the live host you wanted, but Dawsey won't talk to the triangles. Kind of shoots the whole plan right out of the sky.'

In one sentence she managed to combine the success of her idea to send Ogden with the failure of Murray's team to capitalize on it. Okay, so it was actually a compound sentence – that didn't change how effortlessly Vanessa Colburn could make you look like an idiot.

'Montoya can still dissect a triangle before it decomposes,' Vanessa said. 'We're further ahead than we were before, even though Dawsey failed to communicate, so what's the problem?'

'The problem, Miss Colburn, is that for three months we've also been trying to capture a live hatchling. Now we can achieve that objective.'

Vanessa stared at him. 'Achieve that *objective*? What the hell are you saying, Murray? That we should just let this woman die so we can capture a hatchling?'

'It's an option that's on the table.'

'It's an option if you're a fucking *vampire*,' she said.

She was calling *him* a vampire? Priceless. 'We need information. Wars aren't won with guns. They're won with intel.'

She shook her head. 'This isn't a *war*, Murray.'

He'd had just about all he could take from her. *This* woman had the president's ear? *This* woman was part of deciding the fate of the free world?

'Not a war?' Murray said. 'What would you call it, then?'

'It's a crisis situation,' Vanessa snapped. 'No one in his right mind would call this a *war*.'

'And what the *fuck* do you know about war? Huh? With your fucking Ivy League education? *You're* going to tell *me* what a war is?'

'Take it easy, Murray,' Gutierrez said.

'I don't think I will, Mister President,' Murray said. He could hear himself, he tried to stop himself, but he couldn't take it anymore. 'Tell me, Miss Colburn, in your *infinite* wisdom, do you know what it's like to have someone shoot at you?'

'As a matter of fact, I do,' she said. 'I *earned* my Ivy

League education. Earned it while growing up without any money, with drugs all around me and crime all over the place. I saw my fair share of guns, Murray. I've seen friends die.'

Murray laughed at her. 'Oh, is that right? So you grew up in *da hood*, and that means you know what *war* is? After you saw someone die, did you run back to your house and turn on MTV?'

'You don't know me,' Vanessa said. 'You don't know how I grew up.'

'Fine, then educate me. How many people have you killed?'

She said nothing.

'None? Okay, I'll give you a free pass there. How many times have you held your friend's head while he bled out, looked into his eyes and promised him you'd make sure his kids would grow up strong? None? Well then, surely you must have had to wipe your friend's brains off your fucking *face*, right? How many times have you hidden in a rice paddy as your blood seeps into the filthy water? How many times have you had to kill a twelve-year-old girl because she was shooting her AK at you? Huh? Maybe *da hood* don't sound so tough now, *does it*?'

'Murray!' Gutierrez barked. 'Your service to this country is no small matter, but that's *enough*.'

Murray realized he was breathing hard and sweating. In thirty years of being in this room, in front of six presidents, he'd never snapped like that. This woman could push his buttons like no other. He pulled some Kleenex from his pocket and wiped the perspiration from his head.

Vanessa didn't look upset at all. Her poker face was good, but it couldn't hide her main emotion – satisfaction. She'd won. She'd exposed his mistakes. She'd made him lose his temper, big-time. In her eyes he saw a crystal-clear message – if he was going to save any part of his career, he needed to cave in and back whatever she suggested.

Murray cleared his throat. 'I'm sorry, Mister President.'

Gutierrez gave his political smile. 'This is a rough situation. We're all a little short-tempered.'

'Listen, Murray,' Vanessa said. 'Believe me, I'm not some hippie who thinks you were a baby killer or something. I respect your service and your experience, but you're from a different time. This is the reason we came into office. Because people like you think we can just forget someone's civil rights if it fits the moment.'

Murray's temper reignited, but he'd be damned if he'd lose it again. He locked his jaw shut. An uneasy silence filled the Oval Office. Gutierrez finally broke it.

'How controlled would this be, Murray? If we let them hatch, would anyone know?'

Vanessa's head snapped around in confusion. She started to speak, but Gutierrez held up a finger, cutting her off.

'How controlled, Murray?'

All Murray had to do was steer Gutierrez away from allowing the triangles to hatch. All he had to do was fall in line behind Vanessa, and she'd back off.

But they still didn't know the location of the next gate. For that they needed a hatchling. Dawsey would come through – he *had* to come through.

And besides . . . Murray fucking hated Vanessa Colburn.

'Well, sir, I'll be blunt,' Murray said. 'The media already knows about the flesh-eating bacteria. If someone dies from that . . .' He spread his hands. 'These things happen.'

Vanessa shook her head patronizingly. 'These things do not *just happen.*'

'Vanessa,' Gutierrez said, 'do me a favor and shut the fuck up.'

The look on her face might be the same one she'd have if Murray whipped out his cock and asked for a blow job with whip cream and ice cubes.

'On a scale of one to ten, Murray,' Gutierrez said, 'how bad do we need to know what we're up against?'

'One to ten? Try four hundred thirty-two. We're facing some kind of invasion here. I think the time for tea and crumpets is long past.'

He looked hard at the president. Just two weeks in, was John Gutierrez already seeing beyond his idealism?

Only one way to find out, and that was to force the issue. Murray pulled out his phone and held it up.

'Mister President, please, I *have* to get your decision or soon there won't be any point to this discussion. Saying nothing is the same thing as telling me to let them hatch. If you don't mind a little advice from an old man, sir, don't let indecision decide things for you. Make a call and live with it.'

Gutierrez stared off into nothingness, looking at something not inside the room.

'Let them hatch,' he said.

Murray typed LET IT RIDE into his cell phone with a thumb speed that would have drawn admiration from Betty Jewell in her texting prime. He hit *send.*

Vanessa shook her head. She had the look of a person about to explain something obvious to a loved one who just doesn't *get* it. 'Mister President,' she said. 'John, I . . . we can't do this.'

Gutierrez laughed. Murray heard the anguish in that laugh. 'Vanessa, are you flinching? I never thought I'd see the day. I always knew that sooner or later I'd have to send people to their deaths. Every now and then, I'd kid myself, let myself hope that maybe my administration would be the lucky one, that a decision of mine wouldn't result in flag-draped caskets. Sending soldiers to die is difficult, but dying is part of a soldier's job. They understand that when they sign up. You know what's even harder to deal with? Realizing that there is an American woman named Bernadette Smith, age twenty-eight, mother of three, a Christian who volunteers at her church, and that I'm going to knowingly let her die in the most horrible way imaginable.'

Vanessa shook her head. 'Mister President, I *insist* th—'

He pounded the desk with his right fist. 'You insist? *You* insist? Who is the fucking president here?'

'You are, John,' she said quietly.

'That's *Mister President*,' Gutierrez said.

Vanessa looked down. 'You are, Mister President.'

'Do you know *why* I'm the president of the United States of America, Vanessa?'

She shook her head.

'One, because I'm smart enough to hire and listen to people like you. And two, because I'm smart enough to know when *not* to listen to people like you. The hardest decision is usually the necessary decision, and that decision has just been *made*. Now get out.'

Vanessa looked at Murray, then back at the president. Murray wondered if she was going to cry.

She opened her mouth to speak, then closed it, then opened it again. 'You . . . you want us to leave?'

'No,' Gutierrez said. 'Just you. I need to talk to Murray.'

She did the double look again, first at Murray, then at Gutierrez who stared back, his face immobile.

Vanessa Colburn stood and walked out of the Oval Office so fast she almost broke into a run. The door shut behind her. Silence hung in the air.

'What about Montoya's weather report?' Gutierrez asked. 'Any luck finding this invisible satellite?'

'Not yet,' Murray said. 'But we've got a lot of resources focused on it, sir. We're trying to extrapolate possible locations. We're hopeful we can find something soon.'

Gutierrez nodded slowly. He'd asked about the satellite in almost a perfunctory manner.

Murray calmly waited. He'd done this dance before.

'Am I doing the right thing?' Gutierrez asked finally. His stony expression broke. Murray could see the pain, the indecisiveness on the man's face. 'Murray, tell me straight. You've been doing this for a long time, right?'

'Yes, Mister President.'

'Am I doing the right thing, letting that woman die?'

'I don't decide right and wrong. You do, sir. I just give you the information to make decisions, then carry out those decisions.'

'I see. And does that gigantic line of bullshit help you sleep at night?'

'No sir,' Murray said. 'But a Xanax or two sure as hell does.'

Gutierrez sank back in his chair. He drained the glass of scotch, then set it down so hard that one of the ice cubes shot out and skidded across the desk. Murray walked to the drink cart, grabbed the bottle of Macallan, then poured the president a double.

'If it's any consolation, Mister President, it makes me very proud, and very hopeful, that this decision is so hard for you. I've served five presidents before you. For some of them, I watched decisions like this become . . . become *easy.'*

Gutierrez stared at Murray for a second, then raised the glass in a salute. 'Thank you, Murray. Now go take care of this.'

'Yes, Mister President,' Murray said, and walked out.

BOXERCISE

Margaret paced in the computer room, which was tough to do considering she could only walk about five steps before she had to turn a 180. The PVC fabric on her legs *zip-zipped* as she walked. She was still wearing the suit, sans helmet, in order to save time when she had to go back in for surgery. Dew was already out of his. She'd never seen him in scrubs before.

Clarence walked into the control room.

'Did you reach Murray?' she asked. 'Is it *okay* with him if we go ahead and save this woman's life now?'

Clarence looked at Dew, then back at her.

'What's the problem?' she asked. 'Come on, guys, chop-chop. Time's a-wastin'.'

Dew looked at the floor. Clarence's face was a blank.

'You can't operate,' Clarence said.

'What are you talking about? We've got everything we can get from her.'

'Not everything,' Clarence said. 'Not yet.'

She stared at him for a moment. Understanding flared up, but part of her fought it down. She didn't want to believe what she was hearing.

'You . . . Clarence, you can't be serious. You don't think we're going to let those things *hatch* out of that woman, do you?'

'We have orders,' he said.

Clarence had known what Murray's answer would be. That's why he'd insisted they wait, delay the surgery. If he hadn't fed her that bullshit about keeping people in the loop, she'd already have Bernadette Smith on the operating table.

Margaret had heard the phrase *seeing red*. She'd understood it in theory, but she had never actually *seen* red. Until now. A rage exploded inside her like nothing she'd ever felt.

'We are *not* going to let that woman die!'

She took two steps forward and started jabbing her finger into Clarence's broad chest. She could have also screamed at Dew, sure, but she'd almost expected this from a cold-blooded killer like him. But from *Clarence*? A man she'd made love to? 'That woman has a ten-year-old son who just lost his father and two sisters. I can *save* Bernadette, I know it. We are going to operate on her, and *right now*, you rotten bastards. Do you hear me? *Right now.*'

Clarence shook his head. 'We can't, Margaret.'

'That's *Doctor Montoya* to you, asshole. *Doctor*. As in sworn to protect life.'

'We have orders,' Clarence said.

'Orders from who? From that slimy bastard Murray Longworth? From Ogden? From *him*?' Margaret pointed at Dew, who kept staring at the floor. 'Who the fuck thinks they can *order me* to let this woman die?'

'The president,' Clarence said quietly. 'It's from the top. Executive order.'

'Is that right? Well maybe he can order you to gas some Jews while you're at it! How about that for following orders? Or maybe he can order Dew here to tie up some nigger and give him a whippin' just to set an example!'

Clarence's face wrinkled in anger, but she didn't care.

In fact, she liked it. She wanted to get a reaction out of this asshole, this *goose-stepping* asshole. How could she have ever thought she loved a coldhearted machine like this?

'What do you think, Dew?' Margaret screamed. 'If you were *ordered* to do it, that would make it *okay*, wouldn't it?'

'Margaret,' Clarence said, 'please calm down.'

'Didn't I tell you it's *Doctor* Montoya? Didn't I, *Agent* Otto?'

'You don't understand, we ha—'

Margaret threw a straight right jab. He was still talking when she did. Her fist hit the bottom of his left front tooth. His head snapped back, from pain, not from the force of her punch, and his hands shot to his mouth. She had seen anger on his face before, but his new expression went way beyond that. This was *fury*. His eyes cut through her rage a bit, made her realize that no matter how mad she got, she was still a small woman and someone his size could hurt her. Hurt her *bad*, anytime he wanted to . . . or anytime he lost control.

His nostrils flared. He stood up to his full six-foot-three-inch height.

'You broke my tooth,' he said. His voice remained quiet, but it was no longer calm. Agent Clarence Otto, her lover – correction, *former* lover – was about one ounce shy of knocking her right the fuck out.

'Leave, Otto,' Dew said.

Clarence's head snapped to the left and he glared at Dew. For a second, Margaret thought his rage might manifest itself on Dew Phillips.

'That's an *order*,' Dew said quietly.

Clarence glared at him for another few seconds, then looked at Margaret, hate in his eyes. He turned and walked out of the trailer.

'You need to get a grip, Doctor Montoya,' Dew said. 'We're in a very bad situation here, and you're smart enough to understand the big picture. Do you have that first-aid kit in here?'

'Why the *fuck* do you need a first-aid kit?'

Dew pointed down to her right fist. 'Because you're bleeding all over the place.'

Margaret felt the hot wetness a second before she lifted her hand. Only when she saw it did she feel the pain. Her right ring finger was split wide open at the base knuckle, cut by a piece of broken tooth wedged between the torn skin and the bone.

With her left hand, she opened a cabinet and pulled out the plastic first-aid kit. One-handed, she lifted its lid and rummaged for a suture needle and some gauze.

Dew held out his left hand, palm up.

'I don't need your help, Phillips.'

'Yes you do.' His hand was still waiting for hers.

'My left hand is fine,' Margaret said. 'I'll be happy to split that one open on *your* tooth if you push me.'

'Clarence Otto is a gentleman,' Dew said. 'I'm not. I'm a firm believer in equal rights. You hit me and you'll be spitting up blood. Then, if I know Otto, he's going to come after me because I hit his girl. He's bigger than me, so I'll have to knee him in the balls and then probably break his right arm to make him stay down.'

Margaret just stared at him. Dew talked in a slow, steady voice. A smooth voice. Even while he was talking about nothing but violence, his voice calmed her. Every degree her temper dropped, the pain in her hand went up correspondingly.

'Do you want to know *how* I'll break his right arm, Doctor Montoya?'

Images of Perry Dawsey flashed through her mind, images of the huge man curled up on a hotel-room floor, bleeding from Dew's handiwork. Her brain superimposed Clarence Otto over Perry Dawsey.

Dew's left hand was still out, palm up.

'No,' she said. 'I don't want to know.' She lifted her bloody right hand and put it in his palm.

He picked the tooth out of her knuckle and put it on the computer counter. 'Otto might want that back,' he said. 'Aren't you scientist types supposed to be above the fray and all that?'

'I'm not going to let that woman die,' Margaret said. 'What just happened doesn't change anything. I'm *going* to operate.'

'No you're not.' Dew pulled gauze on the wound, pressed hard and held it. Margaret hissed at the pain. 'What you're *going* to do, Doctor Montoya, is what you're told.'

She started to protest, but he squeezed her hand a little bit harder. The pain made her gasp, cutting off her words.

'The president ordered that we allow that woman's triangles to hatch,' Dew said. 'We can't locate the next gate; therefore we can't afford to kill something that might have that information.'

'We can't sacrifice our own citizens, goddamit.'

'Wake *up*, Doctor Montoya. America sacrifices her own all the time. Always has, always will. We sacrificed enough of my friends in Vietnam.'

'We have a volunteer army now, Dew,' Margaret said. 'It's not the same thing. We don't have the draft anymore.'

'Which will last exactly as long as there are enough troops to fight the engagements we have.' Dew removed the bloody gauze and tossed it into a wastebasket. He pressed another batch in place, held it with his left thumb, then pulled out a suture kit with his right hand. He tore it open with his teeth and set it next to the keyboard.

'The very *second* we face a big enough threat, you know damn well that draft will be back,' he said. 'The few die so the many can live. That woman in there, she needs to die for that same reason.'

'I don't give a shit,' Margaret said. 'I'm not military. I am a doctor, and I do *not* sacrifice people. I'm going over your head.'

Dew removed the second batch of gauze, which was less bloody than the first. He pinched her torn skin together, picked up the pre-threaded needle and slid it through the flesh.

His hands were rough but warm. Gentle. She watched his technique: smooth, experienced.

'You've done this before?'

Dew nodded. 'Sugar, I've done this while people were trying to kill me. I've done it to *myself* while people were trying to kill me. This here is just a little ol' barroom brawl cut. Where did you learn to punch like that?'

'Boxercise,' Margaret said. 'I've never actually hit anyone in my life.'

Dew nodded again. 'You go over my head and you're out,' he said as he made the second stitch. 'It's not a threat to say you'll be put in solitary confinement until this thing is all over. I say it's not a threat because I know you don't care about punishment or pissing anyone off.'

'I don't.'

Dew made a third stitch. 'Still, that's what will happen. You'll be off the case and someone else will take over. Maybe that Doctor Chapman fella, maybe your old buddy Doctor Cheng.'

Dew made the fourth stitch, then looked her in the eyes. His face was only a few inches from hers. She felt his hands moving – he was tying off the stitch by feel alone.

'Whoever it is, they won't know as much as you, Margaret. They're going to have to spend time catching up, time we don't have. And they will probably miss something that could make all the difference.'

She looked away. He was right.

'We don't know what's coming through those gates,' Dew said. 'But whatever it is, it would *already* have come through if it wasn't for you. Thanks to your weather theory, we may even find the source of infection. If it's a satellite, we might be able to shoot it down. That's because of *you*. Margaret – we can't do this without you.'

'But Dew, that woman . . . it's going to be horrible.'

He nodded slowly. 'Yeah, it will. But we *need* to know. You're playing in the big leagues now, and part of the game at this level is knowing when you have to make a sacrifice.'

'That's easy for you to say,' Margaret said. 'This is what you're good at, right?'

Dew smiled. It was a smile full of bitterness.

'Among the best, I'm told. Kind of a dubious honor. Look, Doc, no matter what you say, what you do, or who you talk to, Bernadette Smith is going to die. All you can do is put up a useless protest and be pulled off the project. You get to keep your integrity, but at what cost to the country? To *humanity*? Tell me you understand that part at least.'

She did understand. Any protest would just be ignored, accomplish nothing – the Murray Longworth machine would roll over her. Things would continue, only less effectively. And as much as it made her hate herself, she wasn't going to let a wasted gesture take her off this project.

'I get it,' she said.

'If you think Gutierrez is making this call on a whim, if you think it's easy for Otto and me to execute it, then you're a fool. I hope you never have to make a call like this, Margaret. But if you do, you just remember – is one life worth the lives of hundreds? Of thousands?'

'We don't *know* that sacrificing Bernadette Smith is going to save hundreds of lives. Or even *one* life.'

Dew nodded. 'Exactly. We *don't* know, and that's why a decision like this is such a mindfuck.'

He stood up and started repacking the first-aid kit. Her hand was already bandaged. She hadn't even felt it. Had a few different cards been dealt, Dew Phillips could have been a world-class surgeon.

He started to walk out, then turned to face her. 'So shall I get Doctor Chapman to run things, or will you do your job?'

She hated him. She hated him more than she thought it possible to hate a human being, and almost as much as she hated Clarence Otto.

'I'll do it,' she said.

That bitter smile again.

Dew Phillips walked out of the control room, leaving Margaret alone to think about the coming nightmare.

ALL YOU NEED IS LOVE

Colonel Charlie Ogden stood in the command tent, looking over the maps and satellite photos spread across a central table. Corporal Cope sat on a stool. He had the forward-leaning posture of a bird of prey, waiting to pounce on Ogden's next order.

Ogden wondered if he'd get even his customary four hours of sleep that night. Probably wasn't time for it. And if he couldn't sleep, neither could Corporal Cope. Poor guy. But Cope was a young man; he didn't really need sleep. Sleep was for pussies.

Ogden checked his watch: 2130.

'Corporal.'

'Yes sir?'

'Any word from Doc Harper about private Climer?'

'Nothing yet, sir,' Cope said.

'How long ago was Harper in here?'

'About twelve hours, Colonel.'

'How long does it take to wake up from being shot in the fucking shoulder?'

'I wouldn't know, sir,' Cope said. 'I can look it up online if you like.'

'It was a rhetorical question, Corporal.'

'Yes sir.'

Maybe the kid did need some sleep after all.

'Corporal, any hits from the satellite search?'

'No sir,' Cope said. 'I'm all over them, as you requested. I'm on a first-name basis with the squints now, sir, although the name they have for me when they take my calls every fifteen minutes isn't Jeff, if you know what I mean.'

The squints were annoyed with thoroughness? Well, fuck 'em. They weren't on the front lines.

Ogden sipped lukewarm coffee, staring, thinking. He'd expanded the search area, applied every available resource, and still no sign of a gate. All the previous outbreaks had resulted in a construct somewhere within about a hundred miles. Granted, a hundred-mile radius made for a huge area, but they had dozens of air assets and dedicated satellite coverage. If something was there, they should have found it.

What really worried him, however, was the Jewell family. Ogden had no doubt the Jewells were at least partially responsible for the deaths of his men. Thus far the APB hadn't turned up a thing.

So where had they gone?

The tent flap opened. A soldier walked in, shirtless, wearing boots, fatigues and a white bandage around his left shoulder. In his right hand, he carried his M4.

'Speak of the devil,' Corporal Cope said. 'Dustin, how you feeling?'

'Fine,' Dustin said. 'I'm here to see the colonel.'

Ogden put down his coffee mug. 'You're wounded, son, and you're out of uniform. I told Doc Harper I'd come see you.'

'That's okay, Colonel,' Dustin said. 'I came for you. You're the one we need.'

'You get your ass back to bed, Private Climer,' Ogden said. 'I'll talk to you there. I don't want you out of Doc Harper's sight, understood?'

Climer stood tall and gave an exaggerated salute. 'Sir, yes *sir*! Doc Harper is right outside, *sir*!'

The kid was acting strange. Painkillers? Climer walked closer to Corporal Cope. The tent flap opened again and two men entered: Doc Harper and Nurse Brad. Doc Harper's nose was broken, white bone jutting up from a red gash. And yet he was smiling. Nurse Brad was smiling as well, his mouth hanging open at a strange angle. Drool dripped from his jaw, swinging in a long, glistening strand when he moved.

'*Sir!*' Climer screamed. 'We are here on a recruiting trip, *sir*! We want you to be all you can be!'

It all clicked home. How could he have been so stupid? Roznowski had *let* Climer live. The gunshot to the shoulder had just been camouflage to keep Climer under the radar as the disease took him over. That meant the disease was now *contagious*.

Charlie Ogden reached for his sidearm.

Nurse Brad and Doc Harper rushed forward.

Dustin Climer whipped his M4 in a horizontal arc, catching the slow-reacting Corporal Cope in the throat. Cope fell off his stool, coughing.

Ogden fired two shots. The first one went wide. The second one hit Doc Harper right in the forehead just as Brad connected with a flying tackle. Nurse Brad was a big, strong, young soldier, and the hit rattled Ogden's middle-aged body. As they crashed to the ground, Ogden heard Climer rushing toward them. Ogden tried to bring the gun around, but Brad grabbed his wrist with both hands. With his free hand, Ogden jammed his thumb into Brad's right eye. The eyeball popped, spilling clear fluid onto Ogden's hand.

Nurse Brad didn't let go.

He didn't stop drooling.

He didn't even stop smiling.

Another hand tore the gun free and pinned Ogden's arm to the ground. Something slammed into his stomach, and he suddenly found himself unable to draw a breath. Ogden tried to kick, tried to pull, but he couldn't breathe, couldn't fight against the two young soldiers pinning him down.

Climer's face seemed to float over his own, backlit by the tent's lights.

'Sir, yes *sir*!' Climer said. 'I want you to get your mind right, *sir*!'

Ogden felt hands on the sides of his head, holding it so he couldn't turn in either direction. Climer straddled his chest. His right hand held Ogden's forehead, pinning his head to the ground. Climer's other hand grabbed his chin – hard – and pulled his mouth open.

Then Climer leaned forward, leaned close.

Ogden would have said, *What the fuck are you doing?* if he could have breathed, if he could have moved his mouth, but he couldn't do either. All he could do was growl from deep in his throat.

Colonel Charlie Ogden saw Climer's tongue. Swollen. Covered in blue sores.

Triangular blue sores.

Climer's lips closed around his own, and Climer's tongue dove into his mouth. Wide-eyed in shock and confusion, Ogden tried again to get away. He tried to bite down but could not – Climer's strong hand held his lower jaw open.

Ogden felt the hot wetness of Climer's tongue fishing around inside his mouth. He felt the sting of a hundred needles.

Then he felt the *burning*.

Climer sat up, looked down at him, wiped his lips with the back of his hand and smiled.

Ogden's mouth was on fire.

'It won't be long now, sir,' Climer said. 'Not long at all.'

WELCOME TO DETROIT

'Mister Jenkins, are we there yet?'

'I think we're close, Chelsea,' Mr. Jenkins said.

Chelsea was tired of driving. She followed along on the map. The long trip from Gaylord, then driving all over the city, looking for just the right place. The Winnebago rolled down an empty St. Aubin Street. Headlights played off abandoned buildings and lit up broken pavement. A light wind blew wisps of snow, invisible until they crossed in front of the headlights, then invisible again as they swept past. Even with a couple of inches of snow, they saw trash everywhere: newspapers, Doritos bags, chunks of broken wood, piles of broken bricks speckled with bits of mortar like ocean rocks dotted with barnacles.

'You wanted a secret place,' Mr. Jenkins said. 'I think this area will do. This is the kind of Detroit we've been looking for.'

'There's no one down here,' Mommy said. 'It's like a ghost town. You'd think there would at least be homeless, squatters.'

'Winter is hard on them,' Mr. Jenkins said. 'Looks like these buildings don't have electricity, so no heat unless they build a fire.'

'What about gangs?' Mommy asked. 'Will we be safe here?'

Mr. Jenkins shrugged. 'Pretty much. Look around you. What are the gangs going to do here? Freeze their asses off, that's what. If we get out of sight and stay out of sight, we should be okay. It's like most cities, I bet – you don't fuck with people, people don't fuck with you.'

'There's that naughty word again, Mister Jenkins,' Chelsea said.

Mr. Jenkins hung his head. 'I'm sorry, Chelsea.'

The Winnebago turned right on Atwater Street. On their left was a small, mostly empty marina opening onto the Detroit River. Ahead on the right, they saw a lone three-story brick building surrounded by vacant lots filled with rubble, broken fences and tall grass weighed down by snow. A faded blue band ringed the top of the building, flecked with reddish-tan where spots of original brick showed through. The words GLOBE TRADING COMPANY were painted on the blue in faded white letters.

Chelsea liked this building. She liked it a lot.

'What about this place, Mister Jenkins?'

'Looks like no one's here,' he said. 'It's all boarded up. Could be some bums inside, but if so, we can take care of them.'

'Is there . . .' Chelsea searched for the words that Chauncey had given her. 'Is there a lot of concrete? Is there . . . *rebar*? Metal? Those things will make it hard to see us from space.'

'Oh sure,' Mr. Jenkins said. 'There will be lots of that.'

'Good,' Chelsea said. 'I think the dollies will like it here. Let's go inside and look.'

'Okay,' Mr. Jenkins said. 'Let's drive around the building and look for a door we can open up. We need to pull the Winnebago inside, or the police will see it in the morning.'

The Winnebago turned right on Orleans, and its headlights lit a man in the middle of the street. He was dressed in only a T-shirt and jeans, shivering like mad. Even in the dim headlights, they could see that his fingers were swollen and raw. Behind the man they saw the rear of a squat, jet-black motorcycle caked with frozen sludge, dirt and even some ice.

'Holy shit,' Mr. Jenkins said. 'It's freezing outside. That guy was riding a Harley? Is that an Ohio plate on that thing? Look at his fucking fingers.'

'Language,' Chelsea said.

'Sorry, Chelsea,' Mr. Jenkins said.

She reached out. The man's name was Danny Korves. He had lived in a town called Parkersburgh. That was a long ways away, and he was cold to the point where he would soon die.

'Mister Jenkins,' Chelsea said, 'go get that man and bring him inside. We need to warm him up.'

She didn't want Mr. Korves to be cold.

After all, if he felt cold, so would the nine dollies growing inside him.

Now that she had enough of them, she knew how long it would take to build the gate. Construction would begin almost as soon as the dollies hatched.

And that moment was only a few hours away, sometime around dawn.

DAY SEVEN

LEAD FROM THE FRONT

Agony. *Heat*. Brutal, shooting pain, his whole body on fire, his *brain* on fire.

Was he in hell? Charlie Ogden had caused enough death to qualify. Both the enemy and his own men. How many enemy soldiers? His best guess was over a thousand – the kill ratio in Somalia and Iraq had been so ridiculously high that it was hard to keep track.

The exact number didn't matter, did it? *Thou shalt not kill*. One death was the price of admission to hell; everything else was just overachieving.

A snippet of a picture flashed through his mind. Something black, wiggling. A snake? A centipede?

The heat in his brain grew even higher, which was impossible, because it couldn't *get* any higher. Ogden heard himself screaming, or at least trying to, but something in his mouth muffled his sounds.

The picture again. Not a snake . . . a tentacle.

A hatchling.

Were they there to kill him? To take revenge?

Hello . . .

A voice. More pictures, more images. Hatchlings. Hundreds of them, building something, *making* something.

Something beautiful. Something . . . *holy*.

The heat went yet higher. Ogden felt his brain *tearing*. AC/DC had once sung that *'hell ain't a bad place to be,'* yet Ogden knew that was some crazy shit, because he would have done *anything* to escape this endless agony.

Can you hear me?

The voice. The voice of an angel coming for him. The heat seemed to drop. Just a little, but even that tiny bit felt like a miracle.

Ogden made a noise that was supposed to be a *yes*, but through the gag it sounded like *yay!*

Hands touching his head, his *hot* head. The gag lifting. Fresh breath in his lungs. A foul taste on his thick, sore tongue.

Can you hear me?

'Yes,' Ogden whispered. Was the voice making the heat fade away? He loved that voice.

Good. We need you.

Ogden felt hands lifting him, sitting him in a chair. He looked around. There was Corporal Cope, beaming with love. There was Nurse Brad, drooling, smiling, a saggy-lidded socket where an eye used to be. There was Dustin Climer, grinning, nodding as if he and Ogden shared a secret. They *did* share a secret, the best secret the world had ever known.

Ogden took a deep breath, trying to handle the new emotions ripping through his soul. 'What do you need me to do?'

What you were born to do. Protect the innocent.

Ogden nodded. Protect the innocent. He'd done that his whole life.

We need your men in Deeeee-troit, the voice said. *You must hurry, but be careful. The devil will try to stop you. Stop you so he can get to me.*

Ogden shook his head. Cope and Climer shook theirs as well.

'They won't get you,' Charlie said. 'I won't let them.'

Good. Bring your weapons, bring your men.

'But . . . the men . . . they don't all feel like this. I think some won't see.'

Then you must show them love. Hurry, please hurry.

The voice seemed to wash away on a mental wind. It faded, but the love did not. Charlie Ogden knew what he had to do. He looked at Dustin Climer. 'How long did it take for me to see the light?'

Climer checked his wristwatch. 'You went under at twenty-one-thirty-five, sir. It's oh-four-thirty, so about seven hours. It only took Corporal Cope four hours to convert. Maybe because he's younger, sir.'

Ogden knew. He knew exactly when the gate would open. Chelsea had pushed that information into his head, a ticking clock to the beginning of heaven. He had a little over fifty-two hours to make it all happen.

'Corporal Cope,' Ogden said. 'Order all troops confined to barracks. Order First Platoon to prevent access to or egress from camp. No one gets in or out, not even a four-star general. Order Second Platoon to conduct detainment drills. They are to immobilize all men in Third and Fourth platoons. Tie them to their bunks, hands and feet. Inform all squad leaders from Third and Fourth platoons to cooperate without hesitation, that I'm evaluating the ability to restrain large numbers of able-bodied individuals. After this is complete, First Platoon is to return to their barracks and wait for further orders.'

'Yes sir,' Corporal Cope said. He moved to the radio.

Ogden turned to Climer. 'How many of us are there now?'

'Just us four, including you, sir.'

Ogden nodded and checked his watch. It would take about an hour to restrain Third and Fourth platoons and show them God's love. Add four to seven hours for the gestation period, and he'd have the first sixty men fully converted a little after noon.

His DOMREC men owned the airport. They could control all movement in and out. Gaylord was still evacuated – the only problems he might face would come from the police, emergency workers, or the media. Reporters were undoubtedly outside the checkpoints, waiting to come in with lights blazing and cameras rolling. He'd have to take his men out at night, using the same back roads they'd guarded since yesterday.

'Corporal Cope.'

'Colonel?'

'Start planning logistics,' Ogden said. 'At twenty-three hundred hours, I'm taking Platoons Three and Four to Detroit. Climer, you make sure Platoons One and Two complete the conversion process. By tomorrow they need to be ready to head to Detroit when I call them.'

'Yes sir,' Climer said.

'That leaves Whiskey Company,' Cope said. 'What about them, sir?'

The 120 fighting men of Whiskey Company. A wrinkle in his plans. He could convert them, but that would take more time, add risk. Might be best to just avoid them. Leaving them at the Gaylord airport, even after he moved all of X-Ray Company to Detroit, would maintain appearances for Murray and the Gaylord police. Not for long, of course, but now everything was about buying a few hours of discretion here and there.

'Tell Captain Lodge that Whiskey Company is to immediately take over all roadblock work and interaction with law enforcement,' Ogden said. 'Whiskey Company is *not* to interact with anyone from X-Ray Company. Tell

Captain Lodge about our detainment drills, and that I need to test Whiskey Company's ability to operate solo. He and Nails can handle things just fine. That will buy about a day, maybe two, before anyone notices that I'm gone.'

'Yes sir.'

'Come to think of it, Cope, you'd better stay here with Climer,' Ogden said. 'Everyone knows your voice, knows you deliver my orders. Who can come with me and operate as my communications man?'

'The most skilled would be Corporal Kinney Johnson, sir,' Cope said. 'But to be honest, he's not too bright.'

'He'll have to do,' Ogden said. 'Make sure he's in the next batch to be converted. Now get cracking.'

Ogden leaned over the table, staring at the map of Michigan. He could create only so many protectors in the next forty-six hours, and that number paled in comparison to the forces he would face.

Despite the odds, he had to find a way to win. It would take strategy. *Grand* strategy.

The kind that would put you in the history books forever.

DADDY IS SO SILLY

The building was perfect.

Rusted, once-white metal beams held up a peaked ceiling way above. There were holes in that ceiling. Through them Chelsea could see little patches of early-morning sky, tiny stars still flickering their fading light. She could see the *heavens*. It was such a long building – her Mickey Mouse watch said it took her thirty seconds to run from one end of the trash-strewn floor to the other. On one side of the building, a second deck and even a third deck looked out over a long, open, central area. There was lots of graffiti. Some naughty words, too. If anyone else came in to paint bad words, Chelsea would have Mr. Jenkins take care of them.

They'd found a big entrance in the back. Mr. Jenkins called it a loading dock. Up above was a metal roll-up door, stuck three-quarters of the way open. Mr. Jenkins said it worked exactly like a roll of paper towels, that people used to just pull it down, but it was rusty and broken. Grafitti-covered plywood blocked the rest of the entrance. Mr. Jenkins had to drive the Winnebago right into the plywood, and the whole wall fell in like one of those drawbridges in the princess stories. He drove over it, cracking the wood in many places, but then he and Daddy and Old Sam Collins and Mr. Korves were able to put it back up again.

The Winnebago was inside, safely out of sight. Which was good, because right about the time they put that plywood back, Chelsea sensed that the dollies were almost ready to come out and play.

Chelsea made Mr. Jenkins put all the dolly daddies side by side in front of the Winnebago. The rising sun was already spreading a little light into the building through the small holes in the roof, but she wanted the daddies in the headlights so she could see everything. Their heads were closest to the Winnebago, all their tootsies pointed away. Kind of looked like nap time at summer camp.

Mr. Jenkins tied them up.

He tied up Daddy, Mr. LaFrinere, Mr. Gaines, Old Sam Collins and Danny Korves.

Mommy took one of Mr. Jenkins's knives and cut off their clothes.

They all shivered a lot. A little bit of snow had blown into the building, fine white powder drifted up against fallen boards and broken bricks. Every now and then, a gust of wind found a way through the walls and the boarded-up windows, swirling the powder in slow arcs.

Then the dolly daddies all started screaming. That was annoying. Chelsea told Mommy to stuff their mouths with some of the cut-up clothing. That helped.

Chelsea sat down and watched.

They were all tied up, but they still kicked and thrashed around. Everyone except Daddy. Daddy was looking at Chelsea. His eyes seemed very sad. He was trying to say something. He wasn't screaming like the others, even though the dollies on his arm were starting to bounce in and out.

Chelsea stood and walked over to him. She pulled the piece of T-shirt out of his mouth.

'Chelsea, honey,' Daddy said. It was hard to understand his words because he was breathing so hard. 'Please, baby girl, make . . . make them stop.'

Chelsea laughed. 'Oh *Daddy*! You're so funny.'

'No, honey, I'm . . . I'm not joking with you.'

The triangles bounced out farther, making interesting moving shadows on the far wall. Daddy's face scrunched shut. He ground his teeth and let out a little noise.

'It will all be over soon, Daddy.'

His eyes opened again. They blinked so *fast*. He was breathing like he'd just come back from a run.

'Chelsea . . . you have power over these things. You can make them stop . . . you can . . . shut them down.'

One of Old Sam Collins's hatchlings popped free. It arced through the air, lit up by the headlights. How *pretty*!

The muffled screams got louder.

'Chelsea!' Daddy yelled. 'I'm not . . . not kidding around. You *stop them* or you are in *big trouble.*' Tears leaked from his eyes. Snot bubbled from his nose. He started to kick. The triangles on his arm were coming out really far now.

'Daddy, God wants them to come out. Why would I stop them?'

'*Because I'm going to die, you little bitch!*' Daddy's chest heaved. His eyes opened and shut, opened and shut. 'Please, Chelsea! Oh my God it *hurts*! They're screaming in my head. *Please! Make it stop.*'

One of Daddy's hatchlings popped free. Daddy screamed really loud. He was just confused, that's all. Now he got to go to heaven. Anyone who *really* believed in heaven would be happy to die. Why, the longer they lived, the more chances they might do something bad, then wind up in hell. She didn't understand why people prayed to God to stay alive. It just didn't make any sense.

He drew a big breath to scream again, and Chelsea stuffed the T-shirt back into his mouth.

'I love you, Daddy,' she said. 'Say hello to Jesus for me.'

Daddy's screams stopped a few seconds later.

Chelsea walked around, picking up the little hatchlings and taking them inside the Winnebago. She wanted to make sure they were safe and warm.

THE DOLLY MAMA

Bernadette screamed so hard that flecks of blood flew out of her mouth. The containment-cell walls would have muffled most of the sound, but Margaret had insisted that the room's microphones pump the audio throughout the comm system.

If the men were going to let Bernadette Smith die, Margaret would make sure they heard every last second of it.

Dew was there. So was Clarence. Daniel Chapman was there as well, holding a handheld high-def camera. The two fixed cameras built into the containment cell would catch everything, but Dan had his in case they needed specific shots. Dew had asked Perry to come; Perry hadn't shown.

Only an hour earlier, Perry had told Margaret what to expect. She wasn't surprised he'd taken a pass.

'Nine thirty-seven A.M.,' Margaret said. 'The triangles are beginning to move.'

She watched, horrified, as the triangles, now inch-high pyramids, started to bounce up and down under Bernadette's skin.

'Sweet Jesus,' Dew said.

'Don't you look away,' Margaret hissed.

Somehow, Bernadette found the energy to scream even louder.

The triangles bounced out farther, stretching her skin, tearing it. Little jets of blood shot out from the edges.

'Please *help me*! Make it stop! Make them stop *shouting in my head*!'

'Doctor Chapman,' Margaret said, 'put that camera down and sedate that woman.'

'Do *not* do that, Chapman,' Dew said. 'It could damage the triangles.'

Margaret turned to look at Dew. Her anguished soul longed for any excuse to look away from Bernadette, and this one fit the bill.

'Dew, you fucking *bastard*. We're *torturing* that woman!'

'I'm not going to take a chance your potions will kill the hatchlings,' Dew said. 'This will be over soon.' Even as he spoke, he stared unflinching at the dying woman.

'Nine forty-one A.M.,' Dan said. 'Patient is going into V-tach.'

Those words made Margaret snap around to look in the cell, made her instinctively take a step forward before she remembered that she wasn't allowed to save the patient.

But Margaret could take away her pain.

Everyone in the trailer wore a hazmat suit – sealed, airtight, protected. Margaret moved to the containment cell's door and started punching buttons on the touch screen.

First the # sign, then 5, then 4, then 5, then—

Strong hands grabbed her wrists and pulled her away.

Clarence's hands.

'Margaret, stop it!'

She struggled against him, but it was useless. He was too strong.

'Let me go, you *monster*!' How could she have been so wrong about him?

Dew leaned forward to look at the touch screen, then at Dan. 'What was she doing?'

Dan looked away.

'Dan,' Dew said. 'Answer me, now.'

'She was trying to do an emergency decontamination,' Dan said. 'If she hits another five, every decontam nozzle in both trailers starts spraying. It would kill everything not wearing a hazmat suit, including the patient.'

Dew turned to look at Margaret. 'You spell out the word *kill* to do that? Cute. Otto, don't let her go. We have to finish this.'

Dew turned back to the horror show inside the containment cell. Margaret did the same – she didn't want to watch, but she had to.

The triangles bounced out almost a foot before their tails and Bernadette's ravaged skin pulled them back. The one on her chest jumped up and down like the heart of a cartoon boy who's just seen the cartoon girl of his dreams.

The one on her hip tore free first, shooting across the tiny room to hit the wall. Barely an inch high, it wiggled on the floor, black tentacles writhing in a soupy combination of human blood and purple slime.

Her arm went next. The hatchling severed the artery as it launched free, spraying blood all over the clear containment-cell wall. The heartbeat monitor beeped out an erratic, panicked pace without rhythm.

The chest triangle finally broke its fleshy tether, shooting upward on a geyser of blood that splashed against the ceiling.

Margaret heard the droning monotone of the EKG machine sounding out a flatline.

'Shut that fucking thing off,' Dew said.

Dan lowered the camera and quickly punched a button on the panel. The flatline sound vanished, leaving only silence.

Margaret put her gloved hands against the transparent wall. Blood drops trickled down the inside of the glass, rolling toward the floor. They left little see-through streaks of red.

The three hatchlings tried to stand on weak tentacle-legs. They managed a few wobbly steps, filling the air with strange clicking sounds. Gradually they slowed. Their black, vertical eyes blinked slower and slower, heavy-lidded, sleepy, until they closed and the little creatures stopped moving.

Margaret rested her helmeted head against the glass. She checked the red clock on the far wall.

'Time of death, nine forty-four A.M.,' she said weakly. 'I hope it was worth it, Dew. I really hope it's worth it.'

Dew still hadn't moved. He stared into the cell, stared at the body. 'It's not, Margaret. It never is.'

EYES ON THE PRIZE

It was only a matter of time now.

The Orbital had long since mapped all human satellites capable of detecting its presence. It had also identified a few ground-based observatories that might be able to see it. In all, the Orbital tracked eleven devices that could spot it, if only they looked in the right direction.

And now five of them were.

One was unfortunate, but not a cause for concern. Just random chance. Two was pushing the boundaries of coincidence and meant it had possibly been spotted. As the day progressed, the Orbital saw a third, then a fourth, then a *fifth* device point its way.

There was no question: the humans knew.

It was only a matter of time before they attacked. The probability tables rated this at 100 percent. The same tables predicted a 74 percent chance that the first attack would destroy the Orbital.

It had some defenses, but it was small and designed for stealth and reliability, not combat. It could not fight an entire world.

The Orbital had prepared Chelsea as best it could. It would probably be up to her to finish the doorway. Chance of success? Incalculable – the Orbital simply did not have enough data.

The Orbital ran through the tables and arrived at the final entry in its extensive decision tree. If a planet could resist colonization, detect the Orbital and attack it, then that planet qualified as a long-term threat.

A threat that had to be eliminated.

The Orbital began to modify its final probe.

PEEKABOO, WE SEE YOU

Gutierrez walked into the smaller Situation Room like a suit-wearing cage fighter rushing to the ring, aggressive and excited to get it on. Tom Maskill and Vanessa Colburn trailed in his wake, the boxer's entourage shining with their own intense auras.

Ah, Murray thought, *the energy of youth.*

Gutierrez, Maskill and Colburn slid into their seats. Donald Martin and all the Joint Chiefs were already present. A full house once again.

Murray was thrilled that Vanessa had made it – he wanted her to see this.

'Okay, Murray,' Gutierrez said. 'I just cut short a meeting with the Russian ambassador about this Finland crisis to hear your urgent news, so let's go.'

'Mister President,' Murray said, 'Montoya's weather theory panned out. We think we've located the source of the infection.'

Murray called up a map of the Midwest on the Situation Room's big screen.

'This is the location of the first construct,' he said. A red dot appeared at Wahjamega, Michigan. 'These blue dots represent approximate locations of the hosts seven days before we attacked that construct, and the green lines represent wind direction.'

Gutierrez studied the map briefly, then nodded.

'And here is the same information for the hosts associated with Mather, South Bloomingville, Glidden and Gaylord, Michigan.' As Murray spoke each city's name, he added a yellow dot to the map. 'This information provided enough data to triangulate a specific search zone.'

Murray tapped some more keys. The map zoomed in on a grid that included southwest Michigan, northwest Ohio and northeast Indiana.

'But that's still a huge area,' Gutierrez said.

'Yes sir,' Murray said. 'But it helped us focus the hunt. It took our image-processing computers three days to identify visual anomalies, but by doing so, we found this . . .'

Murray clicked the keys again. The map vanished, replaced by a grainy photo of what looked like a translucent, teardrop-shaped rock pointed at both ends.

All of them, including Vanessa, sat back in their chairs. Murray felt like a conductor reaching the emotional apex of a symphony. The room filled with excitement and relief. They finally had a target; they could finally *hit back*.

'Son of a bitch,' Gutierrez said.

'NASA is convinced it's artificial,' Murray said. 'It's very small, about the size of a beer keg.'

'How could we not have seen this?'

'There's a lot here we don't understand, sir,' Murray said. 'The thing is stationary, hovering forty miles above South Bend, Indiana. The object seems to bend light around it – which makes it basically invisible, but the image analysts identified a visual fluctuation. They had to write a program that combined images from five different sources, then create this computer-generated model.'

'So this isn't a real picture?'

'No sir,' Murray said. 'They explained it to me with an analogy. Imagine a contact lens dropped in a swimming pool. It's not actually invisible, but if you don't know the contact lens is there, you're never going to see it. If I tell you to look in one corner at the shallow end, forget the rest of the pool, look for something that might stand out just a little, and you had a dozen people helping you, eventually you'd see the lens and figure out what it is. NASA doesn't know how the thing can just hover there. It doesn't drift. It should take a ton of energy to keep something stationary like that, yet it doesn't give off an energy signature. That's supposed to be impossible.'

'How impossible?'

'As in contrary-to-the-laws-of-physics impossible,' Murray said. 'But it's there all the same.'

Gutierrez stared at the fuzzy double teardrop up on the screen. 'Are there more of these objects?'

'Now that they know exactly what anomalies to look for, they're doing global searches. This object appears to be the only one of its kind.'

'Why us?' Gutierrez asked. 'Why not Russia? Or China? What does NASA say about that?'

'They think it was just bad luck, Mister President. If this really is an alien craft, it probably locked in over the first landmass it found. We'll probably never know, unless you want to try to communicate with it.'

'Communicate?' Gutierrez laughed. 'It's already *communicated*. Its message is loud and clear. This is amazing. Murray, your team is just *amazing*. And no, I don't want to try to communicate with this thing. I want to blow it out of the goddamn sky.'

'We thought you might choose that option,' Murray said. 'General Monroe?'

Murray sat as the air force general rose to discuss his attack plan. Murray looked across the table, and saw that Vanessa was watching him, not the screen. She wore her normally cold expression, but Murray was learning how to read her. On her best day, she couldn't hope to ever match the show he had just put on, and she knew it. Did the corners of her mouth reveal just a touch of envy?

He turned his attention back to the screen and watched General Monroe outline his strategy.

GENERAL CHARLIE OGDEN

No point in calling himself a colonel anymore. As Chelsea's top military leader, now he was truly a *general*. He could promote Cope while he was at it, but why bother? *Corporal Cope* had such a nice ring to it.

'What's the latest from Whiskey Company, Corporal?'

'Captain Lodge reports zero traffic at all checkpoints,' Cope said. 'He suspects that your readiness drill is actually a way for you to get X-Ray Company in heated tents while his men stand out in the cold. Sergeant Major Nealson also called, wanted me to tell him on the sly if you had an op planned and if he could get in on it.'

'And what did you tell him?'

'I told him this was just a boring drill, sir,' Cope said. 'And I took the liberty of suggesting that if he snooped around for more information, you'd have him on the first transfer back to Fort Bragg.'

Ogden smiled. Cope showed initiative, and Ogden needed that kind of person around. Better a clever corporal than a stupid lieutenant.

'Pack up my things, Corporal. I'll be leaving tonight.'

Cope moved off to pack Ogden's clothes and effects.

General Charlie Ogden couldn't wait for nightfall. He couldn't wait to drive down to Detroit, to actually meet Chelsea. But it was only 1430, and he couldn't make the sun move faster across the sky. He needed the time to plan, anyway.

Forty-six hours to go.

If the gate opened up undetected, everything would work out fine. General Ogden's job, however, was to assume that the gate would not go undetected.

The primary threat remained the Division Ready Force from the Eighty-second Airborne. Six hundred soldiers probably eight hours away from parachuting in on top of any trouble spot. He had at best 120 men – no matter what strategy he created, he couldn't hold out for long against five-to-one odds.

That meant he had to make sure any battle ended before the DRF could fully respond. An eight-hour window.

Far inside that eight-hour window, however, sat the other two DOMREC companies waiting at Fort Bragg. Two hundred and forty men he'd led himself. If alerted, they could deploy in Detroit potentially within *two* hours. How could he keep them out of the game entirely?

And even that didn't account for the forces already in the area – Detroit police, cops from surrounding suburbs, SWAT teams and Michigan State Police. Not as heavily armed, not as well trained, but a lot of guns was still a lot of guns. He'd also have to find a way to tie up all of those.

If conflict came, Ogden would have no air support. His men would face Apaches, Ospreys, F-15s and probably even a squadron of A-10 tank-killer fighters stationed at the Selfridge Air National Guard Base thirty minutes north of Detroit.

So that was the scenario. Do everything possible to keep things quiet, to keep a fight from breaking out. If a fight *did* break out, he had to choose the battlefield, delay the troops from Fort Bragg, tie up the Detroit police, keep the gate hidden from air support *and* make sure the gate was wide open and pumping in angels well inside of the eight-hour DRF window.

A general's stars certainly didn't come easy.

'Corporal Cope,' Ogden said, 'when you're finished packing, get on the line with the companies at Fort Bragg. I want to arrange an immediate transfer. The Exterminators have been fighting hard. It's time to rotate out some troops.'

MCDONALD'S RUN

So many dollies! Chelsea sat in the back of the Winnebago, hatchlings crawling all over her. Their black tentacles tickled. It felt like little kisses, like she was covered head to toe in smoochies. They would walk on her, then jump around, maybe cling to a curtain or go eat a piece of the daddies. Mr. Jenkins had put some daddy parts on plastic so his Winnebago carpet wouldn't get messy, but the triangles' tentacle-legs were still tracking spots of blood all over the place.

Chelsea stood, carefully, so as not to startle the dollies, and walked to the Winnebago's small fridge. There was a portable TV on top, black and white with a tiny screen playing the seven o'clock news. She'd watched some cartoons on it, but cartoons didn't really interest her that much anymore. The grown-ups watched the news, and Chelsea was surprised to find that she liked it.

There were only three ice cream bars left in the little fridge. Those, half a jar of mayonnaise, and a wrinkled hot dog that might have been older than Chelsea herself. She pulled out an ice cream bar, tore off the paper and started eating, but her stomach rumbled for something other than dessert.

Mister Jenkins and Mommy, come here.

Seconds later they ran through the door and shut it behind them to keep out the cold. They were both shivering.

'Whoa,' Mommy said. 'They're bigger already.'

'The dollies are growing fast,' Chelsea said. 'Pretty soon they will start building the gate. Are you getting enough stuff?'

Mr. Jenkins nodded. 'There's a lot of wood in this building. I spent the whole night dragging in sticks and bushes, stuff like that.'

'And I found a lot of trash,' Mommy said. 'Mister Burkle is out collecting as well.'

Chelsea smiled. Mommy and Mr. Jenkins sounded like they knew what to do.

'Mommy, I'm hungry,' Chelsea said. 'I want McDonald's.'

'I don't know if there's one around here,' Mommy said. 'Besides, it's dark out.'

'But I *want* McDonald's!'

Mommy took a step back. She was scared. She *should* be scared – Daddy was gone, but Chelsea could make Mr. Jenkins use the spanky-spoon just as well as Daddy had.

Mr. Jenkins pulled out a cell phone. 'Give me a second, Chelsea. I'll Google it and see if I can find one, okay?'

Chelsea nodded. 'And I want ice cream bars. Lots of them.'

'I saw a party store not too far from here,' Mommy said. 'I could go grab food there.'

'Found one,' Mr. Jenkins said, looking up from his phone. 'It's a couple miles from here.'

'Go get me McDonald's, Mommy. I want McDonald's.'

'Your mother shouldn't go,' Mr. Jenkins said. 'This is a bad neighborhood. It's nighttime. A woman on her own out there . . . won't do well. I'll walk, but it's two miles away, so might take me an hour and a half.'

'Can you take Mister Korves's motorcycle?' Chelsea asked.

Mr. Jenkins shook his head. 'No, I don't know how to ride.'

'Then walk,' Chelsea said. 'And make it fast.'

Mr. Jenkins nodded rapidly.

'Do you have enough money?' Mommy asked.

'I'll find an ATM,' he said. 'I'll stock up. We're going to be here for a few more days.'

'Two more,' Chelsea said. 'Two more days, and then the angels come. Now get going, and don't you *dare* forget the ice cream.'

Mr. Jenkins ran off, his fat shaking with every step. Mommy ran out behind him before the Winnebago door could even close. They did what Chelsea said, and that was as it should be.

They *all* did what she said – all but one.

Chelsea closed her eyes and spread her mind, reaching out. Where was he? Where was the boogeyman? Was he thinking of her? Was he *afraid* of her? If not, she would *make* him afraid.

She found him, but she couldn't connect. Something was blocking her.

Chauncey.

What are you doing, Chauncey? Are you stopping me from scaring the boogeyman?

I told you not to connect to him.

And I told you you're not the boss of me.

Chelsea, the destroyer is not a toy. He has stopped

**t h e   a n g e l s   f o u r   t i m e s .   I f
h e   f i n d s   y o u ,   h e   w i l l   k i l l
y o u .   W h e n   y o u   c o n n e c t   t o
h i m ,   y o u   r i s k   e v e r y t h i n g .**

Chelsea felt angry. Not just at the boogeyman but at Chauncey.

No one can tell me what to do. Not anymore.

Chelsea waited for him to reply. He didn't. Instead, hundreds of images smashed into her brain like rapid-fire visual lightning. Images of the boogeyman burning hosts, strangling them, hitting them, *killing* them.

Chauncey, stop it.

She started to shake, yet the images kept coming, images of soldiers shooting dollies, stabbing them, stomping them. Pretty dolly bodies smashing, purple stuff squishing out in long, gloopy jets.

Chauncey, no!

She couldn't breathe, yet still the images came. Images of gates, beautiful gates, exploding, disintegrating, breaking into tiny pieces and the pieces rotting to blackness. She felt that pressure in her bladder again . . .

Okay, I won't contact him. I promise!

The images stopped.

Chelsea took a deep breath. The boogeyman, he wasn't a game at all. He was death. For-*real* death, not movie death.

**N o w   y o u   u n d e r s t a n d .   I f
y o u   c o n n e c t   w i t h   h i m ,   y o u
b r i n g   d e a t h   u p o n   y o u r
p e o p l e .**

She ran her hand down to where her bathing suit went. The front of her pants was a little damp. Chauncey had caused that, but it wasn't his fault. He wasn't the one who killed, who burned, who destroyed. He wasn't the one who had made her pee her pants a second time.

It was the boogeyman's fault.

And sooner or later, she would make him pay.

NO MEANS NO

Another dark night at the ruins of Clan Jewell. Cold as shit. Again. Dew hated the cold. He, Margaret and Perry stood in what had once been the Jewells' kitchen. A bright half-moon lit up the snow in a silvery light. Barely an inch of fluff already covered most of the blackened remains, a layer of white sitting on top of cindered chunks of wood and warped appliances.

They stood there, out there in the cold, because Perry still refused to go inside the trailer. He wouldn't go near the hatchlings.

'Perry, they're locked in individual cages,' Margaret said. 'They can't get to you.'

She had changed; Dew could hear it in her voice. So much anger in her now, so different from the Margaret Montoya he'd met months ago. She'd been devastated after Amos's death, but now? Now an unhealthy dose of rage brewed in her little chest.

'There's no way they can get out of those cages,' she said.

'It's not . . . not that,' Perry said. His words sounded strained, broken, as if he had to work to complete a sentence. He stood still, but his upper body bobbed slightly back and forth.

'Perry,' Dew said, 'you got to sack up.'

Perry shook his head. Shook it *violently*. Made him look like a retarded dog.

'Look,' Dew said. 'Something is blocking you, but if you're close to the triangles, you can hear?'

Perry nodded. 'Yeah, when I was standing right there, I could hear them. I could hear *her.*'

'That's the point,' Dew said. 'We don't know where the next gate is, Perry. The Jewells have to be there. If we find them, we find the gate. Chelsea talked to you. You have to go back in there and see if she makes contact again.'

'You have to do this,' Margaret said, her voice tight and cold. 'We are *not* going to have let that woman die for nothing.'

Perry shook his head again. His eyes remained wide, his nostrils flaring with each breath.

'Perry,' Margaret said, 'you've fought through so much. Tell me why you're afraid of this little girl.'

'She's not a little girl anymore,' Perry said. 'She's something else. She can . . . she can make people do things.'

'We're with you, kid,' Dew said. 'We'll be right there, okay?'

'The answer is *no*, Dew,' Perry said. 'You have to stop asking me to go in there. You just have to.'

'Those hatchlings are in their own little cages,' Dew said. 'They can*not* get to you. You need to stop being such a pussy and—'

Dew never saw Perry's hand. Not even a blur. One second he was shaking and nodding like a rabid Saint Bernard, the next Dew felt a cast-iron vise on his throat and his feet dangled a foot off the ground.

'You don't get it!' Perry screamed. 'You just *don't* get it!'

Dew clawed at Perry's fingers, trying to isolate one, to bend it back and break it, but even the kid's *fingers* were strong. Dew couldn't pry one free.

Margaret grabbed Perry's arm. She might as well have swung from a tree limb for all the effect she had. 'Perry! Put him down!'

Perry shook Dew. *Shook* him. Dew's vision blacked out for a moment, then came back – he only had a few seconds left. He kicked out, clumsily, trying to get his actions under control. One foot connected, but he'd kicked Margaret, not Perry.

She grabbed at her left thigh and fell to the ground. Dew suddenly found himself down there as well, coughing and spitting. Perry was so big, so strong, so *fast*. Dew now knew it had been nothing but dumb luck he'd won that fight.

'I'm not afraid of what *she'll* do to *me*!' Perry screamed. 'I'm afraid of what she'll make *me* do to *you*!'

Dew rolled onto his back and looked up. Sooty snow melted into the seat of his pants. Perry was bent over him, staring down with insane eyes. Saliva flew when he talked.

Perry jabbed his finger repeatedly into his temple, punctuating his words.

'Don't you get it? They *rewrote* my fucking *brain*! And when I go near those triangles, I can *hear* her. She's fucking powerful, man. I don't want you to end up like Bill. She told me to *kill* you!'

Dew hawked a loogie and spit. It came out thick with blood. 'So why didn't you?'

Perry didn't say anything. The insanity slowly left his eyes.

'Why?' Dew said. 'If she's so powerful, why didn't you kill me when she told you to? Why didn't you kill me just now?'

'Because . . . because you can take me. You can beat me up.'

Dew laughed, but the pain in his throat changed the laugh to a cough.

'Kid, you could have broken my neck just now. You didn't. So if this little girl has control over you, why am I still alive?'

The insane look faded away completely. Perry stood straight, stared at Dew for a few more seconds, then turned and walked away.

Margaret rose to her knees. Her hands held her left thigh, and her face was wrinkled with pain. 'You kicked me.'

'Sorry,' Dew said. 'My aim was off. I can't imagine why.'

Dew slowly got to his feet, then reached down and helped Margaret up.

She let out a long breath. 'Jesus,' she said. 'You're not the most sensitive guy in the world, are you? *You need to stop being such a pussy?* Did you really think that was going to motivate him somehow?'

'He's a guy,' Dew said. 'That kind of thing usually works with us.'

Margaret shook her head. 'Can't you men ever just *talk* something out?'

'You're right, women are so much more logical,' Dew said. 'Maybe I should have shown him my boxercise technique.'

Margaret rolled her eyes. 'Fine. You've got me there. But hear me, Dew. Marcus and Gitsh are in the trailer mopping up Bernadette's blood. You *will* get Perry to go in there and talk to those things, or that woman died for nothing.'

She pointed her finger in Dew's face. 'Do you understand me?'

So much anger in those eyes. She didn't even look like Margo anymore. This was a new woman, one he'd helped create.

'I understand,' Dew said. 'I'll get through to him.'

Margaret walked back to the trailer, leaving Dew alone in the burned out, snow-covered kitchen.

TWO ALL-BEEF PATTIES

Rome sat slunk down in the driver's seat of his Delta 88. The car was turned off, but even if it had been on, it would have been cold as hell because the heater hadn't worked in months. His eyes were just high enough to look out the driver's-side window, across Orleans Street, at the fat man with the red beard walking along a waist-high fence. Wasn't even a sidewalk there, just a snow-covered grass strip, the fence, then trees on the other side. White guy in the wrong neighborhood, at night, carrying a big white McDonald's bag in each hand.

'Are you kidding me?' Rome said quietly. 'Doesn't this motherfucker know where he's at?'

In the passenger seat, Jamall shook his head. 'He must not. White guy walking *here* at night? Alone? After hitting an ATM? It's like he *wants* to get robbed.'

'Hope he got some Big Macs,' Rome said. 'I'm hungry.'

The man wore jeans and a long-sleeved plaid shirt. Not only did he seem oblivious to his surroundings, he also seemed oblivious to the cold. Every four steps or so, his breath shot out in a big white cloud that lit up from the few working streetlights.

'I'll tell you what,' Rome said. 'Somebody has a *serious* fucking hankering for McDonald's.'

They'd been watching an ATM on Mack Avenue, looking for an easy mark. This guy had walked up on foot and taken out money. Looked like a *lot* of money. Rome and Jamall then watched him go into McDonald's. Five minutes later he'd walked out with the two big bags. The man turned south on Orleans and had been walking for fifteen minutes straight. Rome even drove a block past Orleans, to St. Aubin, then several blocks south to get ahead of the man, then cut back on Lafayette and finally up the other side of Orleans. Here the street was barren, a parking lot on one side, the long stretch of trees on the other. He'd parked and they'd waited, seeing if the man was stupid enough to keep walking down such a deserted area.

He was.

It just didn't get any easier than this. And that made Rome nervous. 'Am I missing something?' he asked after the man had gone a half block past the Delta 88. 'For real, this guy is *alone*?'

'He's just going straight,' Jamall said. 'Not even enough sense to walk on a main road. Dude must be in a hurry.'

'No one here,' Rome said.

Jamall nodded. 'No one. You said you wanted a sure thing, man. It don't get more sure than this. We gonna do this, we gotta move. Let's go get paid.'

Jamall and Rome got out of the car and left the doors slightly open. That wouldn't give them away, because the dome light didn't work. They pulled their guns, Rome a simple .38 revolver, Jamall his fancier Glock. They ran across the empty street and came up on the man from behind.

He heard them, because he turned – and when he did, he found two guns pointing at his face.

'Gimme your wallet!' Rome said. He held the .38 in his right hand. His left he held out, palm up.

The man just stared at him.

Jamall made a show of pulling back the Glock's slide, then pointed it at the man's face again. 'You give my man that wallet, or it's your ass. And put them bags down – we're takin' those, too.'

The man turned to stare at Jamall. White as a sheet, big red beard – he couldn't possibly look more out of place. Had to be a tourist or something like that. Or maybe a retard, because he didn't look scared. Not even a little bit.

'No,' the man said.

Fury crossed over Jamall's face. Rome got nervous. Jamall didn't like it when people told him no. Especially white people. Rome chanced a quick look up and down the street. No one there, but this was already taking too long.

'I'm only gonna tell you one more time,' Jamall said. 'Put down those bags and give my boy your wallet. If there's enough money in it, I won't kill you.'

'No,' the man said. 'I can't. I still have to get ice cream bars. Chelsea will be mad if I don't come back with ice cream bars.'

Jamall took two steps forward and put the barrel of the gun on the man's forehead.

'I don't give a fuck about your ice cream bars,' Jamall said. 'Put down the motherfucking bags.'

The man knelt a little and set the bags on the snow-covered grass, then stood. He *still* didn't look scared. Rome didn't like this shit, not at all. Usually people crapped their drawers when you pulled a gun on them. This guy looked like he'd had a gun to his face so many times it bored him. Fuck the money, Rome wanted out of there.

The man reached back with his right hand.

'That's it,' Jamall said. 'Real slow, gimme that wallet.'

The man's expression didn't change. He reached up with his left hand, grabbed Jamall's gun and lifted it until the barrel pointed into the air. It wasn't a fast move, but it wasn't slow, either: just smooth. No hesitation. Jamall seemed to freeze for a second, almost in disbelief that someone could be so stupid as to fuck with him, and then he tried to pull the gun free.

It was only then that Rome saw the man's other hand coming out from behind his back, coming out with that same speed, that same confident smoothness – and holding a gun.

The man put the barrel against Jamall's stomach and pulled the trigger.

The sound was like a cap gun. It didn't sound real. Jamall's face twitched, more in surprise than in pain.

Smooth as before, the man raised his gun up under Jamall's chin and pulled the trigger twice.

Then the man's throat started spraying blood. At first Rome thought Jamall's blood was spraying on the man, but Jamall wasn't bleeding that much – he just wobbled for a second, then fell.

The fat man dropped the gun and put both hands to his throat. His expression didn't change. The guy *still* looked bored, even as blood seeped between his fingers.

The man turned to face Rome.

Rome had fired his .38. That's what had happened. Smoke curled from the stubby barrel. He hadn't even known he'd fired, but he must have. He'd shot the man right in the throat.

The man blinked a few times, then knelt, one knee on the ground. He reached back with his hands and eased into a sitting position. Blood continued to pour out of his throat, some of it splattering on the white McDonald's bags. The blood stained his collar and his shirt, dripping from his red beard.

'I wish,' the man said quietly, 'I wish you could know the love.'

Then he lay down on his side and stopped moving.

The blood slowed to a soft pulsing.

Rome saw the man's wallet in his back pocket. He looked at it for a second, then his common sense returned in a flash of panic. He'd just *killed* that man. Armed robbery, that made it murder one. He looked at Jamall. Jamall was dead. *Fuck!* Jamall? How could *Jamall* be dead?

There were no sirens. There wouldn't be. No one called the cops around here for a few gunshots.

Rome's heart hammered away. His breath came fast and deep. This was so fucked up.

He reached down and grabbed the man's wallet. It was thick with cash. Rome put the wallet in his pocket. He looked up and down the street. Cops wouldn't come, not unless someone drove along this street and saw two bodies on the ground. Cops would be out fast then, real fast. Rome looked at the waist-high fence. It was torn open just a few feet away.

Run, or cover it up?

He put his .38 in his pants, grabbed the fat man's arm and dragged him to the fence. Dude must have weighed 250. Rome pulled the cut fence aside and ducked under the cross-post, dragging the man's body through. He ducked back out under the fence, then saw the trail of blood on the snow.

Fuck. Someone would see that as soon as the sun came up. Still, that gave him plenty of time.

But there was one body left.

Rome looked at his dead friend. He'd known Jamall since they'd both been ten years old. Rome had seen people die before, but not *his* friend.

He felt a tear slide down his left cheek.

'I'm sorry, man,' Rome said as he grabbed Jamall's wrist and started to drag. 'I promise I'll look out for your mom. I hate to leave you here, but I gotta get out. I'd expect you to do the same, man, you *know* this.'

Jamall didn't say anything. He just stared up at the sky as he slid along.

Rome dragged Jamall's body under the fence. He didn't put Jamall right next to the fat man, but rather about five feet away. He could do at least that much for his friend. Rome slipped under the fence one last time, grabbed both McDonald's bags and hurled them over. Finally, he grabbed the guns and ran back to the car. He could ditch them in the river.

Less than five minutes after they'd first approached the man, Rome drove his car down the empty street.

LIKE LEGOS

Chelsea made Mommy and Mr. Burkle leave the Winnebago. She sat very still, very quiet, and focused all her attention on Mr. Jenkins.

She could sense his location. She could send Mommy to him . . . but it was too late.

Chelsea felt his life slip away.

Death.

She'd felt the deaths of Daddy, Mr. Beckett and Ryan Roznowski, but this was different. They were vessels, their only purpose to carry the dollies. Mr. Jenkins was like her. He was *converted;* they were *connected.*

She took a deep breath and tried to deal with the amount of information flowing through her mind. It wasn't easy. The infection had spread to many of General Ogden's men. She constantly drew knowledge from them, searching their brains for new information.

Now she knew words that most seven-year-olds would probably never have heard, and definitely not understood.

Words like *collective organism.*

Mr. Jenkins had been part of that collective.

Chauncey, what will happen to Mister Jenkins now?

He will decompose quickly, so that no one can study him and use him against us.

But what will happen to his . . . to his interface? To all the little parts of you inside of him?

They are designed to destroy themselves as his body shuts down.

But we can use them.

No, Chelsea, they must decompose. Do not go near him. Stay hidden.

Chelsea thought. She reached out with her mind, connected with the little things inside Mr. Jenkins's body. Could she? Yes . . . yes, she could.

Chauncey, I can change them. I can put them in different orders, like Legos.

Chelsea, I command you to stop this.

Chelsea ignored Chauncey. She loved God, but maybe God up in Heaven didn't know how things worked down here on Earth. She sent a strong signal to the bits and pieces inside Mr. Jenkins, a signal in the form of two images.

One image of Mr. Jenkins, fat cheeks smiling, as he looked when he was alive. He was to stay that way. They were not to make him decompose.

The other image was of her favorite flower.

DAY EIGHT

ICE CREAM WITH A GOD

At 0315, General Charlie Ogden's Humvee rolled up to a battered plywood wall in a formerly abandoned building on Atwater Street in Detroit, Michigan. The plywood wall moved aside, the Hummer rolled in, and the plywood wall was put back in place.

The other vehicles would arrive soon. Ogden had ordered them to split up, come at the building from different routes, arrive at different times. A convoy would have drawn too much attention, but one green Humvee here, another there . . . at this hour no one would give a shit. As long as his men were under cover by 0500, they'd be fine.

The Hummer rolled deeper into the large, decrepit old warehouse, solid tires crunching on debris of wood, glass, trash and broken masonry. Two vehicles over by the far wall – a white and brown Winnebago and a filthy Harley Night Rod Special.

Standing in front of the Winnebago, a little blonde-haired angel.

The motion of dozens of knee-high hatchlings, scurrying about on black tentacle-legs.

And the most important thing of all.

Eight curving columns in two parallel lines – four on the right, four on the left. The parallel opposites leaned toward each other. When they were finished, they would form four beautiful arches. Fat hatchlings sat on top of the columns. Each hatchling grabbed the top of a column with its tentacle-legs, then squeezed out a foamy brown material that hardened almost instantly. Each squeeze seemed to grow the column by six inches, maybe as much as a foot. If it hadn't been blasphemous to think of such a thing, Ogden might have said it looked like the hatchlings were building the arches with their own shit.

When the hatchlings finished excreting, they looked thinner, triangular sides sunken in. The newly skinny hatchlings scurried down, instantly replaced by other fat ones. The skinny ones ran to piles of wood or to trash or to half-eaten, bloody corpses. They lowered themselves onto these things. Sharp, cutting parts slid out of their triangular bases and they started eating, pulling material up inside themselves with frightening speed.

The gate: never had the world seen something as perfect, as beautiful.

The sound of small feet crunching on broken glass drew Ogden's attention away from the hatchling flurry. It was the little angel, her blonde curls bouncing with each step. She held an ice cream bar in each hand.

'Hello, General Ogden,' the girl said. 'I'm Chelsea.'

He knew this, because hers was the voice he'd heard in his head when he converted, when he'd been planning, driving. Just looking at her filled his heart with love.

We've been waiting for you.

She spoke right into his mind, spoke with that voice of love and wisdom.

'Hello, Chelsea. I like your motorcycle.'

Then it's yours. Mister Korves doesn't need it anymore.

She was love incarnate. She was everything.

We've been waiting for our protectors, General. Are you ready to protect us?

She handed him an ice cream bar.

'Yes, Chelsea,' Ogden said. 'I'm ready.'

COPS, STARRING SANCHEZ AND RIDDER

Officer Carmen Sanchez had a bad feeling about this one. A report of bloody snow and two bodies. He felt grateful for the subzero temperature. Morbid, sure, but dealing with a frozen body was preferable to finding one that had cooked in Detroit's summer humidity for a few days. Sometimes these calls were crap, but after ten years on the force you got a hunch for which ones were the real deal. Sanchez had that hunch now.

The cruiser's bubble lights flashed as his partner, Marcellus Ridder, pulled off to the side of Orleans Street. Headlights illuminated chewed-up snow.

Snow streaked with frozen red. Streaks that led toward a fence and the trees beyond. And just past the torn fence, two bodies – one black, one white.

Neither of them moving.

Ridder put the cruiser in park and grabbed the radio handset. 'This is Adam-Twelve, responding to reports of bodies on Orleans Street,' he said. 'We have two men down. Send ambulance and backup immediately. We're examining the scene.'

A ten-year-old boy had seen the bloody snow, found the bodies, then walked to a gas station and called the police. What a ten-year-old boy was doing up at four in the morning, Sanchez didn't want to know. Strict parenting didn't always happen in these parts.

Ridder put the handset back in its cradle. They both got out of the car, guns drawn and pointed at the ground. Ridder knelt behind the cruiser's open driver's-side door, while Sanchez did the same with the passenger door.

'Police! Do not move!' Sanchez screamed in his loudest cop voice. 'Stay where you are! If you can hear me, kick your right foot!'

Their caution probably seemed silly to most people, because both men looked very, *very* dead, but this much blood meant weapons, probably guns, and Detroit police do *not* fuck around with something like that. Either one of the men might rise up at any second and start shooting.

'I said move your right foot!' Sanchez screamed. That's the way it usually went – Ridder did the driving, Sanchez did the yelling. To each his own special skills.

'We gotta check them out,' Sanchez said. 'Ready?'

'Ready,' Ridder said.

'I'll take the white guy on the left. Go!'

Sanchez scooted around his door and moved toward the prone white man. He kept his gun pointed at the ground but angled forward, so he would only have to raise it a couple of inches should the man pop up with a weapon.

The Caucasian corpse was overweight, with a frost-lined red beard and brown eyes that stared blankly into nothing. The eyes had frozen open. A small bloody hole dotted the right side of his throat. His shirt, especially the collar, looked stiff with frozen blood.

Still-wrapped Big Macs littered the area.

Ridder knelt next to the black guy.

'This guy's dead,' Ridder said. 'No pulse, cold to the touch.'

Sanchez reached down to feel for a pulse, fingers probing

under the beard, feeling the fat man's neck. The skin was cold and firm, but not stiff – the man hadn't frozen solid yet. Sanchez felt the jawline, reached under it and pressed.

Then a sound like a soft cough.

The sensation that his fingers had popped something, a small bubble.

A thin cloud of gray lifted up and away from the man's beard.

Only then did Sanchez see it – little blisters on the corpse's neck, hands, even some on the forehead. He'd popped one, and this gray powder shot out and drifted through the air like fine pollen.

'Aw, *fuck*,' he said. 'What the fuck is this?'

He backed away from the corpse, left arm bent, left hand held away from his body. He flung his hand, snapping his fingers outward. The powdery substance flew from his skin and floated in the air.

Ridder looked at him. 'What the fuck happened, Chez?'

'This guy has blisters,' Sanchez said. 'I think I touched one. It popped like a puffball or something. Fucking *gross*!'

He holstered his pistol 'Get the first-aid kit. Oh man, this is so fucking nasty. Fucking asshole probably has AIDS or something. It's a fucking AIDS blister. I should have been wearing gloves.'

Ridder ran to the cruiser and opened the trunk. He pulled out the first-aid kit.

Sanchez stopped and looked at the hand for a second, wondering if he actually felt what he thought he was feeling. He was. It wasn't his imagination, his hand felt hot. *Real* hot.

'AIDS doesn't have blisters,' Ridder said as he took a clear plastic alcohol bottle out of the kit.

'Yeah? Then why does this fucking *burn*? Hurry up!'

Ridder doused the hand with alcohol, then handed Sanchez some gauze.

'Wipe it off,' Ridder said.

'Oh, ya fucking think?' Sanchez wiped at the hand.

Ridder opened a belt pocket and pulled out surgical gloves.

Sanchez looked at the gloves in Ridder's hand as he continued to wipe his skin. 'That's not going to fucking help me now, you asshole.'

Ridder took a step back. 'Well, *I* don't want AIDS.'

'You said AIDS doesn't have blisters!'

'I don't fucking *know*, okay?'

The burning sensation grew. Sanchez had vacationed in Jamaica once, with his second wife, and while swimming had put his left hand through a jellyfish. That's what this felt like, a persistent stinging/burning pain that steadily increased.

'Oh man,' Sanchez said. 'That was so goddamn sick. Shit, this *burns*.'

Ridder stared at the hand. 'Uh, Chez,' he said. 'Remember this morning's briefing? About that shit in Gaylord?'

Sanchez stopped wiping. His eyes widened in fear.

'Flesh-eating shit? You think I got that flesh-eating shit?'

'I don't know, man,' Ridder said. 'Just relax.'

'*You* fucking relax!'

'Look,' Ridder said. 'We've got that test kit, that swab thing. Go use it on that guy.'

'Me? I think I'm fucked up enough here.'

'Well, if he's got it, then you already got it,' Ridder said. 'Why the fuck should *I* get it?'

Flesh-eating disease . . . was that supposed to burn? If not, what *did* burn? This came out of a dead man's skin, for God's sake.

'Dude, this *hurts,*' Sanchez said. 'You've got gloves on, just check him!'

'No fucking way. Let the paramedics do it, they're trained for that stuff.'

Sanchez could already hear the sirens. The ambulance would be here within minutes, but he couldn't wait. He had to know now. 'Come on, man,' he said. 'Just do the test.'

He took a step toward Ridder. In the blink of an eye, Ridder was backpedaling, drawing his weapon and pointing it at Sanchez.

'You stay the fuck away from me,' Ridder said. 'Stay right there!'

Sanchez did just that. His own partner, drawing down on him. This was messed up. This was how people got shot. 'Okay,' he said. 'I'm not moving. Just relax, Ridder, and stop pointing that gun at me.'

Ridder didn't stop, not until the ambulance arrived and the paramedics took over.

PUTTIN' ON HER
WALKIN' SHOES . . .

Margaret and Dew sat in the computer room, watching the flat-panel screens. *Note to self,* Dew thought. *Never let the sentence 'How can it get worse?' enter your mind again.*

Murray had just sent the live feed from Detroit's Channel 7 News Eye in the Sky. The screen showed a road that ran parallel to a strip of snow-covered trees. Looked like an abandoned railroad track that had long since grown in. Near an area where the old track ran under an overpass, Dew saw a pair of unmarked blue semi trailers.

Another MargoMobile. Parked in the open. In a major city. Shit on a saltine wouldn't have tasted this bad.

The caption at the bottom of the screen said, POSSIBLE CASE OF FLESH-EATING DISEASE IN DETROIT.

Dew put Murray on speakerphone.

'Okay, Murray,' Dew said, 'we've got the picture. What's going on?'

'Be quiet and listen up,' Murray said. 'I've got something else going on over here, something big, so I don't have much time. We have a positive cellulose test in Detroit, but it is not – I repeat, *not* – a triangle infection. This might be similar to the Donald and Betty Jewell case. No ID on the man, fingerprints came up negative. Right now he's a John Doe. As you can see, the story has already leaked, so we're in damage-control mode. I'm sending a chopper for Margaret and her team.'

'But I can't leave now,' Margaret said. 'We *killed* that woman to get hatchlings, and now we've got them.'

'I don't have time for your opinion,' Murray said. 'Just listen. The man didn't die from the disease. He was shot in the throat sometime last night. He has not – I repeat, has *not* – decomposed. The cop who found the body was checking for a pulse when some kind of blister popped. Paramedics didn't go near the body, but they tested the cop a few hours later, and *he* was positive.'

'It's contagious,' Margaret said quietly. 'It finally happened.'

'That's why I need you there ASAP,' Murray said. 'The math is simple. We have triangle hosts killing people in Gaylord, so Ogden stays. Dawsey is the only one who can talk to the captive hatchlings, and since I'm not about to move those things across the state *or* let Dawsey out of Dew's sight, they both stay. This Detroit case doesn't have a triangle infection that we know of. No triangles means no gate, so we need to evaluate before we take any drastic action.'

'I agree,' Dew said.

'I didn't ask for your opinion, either,' Murray said. 'Margaret, it will attract too much attention to drop you right on the site, so we're landing you at Henry Ford Hospital a few miles away. You'll drive in. The MargoMobile crew already has the John Doe and the cop loaded in. They will move the rigs someplace secure.'

'You can't move them,' she said. 'At least not far. We need to check the area, see if the contagion vector is still there.'

'Margaret,' Murray said, 'you're looking at feed from a *news helicopter*. We have to get the trailers out of sight.'

'Then move them someplace close,' Margaret said. 'If there's one case, others could be in the same area.'

'Fine,' Murray said. 'I'll get someone on it. Dew, get Dawsey to talk to those hatchlings again. I don't care what it takes. Cut off his finger if you have to. I need to address something else, so neither of you call me unless you have actionable information.'

Murray hung up.

'Wow,' Margaret said. 'I've never heard him like that before.'

'I have,' Dew said. 'It means he's been up all night working on something big. What you just heard was the normally calm, cool and collected Murray Longworth stressed out to the max.'

The computer room door opened, and Otto rushed inside. 'Margaret, there's a chopper coming in. Pilot radioed down, says he's here to take us to Detroit. He's landing now.'

'Get Gitsh and Marcus,' she said. 'Let's go.'

Otto vanished.

Margaret turned to Dew. Her eyes burned with anger, intensity.

'If this thing is really contagious,' she said, 'we're in a whole different world of shit. The country needs to know. The *world* needs to know.'

Christ on a crutch. As if Dew didn't have enough problems. The New & Improved Margaret Montoya wanted to go public. Trouble was, if it actually *was* contagious, she was 100 percent right. Murray's skulduggery had its place, but the time for that was almost up.

'Examine it first,' Dew said. 'Before you do something silly, can you give it twenty-four hours?'

'Why the fuck should I?'

'Just do your job,' Dew said. 'Evaluate, like Murray says. This time tomorrow, you still think going public is the right thing to do, I'll do it with you.'

She stared at him, her expression a mixture of hatred and disbelief. 'Why would you throw away your career like that?'

'Because Murray has more people like me,' Dew said. 'And if you try to go public against Murray's will, one of them might just pay you a visit.'

EXPENDABLE

Chelsea's knowledge grew and grew.

She now understood why Chauncey had been sent. He wasn't a person. *Organic* material, like people or plants or puppies, couldn't survive the trip, not the way Chauncey had traveled.

Organic material could survive a trip through a gate, but there was a catch – the *gate* was biological. Like a plant. That meant they couldn't send a gate the same way they'd sent Chauncey.

Such a funny problem, and it grew more complicated from there. Each of the hatchlings had a...a...a *template*. What a neat word, although she still didn't understand what that meant, exactly. Some kind of a *template* to make material for the gate. The templates had been shipped with Chauncey. They were a part of each triangle seed. Their number was *finite* (another neat word!), which meant that the hatchlings could not replicate themselves like the crawlers could.

And the little crawlers that spread through people's bodies, converting them? What wonderful creatures! But they weren't creatures at all, not like snails or bugs or kitties. They were just collections of pieces. Like Legos. You could put the pieces together in different ways. You could make the pieces do different things. Way cooler toys than Legos, actually.

She wandered through the minds of the people in her . . . her *network*. So many interesting things! Many naughty things, too. She would address that later. One mind stood out above the rest, a mind that combined logic and creativity – General Ogden's. She found herself spending more and more time in there as she waited for the gate to open. She learned much. General Ogden seemed obsessed with something called *contingency plans*.

Most of her network consisted of soldiers. General Ogden thought that most of those soldiers, including himself, would die defending the gate. He thought of his soldiers as *expendable*. If they all died, though, or even if the numbers of converted dropped just a little, what would happen to Chelsea's mind? To her knowledge?

She did not know. And therefore she needed a contingency plan of her own.

The soldiers were very, very important, with training and experience at shooting things. There were only two people left in her network who were not soldiers.

Mommy and Mr. Burkle the Postman.

Mr. Burkle was a man. He was stronger than Mommy. That made Mommy the weakest person in the network.

Which meant Mommy was the most *expendable*.

Chelsea breathed slowly and reached out with her thoughts. It wouldn't be that hard, really, to modify Mommy's purpose. It had worked with Mr. Jenkins.

Chelsea concentrated, connected with Mommy's crawlers and began to move the pieces around.

MARGARET ARRIVES

The trip to Detroit felt like an eternity, even though it took just over an hour.

She had spent so much time cooped up in the MargoMobiles, or out in the middle of nowhere, that she'd almost forgotten what a city looked like. Detroit wasn't much of a skyline city, not a lot of tall buildings, although coming in you couldn't miss the five towers of the Renaissance Center and a few other downtown skyscrapers she couldn't name. The city seemed to radiate from there, spreading north and west from the Detroit River, suburbs stretching out for miles and miles.

Margaret, Clarence, Dr. Dan, Marcus and Gitsh landed at the Henry Ford Hospital helipad. From there, two agents whisked them to an unmarked van, and ten minutes later they drove down East Lafayette Street.

'We're coming up on the intersection of Lafayette and Orleans,' the driver said. 'The crime scene is on your left. CDC has it locked down nice and tight.'

Big concrete dividers, the kind used in highway construction, completely blocked the entrance onto Orleans. About a half block farther, she saw the biohazard tent that had been erected over the murder location. That tent would stop any breeze from spreading the contagion, if it hadn't blown around already. It also blocked curious eyes. A few people in biohazard suits moved in and out of the tent. The site was as secure as it could be.

The next street was St. Aubin, and they turned south. That put the tree-packed old railroad track on the van's right side. More trees and apartment buildings ran along the left side of the road. Apartments, cars everywhere – so many people moving about, a recipe for disaster if this contagion was wind-borne, like the strain that had infected Perry. A left on Jefferson, six lanes of major traffic rolling through Detroit, then a quick right (which was, curiously, still St. Aubin). Abandoned factory buildings stood oppressive and desolate. A right on Woodbridge, and then a right after another abandoned factory, and the van turned into a wide dirt lot. The overpass directly in front of her was Jefferson again, she realized, and they drove under it into a long ditch. Steep, tree-packed slopes rose up on either side, ending in black chain-link fences. Margaret realized that now they were *in* the old railroad track that ran parallel to Orleans. Under the next overpass, wedged in past the thin trees, Margaret saw two blue semis parked side by side.

'Nice work,' Clarence said to the driver. 'You can't see this from up top.'

The driver nodded. 'Yes sir, and it's only a thousand feet from the crime scene.'

'What about the news helicopters?' Margaret asked. 'Anyone see the trailers pull in down here?'

'No ma'am,' the driver said. 'We called an air-security alert, forced the news choppers to clear out. And your two semis took a pretty roundabout route to get here. We made sure they weren't followed.'

They parked beneath the deep shade of the overpass. Snow-speckled trash littered the area. Graffiti-covered walls sloped up either side to support the road above.

'Nice little vacation spot,' Dr. Dan said. 'I should bring my girlfriend here. Impress her with my metropolitan style.'

'Not the time for humor,' Margaret said. 'Let's get in there and get samples from Officer Sanchez and the John Doe, ASAP. We need to see if they have crawlers, and if they do, how we can kill the things.'

She hoped her hunch was right, that she could disrupt the cytoskeleton of the crawlers and stop this new infection. She hadn't been able to save Betty Jewell. She'd lost Amos. She'd stood by while Bernadette Smith screamed for help.

Even though she had yet to see him, she'd be damned if she had to lose Officer Sanchez as well.

CLIMER SPREADS THE FAITH

Private Dustin Climer peeked out of the tent that held Second Platoon. Some of those Whiskey Company guys were lurking around out there. Maybe they knew. Maybe they were spying.

They'd get theirs soon enough.

Climer turned back to look at his handiwork. He was behind schedule, but in a few hours the last of the Exterminators would be ready to roll. Most of them had already been converted. Those who hadn't were sleeping, sweating, trying to twitch, but they couldn't move much with their hands and feet zip-tied to their cots.

He turned to look at Private Pickens and Private Abbas. They'd been out on a patrol, filling in for a couple of sick Whiskey Company guys. Climer had had to wait for them to get back. As soon as they did, he ordered them in here, where ten soldiers jumped them, gagged them, tied them down.

Pickens was squinting and blinking, shaking his head, trying to scream through the sock stuffed in his mouth. Looked like he'd just received the smoochies.

Abbas was fighting his ass off. Even with his arms and legs tied down, it took two men sitting on his chest and thighs to control him. A smiling, one-eyed Nurse Brad bent over Abbas's head. Brad leaned closer for the kiss. Abbas fought even harder. Two sets of hands grabbed his head, pried his mouth open. Brad pulled the sock out of Abbas's mouth – the bound man made a strange kind of coughing noise, maybe meant to be a scream, and then Brad gave him God's love.

That was the last of them. Another five to seven hours and all of X-Ray Company would be ready and able to serve General Ogden and Chelsea.

JOHN DOE

Margaret Montoya had her hands full.

A naked, overweight, red-bearded John Doe lay on her autopsy trolley. Golf-ball-size pustules dotted his body. When she'd entered the trailer three hours ago, the pustules had only been the size of big marbles – even though he was dead as dead can be, the shiny, thin, air-filled growths had continued to slowly expand.

While they'd been preparing him for examination, many of the pustules had popped or torn open, leaving gaping pink sores all over his skin. Each burst spread a pollenlike substance that drifted in the air, coating the walls and counters and equipment with thin layers of gray dust.

When she looked at that dust, she saw her worst fears. This dust, this *contagious* dust . . . it might very well be the end of the world. It was nothing but pure luck that Officer Sanchez had found the body when the pustules were still small, the size of pencil erasers. Pustules that size didn't contain as many spores. The longer the corpse sat, the more the pustules grew, the more dust they contained. They might grow so large they could infect multiple people in one shot. And if some of those people moved to other parts of the city, or beyond into the state, to other cities . . . then there would be no stopping it.

Gitsh mopped the floor while Marcus sprayed the other surfaces down with concentrated bleach. Dr. Dan had already taken samples from the unconscious Officer Sanchez and was now gathering them from the John Doe's body. Dan leaned in close, trying to cut free one of the air-filled pustules without breaking it. This was his third try, as evidenced by the two thin spots of gray powder already dotting his face shield.

The John Doe had tested positive for cellulose, yet he wasn't rotting. No apoptosis. Why? The disease *knew*. It knew it had found another way to spread. Rapid decomposition no longer served a purpose.

Margaret dragged her gloved finger across the surface of the autopsy trolley. She held the fingertip in front of her, examining the gray powder.

Correction, the gray *spores*.

'Dan,' she said, still staring at the powder on her fingertip. 'Keep gathering samples. I'm going to run the battery of tests to see what can kill the crawlers you got from Officer Sanchez.'

'You better take a look at this first,' Dan said. He was standing now, no longer hunched over. He had one hand on John Doe's jaw and was peering into the dead man's open mouth.

Margaret walked to the other side of the trolley and looked in. The man's tongue was swollen and covered in small blue triangles.

'Smurf tongue,' Dan said. 'Nothing else on his body looks like this. What do you think it is?'

Margaret grabbed a scalpel and a sample container.

'I think,' she said as she sliced out a little chunk of tongue, 'that we're looking at a contagion vector.'

'But what about the pustules?'

'The pustules form after death,' Margaret said. 'The tongue must spread the disease while the host is still alive.'

'Ewww,' Dan said. 'You're thinking they *lick* you?'

She shrugged. 'No way of knowing. We'll have to see if the same sores develop in Officer Sanchez. If they do, we know we have a continuing vector, one host to the next. Marcus, assist Dan. Gitsh, keep mopping and wiping everything down. Clarence, are you suited up?'

'Yes ma'am,' she heard in her earpiece. 'I'm in Trailer B right now, with Officer Sanchez.'

'How is he?'

'Conscious now, but still kind of out of it. Complaining of a fever and body aches. He doesn't want to be strapped down, but he understands. I think as long as I'm here with him, he'll be okay. I can do that unless you need me to do something else.'

'I don't need anything from you,' Margaret said. 'Just stay there and stay out of my way.'

She hadn't forgiven him for Bernadette. She wasn't going to. Clarence Otto was just like the rest of these heartless butchers.

Dew, Murray, even Perry. Their business was death, and Clarence was one of them. Margaret's business was life.

And that's what she would give to Officer Carmen Sanchez.

PERRY GETS HIS GUN

Perry did pull-ups on the branch of a fat oak tree in the Jewells' front yard.

One after another, pull, lower, pull, lower. He didn't cheat, either, didn't let his body just drop – the let-downs took twice as long as the actual pull-ups. His breath crystalized in front of him each time he reached the top. Everyone kept bitching about the cold, but he loved it. He wasn't far from where he'd grown up. Hell, he'd played against this town back in high school, the Cheboygan Chiefs against the Gaylord Blue Devils. This weather wasn't *cold*, it was *home*.

Pull, lower.

He looked at the rope swing farther down the branch. Snow covered the little wooden seat. He wondered if Chelsea had sat on that.

Maybe her dad had pushed her.

Maybe she'd laughed.

Pull, lower.

He had to find her. He knew that, but at the same time he didn't want to go anywhere near her. He'd felt her power, exponentially higher than that of the hatchlings that tried to tell him what to do. They were merely a nuisance, but she . . . she pulled at something deep in his soul.

He didn't know why her commands felt different. They just did. If she grew more powerful, he really didn't know if he could stand against her.

The sound of footsteps in the snow. He recognized the heavy-footed rhythm of a man with a limp.

'Dawsey,' Dew said. 'I have something for you.'

'You missed Christmas,' Perry said. 'Trying to make up for lost time?'

'Something like that. You know why I'm here.'

Pull, lower.

'I'm not fucking going in there, Dew, so forget it.'

'It's contagious now.'

Perry stopped in mid-pull. He looked at Dew, then dropped to the ground. He stumbled a little from the pain in his knee, then stood tall and crossed his arms.

Dew nodded. 'They found some John Doe in Detroit. Cop found his body. Cop touched him, then tested positive for cellulose. Things just got even worse. You have to go in there and talk to the hatchlings, maybe see if you can reach Chelsea again – Perry, you have to find the gate.'

'I . . . I can't, Dew. I can't face them.'

'You can,' Dew said. 'I'm not much for emotional stuff, kid. But I got to tell you, I think you're the toughest bastard I've ever met. The shit you've fought through would have broken guys like Baum and Milner, probably even guys like me. You have a warrior's soul, Perry. You've got my *respect*. I will fight with you against this shit, and I will die before I let anything get you. Do you understand that?'

Dew's eyes burned with intensity. Perry wasn't much for emotional stuff, either, but Dew's words kicked up a knot in the back of his throat. Bill Miller was the only guy who'd ever stood by him like that. So had Perry's father, in his own fucked-up way. But Bill was dead. So was Daddy.

'I can see you're about to sob like a little girl,' Dew said, 'so let's get this conversation out of borderline-gay land and move it back to practicality. You're scared of what these things might make you do, but I *know* you can beat them. In fact, I'm willing to bet my life on that. So here's your present.'

Dew reached into his shoulder holster, pulled out his .45 and handed it to Perry butt-first.

Perry looked at it. 'You want me to shoot my present?'

'No, college boy, this *is* your present.'

Perry stared at the scratched weapon. It seemed to glow with well-oiled love. Dew had shot Perry in the shoulder with that gun. And in the knee.

Dew had carried that .45 in Vietnam, and every day since.

This wasn't just a *present*. Perry was a worthless psycho, a failure. He didn't deserve something this significant.

'I can't take it,' Perry said. 'You've had that for like thirty years.'

Dew nodded. 'That's long enough, I think. It's yours now. It's fired thousands of rounds without a problem. Guaranteed to work. So you take this gun. You go in there, and you sack up. You do what you have to do, no matter how scared you are. And if you can't take them jabbering in your head, you've got my permission to send them back to whatever hell they come from.'

Perry reached out and took the gun. The grip felt cold, worn and smooth.

'Yeah, it's loaded,' Dew said. He extended one finger and gently moved the barrel away from his chest. 'So how about trying not to kill me by fucking accident, okay?'

Perry laughed. It sounded strange to him. He looked at the gun, then looked at Dew.

'Let me spell it out for you,' Dew said. 'The Jewell family has been at large for at least thirty-six hours. They could be in any of two dozen states, even Canada. Maybe they already popped and their hatchlings are building a gate as we speak. We also have a second strain of infection that's contagious. We're out of time. We need to find the Jewells. We need to find that gate. So I'm only going to ask you one more time – do you want to go in that trailer and face these things that have fucked you right in the ass, or do you want to go hide your head for the rest of your life? My respect you've got, but my time? I don't have any left. You either step up, right now, or you just leave and let me do what needs to be done.'

Dew was on his side, but Dew also had a job to do. Perry understood – he was either part of that job, or Dew wanted him gone.

Perry felt like maybe, just maybe, he actually did deserve some respect. He felt human again, and there was only one person responsible for that.

His friend, Dew Phillips.

'Whatever you need,' Perry said. 'I've got your back, whatever it takes. Let's get this over with.'

PERRY PULLS THE TRIGGER

Before they went in, Dew gave Perry a side holster for the .45. He also gave him four full magazines, which fit into little canvas pouches fixed to the holster's straps. At seven rounds a magazine, that gave him a total of thirty-five rounds. Not that any amount of bullets could make him feel safe.

Perry walked into Trailer B, Dew right behind him. They both wore biohazard suits. Perry's felt even more suffocating than before. This was it, his dramatic showdown with the monsters – he felt as if the trailer should have been poorly lit, half dark, maybe a bulb or two flickering sci-fi movie style, but everything was bright-white as fuck. The first thing he saw was the empty containment cell. Gitsh and Marcus must have hosed it down or something, as all of Bernadette's blood was gone.

Perry turned left, toward the back, toward the body lockers. On the floor in front of those lockers sat three small glass cages, each a two-foot cube.

Inside those cages, he saw them.

They saw him.

Sonofabitch.

Things just like this would have ripped out of his body if he hadn't destroyed them first, if he hadn't cut up the Magnificent Seven. They would have killed him just like Fatty Patty's triangles killed her. That's how close he'd come to death. His body shook. He forced himself to look at the .45, to make sure the safety was on – he was trembling so bad he might squeeze the trigger without even knowing it.

'Easy, kid,' Dew said as he came around to stand on Perry's left, close to the gun hand. 'Just breathe. They can't get out of those cages. You're in control.'

We will kill you.

The hatchlings had grown massively since tearing out of Bernadette Smith's body the day before. Then their triangular bodies had been maybe an inch from top to bottom – now they were a foot high or more. Each tentacle-leg looked as thick as a fat baby's arm, long and flexible, full of speed and strength.

Kill you kill you killyoukillyou.

Their eyes *stared* at him, all black and shiny and full of hate, one vertical eye on each of their three pyramid sides.

His hand tightened on the gun.

Yessss, use the gun. Kill the man.

'Perry, are you hearing them?'

Perry nodded.

Shoot him. Shoot him, shoot him shoothimshoothim.

Their words meant nothing, the delusional jibber-jabber of pure evil. The hatchlings were just worker ants – Chelsea was the queen.

'Where is she?' Perry said.

Silence.

'Tell Chelsea I'm coming for her,' Perry said. 'Tell her I'm going to help her.'

He still felt that grayness, that fuzziness, although he could hear these hatchlings clear as day. But *just* them.

Beyond them, nothing. Maybe he could antagonize them, get them to connect to Chelsea. They were like antennae into the larger network, a way to punch through the jamming if only Chelsea would do her part.

He is the Columbo, kill him kill him now killllhimmmmm.

'Dew, they want me to kill you,' Perry said. 'Why don't you say hi?'

'My name is Dew Phillips. I have the authority to speak on behalf of the president of the United States of America. Cease your hostile actions, and we can negotiate. What is it you want?'

The hatchlings stopped staring at Perry. Instead, they stared at Dew.

Kill him.

'What did they say?'

'They still want me to kill you,' Perry said. 'They don't have much of a vocabulary, I'm afraid.'

Dew nodded. 'First of all, you nasty bastards are the ugliest pieces of shit I have ever seen.' His voice built in intensity, a hoarse gravel coloring his words. 'I don't know if you little fuck-stains can think for yourselves, but I will tell you that my patience is already gone. Now, last chance . . . what do you want?'

We want to kill you. We want to kill you all. Kill Columbo, kill him nowwww!

'More of the same?' Dew asked.

Perry nodded.

'Shoot one,' Dew said.

Perry turned to look at Dew. 'What?'

'Shoot one of these fucking things.'

No! Shoot him shoothimshoothim shoot yourself do it doitdoit

'Perry, you need to show these things who's boss,' Dew said. 'You've got to show them some discipline.'

Yes. *Discipline*. These things had fucked with a Dawsey, and you did *not* fuck with a Dawsey. Perry raised the gun. He noticed that his hand wasn't shaking anymore.

No no no no no no no no no

He emptied the clip into the middle cage. Bullets punched through the thick glass in spiderweb-crack splashes and shredded the hatchling's plasticine body. Seven .45-caliber bullets, all direct hits. The creature twitched a little, spasming amid splatters of purple fluid before it slumped, motionless.

Perry felt the adrenaline gush through his chest, felt a tingle in his fingers and toes. It felt like crushing a quarterback. Oh, God, did that ever feel *good*.

The two remaining hatchlings flailed inside their cages, trying to get away. They slammed themselves against the glass over and over, tentacle-legs whipping so fast he could barely make them out.

'What do you think, kid?' Dew said. 'How did that feel?'

'My freshman year we were at Notre Dame,' Perry said. 'I blindsided Tommy Pillson, knocked him out cold, caused a fumble that I ran back for a touchdown. The whole stadium booed me. Pillson had a concussion. I ended his season. They showed the hit over and over again on ESPN. Chris Berman said I was *made of mean*. On national TV, said I was *made of mean*. And that feeling was nothing compared to this.'

Dew smiled and nodded. 'Now you're getting it. Let them ponder what just happened. We'll come back later and see if we can make any progress.'

'Do we have to kill another one?'

Dew shrugged. 'One can always dream. I imagine that's enough personal growth for one day. Come on, *made of mean*, you need a beer.'

DANDELIONS

Margaret stared at the flat-panel monitor mounted on the wall of the narrow autopsy room. The picture showed a split screen of two microscopes, the right side containing the powder from one of John Doe's pustules, the left containing a tissue sample from Officer Sanchez's hand.

'Oh man,' Dan said. 'That is so totally fucked up.'

The sample from Officer Sanchez's hand showed motion similar to what she'd seen in Betty Jewell's blackened facial sore before the girl killed Amos. It looked like a moving, crawling nerve cell. Who knew how many of those things were in Sanchez's system, creeping toward his brain. Maybe they were already there.

The samples from John Doe's pustules looked similar, but different in one key way. Where the crawling nerve cell looked flexible and streamlined, John Doe's pollen looked fuzzy. It moved only when it landed on something, and then with an awkward stiffness that spoke of an internal rigidity.

Under high magnification she saw the cause of that fuzziness – hundreds of tiny cilia-like hairs sticking out from the stiff dendrites. It reminded Margaret of a fluffy white dandelion seed.

'So this is how it spreads,' she said. 'It rides air currents until it lands on a host.'

'Then it burrows in somehow,' Dan said. 'And once under the skin, it becomes a crawler just like the one on the left. Good God, what would the range be on this thing?'

Margaret didn't want to consider the answer, but she already knew it. 'Depends on the winds,' she said. To think that the difference between a localized infection and a pandemic might be nothing more than a good, strong breeze . . .

She wished Amos were with her. He was the parasitologist. He would have quickly created working theories on range and contagion mechanics. But Amos was gone, gone because of the very things that moved up there on the screen.

'Let's run the tests now,' she said. 'Give me all the samples.'

Dan went to the wall screen and typed in commands. The flat-panel's image changed from one set of side-by-side pictures to twenty-five sets, five rows of five spreading a checkerboard across the screen.

They had identified twenty-five possible cures to kill the crawlers. Now they could try all of them on crawlers and dandelion seeds at the same time. Multiple caustic solutions, heat, cold, antibiotics, Sanchez's own white blood cells and six kinds of chemicals that might damage the cytoskeletal structures.

Somewhere in those twenty-five options was a way to save Officer Sanchez and stop this whole thing in its tracks.

There had to be.

'All right,' Margaret said. 'Let's find out what kills these little bastards.'

OGDEN SEES TRAILERS

Charlie Ogden watched the Winnebago's little TV. Every word the newscaster said seemed to increase his anger, his desire to kill the enemies of God. If only he'd arrived sooner, stopped Jenkins from making that McDonald's run.

'This is footage from this morning,' the newscaster said. 'Police were investigating two bodies found on Orleans Street. We have unconfirmed reports that one or both of these bodies had the flesh-eating bacteria that has been found in several places in Michigan, including Gaylord, where it caused at least two deaths. Homeland Security has elevated the alert status to orange, although they say there is no evidence of terrorist involvement. The no-fly zone over Detroit is still in effect, and we will bring you live aerial pictures as soon as that ban is lifted.'

Ogden turned off the volume. He just stared at the image of Orleans Street, dozens of police, white CDC vans, and two semi trailers.

Chelsea's lovely voice in his head: *Why does this make you so angry?*

He pointed to the screen, his fingertip tracing an oily mark on the glass.

'These two trailers,' Ogden said. 'It means they found Jenkins. The people in those trailers, Chelsea . . . they work for the devil.'

Are they coming for us?

Not yet. They couldn't. Sending troops to a town like Gaylord was one thing; a major city was a different story.

'I think we have enough time,' Ogden said. 'We just have to make sure we stick to the timeline. You're sure the gate will open exactly when you say it will?'

When Mickey's big hand is on three and his little hand is on one.

Thirteen-fifteen. Just eighteen hours away.

That spot is only a few blocks from here. If the trailers make you angry, destroy them.

'They moved them,' Ogden nodded. 'I sent Sergeant Major Mazagatti out in street clothes, and the trailers are gone. They have to be around here somewhere, but we can't send people out to search. It's too risky. The longer we stay quiet and unnoticed, the better.'

You're so smart, General.

He felt his face flush red. 'Thank you, Chelsea.'

But tomorrow, once things begin, we should find the trailers and kill the people inside.

Ogden nodded. 'Absolutely, Chelsea. I'll send Mazagatti and my personal guard to make sure it happens. We just have to find them first.'

MACH 10

Captain Patrick 'P. J.' Lindeman felt ridiculous G-forces smash him into his seat, and he wondered if his ass would explode.

Well, not his ass per se, but the HTV-6Xb hypersonic fighter in which his ass was currently sitting, the same fighter that had that same ass hurtling through the night sky at Mach 10.

Mach motherfucking *10*.

Seven thousand miles per hour.

That shattered the official record for manned flight that had stood since 1967, when Major William J. 'Pete' Knight took his X-15A-2 to Mach 6.7. Put that in your pipe and smoke it, Pete.

Knight's flight had been very different. For starters, Knight's X-15 dropped from the bottom of a B-52 bomber, while Lindeman's HTV-6Xb took off under its own power from a military airbase at Groom Lake, Nevada. Knight's X-15 was basically a rocket with wings and a cockpit. Lindeman's plane used fairly standard turbojets for takeoff and landing, combined with scramjets to hit such obscene speeds. The most important difference? Knight's plane was built for speed only. It couldn't fight.

The HTV-6Xb was a bona fide war machine.

Known by its nickname, 'the Wasp,' the HTV-6Xb was

the world's premier air-superiority weapon. The world didn't know of its existence, of course, but that didn't change the fact it could eat a couple of M16s for breakfast, wash them down with the best Mirage the French had to offer and then casually pick its teeth with an F-22 Raptor. The Wasp could reach any target zone faster than anything on the planet and outfly anything it found in that airspace.

This particular combat mission didn't require a great deal of skill. Lindeman had taken off on a northwest heading, flown to ten thousand feet, then came around in a slow turn that pointed his nose toward South Bend, Indiana. The conventional jet-turbine engines drove the Wasp to Mach 2. At that speed, the turbines' air inlets closed off, forcing that same air intake into the scramjet engines. The turbines had to shut off, because once the plane reached Mach 3 or so, air friction would melt the spinning intake fans. The scramjet portion, however, acted more like a funnel – it had no moving parts. Air shot in at supersonic speeds, compressed, mixed with a gaseous fuel and ignited in a highly controlled reaction that drove the plane to Mach 10.

Lindeman's record-breaking flight would take him from Groom Lake to South Bend in fifteen minutes. Almost seventeen hundred miles. In *fifteen minutes*.

Twelve minutes into the flight, Lindeman released an ASM-157 antisatellite missile. His speed of Mach 10 wasn't even half that of the ASM-157, which would max out at Mach 22.7 – fifteen thousand miles per hour.

Aircraft normally come nowhere near Mach 5, let alone Mach 10. As a result, anyone or anything watching the skies for unusual flight patterns would notice the Wasp. Hard to miss something like that.

Which was precisely the point.

There was no way the Orbital could track every plane in North America. It couldn't even track all the military planes in that area – far too much traffic to monitor. It did, however, try to keep tabs on particular military bases. So when the HTV-6Xb took off from Groom Lake, the Orbital noted the flight and marked a subroutine to watch its direction.

When the HTV-6Xb turned and accelerated to Mach 1, that didn't merit the Orbital's primary attention. At Mach 2 the Orbital changed the marking status to potential threat. By the time it hit Mach 5 and was flying straight for South Bend, the Orbital knew it was under attack. When the jet launched a missile, it was only 350 miles away.

At Mach 22, traveling 350 miles – the distance from San Francisco to Los Angeles – takes just under a minute and a half.

The Orbital ran through protocols, checking the decision tree for responses. As it did, it picked up another inbound threat.

Military engineers built the NFIRE satellite to do two things. The first was the difficult task of tracking intercontinental ballistic missiles. The second was even more complex – shooting those missiles out of the sky.

The NFIRE orbited at an altitude of 240 miles. It targeted an ICBM's apex, typically about sixty miles above the Earth. The part of the NFIRE that actually shot down an ICBM was known as a *kill vehicle,* a small missile that got close to a target, then launched a high-speed spray of dense shrapnel. In basic terms, the kill vehicle was a high-tech, $560 million exoatmospheric hand grenade.

Certain senators, however, objected to putting a kill vehicle in the NFIRE. Such an act would open up a new arms race, they said. It would begin the 'weaponization of space,' and that was something the world could do without.

Defenders of the project said Congress was a bunch of myopic, tree-hugging hippies who deserved to die the radioactive death they would surely bring upon all freedom-loving Americans. The defenders said that only to themselves, of course. What they said *publicly* was that the kill vehicle had a range of only four miles, a minuscule distance compared to the vast ranges of space, so the kill vehicle could really only be used to shoot down a rocket aimed directly at the NFIRE. It was strictly for self-defense, and how could that be a bad thing?

Congress didn't care. Senators insisted the kill vehicle would cross a line. So to secure funding, NASA and MDA (the Missile Defense Agency) had agreed to remove the kill vehicle and instead include a laser communications terminal, also known as an LCT.

The thing was, military engineers are pretty sharp cats, and they quietly figured out how to fit *both* the kill vehicle and the LCT into the NFIRE. So Congress, and the public, was told that the NFIRE did not include the kill vehicle.

That was the first lie.

The second lie was the four-mile killing range. Of the two whoppers, this might have been the big one because the NFIRE's killing range was actually *thousands* of miles. Thanks to triangulation data piped up from NASA, the NFIRE could both target and hit the Orbital.

Exactly ten seconds after P. J. Lindeman released his ASM-157, the NFIRE launched its kill vehicle.

Primary threat: the missile launched from the Mach 10 jet. The Orbital tracked the missile's trajectory, then fired a supersonic stream of pellets made from an iridium alloy. The pellets spread out like a tight cloud, a cloud traveling at several thousand miles per hour. Air friction melted the pellets. By the time they intersected the missile's path, they were globs of dense, molten metal that tore through the ASM-157 like twelve-gauge shot through rice paper. The missile shattered into dozens of useless pieces.

The Orbital switched its targeting solution to the NFIRE kill vehicle. As it did, temperature sensors suddenly registered a spot on its beer-keg-size surface that almost instantly shot from normal to five hundred degrees, then a thousand, and kept climbing. . . .

Four hours earlier a heavily modified Boeing 747-400F cargo plane had taken off from Edwards Air Force Base in California. The flight plan called for a normal trip from Edwards to Langley Air Force Base near Hampton, Virginia. Unlike the HTV-6Xb, this 747 flew at normal speeds. It attracted exactly zero attention from the Orbital. Just another big cargo jet, just another cross-country flight.

This particular 747, known as the YAL-1, carried the YAL-1A airborne laser. The YAL-1A was designed to shoot down incoming missiles, including nuclear-tipped ICBMs or any other kind of ballistic missile. This *chemical oxygen iodine laser,* or COIL, could also theoretically be used against hostile bombers, fighters, cruise missiles – or even against low-Earth-orbit satellites.

Thirty seconds before P. J. Lindeman released his antisatellite missile, the crew of the YAL-1 had activated the COIL by combining chlorine gas, hydrogen peroxide and potassium hydroxide to create highly energetic oxygen molecules. Pressurized nitrogen then pushed the oxygen molecules through a mist of iodine, transferring the oxygen's energy to the iodine molecules. These fired-up iodine molecules shed the excess energy in the form of intense light.

Intense light that created an infrared laser.

This light bounced between mirrors, forcing more iodine molecules to give up their energy as photons, further increasing the laser beam's intensity. From there the beam traveled into a chamber where mirrors instantly adjusted to compensate for movement of the airplane and for atmospheric conditions. Finally the beam moved into a swiveling pod on the YAL-1's nose. The pod focused the laser to hit the Orbital as a tiny, concentrated pinpoint of immense energy.

Within three seconds a spot on the Orbital's hull superheated to almost three thousand degrees Fahrenheit. The Orbital abandoned all calculations and just moved, gaining altitude as it shot due north. At fifty miles above the surface, the YAL-1A beam tracked on-target again, this time hitting a different spot on the Orbital's hull. A four-second cat-and-mouse game ensued as the Orbital changed headings five times and climbed to an altitude of sixty miles. After each turn the YAL-1A's targeting system instantly compensated and reacquired, but only for a second each time, and always in a different spot as the Orbital rotated to mitigate heat buildup.

The NFIRE satellite's kill vehicle tracked the Orbital's evasive action. With a nice three-thousand-degree hot spot on its hull, the Orbital could bend all the light it wanted and still stand out plain as day to an infrared sensor. The kill vehicle marked the Orbital's sudden acceleration and climb, course-corrected, then detonated a warhead that released an expanding cloud of shrapnel traveling at thirty-three thousand feet per second.

The Orbital was still accelerating when the kill vehicle landed the technological equivalent of a money shot.

Dozens of depleted uranium ball bearings punched through the Orbital, shredding its fragile interior, including the computer system that had caused humanity so much trouble. The multiple impacts instantly rendered the Orbital inoperative. The YAL-1A laser reacquired and started heating up another hot spot, but the Orbital performed no further evasive maneuvers.

The Orbital's desperate actions had taken it out well over Lake Michigan. Cracked and shattered, a hollowed-out husk, the Orbital started to descend. As it reached terminal velocity, the surface heated to over a thousand degrees Fahrenheit. Air friction dug at the cracks, ripping free small bits and pieces of the once-pristine hull.

It didn't melt. While a few pieces trailed behind, there was no cometlike flame trail. The Orbital just *fell*.

Three hundred pounds of broken machine hit the surface of Lake Michigan at well over two thousand miles an hour.

It made a pretty big splash.

The impact shattered what was left of the Orbital, breaking it into hundreds of pieces that spread and sank and sizzled as the water rapidly cooled them off.

The Orbital was truly dead.

Not that it had ever really been alive.

Perry stopped drinking in mid-sip.

The grayness vanished.

For the first time since his triangles had started talking to him months before, his brain felt . . . clear.

He was so focused on this new sensation, or rather the absence of a sensation, that he didn't notice the beer spilling out the corner of his mouth and down his chin.

'Kid,' Dew said. 'Should I get you a sippy cup?'

Perry put the beer down on the computer-room console. He absently wiped his chin with the back of his hand.

'The jamming is gone,' he said. 'Whatever was blocking me, it's gone.'

Dew clapped once. 'Fan-fucking-tastic! So where's the next host? What direction?'

Perry closed his eyes, trying to hear, trying to *sense*. Trouble was, he didn't sense jack squat.

'I don't know,' he said. 'I'm not picking up anything. Nothing at all.'

Dew's satphone buzzed. He pulled it out of his coat and answered, then just listened.

'Yeah?' he said after a few seconds. 'No shit? Dawsey said the jamming is gone. We'll keep you informed.'

Dew hung up.

'That was Murray,' he said. 'Tight-lipped bastard has been up to all kinds of antics without filling me in. They found the mystery satellite and took it out. Just now, so gotta be the satellite that was blocking you.'

Perry smiled and grabbed Dew's shoulder. 'I'm not getting *anything*, man! Dew, I think that's it. I think the *whole thing* is over! Guess what? Fuck their fourth-quarter comeback, because *we won*!'

Chelsea felt something. More accurately, she *stopped* feeling something. It was as if she'd had a ringing in her ears, a steady, low noise that had been there so long she didn't even notice it until it vanished.

Chauncey?

No response.

Chelsea felt weak. She sagged to the floor of the Winnebago. What was happening? She couldn't hold the connections. The network flickered in and out, fading.

Blackness replaced her vision.

Chelsea Jewell passed out.

Out on the warehouse floor, Ogden's soldiers sagged and lowered themselves to the ground. He felt a blankness, a twofold void, the second one far more powerful than the first.

He sat. A chunk of brick dug into his butt. One by one, his men passed out as if they'd been gassed.

The hatchlings didn't seem to notice. They kept building.

Ogden watched them for the final few seconds he remained conscious, hoping they could complete the gate on their own.

Margaret stared at the autopsy room's flat-panel screen and smiled in grim satisfaction. There were twenty-five squares up there, but only one square held her attention. It showed a side-by-side picture of a crawler and one of the pollen pieces that looked like a fluffy dandelion seed.

A caption at the top of that square read LATRUNCULIN A. A toxin produced by a group of sponges found in the Red Sea that disrupted filaments of the cytoskeleton. Amazing to think that might make the difference in this battle, that one word, *latrunculin*.

She *loved* that word.

Because below that word she watched both alien structures dissolve into smaller and smaller bits. The crawler's long, firm, musclelike strands twitched, then seemed to morph into slack, lifeless little sacks of fluid. The dandelion seed was even more entertaining – the latrunculin made the stiff structure break apart, crumble and liquefy.

'I've got you, motherfucker,' Margaret whispered.

She had never really wanted to kill anything before. She stopped disease because that was how you saved lives. This was different. She wanted the *disease* dead, all of it – crawlers, dandelion seeds, triangles and hatchlings. She wanted to kill every last bit of it, in as painful a way as possible. Watching those things break apart on the screen filled her soul with a dark satisfaction. She wondered if this was what Perry felt when he killed an infected host.

'Hey Margaret,' Dan called. 'Did you do something to the samples?'

'Yeah,' Margaret said without looking away from the sheer beauty of a dead crawler. 'I gave them a nice latrunculin bath and killed them.'

'No, not that one,' Dan said. 'I mean *all* of them.'

She stepped back and took in the whole screen. In all twenty-five side-by-side samples, nothing moved. They'd successfully killed many of the crawlers, but until a few seconds ago over half the boxes had still shown activity. Now, no movement at all.

'Gitsh,' Margaret said, 'check this monitor. Is it frozen or something?'

Gitsh looked at the screen, then moved to the computer that fed the images. As he checked it, Margaret's eyes slid over the twenty-five test pairs. Each had a word across the top. Words in red indicated no effect on the crawlers. Words in green showed successful kills.

Chlorine killed them, and in far lower concentrations than the MargoMobile's decontamination mist. In fact, basic bleach killed them instantly. That was great for sterilization but didn't do much for a living victim. Antibiotics, unfortunately, had no effect, and Sanchez's immune system completely ignored the things.

Reducing the temperature did nothing – freezing them might work, but that would also kill the host. Heat at two hundred degrees Fahrenheit or higher killed them, but that wasn't a solution either, as those temperatures would also kill the host. Heat did, however, provide another way to decontaminate any area exposed to the dandelion-seed spores.

'The picture is live,' Gitsh said. To punctuate the point, he changed the screen from twenty-five small squares to one big square containing a nerve crawler. He slid a needle into the sample. Up on the screen, she saw the needle magnified thousands of times. It looked like a giant sword poking into a hydra.

'Huh,' Margaret said. 'It's like they just shut off.'

'They quit,' Dan said. 'They have seen the new Mightily Pissed-Off Margaret, and they threw in the towel.'

Suddenly, Clarence's voice crackled in her earpiece, anxious and rushed. 'Margo! Murray found the satellite! They just launched an attack, and they think they got it.'

'Oh my,' Margaret said. So that's why Murray had been in such a hurry. 'When? Like two minutes ago?'

'Yeah, exactly.'

'The samples, they shut down,' Margaret said. 'Even at the smallest level, they must have been controlled by the thing. Is there any effect on Sanchez?'

'He's out cold,' Clarence said. 'He was babbling incoherently, then started getting groggy and just dropped off. He's snoring.'

Margaret didn't know what to think. The crawlers' sudden shutdown, Sanchez falling asleep, both things coinciding with the satellite's destruction. Could it all be over?

No. It wasn't all over. She knew that.

'Dan, how much latrunculin do we have?'

'Plenty, if it's just Sanchez,' Dan said. 'If we need more, the supplier could medevac it right to us.'

'Let's see if it works first. Start an IV drip of latrunculin on Officer Sanchez. I'm not going to get caught with my pants down. These things might reactivate at any second.'

'But latrunculin is toxic as hell,' Dan said. 'We give Sanchez too much, he could lose the ability to breathe, his heart could stop. Shouldn't we wait to see if these things are really dead?'

'No. We'll watch Sanchez carefully, but get him on it right now.'

'But Margaret, he—'

'That's a fucking *order*, Dan,' Margaret said. 'Now start the goddamn drip.'

Dan looked at her for a second, then snapped a smart salute and walked out of the autopsy room.

Were his little feelings hurt? Margaret didn't care. She finally had a potential weapon, and she was going to use it.

DAY NINE

MOVEMENT

Margaret sat down at the computer desk, utterly relieved to finally be out of the hazmat suit she'd worn for fifteen hours straight. She typed commands to call up the new Sanchez samples.

What was that *smell*? Had someone left food in here? She looked under the desktop, then under the chair before she realized what it was.

The smell was *her*.

Damn, she needed a shower something fierce. Nothing she could do about that now, though.

She looked at the readout. The latrunculin was working – Sanchez's crawler counts had fallen. The chemical's side effects were taking their toll, but he wasn't in any serious danger. Not yet. She called up a feed from one of the latest samples. It showed three crawlers, still motionless, just as they had been since Murray's people shot down the satellite. As she watched, one of the crawlers slowly dissolved into little bits, courtesy of the latrunculin.

The second crawler started to disintegrate. Margaret had never seen anything so beautiful in her entire life.

And then . . .

. . . then the last crawler twitched.

She stared, wondering if she'd imagined it, hoping she had. It twitched again, kept twitching. It reached out, looking for something to grab. A dendrite arm locked onto the surrounding muscle tissue and *pulled*.

The crawler was crawling again.

The intercom buzzed.

'Margaret, you there?' Dan's voice, urgent.

'I'm here.'

'Something's up,' he said. 'I'm looking at the side-by-side samples. Everything that wasn't already dead is moving again. They just woke up, *all* of them.'

THE REBOOT

So many thoughts. So many voices. No organization. No *cohesion*. Did she know what that word meant? Yes, she did.

Chelsea blinked and opened her eyes. Slivers of early-morning light poured through cracks in the roof and the boarded-up windows. She felt sleepy. She felt sad.

Her special friend was gone.

She needed Chauncey's wisdom, needed to know what God wanted her to do. She sensed the minds of the soldiers, the hatchlings, the converted. They were all very still. Random thoughts . . . they were dreaming. No one there to tie them all together.

That's what Chauncey had provided. He'd made them *one*.

A sneaking suspicion grew in her mind. What if *she* could connect everyone? She could replace Chauncey.

He had been God, but he was gone.

Now *Chelsea* was God.

She sensed all the soldiers, Mommy, Mr. Burkle, the Postman, General Ogden . . . she sensed the two hatchlings back in Gaylord . . . and she sensed one more voice, a new voice, very faint, very *weak*, but also very close.

The two hatchlings in Gaylord remained prisoners.

Prisoners of the boogeyman.

Chauncey had told her to leave the boogeyman alone. Chauncey had *blocked* her, but Chauncey wasn't around anymore.

And besides, no one could tell Chelsea what to do. She wasn't afraid of the boogeyman. God shouldn't be afraid of anyone.

Could she block the boogeyman, like Chauncey had done? Maybe, but it would take time to learn how, to experiment. If she couldn't block him fast enough, the boogeyman would come for her.

Unless she got to him first.

She summoned General Ogden. It was time to put the pieces in place for his contingency plan, just in case the boogeyman escaped.

PERRY HEARS AGAIN

I'm going to kill you.

It started as a mental tickle, or maybe a ringing. Something faint. At first he wished it away. He just wanted to sleep.

You will scream . . . and scream . . .

The ringing grew louder. He heard a voice but couldn't register it. What he *could* register was a serious hangover. Holy God, did his head hurt.

. . . and scream.

Perry sat up and tried to rub the sleep from his eyes. The movement produced a metallic sound. The bed felt wobbly. Both hands held his head as he looked around. He wasn't in a bed. He was on an autopsy trolley in the examination room. Someone's idea of humor? Well, yeah, that *was* kind of funny.

The mental tickle grew. With a sinking sensation, he recognized the feeling.

Chelsea.

Are you afraid?

She'd grown stronger. His breath came in short gasps. He *was* afraid.

I'm gonna get you, boogeyman. Maybe I'll make you shoot yourself . . .

Fuck. Fuck-fuck-fuck.

Perry's hand shot to his waist, to the holster. The .45

was there. His hand gripped the cool handle. He didn't draw it, just held it.

Soon, boogeyman . . .

He hadn't experienced her this clearly before. The intensity shocked him. It felt as if her every little emotion was the most important thing that could possibly happen. And yet behind the intensity lay a curious blankness, the feeling that she wasn't good, or evil.

Chelsea didn't know what good and evil were.

She would do whatever she wanted, without remorse, without conscience.

Soooooon . . .

Perry had to find her. Find her and help her.

He jumped off the trolley and ran to find Dew.

CRAVING MCDONALD'S

Private Alan Roark parked the Hummer on the shoulder of North Chrysler Drive. He hopped out. So did Private Peter Braat, who carried the map. They both walked to the back bumper and looked at the massive overpass.

'Fuck,' Peter said. 'That's a lot of road.'

Alan nodded. It was a lot of road.

To their right, three lanes of I-75 heading north, then just past it three more lanes heading south. Those six lanes slid under the overpass of another six-lane highway, this one M-102, also known as Eight Mile Road. The sound of tires whizzing over wet pavement combined with hundreds of passing engines to create an almost riverlike, tranquil babble.

'That's a lot of lanes,' Peter said.

Alan nodded again. 'Yep. Sure is.'

He turned and looked into the back of the Humvee. He'd already counted what was back there five times, but God was in the details, so he counted again.

'Seems like a long ways off for a perimeter,' Peter said. 'We're ten miles away from the gate. How are we gonna hold a perimeter ten miles out with just two fucking platoons, you know what I mean?'

'The general knows what he's doing,' Alan said. 'So does Chelsea. They're bringing in the other two platoons from Gaylord, so we'll have that. Besides, the bigger the area we control, the harder it is for them to find Chelsea.'

Peter nodded. 'Makes sense, I guess. Still, I wish we got to do the airport thing.'

'Willis and Hunt got that one.'

'I know,' Peter said. 'I hate those guys. We should have got that gig. Let's just hope we make it back to watch the angels come through. That will be such a glorious moment.'

'Truly,' Alan said. 'But if we don't see it, I'm sure it's all part of the plan.'

Peter nodded, slowly and solemnly. 'Okay, so we've seen these roads. Where is our spot?'

Alan pointed up to Eight Mile. 'We'll just drive up there and get to work.'

'Easy peasy,' Peter said.

Alan nodded. 'Easy peasy bo-beasy. Let's go. We'll just drive around and see if we get the call. You hungry?'

'I could go for some McDonald's,' Peter said. 'I have the biggest craving for it lately. That, and I can't stop jonesing for ice cream on a stick.'

'You too? Man, that's weird. I never liked ice cream before, but now I wanna fucking *bathe* in that shit. Let's eat.'

They got back in the Hummer. Alan waited for traffic to clear, pulled onto the road and headed north, looking for the golden arches.

GO SOUTH, YOUNG MAN

Take some lumpy shit from horses, the smelly kind that's peppered with half-digested hay. Mix that with gravel. The jagged kind. Now cover it all in kerosene and light it on fire.

That's what it felt like inside Dew Phillips's skull. He'd slept on the floor of the computer room, right after Baum and Milner convinced him it would be funny to put a passed-out Perry Dawsey on the autopsy trolley.

Well, that *was* kind of funny.

A headache like that and a hyperactive Perry Dawsey jabbering a mile a minute? A match made in hell.

'Perry, you gotta talk slower,' Dew said. 'Seriously, my head.'

'Yeah, mine too,' Perry said.

'There's a difference. You and Baum and Milner, you're all young. I'm old enough to know what will happen if I drink that much, which means I'm old enough to know better.'

'You seemed to be down with it last night.'

Dew nodded and instantly regretted doing so. 'Last night I was awash in the glory of victory. And now that it's morning, my head feels like ass, and you're telling me that victory was no victory at all?'

'She's talking to me,' Perry said. 'She says she's gonna kill me.'

'Where is she?'

Perry shrugged. 'South.'

'How far south?'

'I don't know,' Perry said. 'Could be Ohio, could be Indiana, fucking Kentucky for all I can nail it down.'

'So how do we find her?'

'Like before, I guess,' Perry said. 'We start driving south till I feel it getting stronger, then we go in that direction. The signal is fucked up, though. I feel something *moving* south, something big, and something even stronger beyond that. We should start driving right now.'

Dew thought that over. It would work, it had before, but how long would it take?

'I don't know if we have that much time,' he said. 'Now that the jamming is gone, now that you feel something, you can focus on the hatchlings. Maybe we'll find out exactly where this thing is.'

Perry thought for a second, then nodded. 'It's worth a shot.'

'So will you go in there and talk to them again?'

Perry took a deep breath, then let it out long and slow. 'I don't want to. She's so *strong*, Dew. She might be stronger coming through the hatchlings, I really don't know.'

'You didn't answer the question,' Dew said. 'Will you or will you not go talk to them again? I'll be right there with you.'

'That's what I'm afraid of,' Perry said.

Dew smiled. 'We'll do it just like the shooting range, okay? I'll have a gun at your back. You get silly, I'll put you out of your misery.'

Perry chewed his lip for a second. 'Okay. I'll do it. But Dew, you better not be lying about shooting me in the back. If I have to die, I have to die, but . . . I couldn't handle it if I hurt you.'

Hard to believe this was the same kid who had butchered a family only eight days ago. But people couldn't change that much in that short of a time. This version of Perry had always been there, waiting for a reason to come out.

Pride swelled in Dew's chest – once again Perry Dawsey was going to stand face-to-face with his nightmare.

MOMMY IS A BIG BABY

Chelsea Jewell sat at the Winnebago's back end, in the couch that faced the front. Her small body made the couch look like a giant throne. She had a little blood in her hair. A hatchling sat on her lap. She'd named it Fluffy. Chelsea slowly petted Fluffy, feeling the nice texture of his stiff, triangular body. Fluffy's eyes stayed mostly closed, and when they opened, they opened only a little bit.

Chelsea wanted to stay calm, but General Ogden was making her so angry.

'Chelsea,' the general said, 'we should just leave him alone.'

She said nothing. He stood there, waiting for her to speak. The plastic on the Winnebago's floor was torn in places, kicked aside in others. Covered with tacky blood, it still crinkled under General Ogden's feet. Little bloody tentacle tracks lined the walls and the burnt-orange fabric on the seats and couches.

I want the boogeyman dead.

'Can't you block him? Like Chauncey did?'

I'm trying, but it's hard. I don't know how yet. He could come for me before I figure it out.

'The gate will be done in about three hours,' he said. 'We don't have to show our hand. Even with the rest of the men driving down from Gaylord, we have too few soldiers for a real fight.'

She just stared at him. What did he know, anyway? He was just the general. Chelsea was in charge. If she said they had enough soldiers, they had enough soldiers, and that was that.

What about the other soldiers back home? The ones you left to deal with Whiskey Company?

'That's just eighteen men, Chelsea,' Ogden said. 'They have to go up against a hundred twenty men and do enough damage to take Whiskey Company out of the picture.'

Well, if you have eighteen, then—

A voice called from outside the Winnebago, stopping Chelsea in midsentence.

The strange, deep new voice of Mommy.

'Chelsea! May I *please* talk to you?'

Mommy used her mouth, not her thoughts, which meant she was upset, confused.

Chelsea sighed. She would have to get up and walk outside. Mommy was already having trouble fitting through the Winnebago's door. Chelsea lifted Fluffy and set him down on the couch.

'You *stay*, Fluffy. Stay!'

She didn't have to speak out loud to Fluffy, but it was more fun. That's how you talked to puppies, in the special voice so they knew you loved them.

Come with me, General.

Chelsea walked out of the Winnebago's side door and into the building's cold winter air. Ogden followed her. They both looked at Mommy.

Mommy seemed sad.

'Hello, Mommy.'

'Chelsea, honey,' Mommy said. 'Something's wrong. Wrong with me. Maybe with my crawlers?'

Chelsea shook her head. 'No, Mommy. Nothing is wrong.'

Mommy started to cry a little. She was such a baby.

'But . . . *look* at me,' she said. 'It hurts. I'm not pretty anymore. It hurts so *bad*.'

'Pain brings you closer to God, Mommy. Don't you want to be closer to me?'

Mommy nodded. 'Of course, but baby, just look at Mommy for a second. If this keeps going, Mommy is going to . . . to . . .'

'You'll serve God, Mommy,' Chelsea said. 'You'll see, it will be so cool. Bye-bye now, Mommy. Bye-bye.'

Mommy turned, slowly, and walked away.

Chelsea turned to stare up at General Ogden. 'You don't know anything,' she said. 'You're just a general. I'm the boss of you. I *want* you to kill the boogeyman. *I want it!*'

'But Chelsea . . . most of our men are already on their way here.'

Then take some of the eighteen you left back home and send them to kill the boogeyman. And tell them to rescue my hatchlings, too – we can't make those anymore.

'But Chelsea, that will leave only nine men for the sneak attack on Whiskey Company. That's just not enough.'

You think you're so smart. Beck Beckett thought he was smart. If you don't start behaving, I can make you look just like Mommy.

Ogden's face turned white. He opened his mouth to speak, then closed it. The general glanced at Mommy. She was still walking away, still crying. He looked back at Chelsea.

'Tell Dustin Climer to split his eighteen men,' he said. 'Tell him to lead the attack on Dawsey. Corporal Cope can continue to Detroit as planned.'

Chelsea closed her eyes, then pushed her thoughts to Mr. Cope and Mr. Climer. It was so much easier now, so much faster.

It is done. Now go make sure the rest of your men are ready for the contingency plan.

She turned and walked back into the Winnebago's heat. Mommy started to cry louder, but Chelsea shut the door and then she couldn't hear it anymore.

DOUBLE DOSE

The little bastards were fighting back.

She was in the damn suit again, in the cramped containment cell with Dr. Dan. Clarence stood outside the open glass door. If Sanchez could somehow pull free from his restraints, Clarence wouldn't even have a clear shot. That pissed Clarence off, but Margaret didn't give a shit.

The latrunculin had worked, no question, but Sanchez's body wasn't the wide-open killing field it had been at first. Some of the crawlers seemed resistant to the drug, and those were splitting, dividing. It wasn't mitosis, nothing so elegant – the little bastards simply split into two smaller versions, each of which grabbed and incorporated free-floating muscle strands that broke away from dead crawlers. Under the microscope it was like watching a mass of tiny snakes entwining with each other, merging, becoming a collective organism.

She felt a sensation of dread – if the crawlers developed resistance to latrunculin, then she had no weapons that could keep Sanchez alive. If that happened, the only way to stop them was to kill the host.

'He's getting weaker,' Dan said. 'Breath rate is increasing, pulse is getting a little erratic.'

She'd doubled the dosage, and that had helped, but the crawlers were still in there, still heading for his brain.

How many had already made it?

She'd stayed ahead of this whole thing by trusting her instincts, following her gut. And right now her gut told her that if enough crawlers reached Sanchez's brain, there would be no coming back.

He'd be permanently changed. Just like Betty Jewell. And wasn't death better than that?

'Double it again,' Margaret said.

Dan turned his shoulders to face her square-on. 'No way. Didn't you hear me? He's got an erratic heartbeat.'

'He's a strong man, Doctor,' Margaret said. 'He can handle it. Now double the dosage.'

Inside his helmet, Dan shook his head. 'No fucking way.'

'Damnit, Daniel,' Margaret said. 'If these things mass in his brain, he's screwed. We've got to cure him.'

'Is killing him the same as curing him? Because that's what's going to happen if you jack up the dosage again.'

'Get out of here,' she said. 'I'll do it.'

He stared at her. 'I don't know you very well, but you're a *doctor*. What the hell happened to you?'

'*They* happened to me,' Margaret said. 'We have to know if this works. If we don't find a cure, one life won't really matter. Now get the hell out of my way.'

Daniel pushed past her, past Clarence, and opened the airlock door to Trailer A. As she turned back toward Sanchez, her eyes caught Clarence's.

In his eyes, she saw sadness. More than that, she saw pity. She finally understood why Bernadette Smith had to die. And she hated herself for it.

She looked away from Clarence and started increasing the dose.

11:50 A.M.: THE INTERROGATION

Dew hated the biohazard suit almost as much as Perry did. He'd always made fun of the human condoms, but now that he'd actually caved in and worn one, he felt jinxed, as though the next time he *didn't* wear one he'd catch something for sure. With a new .45 in a hip holster worn outside the suit, Dew imagined he looked like a total douchebag.

Perry just stared at the two caged hatchlings. They looked lethargic, defeated. Maybe sitting next to the center cage containing Perry's decomposed shooting victim mellowed them out. They'd barely moved in the last twenty minutes.

'What do they say, kid?'

'They're still not saying anything,' Perry said. 'They just seem to be out of it.'

'Can't you read their minds or something?'

Perry shook his head. 'It's not like that. The triangles are still connected to human brains, I think that's why I can hear that chatter from hosts. But the hatchlings aren't connected to human brains. They can talk to me, but only when they want to.'

'But you're still hearing that triangle chatter?'

Perry nodded. 'Yeah. It's getting stronger, too, which is kind of weird. It usually only gets stronger when I'm tracking them down, getting closer. Maybe they have more power now? I don't know, Dew – maybe we don't need these fuckers at all. Can I shoot another one?'

Dew leaned down to look into the cage on the left. 'What do you say, champ? Should we shoot you?'

Both of the hatchlings stirred. They blinked their black eyes, seemed to gain a little life.

'Something's getting them moving,' Dew said. 'They afraid of the gun?'

'No, that's not it,' Perry said. He closed his eyes, seemed to concentrate. 'The chatter is getting louder. A lot louder. Wait, Dew, I'm picking up thoughts of a gate . . . and a tall building.'

'You recognize it?'

Perry's eyes stayed closed, but he shook his head. 'No, not really. This is weird. Usually everything feels so chaotic, like the hosts are scrambling, trying to figure out what to do, but this . . . this feels organized. One-fifteen P.M.'

'One-fifteen?' Dew said. 'What the hell happens at one-fifteen?'

Perry opened his eyes. 'They've got a timeline. That's when the gate will open up. And I don't know why this is so strong. I mean, it's *really* strong, and it's got nothing to do with the hatchlings.'

'It's eleven-fifty right now,' Dew said. 'We've got less than ninety minutes. Perry, focus on that building. See if you can recognize it, or at least describe it to me.'

Milner's voice in his earpiece. 'Dew, can you talk?'

Perry's eyes opened – he had the same earpiece, so he also heard Milner's voice.

'Jesus, Milner, not now!'

'Some of Ogden's men are coming down the driveway,' Milner said. 'Two Hummers. You want to come out?'

'Handle it,' Dew said. 'Tell them whatever it is it has to wait.'

'I've got it,' Baum said. 'Heading out now.'

'Come on, Perry,' Dew said. 'Concentrate.'

Perry closed his eyes. His face started to crease. 'This is confusing,' he said. 'Now I'm getting a bunch of feelings, emotions. Hatred. Anger.'

'Just breathe, kid,' Dew said. 'Take your time, just breathe, and figure it out.'

Dustin Climer waved from the passenger seat as the Humvee slowed to a stop on the Jewells' icy dirt driveway. His driver eased over to the left side, allowing the Humvee behind to pull up on the right. The burned-out husk of a house sat before them. Off to the left, the two MargoMobiles, side by side and connected. To the right, a big, bare tree with a rope swing.

Five men in his Hummer, four in the other. More than enough to get the job done.

He waved again to the man standing in front of the MargoMobile. Climer hopped out and walked forward. He recognized the mustached face of that CIA puke Claude Baumgartner.

'Afternoon, gents,' Baumgartner said. 'What's up?'

'We came for the hatchlings,' Climer said. 'Ogden wants them moved to the camp.'

Baum shook his head. 'Uh, I don't think we can do that right now.'

Climer smiled. 'Sure we can, Baumer. It's just a matter of who calls the shots.'

Perry knew that building. Black. Tall. Glossy. Usually he had to listen very carefully to sense anything in the chatter, but this was different – now he had to block things out, try to ignore the random thoughts ripping through his head. But that could only happen if there were a bunch of hosts, way more than the three he'd sensed in Glidden.

The image of the building crystallized.

The Renaissance Center.

Perry's eyes shot open. The chatter wasn't getting louder because the hosts had more power – it was getting louder because, just like before, he was getting closer to the hosts.

More accurately, the hosts were getting closer to him.

'Oh shit, Dew,' Perry said. 'I'm hearing *Ogden's men*! They're here to kill me!'

A muffled gunshot from outside, then another, then another.

Milner's voice blasted in Perry's earpiece. 'Ogden's men just shot Baum!'

Dew drew his .45. 'Milner, defend yourself. These guys are with the hatchlings.'

More gunshots. Perry heard them both from outside the trailer and in his helmet speakers. That meant gunshots inside the computer room – Milner trading fire. Just as quickly as it started, the gunfire stopped. Milner was likely dead. The men would come through the decontamination area, into the autopsy room, then across the collapsible connector and into Trailer B.

Then they would kill Perry and Dew both.

Dew ran to the airlock door, reached to open it, then paused. He turned to face Perry.

'What about the hatchlings?' Dew said. 'Do they want those?'

'Yeah, but I'm the main target.'

Men shouting, things falling. The airlock door's light changed from green to red – someone had just opened the opposite door on the other side of the walkway. Foosteps on the collapsible grate outside – they were right outside the door to Trailer B.

'Don't try to open this door!' Dew shouted. 'We've got two hatchlings in here, and we'll kill them.'

The man on the other side of the airlock door sounded both happy and angry at once. 'If you do that, we're going to torture you for a looooong time. Give them to us, and we'll let you go.'

More footsteps outside, more men packing into the collapsible hallway.

Perry didn't know what to do. He waited for Dew to say something, *anything*. They were so fucked.

'Perry,' Dew whispered, too quietly to be heard through the airlock door, but Perry heard him in his earpiece just fine. 'On the containment cell's control panel, type in pound, five, four, five, and then as soon as the airlock light turns green, hit five again.'

Perry ran the four steps to the isolation chamber's door. He typed in the numbers. His fingertip hovered over the final 5.

A pounding on the airlock door.

'Time's up, asshole!' the man outside yelled. 'We've got a lot of firepower out here!'

'And I've got some in here,' Dew said. He raised his .45 and emptied the magazine at the hatchling cage on the left. Just like Perry's shots from the day before, the glass spiderwebbed as bullets tore the hatchling to splattery pieces. Dew's empty magazine hit the floor and he reloaded.

'You *fucker*!' the man screamed.

More footsteps outside the airlock, then a solid thump – the airlock door from Trailer A, closing.

The light above Dew turned from red to green. That equalized pressure in the walkway. Ogden's men were coming in.

Perry pressed the 5.

Spray nozzles in the ceiling, the floor and the walls erupted with a heavy mist of concentrated bleach and chlorine gas. Perry's visor instantly beaded up with the deadly liquid. They heard initial noises of confusion from outside the door, then screams of panic, coughing and vomiting. Gunfire erupted, but no bullets hit the airlock door.

'Make sure your safety is off,' Dew said. 'Follow me, watch my back, and *make sure* you don't point your gun my way, got it?'

Perry nodded quickly.

Dew opened the airlock door. Perry followed onto the collapsible walkway, the chlorine fog so concentrated that he could barely make out the three bodies lying on the grate, tearing at the small holes they'd shot in the walkway's collapsible walls.

Dew pulled the trigger six times. Two for each man. They stopped moving.

Perry followed Dew but felt a slight pressure on his right thigh. His heads-up display flashed a message in orange letters – SUIT INTEGRITY BREACH.

He looked down at his thigh. A piece of metal in the shot-up, torn walkway had ripped a three inch gash in the suit. Chlorine gas roiled around the tear. Perry froze for just a second, thinking this was it, that his lungs would burn, before he realized that air was shooting *out* of the cut, not *in*. His suit's positive air pressure.

Perry heard four more gunshots from inside the autopsy room.

'*Dawsey, move it!*'

He reached down with his right hand and grabbed the cut, bunching the material and sealing off the hole as best he could. He ran into the autopsy room.

Two more bodies. Dew reloading again.

'You idiot,' Dew said. 'Did you tear your fucking suit?'

'Just go already!'

Dew turned and ran into the main decontamination chamber. Two more men clawing at themselves, trying to break free of the chlorine spray that shot into their noses, their screaming mouths, their eyes.

Dew killed them both.

A roar from outside and the tearing of metal.

'Get down!' Dew screamed as he dove to the bleach-wet floor. Bullets tore huge holes in the decontamination chamber's wall. Someone outside opening up on the trailer. Perry hit the deck hard, adrenaline raging through his body. His hand came off the hole in his thigh as he hit, and he scrambled one-handed to close it up again.

Machine-gun fire sawed through the trailer walls. The air filled with flying chunks of white epoxy, yellow insulation and a disturbing amount of thin, jagged metal torn from the trailer's exterior. An explosion rocked the trailer on its suspension, throwing Perry up in the air and smashing Dew headfirst against the wall. The walls buckled and twisted. Perry landed hard on a bent floor. Dew slumped to his belly, then rolled on his side.

'Dew! Dew, are you okay? What the fuck was that?'

'Grenade,' Dew said, his voice oddly calm. 'In the computer center. They'll throw one in here next.'

Perry saw chlorine gas roiling away from three spots on Dew's helmet. His faceplate was cracked. Higher-pressure air pushed out from the new holes.

'That's not good,' Dew said.

'No fucking *shit!*'

They were both leaking air. The compressors on their suits could only compensate for so long.

'Take the guy outside,' Dew said as he scrambled to his feet. 'Hit him or we're dead.'

Perry saw a gaping bullet hole at the base of the wall. Sunlight poured through, lighting up a beam of green mist. He crawled toward it and forced himself to look out. The guy was on top of a Humvee, shooting a *huge* gun mounted in a turret. Perry was wearing bulky gloves, spraying mist kept beading up on his visor, he held his right thigh with one hand and someone was shooting at him – but the guy was only about twenty feet away.

Perry rolled to his side and extended his left arm. He aimed Dew's .45 at the man's head and pulled the trigger until the slide locked on empty.

The machine-gun fire stopped.

The man went limp and fell sideways. He half-hung off the turret's right side. He didn't move.

Perry heard the seven-shot report of another .45.

'Perry, I'm outside!'

Perry scrambled to his feet, a little too fast – he caught another piece of ripped wall on his left arm, and the suit tore again. He didn't bother looking at it, just ran out of the decontamination room and into the final airlock walkway. The last door hung partly open, bent and twisted, full of small holes. Perry sprinted the last ten feet, shouldered the door without breaking stride and found himself outside in a sunny winter afternoon.

Dew stood in the middle of the burned-out house, crouched in a wide stance, .45 in front of him as he swept it back and forth.

Not knowing what else to do, Perry did the same.

Dew emptied a magazine into the dead man in the Humvee turret. Just to be sure, apparently. He reloaded, then let out a long sigh.

'Fuck,' he said. 'This is completely fucked, kid.' He took off his helmet and looked at it. Perry saw four or five cracks – the thing was useless.

'At least it served its purpose,' Dew said, and tossed the helmet away. He looked at Perry's suit. 'I don't think brown sticky tape is going to help that.'

Perry looked at his left arm. Something had hooked the PVC just past his wrist, then torn the fabric almost to the shoulder.

'Perry, you sure that gate opens at one-fifteen?'

Perry nodded. 'Yeah, totally.'

They heard engines, heavy vehicles coming down the driveway.

General Charlie Ogden stood in the back of the Winnebago, waiting for Chelsea to say something. She just sat there, petting Fluffy. She no longer looked like an icon of love. She looked flat-out pissed, her small face furrowed with anger.

He knows we are here. He is coming.

'Are you sure? Sure they didn't get him?'

I can sense him. You failed.

'What about the men we sent to attack Whiskey Company?'

They are dead. You failed.

Ogden said nothing. He'd known that all the men would die. Even with the element of surprise, the odds were just too great. But if he'd kept all eighteen men together, they would have crippled Whiskey Company. This was Chelsea's fault.

Ogden pushed the thought away. Chelsea knew best – he seized that belief and held it, because it was far better than imagining himself suffering the same fate as her mother.

'Chelsea, what now?'

There is nothing we can do to stop the boogeyman from coming. We need more time. Start the contingency plan.

Ogden nodded. 'Yes, Chelsea. I'll begin immediately.'

Dew scanned the Jewells' yard for a place to hide. The vehicles out on the road sounded like approaching Humvees. More of Ogden's troops. He holstered his .45 and ran to the man he'd killed outside the computer room. He slung the man's M4 and pulled at his ammo belt.

The goddamn biohazard suit was getting in the way. He couldn't possibly run through the woods in that. They'd catch him in minutes. He unzipped and started taking it off when Perry called out.

'They're coming!'

Dew turned and looked. His balls shriveled up – five Humvees roaring down the long driveway.

He was out of time.

Dew looked for cover. A sagging, charred wreck of a refrigerator. He ran behind it, then aimed his M4 at the lead vehicle.

'Dew, don't shoot,' Perry said. 'I'm not hearing any chatter.'

Dew looked at him, then back to the Humvees that were almost on top of them.

'Well, too late anyway,' Dew said.

The front Hummer slid to a halt behind the two that had brought their attackers. Soldiers pointing M4s poured out, led by the blocky figure of a man almost as big as Perry. A bandage circled his head, bright white against his black skin, a red spot on the left temple. He wore a sergeant major's chevrons and star. Dew saw that some of the other men also had fresh bandages. The man looked at Perry, then strode toward Dew.

Dew scrambled around the melted fridge. He felt silly standing there in his scrubs, the biohazard suit dangling off at the waist.

The sergeant major snapped a salute so rigid and perfect that it was damn near comical. Dew returned the salute, only because he'd seen men like this many times – this guy would hold that ridiculous salute all damn day if he had to.

The man lowered the salute and slid into an at-ease stance. 'Are you Agent Dew Phillips?'

'I am,' Dew said, wincing at the man's bellowing voice.

'Sergeant Major Devon Nealson, *sir.* Domestic Reaction Battalion, Whiskey Company.'

Dew would have described Devon as *huge* if he hadn't been hanging around Perry Dawsey as of late. Devon's big neck supported a pitch-black head. A graying high-and-tight peeked out from the bloody white bandage around his head. His eyes seemed extremely wide – Dew could see all of the man's irises. The look bespoke rage, or shock, but seemed to be Devon's normal expression. His lower lip was too big for his mouth and stuck out in a perpetual pout.

'Whiskey Company?' Dew said. 'Can you get me Captain Lodge? He's the commander, right?'

'Was the commander, *sir*. Captain Lodge is dead.'

'What happened?'

'*Sir,* an X-Ray Company squad came into our area of the airport, then just started shooting, throwing grenades and launching AT4 shoulder-fired rockets. After we dealt with them, we attempted to locate Colonel Ogden, but his portion of camp was empty and his men will not answer our calls. We called Deputy Director Longworth. He told us to find you immediately.'

'This is bad news, Nealson,' Dew said. 'How many casualties?'

'Thirty-two dead, *sir,*' Nealson said. 'The X-Ray squad had complete surprise, and they were very efficient. Another twenty-five wounded that need to stay put. We've got sixty-three men fit for duty. Just tell us what to do, *sir.*'

'Stop calling me sir,' Dew said. 'I work for a living. Sergeant Major, have you seen any real combat action?'

'Action in Somalia, Yugoslavia, Afghanistan and Iraq,' Nealson said. 'I have busted heads and killed on three continents, and if there are any more members of X-Ray Company that need to be dealt with, I'll add North America as my fourth.'

If it had been possible to relax in the current fucked-up situation, Dew would have done so. Devon Nealson was a gift from above. His men would follow him anywhere.

'Sergeant Major, something tells me you have a nickname?'

'At times, people call me "Nails." '

'Nails, you're now officially in command of Whiskey Company. I'm going to venture a guess that you already established our transport options?'

'We have three Ospreys including the one assigned to you,' Nails said. 'Sixty-five men, including the two of you. It'll be a little snug but the Ospreys will take us all.'

'Load them up,' Dew said. 'We're all heading to Detroit.'

11:55 A.M.: THE FIVE-SECOND RULE

Alan Roark stopped the Humvee right in the middle of the I-75 overpass. Horns immediately started honking from behind. He ignored them and finished cramming the rest of his Big Mac into his mouth. The things were so fucking good. He tried to drink from his Coke, but all he got was the bottom-of-the-cup straw sound.

Peter passed over his Coke, which looked half full. Alan smiled a thanks, then drank. It soaked the giant bite of Big Mac sitting in his mouth.

The horns kept honking.

Alan swallowed and let out a big *ahhh*.

'Dude,' Peter said, 'you need to take smaller bites. Seriously.'

'True,' Alan said. 'Just got carried away. You ready?'

Peter nodded. 'That guy's horn is bugging me. Maybe we should show him what it means to love instead of hate?'

'Chelsea would like that,' Alan said. 'But we don't have time. I'll talk to him.'

He opened the door carefully and stepped out into the hazy gray light of a frigid winter afternoon. Cars whizzed by on the second lane, missing him by inches, kicking up fine sprays of dirty slush.

The guy kept honking.

Alan reached back in and grabbed his M4. He saw a French fry on the seat and popped it into his mouth. It was still warm – five-second rule and all. As he chewed, he walked to the Hummer's back bumper.

The car behind him was an SUV. Who still drove those things? Pretty fucking tough on the environment.

The driver saw Alan, saw Alan's gun.

He stopped honking.

Alan pointed the M4 and squeezed off a burst. The SUV's windshield spiderwebbed, splattering with red from the inside.

Tires screeched. People saw him and swerved, not thinking about the fact that they were on an overpass and there was nowhere *to* swerve. Cars smashed. Metal ground. Plastic cracked. Glass scattered.

Alan turned and saw Peter leaning over the overpass rail, an AT4 rocket on his shoulder. A cone of flame belched out the back as a rocket streaked down, trailing smoke for two seconds before it hit a gray Chrysler. The car turned into a fireball rolling along at sixty-five miles an hour, spewing parts and burning tires as it went. Peter dropped the empty rocket tube, aimed his M4 and started firing on the panicked traffic below.

Alan would join him in a second, but first he had to take care of all the people suddenly stuck in their cars. In only ten seconds, the Eight Mile Road overpass was already shut down.

Alan pointed, squeezed off a burst, turned to the next target and repeated.

NOON: IT HITS THE FAN

Murray Longworth hated the goddamn Situation Room. He'd had it, just *had it*. Maybe Vanessa Colburn was right. Maybe it *was* time for a new generation. Let the kids have the country – it was time for Murray Longworth to go golfing.

They'd killed the satellite, goddamit. They'd *won*. It should have been over, and now a wave of bad news so high he could drown in it. A sense of hopelessness, a feeling that no matter what you did, the enemy was going to keep coming, keep trying to kill you – it didn't just depress him, it exhausted him.

Thirty-three soldiers dead at the Gaylord airport. Thirty-three *so far,* because some of the wounded weren't going to make it. Ogden gone AWOL. The Exterminators unaccounted for. And now Detroit.

They had all gathered in the Situation Room; the Joint Chiefs, the secretary of defense, Tom Maskill, Vanessa. Gutierrez himself would be there soon.

The main flat-panel screen changed to a news helicopter's shot of a highway. The bottom left corner of the screen showed a logo for Detroit's WXYZ-TV. The bottom center of the screen read EIGHT MILE OVERPASS AT I-75. Hundreds of cars sat motionless on the three lanes heading north as well as the three lanes heading south. On I-75, cars had driven up the inclined shoulder, some stopping there, others rolling back down to land on their sides or roofs.

The traffic on the overpass itself looked much the same – motionless cars, smoke, flames and bodies sprawled everywhere. The only movement was near one green vehicle.

A Humvee.

Even from the high angle, Murray could see two men in fatigues. Wherever they moved, little puffs of smoke from automatic weapons soon followed.

The speakers suddenly played the sound that accompanied the image.

'. . . we don't know who these men are or how many people are hurt. We can see bodies from here. The vehicle is army green, but there is no unit insignia.'

An air response was already on the way. A-10 tank killers from Selfridge would be the first to engage, then Apache attack helicopters. Murray had even scrambled Ogden's squadron of four dedicated Strike Eagles – he just prayed he wouldn't have to use any bombs on Detroit.

'Murray,' Tom said.

Murray tore his eyes away from the screen. Tom had a phone in his hand again.

'Dew Phillips on line two, said it's mission-critical.'

Murray nodded, grabbed the nearest phone and hit line two as he looked back to the surreal carnage on the screen.

'Dew,' Murray said. 'You okay?'

'Yeah, so is Perry, but a squad of Ogden's men tried to kill us. They took out Baum and Milner. Perry identified the gate location – it's in Detroit, and apparently it opens up at one-fifteen sharp.'

'We've got a lot of gunfire in Detroit,' Murray said. 'Rockets, too. Looks like more of Ogden's men. He's AWOL, so he's either dead or hiding somewhere and calling the shots.'

'We know,' Dew said. 'It's all over the news.'

'Where are you?'

'With Whiskey Company,' Dew said. 'Two platoons in three Ospreys, headed for Detroit. We'll be there in thirty minutes. We'll set down, then Perry will find the gate.'

Murray popped four more Tums into his mouth and chewed. This couldn't be happening. They'd had it *won*.

'Another one,' Tom called out.

'Dew, hold on,' Murray said. He looked at the screen. The bottom left corner of this one showed Fox-2 News. The center bottom of the screen read 8-MILE OVERPASS AT M-10 JOHN C. LODGE FREEWAY. The scene looked like a mirror image of the other, hundreds of cars piled up on the road, a Humvee on the overpass with soldiers firing away.

Nothing could get through that tangled mess of cars. Ogden was shutting down the highways into and out of Detroit.

Murray turned his attention back to the call. 'Dew, if this is Ogden's doing, what the hell is he up to?'

'Causing chaos,' Dew said. 'Looks like he's trying to block all traffic in and out. He wants a big perimeter with lots of civilians inside it so you won't drop bombs if we find the gate.'

'Motherfucker,' Murray said.

'Are the other two DOMREC companies still at Fort Bragg?'

'They're already on their way to Detroit,' Murray said. 'They should land at DTW in about thirty minutes. I'll also activate the Eighty-second Airborne. It will take them eight hours, but . . .'

His voice trailed off. He didn't need to finish. If the gate opened and something came through, the Eighty-second would be the first organized unit to tackle it.

'I hear you,' Dew said. 'One more thing. Sergeant Major Nealson said he saw at least two platoons of X-Ray Company at the airport this morning. They aren't there now, and there's only two squads accounted for – that means a platoon and a half has to be on the way to Detroit. Roughly forty-five men. Get some birds in the air to take them out.'

'Take them out?' Murray said. 'We don't know those men are infected. We can set up a roadblock, test them. If they're negative, we use them to go after whatever Ogden has in Detroit.'

'A roadblock?' Dew said. 'Are you *insane*? Do you really want heavily armed, combat-tested soldiers going up against some state troopers in a roadblock?'

Dew was right. 'I'll take care of it,' Murray said.

'Get on the offensive, Murray. Pin them down, whatever it takes. We have to get Perry on the ground in Detroit so we can find the gate.'

'Wait for Yankee and Zulu companies to arrive from Fort Bragg,' Murray said. 'Ogden's units have ten Stinger missiles, and you can bet he took them all to Detroit. We need to account for those before you go in. We can't afford to lose Dawsey.'

'L.T., if Perry's right about the time, that thing opens up in seventy-five minutes. Whatever you do, don't drag your feet.'

'Just hold outside the city,' Murray said. 'We'll get to work softening up his positions, tasking satellite coverage to see if we can spot the gate and find you someplace to land.'

12:15 P.M.: DEW WARNS MARGO

Margaret stood in the isolation chamber, looking down at Officer Carmen Sanchez. Clarence stood outside the chamber – patient, quiet, clearly ready to act if Sanchez sprang to life.

But that just wasn't going to happen. Sanchez was having difficulty breathing, and it was only getting worse. She might have to intubate him soon. That, or take him off the latrunculin altogether, because he wouldn't live through another hour of the treatment.

His tongue still looked normal.

His tissue samples no longer showed crawlers. Either the latrunculin had worked or the last ones had moved into his brain. But if they *had* reached his brain, was the chemical stopping them from forming that mesh? Could the mesh form despite the chemical?

No. She refused to believe that. It had worked. This was so much bigger than just Sanchez. Latrunculin *worked*. It killed them. Not all of them, but a lot, and that meant she had a weapon. The weapon needed development, true, but at least she had a starting point.

And if it didn't work, then she had nothing. No cure. Sanchez had been exposed to a small amount of the vector. If she couldn't defeat that much, what could she do against higher amounts of exposure? Some of the John Doe's pustules had grown to the size of baseballs – a hundred times the size of what had popped on Sanchez. Someone hit with that much contagion and she'd have no chance at all.

Fuck Murray's secrecy. Margaret was going public, and she'd call Dew out on his offer to back her up. Would Clarence also back her, or would he continue to *obey orders*?

Gitsh's voice in her earpiece. 'Otto, Dew's calling in.'

'Patch him through,' Clarence said.

'You're connected, Dew,' Gitsh said. 'Otto and Margo are listening in.'

Dew's voice, urgent and excited. 'Otto, have you or your people had any contact with Ogden's men?'

'No sir,' Clarence said. 'We've been working all night on the John Doe and the police officer. We didn't even know Ogden's men were in Detroit.'

'They are,' Dew said. 'And you are to avoid him at all costs. Your trailer, is it visible from a main road?'

'No. We're tucked under a little railroad overpass, trees on either side. Excellent concealment. You can't see us at all.'

'Okay,' Dew said. 'Then maybe you should just stay put.'

'Dew,' Margaret said, 'what's happening?'

'Ogden is working for the triangles.'

Margaret looked at Clarence, her anger at him forgotten for the moment. '*Ogden?* How . . . how do you know?'

'His men tried to kill Perry. Perry's okay, but they got Baum and Milner. Ogden's men are shooting the fuck out of the highways in Detroit, murdering people left and right. The gate is somewhere in Detroit, and Ogden wants to protect it.'

She shivered at the implications – just like that, Ogden and his men, converted, working for the enemy. She'd missed something back in Gaylord, clearly. And even if her new drug worked, was it already too late?

'We're coming in,' Dew said. 'Perry is going to find the gate. If we can get to you, we will, but otherwise stay put.'

'Watch out for infected bodies,' Margaret said. 'That's how the contagion spreads. Bodies can have big, puffy pustules, filled with spores. Those pop on you, you have the new strain. And they can spread it through their tongues, so make sure no one licks you.'

'Understood. You have a cure for this shit yet?'

Margaret looked down at Sanchez. 'We're very close.'

'Get your info to Murray, Margo, in case Ogden finds you and takes you out. You guys are in a bad spot. I'm pretty sure you're *inside* Ogden's perimeter.'

'Understood,' Clarence said.

She couldn't stop now. She had to get Sanchez out, away from the danger.

'Dew,' Margaret said, 'I appreciate what's going on, but we have to evacuate the patient. He could be the key to stopping this.'

'If Ogden finds you, he'll kill you,' Dew said. 'He's hit all the major roads out of Detroit. Surface streets are jammed with people trying to leave, so there's no fucking way you can get a semi out of town. You guys either stay where you are, or you leave the trailer, find a hidey-hole and lay low till I know I can get transport to you. You got it?'

'But Dew, this is a critical phase—'

'We've got it,' Clarence interrupted. 'We'll evaluate the situation and act accordingly.'

'Good,' Dew said. 'No offense, Margo, but let Otto handle this unless you like the taste of bullets. And how about you guys put away the nerd gear once in a while and watch the fucking news.' He hung up.

'Uh, guys?' Gitsh said. 'I think you better come to the computer room. We just turned on the local news, and we're in a lot of trouble.'

Clarence looked at Margaret, then held an arm toward the airlock door – *After you.*

Margaret took one more look at Sanchez, then headed to the airlock.

12:20 P.M.: BONUS POINTS

Northwest Flight 2961 from Detroit to Bangor never had a chance.

The Airbus A319 jet carrying 193 passengers took off from Detroit Metro Airport. Michelle McMichael, age sixty-three, had the window seat because Bernie, her husband of forty years, basically had to pee every twenty minutes. He got the aisle. That was fine by Michelle. She liked to hold a map and look out the window when they flew. Using the map to identify landmarks was a fun way to pass the time. As the A319 banked to the right, it gave her a nice view of a long stretch of I-94. The map said she was looking south at Taylor, Michigan. She craned her head to look back at the airport.

That was when she saw it.

Michelle was no military expert, but she'd seen enough movies to know a missile's smoke trail when she saw one. And just like that, she knew that this was the end.

Michelle had time to reach out and grab Bernie's hand. She looked into his eyes and said, 'I love you,' and then the Stinger missile hit the A319 just behind the right wing.

The warhead penetrated and erupted, splitting the plane in two and ripping the right wing free from the fuselage. Michelle died on impact, she and her seat torn into three separate pieces. Bernie actually lived through the initial blast, barely, but was quickly incinerated as a fireball rolled through the broken cabin.

The A319's tail spun away and started to drop. A secondary blast disintegrated the midsection. From row ten forward, the A319's nose arced toward the city, trailing fire and smoke as if it were a second, gigantic rocket.

At the northwest corner of Detroit Metropolitan Airport, also known as DTW, Vining Road passes over a parallel set of railroad tracks. Under this overpass stood Brian Hunt and Jordan Willis, formerly of Domestic Reaction Batallion's X-Ray Company, now proud members of Chelsea's Army. The overpass hid them and their Hummer from view yet still gave them a clear field of fire on several of DTW's runways.

Jordan had watched Flight 2961 take off, waited for it to come around and start curving north. He knew that it would, because he knew that it was heading to Bangor – he'd used his cell phone to look it up on a travel website. Once that curve carried the jet close to Detroit, he had aimed his Stinger missile, acquired the target and fired. Bye-bye, Flight 2961.

'Fuckin'-A, Jordan,' Brian said. 'Chelsea will love you so much. That was a great shot.'

Private Jordan Willis nodded. He could only hope his actions pleased Chelsea. And it *was* a great fucking shot.

'Wait for it,' he said. 'I think I double-dipped.'

Fifteen miles away from their position, the A319 trailed a thick, curved column of smoke as its nose dropped toward downtown Detroit. It sailed down into the city. Seconds later, a ball of flame rose into the sky.

'Bonus points,' Brian said. 'Nice work.'

'Thanks. Wow, look at all the planes bailing out. I'm betting they aren't asking the tower for permission to change their flight plans.'

One jet had been approaching and another had been circling, waiting for clearance. Both now turned away from DTW. Those suckers were big beasts, sure, but it looked like they could still haul balls when they kicked in the engines.

Brian shouldered his own Stinger, looking for just the right target.

'You gonna shoot that thing or just pose with it?' Jordan asked.

'I think I better save it,' Brian said. 'The general says they could still try to bring in C-5s or some C-17s. They do that, I'll hit one on the way in.' He set the Stinger down and picked up one of five AT4 antitank weapons.

Jordan shook his head. He liked Brian, but sometimes the guy just didn't think. 'That's an antitank missile, dumbass. Ain't no tanks here.'

'How about a fuel tank?' Brian pointed to a 747 sitting at a runway's back edge. 'I think that plane was probably going to take off before you shot down the other one. They can move pretty good in the air, but something tells me they can't exactly turn on a dime when they're on the ground.'

Jordan looked at the plane, a giant white sitting duck. Huh.

'I should have never doubted you,' Jordan said. 'In fact, you've inspired me. I think I'll see if one of these AT4s can hit the tower. I apologize for calling you a dumb-ass, good sir.'

'Don't mention it,' Brian said as he sighted in on the stationary 747 and pulled the trigger.

12:25 P.M.: HOME BASE

Clarence, Gitsh, Marcus, Dan and Margaret sat in the computer room of Trailer A. Each of the three computer screens played a different local channel. The left screen showed a live shot of a fire burning just east of Dearborn. The news anchor said a plane had been shot down by a missile. The middle screen showed jittery shots of panicked people rushing away from the towering Renaissance Center, the broken-glass top of which belched smoke from some large internal fire. Apparently gunmen had rushed into the center tower, killing everyone in sight, then started shooting the place up with shoulder-fired rockets. The screen on the right showed a bulky A-10 fighter sweeping in, strafing a green vehicle up on the Eight Mile Road overpass. Even with the poor camera work, Margaret saw the Humvee shake and shudder as bullets tore through it.

'This is insane,' she said. 'It looks like footage from Iran or something.'

'I think we stay here,' Gitsh said. 'There's people all over out there, cars whipping down the streets and smashing into each other. Ogden's men could spot us anywhere.'

'No, man,' Marcus said. 'People all over is *why* we need to go now. Then we're just more civvies running around looking for a place to hide our heads.'

'We're on a railroad track that hasn't been used in decades,' Gitsh said. 'We're tucked under a fucking overpass, man. You can't even see us from the road. We just stay right here and we ride this out.'

Marcus shook his head. 'Look, that John Doe in the autopsy room? He was found not a block from here. That was fine when it was just him, but now there's infected all over the place. These people pack together, which means their base or whatever has to be close. All it takes is one rocket hitting this trailer and we're *all* dead. We get out there on foot, find a building to hide in, maybe we live.'

'You mean maybe *some* of us live,' Gitsh said. 'You just want to get out there because you know this urban-combat bullshit and you want to save yourself.'

'Motherf—'

'Enough,' Clarence said. He spoke quietly, but his voice carried command. 'It's my call, and we stay. Those highway interchanges they attacked are ten miles from here. That probably means most of Ogden's men are nowhere close to us. We're not equipped to take them on. They see us, we're screwed, so we stay right here under cover.'

'What about the cop?' Gitsh asked.

'What *about* him?' Margaret said.

'Come on, Doc,' Gitsh said. 'What if he wakes up and starts screaming?'

Dan shook his head. 'He's not going to be screaming anytime soon. He's in pretty bad shape.'

Gitsh laughed. 'Yeah, well, Betty Jewell was in pretty bad shape too, right? Besides, these fucking things can talk to each other mentally and shit.'

'Not him,' Margaret said. 'We cured him.'

'You *think* we cured him,' Dan said. 'You don't really know.'

'We've got to kill him,' Gitsh said.

'He's right,' Marcus said. 'We have to kill him.'

'You can't,' Margaret said. 'This isn't just about the five of us. Officer Sanchez could be the key to a cure for the new strain. I'll watch him.'

'I agree with Gitsh,' Dan said. 'He starts talking, we're screwed. I vote we kill him.'

Margaret sneered at Dan. 'And what happened to being a doctor?'

He shrugged. 'He's going to die anyway from an overdose of latrunculin, so what's the difference? Kill him now.'

Gitsh nodded. 'That's three votes. Majority rules.'

'This isn't a democracy,' Clarence said. 'It's a dictatorship, and I'm the dictator. Sanchez is a civilian, a cop. He caught this shit in the line of duty. And Margaret is right – he could be the key to a cure. Unless we know he's a threat, he stays where he is. Margaret will watch him. I'll stay with her. If he poses a threat, I'll kill him myself. Cool?'

Gitsh, Marcus and Dan all traded looks, then nodded. None of them doubted for a second that Clarence would kill Sanchez if it came to that. Margaret wondered if she'd saved her patient or only delayed his execution.

'Margaret and I will suit up,' Clarence said. 'When we're done, you guys do the same. I want everyone sealed up nice and safe. Dan, you stay in here and keep an eye on the news. Holler if there's anything major we need to know about. Gitsh, Marcus, you take up positions at the front and back of the trailers. Watch for trouble. You see anything fishy, call it out over the comm system. Do not engage without the rest of us, got it?'

Gitsh and Marcus nodded.

'Come on, Doctor Montoya,' Clarence said. 'Let's get to work on your patient.'

12:30 P.M.: A CITY PARALYZED

The cacophony of a dozen animated phone conversations filled the Situation Room. Satellite images of Detroit lit up the main screen. Other monitors showed live feeds from news cameras and tactical maps dotted with unit symbols. One screen showed two tallies: one for dead, one for wounded.

The top of every screen showed a countdown: forty-five minutes and fifteen seconds, the time remaining before the clock struck 1:15 P.M.

President John Gutierrez sat at the end of the table, his face an expressionless mask. He looked at the monitors one by one, then circled back again. Murray was sweating like a pig, damn near hyperventilating, and Gutierrez sat there looking calm, collected – like a leader.

The unflappable Vanessa Colburn wasn't sweating at all. She worked the phones, quietly offering advice to Gutierrez, but only when he asked for it. As Murray's World of Secrets crumbled around him, he started to wonder if maybe she *wasn't* the political vampire he'd made her out to be. For the first time, Murray wondered if his way was wrong and Vanessa was right for wanting him out.

General Cooper had a phone pressed to each ear. He nodded once, then put a phone on each shoulder and called out to the room.

'A military convoy has been spotted heading south on I-75,' he said. 'Seven vehicles, including two troop trucks. Around sixty men. I've got a squadron of Apaches moving to a good kill point.'

'On a highway?' Gutierrez said. 'What kind of civilian damage will we face?'

'Moderate,' General Cooper said. 'But a hell of a lot less than if those two platoons get off the road and into the countryside.'

'Do it,' Gutierrez said.

No hesitation. This guy might turn out to be okay after all. Murray certainly hoped so, because it was high time to pass the baton to the next generation. He didn't know how much more of this he could take. It was one thing to go Cold War or cross swords with the Iranians, but Ogden's men were tearing Detroit to pieces.

Detroit.

Eight Mile Road passed over every major highway to the north of the city. At each interchange a massive pileup blocked the roads. Hundreds of cars, some burning, along with the sprawled bodies of people who had been gunned down trying to escape on foot. Ogden's men had also hit the major arteries on the west side: the I-96 and I-94 interchange, the interchange of I-96 and I-75. Surface roads were the only way in and out of the city, and those were choked with traffic from panicked citizens trying to escape the burning buildings and the random automatic-weapons fire that hit every few minutes. The citywide traffic jams had the Detroit police scattered and disorganized. When isolated police units did encounter Ogden's gunmen, the gunmen either cut them down or blew up the cop cruisers with shoulder-launched rockets.

Ogden hadn't stopped with the roads.

Fire poured from the top ten floors of the Renaissance Center's middle tower. A westerly wind carried the thick, heavy black smoke plume across the city in the direction of Ann Arbor. The Fisher Building and the Penobscot Building were also in flames – three of the city's tallest skyscrapers burning out of control. Firefighters were working on those blazes as well as a half dozen raging infernos caused by the crash of Northwest Flight 2961.

Two burning wrecks blocked the runways of Detroit Metro Airport. The main air-control tower was destroyed. Random gunfire. Hundreds dead. Airport security hadn't found the attackers, which meant they were still out there. Some witnesses estimated five gunmen, others claimed ten or even twenty.

The smaller Detroit City Airport? Same deal – blocked runways, burning wrecks, tower destroyed. Totally out of commission.

The attack was less than forty minutes old, yet Ogden had taken out the airports, clogged the roads and tied up every cop, firefighter and paramedic.

'Look at this,' Gutierrez said. 'Look at what's happening. How many men does Ogden have in Detroit?'

'Maybe sixty,' Murray said. 'We're not sure.'

'Sixty men,' Gutierrez said. 'Two platoons and he's paralyzed a major city. What happens to America if the contagion spreads to six hundred people? Six *thousand*? We have to bottle this up here. We can't let it get out.'

Murray looked at the screens and cursed Charlie Ogden. That man knew *exactly* what he was doing. All that would end when the five C-17s came in from Fort Bragg. Those planes carried two full companies, plus vehicles and heavy weapons. Ogden's party was about to come to an end.

'General Cooper, we need an airport,' Murray said. 'We have to assume that Ogden will take out anything that comes near DTW.'

'God*damit*!'

The room fell silent as all eyes turned to General Luis Monroe. The normally soft-spoken, God-fearing Monroe had just cursed at the top of his lungs. He held a phone with both hands, squeezing it as if it were the cause of all this misery.

'The C-17s,' he said. 'Two of them just went down. There were reports of automatic-weapons fire in the cargo sections, where the troops were. Some explosions, possibly grenades. We've lost most of Zulu and Yankee companies, plus the crews. At least two hundred men.'

Silence fell over the Situation Room.

Another gift from Ogden — that guy really knew his stuff.

Gutierrez glared at Murray. 'What else do we have that can get there before one-fifteen?'

'Dew Phillips and the sixty-three men left from Whiskey Company,' Murray said. 'With the shape Detroit is in now, that's all we've got.'

'We have no idea where the gate is,' Gutierrez said. 'We have no forces on the ground. We have little or no communication into the city, and we have no reinforcements that can be deployed in less than six hours. I want Phillips in there now. Let's not leave it up to our Strike Eagle options, shall we?'

Murray nodded. 'General Monroe, you need to saturate the area with air assets, see if we can take out more of Ogden's men and draw fire from the Stingers he has left.'

Monroe nodded and went back to his phone.

Dew and Perry had to find that gate and shut it down, because Murray most certainly did not want to leave it up to the Strike Eagles. They carried both the big two-thousand-pound bombs . . . and the nuke.

Gutierrez, he noticed, hadn't specified which option he'd use.

12:32 P.M.: OFFICER SANCHEZ

Wake up, sleepyhead.

Detroit police officer Carmen Sanchez opened his eyes. It took him a second to get his bearings. He was weak, could barely move. Well he *was* weak, sure, but the reason he couldn't move was that his wrists and feet were tied down.

'He's awake,' he heard a muffled voice say. There was a woman to his left, dressed in some crazy black Halloween costume.

It hurt to breathe. How messed up was it when it hurt to breathe? Pretty messed up, true, but not as messed up as God talking in your head.

'Officer Sanchez, can you hear me?'

He nodded. He could hear her, from speakers in the walls, and that was weird because she was standing right next to him.

Ahhh, there you are!

He'd never bought into the whole God thing. Never. He got married in a church, sure, but that didn't mean shit – *everyone* got married in a church unless you were a fucking hippie. Now that God was chattering away, right in his head . . . well, that made it just a wee bit easier to believe.

'Officer Sanchez, my name is Doctor Montoya. You are very sick. Nod if you understand.'

He nodded.

Would you like to join us?

'Can't,' Sanchez said. 'Tied down.'

'Ah, you can talk,' Montoya said. 'That's great. Do you think you can answer a couple of questions about how you feel?'

Sanchez nodded.

Your thoughts feel very weak, Mr. Sanchez. I'm not sure you'll be of much use to us.

'So try to take a deep breath for me,' Montoya said.

'Maybe . . . not,' Sanchez said.

'Maybe not what?' Montoya said. 'You can't take a deep breath?'

Well then, Mister Sanchez, the people who are with you are very bad. What should we do about this?

'Kill me,' Sanchez said.

'Mister Sanchez, we're not going to kill you. You're going to make it.'

I understand. We are on our way.

He turned his head to look up at the woman. He smiled at her. 'She's . . . coming,' he said. 'Isn't that . . . nice?'

Montoya leaned back, away from him. She suddenly looked guarded, afraid. 'Who's coming?'

'Ch . . . Ch . . . Chelsea.'

He didn't see her hand move, but he felt gloved fingers on his jaw, forcing his mouth open.

'No,' Montoya said. She sounded like she might cry. '*No.*'

'Margaret, what is it?'

A man's voice. God would probably kill him, too.

'His tongue,' Montoya said. 'Blue spots, he's got it.'

'Get to the decon chamber and wait for me,' the man said. 'Move.'

Sanchez heard footsteps, a door open, then a little farther away a bigger door open. It was all kind of a whirl. He hurt *soooooo* bad, and his brain wouldn't process things fast enough.

I'm sorry you can't join us, Mister Sanchez, but you really helped out, because we've been looking for the bad people who are doing this to you.

'I'm . . . glad,' he said.

Another black suit on his left. Bigger. A black man inside. A black man with a broken front tooth. Pointing a pistol.

'I'm sorry about this,' the man said.

Sanchez saw a flash, and then he was gone.

12:35 P.M.: ON THE ROAD AGAIN

Margaret waited in the decontamination chamber for Clarence. She knew what he was going to do, and she knew that it would only take a couple of seconds.

She needed out. She just wanted to go home to her apartment in Cincinnati. She wanted to spend way too much for a Starbucks and sit down and read *People* or *US Weekly*, something truly brain-dead, because she wanted to *be* brain-dead.

Maybe she already was.

Her brain didn't seem to amount for much anymore. It hadn't saved Amos. It hadn't saved Betty Jewell or Bernadette Smith. And it hadn't saved Officer Carmen Sanchez.

Too much death. Too much failure.

Clarence entered the decon chamber and closed the airlock door behind him. She activated the spray. Thanks to her earpiece, she could hear Clarence's orders despite the high-pressure spray.

'Dan, get outside, back of Trailer A,' Clarence said. 'Gitsh, Marcus, we're out of here. Check north, up by the tractors. Make sure no one is coming down the old train tracks.'

'Got it,' Marcus said.

Margaret shut off the spray, then opened the other door. Seconds later, dripping with bleach, they both walked out of the trailer and into the shade of the overpass. Dan was standing there in his biohazard suit, holding a pistol, looking scared.

'Okay,' Clarence said. 'We're going to walk out the way we drove in and head for the water. There we only have to watch for attacks from three sides. I'll take point. Gitsh and Marcus, you've got the rear. Dan, you're in the middle with—'

Gitsh's voice, urgent and sharp in her earpiece, cut off Clarence in midsentence.

'Company!'

Gunfire erupted, amplified by the overpass's brick walls. Margaret's arms flew up around her head, an instinctive reaction, a panicked reaction. A hand grabbed her wrist, yanking her into a run.

Sunlight. She came out the far side of the underpass before she even knew that it was Clarence who'd pulled her along.

'Margaret, *come on*!'

Breath locked in her throat; she stumbled, then regained her feet and ran. That put the sound of gunfire behind her.

In front of her, below the next underpass, two cars. A compact and a convertible. Just people looking for a place to hide, probably, but apparently Clarence didn't want to find out for sure.

'This way!' he yelled, then he turned right and started sprint-climbing up the steep, tree-spotted, snowy-dirt slope. Margaret followed, arms pulling, legs pumping, heart hammering.

A hissing sound from behind.

Then a shattering roar.

She looked back – a ball of fire and smoke billowed

out from the underpass, so thick she couldn't even see the MargoMobiles.

A hand on her ass, pushing her.

'Move!' Daniel said. 'They've got fucking rockets!'

She scrambled up the hill, knees grinding into the dirt and rocks until she remembered the hazmat suit, and then she ran on feet and hands only. Sharp bits poked through the PVC into her palms and fingers, but she could tape those later. They reached the black fence on top of the incline. Her gloved fingers clawed at the rubber-coated chain-link, and she swung over the top before she even knew what she was doing.

More gunshots from behind. Things whizzing past her head.

Daniel crying out.

Margaret pushed off the fence and hit the ground hard. She stood and looked around. White building, Ford dealership. Behind her, the fence, behind that . . . Daniel, rolling limply back down the incline.

Clarence's hard grip on her wrist again. 'Move!'

They ran away from the dealership and into an eight-lane road choked with bumper-to-bumper traffic. No buildings on the other side of the street – an empty lot to the left and a parking lot to the right. Some people were looking out of their car windows, but most had heard the explosion or seen the rising smoke and were already abandoning their vehicles, sprinting for cover anywhere they could find it.

Margaret finally regained her balance and yanked her hand away from Clarence.

'Just go. I'll keep up. What about Gitsh and Marcus?'

'Dead,' Clarence said. 'And Dan took a round in the head. He's gone.'

They skirted cars and ran into the half-empty parking lot ringed with trees growing up through the asphalt. On the far side, they hopped a smaller fence and found themselves on a cobblestone street, old bricks bumping under the soles of their thick biohazard boots. Two blocks straight ahead, across yet more tree-dotted, wreckage-strewn vacant lots, she saw an abandoned three-story brick building. Faded white letters on faded blue paint at the top of the building spelled out GLOBE TRADING COMPANY. She started toward it, then stopped when Clarence again grabbed her.

'No, don't,' he said. 'Look at the bottom there, by the corner.'

She did and saw two men in army uniforms running out of the building. A second later, two more.

'They have men stationed in there,' Clarence said. 'That's their fucking headquarters for all we know. We gotta get out of here. Come on!'

People ran in all directions. It wasn't the screaming sprint of a monster movie, but rather silent running, people moving fast in a half-crouch, looking every which way for the next threat. Margaret and Clarence must have appeared to be such a threat, because one glance at them sent people running the opposite way.

Margaret and Clarence ran left down the old brick road, putting the abandoned lot and the Globe building beyond it on their right. She heard gunfire behind her again – the men who'd killed Gitsh, Marcus, and Dr. Dan, they were giving chase. Shit-shit-*shit*, was this how her life would end? A bullet in the back?

The road changed from bumpy brick to bumpy pavement. On their right a red brick building, one story, loading-dock doors open. Clarence aimed for it.

Margaret was already exhausted. 'Where are we *going*?'

'Away from the bullets.' Clarence stopped at the loading dock, lifted her by her waist and set her on the ledge, then hopped up behind her.

'Just run, Margo. We have to find a place to hide or we're dead.'

12:38 P.M.:
CORPORAL COPE'S BIG DAY OUT

The convoy roared down I-75. Three Humvees, followed by two M939 five-ton troop trucks, followed by two more Humvees. With that much heavy vehicle ripping along at ninety miles an hour, cars just got the hell out of the left lane and let the convoy roar by. Farmland spread out on either side, snow covering the broken remnants of last year's crops. Beyond the fields, rows of trees, at least a quarter mile from the highway. Beautiful scenery.

Corporal Cope rode in the third Hummer, feeling his connection with God. Soon they would see the glorious gateway and, God willing, would be there when the angels came through.

God, it seemed, was not willing.

The lead Humvee suddenly morphed from a hardy piece of military gear into an orange blossom of fire, spewing bits of metal and body parts all over the highway. The explosion engulfed a slow-moving VW Beetle in the right lane, and sent part of a rear axle through the windshield of the Ford Explorer directly behind it.

The second Humvee swerved to the right, around both the suddenly tumbling Explorer and the newly burning Beetle. The Hummer driver showed amazing reaction time, but at ninety miles an hour the heavy vehicle quickly lost traction. Its rear end fishtailed, making it almost perpendicular with the road when the wheels dug in and it flipped violently, barrel-rolling into the ditch. Cope saw a freeze-frame image of a man thrown free, already missing an arm and part of a leg.

Cope's driver swerved into the left shoulder, past the still-moving, burning wreck of the lead Hummer. If this had been Iraq, with insurgent-launched rockets raining down from rooftops, hitting the gas would have been the right thing to do. But this wasn't Iraq, and here hitting the gas just made Cope's Hummer the lead vehicle – the primary target.

'Stop this thing!' Cope shouted at his driver. 'We're sitting ducks!'

The Hummer's brakes hit hard, throwing Cope forward.

'*Go-go-go!*' Cope screamed. 'Get to cover!'

He jumped out the passenger door and started sprinting. He looked up at the sky to see what was killing his people. Apache Longbow attack helicopters. Compact, dark shapes, like flying tanks with that signature radar dome sticking up above the blurring rotor blades.

He was in some deep shit.

As he ran off the pavement and onto the right shoulder, he looked back to his Hummer. Private Bates hadn't jumped out. Instead, Bates had turned the M249 turret, trying to return fire. The man didn't even have time to pull the trigger before a Hellfire missile slammed home. The Hummer erupted in a semi-trailer-size fireball. The blast threw Cope into the ditch on the side of the road. He hit hard, but adrenaline drove him on – he scrambled to his feet and up the five-foot-high slope of the ditch's far side.

In front of him, a snow-covered cornfield, irregular white spotted with knee-high, rotting-yellow stalks. At least a hundred yards to the trees.

Cope snapped another quick look around him. A few soldiers were sprinting across the fields, headed for the woods. On the road behind him, tall black columns of smoke rose into the air. Five Hummers, two trucks, all destroyed. Looked more like the road to Baghdad than a Michigan highway.

All this open space. If the Apaches' pilots couldn't see him in the afternoon sun, they'd just lock on with infrared targeting – a soldier's body heat stood out clearly against frozen ground.

A trap. This was a kill point. The Apaches had been waiting, probably just out of sight behind a hill.

He had no chance.

He ran anyway.

Thirty yards to his right, another soldier running. A wavering line of glowing red reached out toward the man, like some science-fiction death ray – tracer rounds from an Apache's thirty-millimeter chain gun. The rounds erupted when they hit the ground, harsh explosions launching man-size clods of frozen dirt and smoke. The initial shots went wide, but in a fraction of a second the red death ray closed the gap – the soldier exploded in a literal cloud of blood.

Corporal Jeff Cope kept sprinting.

He'd made it almost fifteen yards when he heard a roar on his left. He turned and saw the tracer-round death ray plowing a path toward him.

He didn't even have time to look away.

12:39 P.M.: WE BE JAMMIN'

She could feel them dying. Her soldiers, her protectors. The enemy was too powerful, too many devils out to stop her.

Chelsea Jewell began to realize that maybe, just maybe, she should have listened to Chauncey. Should have listened to General Ogden.

But that didn't matter.

She still had Mommy.

Together they could build a new network, a *bigger* network – one that would eventually spread all over the whole planet.

The gate to heaven?

Fuck the gate to heaven. Fuck the angels.

Bad words, she knew, but not really, because God decides what is bad and good. God *can't* do anything bad.

Chelsea didn't need the angels. If she escaped, she could use the Legos to make her *own* angels.

If she escaped. And that was a big *if*, because the boogeyman was coming.

If he found her, nothing mattered. She had to block him.

Block him . . . or maybe *control* him.

She could do that, she knew she could. She could make him do things. And who could be a better protector than the boogeyman?

Still, she didn't want it to come to that. She didn't want to face him. Killing him had sounded like fun when he was a long ways away. Now that he was so close, none of this was fun anymore.

12:40 P.M.: LANDING FIELD

Dew held the satphone to his right ear. He covered his left ear with his left hand and leaned his head forward, his belly pressing into the camouflage helmet sitting on his lap.

'Yeah,' he said. 'Look, Murray, we can secure whatever area you want when we land, but first you have to find us a spot to put down.'

Perry couldn't get comfortable. They'd found him a flak jacket and a helmet. He was used to not having anything in his size, so he found it odd when both fit. The helmet in particular would take some getting accustomed to. It had a microphone mounted on the side, connected to a little push-to-talk switch clipped to his vest. Small speakers mounted inside let him hear the tinny voices of soldiers preparing for the coming fight. Some were joking, some were serious, but up and down the facing rows of seats they all looked very pissed off. They'd lost friends during X-Ray Company's sneak attack. Most of the conversation revolved around finding Ogden and what they would do to him when they did. The men had also offered Perry an M4, but Dew said Perry would stick with the .45, and that was that.

Dew looked up, eyebrows raised, sweat beading on his bald head despite the cool temperature inside the Osprey. He turned and regarded Perry.

'You saw the Renaissance Center in your vision, right?'

Perry nodded.

'Where was the river?'

Perry tried to think. So much shit had gone down so fast. That image had flashed from multiple minds, like a strobe-light dance from different cameras all hitting at once. But in each of the images, the angle had been pretty consistent.

'On the left,' Perry said.

'How far away would you say it was?'

Perry shrugged. 'I'm not great with distances, Dew.'

'Take a guess, college boy.'

'Maybe a mile? Maybe a bit less.'

Dew relayed the information, waited, then laughed. 'You've got to be shitting me, L.T.'

He listened, then nodded. Apparently Murray wasn't shitting him.

Dew tucked the satphone back in his flak jacket. 'We're going to put down and secure the LZ. Then Murray is going to fly in another MargoMobile set behind us. They've lost contact with Margaret and Otto, so he thinks their trailers were destroyed.'

'Is Margo dead?'

'I doubt it,' Dew said. 'They had plenty of warning. Otto is a sharp guy, so let's hope for the best.'

'Well, where are we landing, then?'

Dew smiled a shit-eating grin. 'Perry, my boy, you're going to love this landing field. The irony is so thick you could spread it on toast.'

'What? Where are we landing?'

Dew kept smiling and shook his head. 'You'll just have to wait and see.'

He thought this was funny. *Funny.* They were heading into a firefight, Detroit was burning, Margaret might be dead, and Dew was laughing.

'Just sit back and enjoy the ride,' Dew said. 'This might be the last time you ever fly in one of these things.'

Perry sat back and hoped that was true. But he hoped it would be because they walked away and just never got on one again – not because they crashed and died.

12:42 P.M.: OGDEN'S PLANS

General Charlie Ogden made another mark on his paper map of Detroit. He'd lost contact with the men at the 94/75 intersection. They'd done their job, but the fact that he'd lost contact meant two more men gone. Fifty minutes into the attack and losses were higher than he'd expected.

Those low-flying A-10s were a real pain in the ass. Small-arms fire just wouldn't take them out. He'd had only ten Stingers to begin with – five for the various airports and five in the city. Three of the latter set had already fired – two misses and a hit, bringing down an Apache right on Woodward Avenue. He'd ordered the last two Stingers held in reserve. It was possible, however improbable, that Ogden had missed something. Giving up air superiority wasn't an issue. What he couldn't handle was troops on the ground. His men were too spread out, too dispersed to repel infantry.

Ogden could sense it now. He could sense how close they were. Thirty-two minutes, give or take, and the hatchlings would activate the gate.

The angels would descend upon Detroit.

He was in the Globe building with Corporal Kinney Johnson, a sorry excuse for a communications man. Just the two of them, the hatchlings busting ass to finish the gate and Chelsea still sitting inside the Winnebago. Mr. Burkle continued to run in and out, finding whatever material he could for the hatchlings.

'Sir,' Johnson said, 'we're getting reports of massive air traffic off Belle Isle, less than a mile up the river. A-10s, Apaches, even F-15s, flying low.'

'Flying low . . . are they attacking anything?'

'It looks like just targets of opportunity, sir,' Johnson said. 'Some of our men tried volley fire with AT4s, even brought down an A-10, but as soon as our men fire, one of the gunships takes them out.'

He's coming.

Chelsea's voice, tinged with fear. That instantly made Ogden sweat, made his stomach churn – how could God be afraid?

The boogeyman, he's coming. Stop him.

His men had failed to kill Perry and Dew. What if they had also failed to do enough damage to Whiskey Company?

'Johnson, call out to everyone who's left. Look for Ospreys. Repeat, Ospreys.'

Johnson bent to the task, and Ogden waited. Perry and Dew were on the way. The only question was, who was coming with them?

'Sir, visual confirmation of three Ospreys – I repeat, *three* Ospreys – coming in fast from the north.'

'Concentrate all remaining Stinger fire on the Ospreys,' Ogden said. 'Tell any unit that can see the Ospreys to move toward them, set up sniper positions. If any of the birds land, concentrate all fire on whatever comes out.'

12:44 P.M.: INCOMING

Perry Dawsey wanted to puke.

Downtown Detroit spread out before them. Urban sprawl stretched out to the right, while Lake St. Claire filled the left-side view. Plumes of smoke rose from the city, some from skyscrapers, some from the ground, wind carrying the black smoke from left to right, due west across the heart of the city toward Ann Arbor. He wondered if the smoke would reach that far, spread soot on the University of Michigan Stadium where he'd once been a star. The three skyscrapers looked like smokestacks, as if the whole city of Detroit was a giant ship steaming eastward.

He was in the last of three Ospreys. Dew had told him why – any missile fire would probably hit the lead helicopter. That strategy, of course, was only as good as the guesswork of the guy firing the Stingers.

The closer Perry got to Detroit, the more he sensed the infected. This was so different from before. Mather had been one guy, really hard to locate. It had been easier to track down three hosts each for the South Bloomingville and Marinesco gates. The Detroit signal felt huge, undoubtedly more hosts there than he'd ever encountered.

It was also stronger for another reason.

Chelsea Jewell.

He could *experience* her, *taste* her blank soul. He would find her, he would help her, because she had tried to fuck with his head – and nobody fucks with a Dawsey.

An alarm blared through the cabin.

'Incoming!' the pilot shouted. 'Missiles inbound!'

Perry gripped hard on the bottom of the seat. The Osprey's nose tipped down, allowing him a view of the ground far below and the other two Ospreys out in front. The smoke trail started low, from a house way off on the right. It curved, course-correcting to match the Osprey's velocity.

'Hold on, kid,' Dew said. 'It's out of our hands now.'

The missile seemed to pick up speed as it closed in, covering the final bit of distance in the blink of an eye. Up ahead the lead Osprey ejected a spray of flashes with white contrails. Countermeasures of some kind.

They didn't work.

The Osprey rocked to the left, a fireball spewing out of its right side. Amazingly, it didn't disintegrate. Perry felt a flash of hope that the pilot had lived, that he might be able to set her down. Then the Osprey's right engine fell away. The half-plane/half-helicopter simultaneously rolled to the left and tumbled forward as it plummeted. It disappeared beneath Perry's line of sight. He didn't get to see it crash, but those guys were gone. Twenty members of Whiskey Company, plus the Osprey crew.

Dead. Just like that.

'Let's hope they're out of Stingers,' Dew said. 'Our chances of survival just dropped from sixty-six percent to fifty-fifty.'

The alarm beeped again.

'I guess they're not out,' Dew said. He looked semi-relaxed, not in the least concerned that he had a 50 percent chance of dying in the next ten seconds.

The alarm changed from a beep to a steady blare.

'That's not good,' Dew said.

Perry heard whooshing sounds, something shooting off of his Osprey. Two seconds later he heard an explosion. The Osprey tilted to the left a little, then came back to normal and kept descending.

Dew looked a little bored.

'How can you be so calm?' Perry said. 'The next one could be us.'

Dew shrugged. 'When your number is up, your number is up. Besides, you're here, and you're like a cockroach – you survive anything. I'm sticking close to you. You're like a big death umbrella.'

Perry nodded and tried to control his breathing. Dew was going to stick close to *him*? Screw that. More like the other way around. This was Dew's world, and Perry wasn't going to leave his side.

Dew nudged him. 'Take a look out front. We're coming in for a landing. Right up your alley.'

Perry looked, then shook his head.

Dew started laughing.

12:46 P.M.: OTTO ON THE RUN

Clarence turned, aimed and fired, squeezing off four rounds as Margaret sprinted toward the long, two-story, tan brick building. She glanced at the street signs – Franklin and St. Aubin. Cinder-block walls filled the building's windows. The place looked like a miniature fortress.

She ran for the door. Clarence passed her; he was so much faster. He reached it, stood at an angle, shot the deadbolt lock and then kicked the door open. They were only a block from the loading dock in which they'd first hidden. Ogden's men had followed them in. Clarence hadn't found any hiding places he thought were defensible, so they'd run again, bullets hitting all around them. If this building didn't give them some protection, it was over.

She ran inside. He shut the door just as more bullets reached out to them, tearing into the door's heavy wood, ricocheting off bricks on the outside wall. One step slower and they would both have been cut down.

Margaret was so scared she wanted to pee, but she kept moving, one thought in her head keeping her feet pumping – this wasn't as scary as a one-cheeked Betty Jewell.

Clarence turned and ran farther into the abandoned building. Rusted metal machinery dotted the cracked floors amid stagnant puddles of standing water. Margaret saw trash and discarded crack vials everywhere, as well as a rusted shopping cart and half a blue toilet seat. It was a big building, a lot of halls and rooms. If they could find the right spot, it might take their pursuers a long time to track them down.

Clarence saw some stairs and dashed toward them. Margaret followed him up, both of them looking for a place to hide.

12:48 P.M.: THE LANDING

The Osprey slowed quickly as they came in for a landing. Perry heard a plinking sound, bullets hitting the craft's armored sides. His body screwed tight with raw anxiety as he waited for a Stinger to hit.

But none did.

Nails spoke loud and calm, his words picked up by the little microphone curling around from the side of his helmet.

'We're taking fire, possibly from a ten- or fifteen-story building south-southeast of the landing area,' Nails said. 'I need air cover right now!'

Nails turned to face his men. Apparently he didn't trust the microphone to pick up everything, because he started screaming at the top of his lungs. 'All right! We're coming in under fire. The Osprey will land with its nose facing the fire to give you a little cover as you go down the ramp. Hit the ground, go left. There are some bleachers there. Get under them. Find cover, return fire. Once our air support kills the snipers, we will move out. We have twenty-five minutes to destroy the target. We're maybe a mile away, but we're not sure where we're going. I'm guessing we'll be under fire as we run. We *must* press forward, no matter what, understand?'

'Yes sir!' the men barked in unison.

Dew leaned in to talk in Perry's ear. 'All these guys are expendable. You are not. They will draw fire and give you enough cover to move out. Hopefully, they'll pin down the shooters.'

'Hopefully?'

Dew smiled and slapped Perry on the shoulder. 'Like I said, kid, it's all just odds. I put us at about eighty percent to make it.'

'Which means there's a twenty percent chance we *won't* make it.'

Dew winked and pointed a finger at Perry's face. He flicked his thumb down twice – *bang-bang*. The face under his helmet showed electricity, excitement. As if someone had just sliced twenty years off his soul.

He likes this shit, Perry thought. *He likes it, and this is the man I'm counting on to keep me alive?*

Perry felt something. The sensation of the hosts flickered. Faded just a little. Another sensation flared up, very weak, but unmistakable.

The grayness.

'Dew,' Perry said. 'I think they're trying to jam me again.'

Before Dew could respond, the Osprey landed hard, throwing men against their seat restraints.

'Get up and *move!*' Nails screamed. The rear ramp dropped open, and men rushed out. Perry started down the ramp, looking out at what had to be the most surreal thing he'd seen yet.

The open, green expanse of a high-school football field.

'You should feel right at home, Dawsey!' Dew shouted.

Perry hit the green artificial turf and cut left along with the other men. They'd landed almost on the fifty-yard line. He ran across a black circle decorated with the yellow letters MLK, and then he was on the green again.

Somewhere in the back of his head, the ghosts of his past cheered for Scary Perry Dawsey one more time. He was even wearing a helmet.

In front of him, a man's head snapped to the left. The man stumbled and started to fall. Perry reached out and grabbed his jacket, then flipped the limp body up onto his right shoulder. He never even broke stride.

From far off to his left, a deep stuttering sound, then an explosion. He only semi-heard these things – all he could think of was reaching the empty aluminum stands that stretched out in front of him. Suddenly he was on the red track, heading for the corner of the stands, then curving around them – their bulk shielded him from more bullets. Men surrounded Perry, helping him lower the wounded man. As soon as Perry set him down, it was clear the man wasn't wounded.

He was dead.

A bullet had hit him on the right cheekbone and gone out the other side, the exit wound much larger than where the bullet had entered.

'Nice try, Perry,' Dew said. 'An A-10 went after the snipers on that building. We're probably okay for now, but we have to move.' Dew checked his watch. 'According to you, we've got twenty-three minutes – so which way do we go?'

Perry looked away from the dead man. Forty-odd soldiers stared at him. Some were breathing hard. All were waiting.

'Perry,' Dew said. 'Now or never.'

Perry closed his eyes and just *felt*. Without looking, he raised his right hand and pointed. When he opened his eyes, he saw that he was pointing toward the smoking Renaissance Center.

Nails drew in a big breath. 'Let's *moooove*! Time to get some payback, men. Fall out by squads, and let's make time!'

The men turned and started to move out by squads.

Perry took one more look at the dead man, then stood and began jogging after the men of Whiskey Company.

1:00 P.M.: THE PYTHAGOREAN FUCKING THEOREM

Corporal Kinney Johnson was no Corporal Cope. That was for sure.

'Talk to me,' Ogden said. 'This isn't the Pythagorean fucking theorem here – just give me a fucking *head count*.'

Kinney was on one knee, handset held to his ear, trying to contact the remaining soldiers. He scribbled away on a notepad as he talked.

'Johnson!'

He looked up, his face showing anguish, panic and fear all at the same time.

'My guess, sir, twenty men. That's the best I can do.'

Twenty. That was not good.

'Sir,' Johnson said, 'I'm also getting reports from the inner perimeter. Large force of maybe fifty men moving southwest down Lafayette, toward our position. Regular army. Snipers are slowing them, but we can't stop them.'

Ogden hung his head. Whiskey Company had found a way. So close to success. Fifteen more minutes, that's all they needed. As long as Murray didn't know what building they were in, he'd have to bomb half the city. Or drop the nuke, and Gutierrez didn't have the grapes for that.

But the attackers probably had Dawsey – he would sniff out the gate, and that would be that.

Ogden had to protect Chelsea.

'Tell all units to fall back to Bravo positions,' Ogden said. 'That includes Mazagatti and my personal squad.'

Ogden closed his eyes and reached out. He had to prepare Chelsea.

1:02 P.M.: BRAVO POSITIONS

Margaret and Otto sat motionless beneath a loose chunk of plaster and lath. They were in what had once been a small closet, or a smaller bathroom, she wasn't sure – some of the holes in the floor might have been for plumbing.

She hoped their black suits would let them fade into the shadows. Clarence was down to one bullet. If the three soldiers found them here, it was all over.

When they'd entered this room, they'd been careful to avoid the crack vials that littered the floor. Even with the gunfire echoing through the city, any noise might give them away. Ogden's men had been searching for ten minutes, rummaging through the ground floor while Margaret silently prayed they would leave. They hadn't. Now they were going through the second floor. Every few seconds the men shot something. Probably firing into shadows, just to make sure.

Soon they would fire into *this* shadow.

'They're coming,' Clarence whispered. 'Our only chance is for me to shoot the first guy in and take his weapon.'

'*No*,' Margaret hissed. 'They're moving as a team.'

'We have to try something. When I move, you stay here. Maybe if they get me, they'll think we split up. After they leave, you sneak out as best you can.'

Margaret couldn't speak. If they *got him,* meaning if they *killed him,* he hoped it would give her a chance to live.

Clarence Otto was willing to die for her.

She heard a crunching pop of glass, a foot stepping on a crack vial. She grabbed Clarence's hand and squeezed it tight. Then she remembered he needed the hand to shoot, and she let go.

Moments later, feet softly crunched the broken glass as a second man entered the room. Even through the suit, she felt Clarence's body stiffen.

'Hey, Sergeant Major, hold up,' one of the men said. A pause, then: 'That douchebag Kinney says the general ordered us back to Bravo position.'

'Now?'

'Yeah, of course now.'

'What about Montoya?'

'Forget her, man. We gotta get ready for the counterattack. If the general beats us there . . .'

'Fine. Let's go, men. Haul balls.'

Creaking boards. One last faint crunch of glass. Footsteps descending the stairs. Margaret and Clarence waited, but heard nothing. Her body sagged as if her soul had slid free and taken her skeleton with it.

Her body relaxed, but Clarence's did not.

'I want you to stay here,' he said. 'I'm going to follow them and see if I can spot this Bravo location.'

'Clarence, *no.* You've only got one bullet. We need to get out of here.'

'I'm not discussing this with you. I have to see what it is.'

'Fine,' Margaret said. 'Then I'm going with you.'

'Margaret, goddamit, knock it off. There is some serious

shit going down. It's not just Ogden's men. It's total chaos out there. You could get hit by friendly fire. Stay here, and as soon as I make contact with someone, I'll have Murray send people right to you.'

'I'm not leaving your side,' she said. 'I don't want to get shot at anymore, *believe me*, but if you go, I'm following you. So it's your call. If you want *me* out of harm's way, that's exactly where *you* need to be.'

He glared at her. He looked even angrier than when she'd broken his tooth.

She glared right back.

He shook his head and sighed. 'You stay behind me and be ready to run, got it?'

Damn it. She assumed he would stay with her. Well, she'd opened her mouth, and no matter what, she wasn't letting him go alone.

'I got it,' she said. 'After you.'

He walked out of the room, quickly but carefully, letting his pistol lead the way. Margaret stood and followed.

1:06 P.M.: TARGET LOCKED . . .

Dew popped up over the trunk of a Ford, fired off a burst, then ducked back down. Bullets peppered the car, hitting metal, glass and rubber. Whiskey Company had cut through most resistance up until now, but Ogden's men seemed to have concentrated in this area. The fighting grew nastier by the second, racking up casualties – about fifteen so far. With the uncontested and constant air support, that left plenty of fighting strength to push forward. When Ogden's men did fire, Apache chain-guns quickly ripped into their positions.

'Come on, Perry,' Dew said. 'They're digging in here. We've got to be close. Which goddamn direction do we go?'

Perry lay curled up half under the Ford, slush-wet pavement coating him in black winter road grime.

'I'm trying,' he said. 'They're jamming me. It's getting bad. I think it's Chelsea, Dew; I think that little bitch is doing it.'

Another burst of plings and cracks as bullets ripped into the Ford.

Dew heard the buzzing roar of a chain gun, then the firecracker-on-steroids blast of thirty-millimeter rounds tearing through brick and wood and glass.

Then nothing, a pause in the action. Dew pulled Perry back up to a sitting position and leaned him against the ruined Ford.

'Look at me, Perry,' Dew said. 'We've got nine minutes. Come on, kid, *focus*.'

Perry nodded and closed his eyes. 'It's blurry, Dew. It's two signals, and . . . and one of them is *moving*.'

'Key on the signal that is *not* moving,' Dew said. 'They can't move the gate.'

Perry nodded. He breathed in deeply through his nose and let it out slowly from his mouth. Eyes still closed, he raised a hand and pointed over the hood of the battered Ford.

He was pointing down Atwater Street, toward downtown. A snowy field stretched along the left side of the road, and past that, the Detroit River. On the right side of the street, he saw a dilapidated three-story brick building surrounded by empty lots. Faded blue paint up on top had a barely legible sign painted on it: GLOBE TRADING COMPANY.

'That way?' Dew said. 'Where, behind that building?'

'No, in it. I think.'

'You *think* or you *know*?'

'I think,' Perry said. 'I told you, the signal is fading really fast.'

Dew scratched at his face, then looked around. Even in the middle of the firefight, he could see civilians scrambling for cover, cowering in doorways, frightened eyes peeking out from windows.

Apache HEAT rounds would destroy the building, but that didn't guarantee destruction of the gate. Was there a basement? Had Ogden built protective berms or other support structures to harden the target?

Dew could have one of the F-15s drop a two-thousand-pound bomb, but again he wouldn't know *for sure* if that took out the gate. Not to mention inevitable civilian casualties. Those bombs could kill people as far as a hundred yards from impact. Dew's *conservative* guess was that a bomb would kill at least fifty people: men, women and children.

He checked his watch – 1:08 P.M. Five minutes to go.

Dew pulled out his satphone. 'Murray! Come in!'

Murray's scratchy voice came back immediately. 'Murray here, over.'

'We think we found the gate,' Dew said. 'Corner of Orleans and Atwater.'

'Understood,' Murray said. 'Can we bomb it?'

'Negative. Do not take out the building. There are too many civilians around. I'll take Whiskey Company in and make sure this is the real deal. We'll capture it, blow it manually if it gets hot.'

There was a pause.

'Dew, this is President Gutierrez.'

'Uh . . . hello, sir.'

'It's admirable that you want to protect civilian life, but I was informed that Dawsey is one-hundred percent sure that gate opens at one-fifteen.'

'That's correct.'

'I'm ordering the bomb run for one-fifteen,' Gutierrez said. 'If you want to stop it, enter the building and capture the gate in the next six minutes.'

Fuck. Dew shoved the satphone into his flak jacket, then thumbed the transmit button on his helmet mike. 'Nails, Nails, come in, over.'

Dew heard the response in his helmet's earphones. 'Nails here. What are your orders?'

'Building at the corner of Orleans and Atwater,' Dew said. 'That's the target. Get in there right now, kill everything that moves. We have four minutes to secure that building or they're going to drop a bomb that will level about five square blocks.'

'Yessir!'

Dew looked at Perry. 'Well, kid, you ready?'

'No,' Perry said. 'Not even close.'

Dew slapped him on the shoulder. 'Tell you what. We go out there, we get this bullshit done, and then tomorrow you and I go fishing. How about that?'

Perry stared at him for a second, then nodded. 'Okay.'

Maybe Dew's daughter wouldn't go fishing, but Perry was probably the closest thing he'd ever have to a son.

1:11 P.M.: HOSTAGES

Following the three gunmen turned out to be much easier than Margaret had thought possible, for a very disturbing reason. They had run back to the eight-laned Jefferson Avenue, turned west and started collecting hostages. Herding them along at gunpoint, like cattle. Sixteen so far. Women, children, a few men. Some people had resisted – and had been gunned down instantly. A few had shot back, men in their twenties and thirties, firing handguns and even one shotgun. Gangbangers, maybe. They didn't stand a chance. The body-armor-clad soldiers worked as a team, moved as a unit and gunned down any resistance. They even collected the resisters' weapons, leaving nothing behind.

Margaret and Clarence followed at a distance, staying out of sight, feeling completely helpless. Clarence kept cursing in a low growl. He wanted to kill those men. So did Margaret, but Clarence still had only one bullet.

Attacking the gunmen would be suicide, plain and simple. There was nothing he could do but wait for an opportunity. So he followed, and Margaret stayed by his side.

1:12 P.M.: . . . AND FIRE

Perry didn't know jack shit about military tactics, but as a football player he knew great team play when he saw it. Right before Dew called in the attack on the old factory building, Perry could spot maybe four Whiskey Company soldiers. They popped up, shot, dropped back down, moved from one spot of cover to the next. They grabbed wounded comrades and civilians alike, dragging them to safety. Fifteen seconds after Dew's call to Nails, Perry saw at least two dozen soldiers. They seemed to materialize out of nowhere, charging forward, shooting at the Globe building's boarded-up windows. The building grew hazy as bullets pounded bricks into little puffy tan clouds. Perry's helmet radio buzzed with the excited talk of soldiers on the attack.

'Sniper, third floor!'

'Got him!'

'Keep that fire on the second-floor windows. They're chucking grenades!'

Dew stood, groaning a bit as he did, then scooted around the front of the Ford and ran toward the building.

Perry drew his .45 and followed. This was insanity. But if Dew was going, Perry was going with him.

Dew's sprint wasn't much of a sprint at all. Mentally, maybe the guy had shed twenty years, but physically, not so much. Soldiers raced across the empty lot on either side, passing Perry and Dew as if they were standing still. Each step felt like it took five minutes, five minutes during which a bullet might connect at any second.

Yet no fire came his way.

Perry saw only one enemy gunman. Didn't actually see *him*, really, just four or five muzzle flashes from behind a cracked piece of plywood covering a third-floor window. About two seconds after that shot, the plywood disintegrated thanks to a massive concentration of fire that kicked out a rain of splinters and paint chips. The gunman didn't fire again.

Dew followed a dozen soldiers toward a rusted roll-up garage door that was closed only a quarter of the way. A battered plywood wall blocked the rest of the opening. Perry heard a *whoosh* from behind and instinctively ducked. A rocket shot past, at least twenty feet to his right. It hit the plywood wall and erupted in a cloud of fire and wooden shrapnel.

Nails's voice in his helmet speakers. '*Take that building!*'

Perry moved forward, still right behind Dew. Whiskey Company soldiers were thirty yards ahead of them, rushing toward the now-gaping door. For what must have been the hundredth time in the past hour, Perry tried to comprehend the bravery of a soldier, someone who *chose* to rush headlong into enemy fire.

The first soldiers reached the open door. One tossed in a grenade. Like an optical illusion, someone from inside the building tossed *out* a grenade at the same time. The two devices actually passed by each other, going opposite ways. The charging Whiskey Company men scattered and dove for cover. Two didn't make it far enough. The grenade exploded. No fireball like in the movies, just a hellacious bang, an instant cloud of smoke and a fist-hard hit of air.

The two men were standing one second, falling the next. One hit the ground face-first and didn't move. The other turned as he fell, landing on his right side, hands reaching behind his back and grabbing madly as if his clothes were on fire.

Automatic gunfire erupted from the boarded-up second-floor windows, one gunman on either side of the roll-up garage door. Another Whiskey Company soldier went down, screaming, grabbing at a thigh instantly soaked with blood.

Dew kept running forward.

Perry stayed on his heels.

Dew raised his M4 and fired. Perry pointed his .45 at one of the windows and emptied the magazine. Plywood splintered where he shot. Behind him, to the right, he heard a *whuff,* then a second later a heavy crunch as something ripped through the plywood window right before a concussive *bang* blasted it outward in a fiery cloud of pulverized brick and wooden splinters. Perry reloaded, debris raining down on him and Dew as they followed soldiers beneath the roll-up garage door.

Once they were inside the long open space of the Globe building, there was no subtle strategy, no effort to capture a hatchling alive, only the brute force of twenty-five pissed-off soldiers, one old CIA agent with a bad hip and one former all-American linebacker with two bum knees.

The fight didn't last long. Only a few of Ogden's men remained alive, and most of them were already wounded. The hatchlings attacked, of course, but they had no cover and were quickly mowed down by concentrated fire.

Perry killed three of the little fuckers himself.

Each shot felt better than the last, a tingling trip of adrenaline ripping through his body. He'd killed the infected because they needed to die – killing hatchlings was just plain fun.

All eyes had been focused on the soldiers, their guns, the hatchlings. When the last hatchling fell, shivering in its sickening death throes, Perry and the others took in the massive brown and green construct arching to an apex some twenty feet high. Strands of the brown material ran from the arches up to the roof's metal framework forty feet above, supporting some of the construct's weight.

And past the gate, a white and brown Winnebago. From inside, even through the jamming, he sensed the infected.

'She's in there,' Perry said, and pointed.

Dew shouldered his M4 and opened up on the Winnebago. Within seconds, four other men unloaded on it as well. Shiny dots appeared as bullets tore through the thin walls. One tire popped, then another.

Dew stopped firing and put in a fresh magazine.

'Secure the building!' Nails called. 'No prisoners, make sure they're dead, and *do not* touch the bodies. And find Ogden! I want to piss on his fucking corpse.'

The men spread out.

Perry walked right under the gate toward the Winnebago. Behind him he heard Dew.

'Murray, we have the building, abort bomb run,' Dew said. 'Repeat, abort bomb run, keep the F-15s on-station, just in case. We'll rig the gate to blow manually.'

Perry kept walking. He held his .45 tight but was careful to keep his finger off the trigger. The Winnebago had so many holes it looked darkly comical. He stepped toward the small side door.

Blood leaked from it.

Dew kept shouting. 'Nails! I want C-4 at the base of every arch, and don't be stingy with it on those other parts.'

Perry stared at the blood dripping from the bottom of the RV's door, lightly pattering onto the dirty, cracked concrete below.

More commotion behind him, Nails screaming, men yelling back and forth, but little of it registered in Perry's thoughts.

He still sensed that other presence, but barely – the jamming had grown during the firefight, so bad now that it was almost all gray again.

This was it. It *had* to be.

He opened the bullet-ridden door and looked inside.

A body, but not Chelsea. A man in a postal worker's uniform, dead and still oozing blood onto crinkled plastic that partially covered the narrow floor.

Perry leaned over the body and quickly looked around.

Chelsea wasn't there.

No, *no-no-no* . . . Chelsea had been the moving signal. She was gone.

'Perry!' Dew yelled. 'Get your ass out here!'

Perry shut the door and turned back to the others.

The gate was glowing, like white frosted glass illuminated by countless tiny, slow-moving, high-powered bulbs. It lit up the warehouse interior, filling it with a beautiful glow.

Perry walked up to the gate. He could already feel the heat. It was the most beautiful thing he'd ever seen. A biological jewel glowing with light drawn from a million stars. Texture like a rough tree trunk. A smell like leftover barbecue. Emotions of love, admiration, even awe, they rolled through him, too strong to deny.

Perry saw it, felt it and sensed it all at the same time. The vibration. The *opening*. The spongy green door from his dreams of six weeks ago, an *eternity* ago. A connection from infinite distance, the threads of the universe binding, entwining, coalescing into something that blended all existence. *Purity*.

'Nails, how much longer?' Dew said. 'It's one-fourteen. This thing opens up in sixty seconds.'

'Almost there, *sir*!'

Perry stroked the gate one last time. It wouldn't be long now. He left his hand there, feeling the growing heat.

'Okay, it's ready!' Nails screamed. '*Moooove* out! *Go-go-go-go-go!*'

Men sprinted out of the warehouse. Perry marveled at their energy, their intensity. Someone hit him on the shoulder.

'Stop staring at their asses, kid,' Dew said. 'Let's go.'

Dew hobble-sprinted toward the door. Perry followed, barely needing to jog to keep up. They ran out and across the field. He tried to concentrate as he ran, concentrate on the fading sensation that had to be Chelsea Jewell. What direction? He couldn't tell.

Nails's men squatted in a wide, loose circle, each man facing out, guns at the ready. Nails pulled a small black plastic clicker from his breast pocket.

'Fire in the hole,' he said, then clicked the clicker three times.

The walls of 1801 Atwater blasted outward at the base. The last surviving bits of glass shattered, along with the plywood that covered most of the windows. Pieces of the roof shot into the sky, trailed by thick tendrils of expanding black smoke. The building collapsed upon itself, hundred-year-old brick walls falling in and down. A second later, rolling smoke and dust billowed out, obscuring everything.

'Holy shit,' one of the men said, laughing. 'That's awesome.'

'Crap,' Dew said. 'I sure hope there's nothing contagious in this dust.'

He pulled out his satphone. 'We got it, Murray.'

Perry felt her, just a bit, the last trailing of sensation. Chelsea. Moving, still blocking him . . .

. . . then she was gone.

And he knew, with absolute certainty, that he'd never get her back, not unless she wanted it to happen. She had become too powerful.

'I lost her,' Perry said. 'I lost Chelsea.'

1:16 P.M.: BRAVO POSITIONS, PART TWO

Margaret crouched at the base of a small abandoned building, watching dust roil through the air around her. A block away, the Globe building had just exploded and collapsed, sending a thick dust cloud rolling through the abandoned lots. She wondered if the cloud carried the contagion – but she and Clarence were safe in their suits. The sticky tape on her hands would keep the glove cuts sealed. A white-trash version of BSL-4 safety, but it worked nonetheless.

Clarence moved along the sidewalk. His right shoulder stayed close to the graffiti-covered brick wall, but he didn't touch it – she had warned him about sliding across anything, even leaning on things for cover should he wind up in a shoot-out. The tough hazmat suit could still tear if dragged across any jagged metal.

Helicopters soared overhead, guns fired, explosions made the ground vibrate – war had come to Detroit.

Clarence peeked around the corner. He watched for a few seconds, then reached back and gently pulled her hand, urging her forward until she could see for herself. Down the block, on the other side of the intersection, stood yet another abandoned building. A corner unit, battered front door opening out at an angle toward the intersection of Franklin and Riopelle. Light gray, two stories, boarded-up windows; it looked like an old restaurant or bar, maybe a corner store from decades past when this area had more buildings than abandoned lots.

'That's where the gunmen took the hostages,' he said.

'What's in there?'

'I don't know. If the gate is gone, Ogden has to know it's over, that he lost. He filled the building with hostages so we can't drop a big fucking bomb on his ass.'

'Or maybe they're trying to convert those people? Infect them?'

'Maybe,' Clarence said. 'Maybe some of them, but it makes more sense to have regular people as hostages. Otherwise they have no negotiating power.'

'What do we do now?'

'We've got to get help. Listen, you watch where those soldiers went in, and *don't move*. Ogden's headquarters blew; our guys had to cause that. I'll slide around to the other side of this building – the gunmen can't spot me from there – see if I can flag down our guys and get them over here.'

Clarence slowly ducked away from the corner. Margaret knelt and watched. Every twenty seconds or so, a car drove through the settling dust, full of people hunting for a place to hide. When they saw her or Clarence, saw their biohazard suits, the cars instantly sped up to get away. The faces inside looked terrified, shell-shocked. Nothing she could do for these people, not without making a scene, making herself visible to the gunmen in the building across the street. She silently prayed that all the cars would just keep driving.

Then, coming up Riopelle from the direction of the river, a motorcycle. A squat one, American and loud, kicking up a low cloud of the still-falling dust. A man driving, someone behind him, someone small.

'Keep going,' Margaret whispered. 'Don't stop here, *keep driving.*'

The motorcycle stopped right in front of the hostage building.

Margaret tensed. She couldn't let those people go inside. They got off the bike, and Margaret saw the small person was a little girl with curly hair.

Blonde.

Chelsea Jewell.

And the man – Colonel Charlie Ogden in street clothes.

They ran into the building.

Margaret whipped behind the corner, out of sight.

Clarence was already coming back from the other side. He wore a wide smile, an expression of near disbelief.

She grabbed his arm. 'I just saw Chelsea Jewell.'

His smile widened. 'Are you sure?'

'Yes, I'm sure! It's her. Why are you smiling?'

He actually laughed. 'I don't know. Too much death, stress, something good finally happens, and now I can't stop grinning. Go take a look – you won't believe who's coming this way.'

Margaret traded places with him. Still moving slowly, cautiously, she walked to the other side of the building and looked around the corner.

And understood Clarence's joy.

Because she felt it, too.

Coming across an empty, abandoned city block, running through the settling dust, she saw Dew Phillips, Perry Dawsey and soldiers carrying machine guns.

THE CAVALRY

If you went back in time, say, six weeks, to a point when Margaret Montoya stood in an apartment parking lot in Ypsilanti, Michigan, scared for her life because a gigantic, burned and brutally wounded infected man named Perry Dawsey was trying to tear through her biohazard suit, his wild eyes staring, his spit and blood smearing her visor, his cracked lips screaming *open that fucking door and let 'em in* . . . if you could go back to that moment and tell her there would come a time where she would feel infinitely happy and relieved to see his face, she wouldn't have believed you. You could have bet her on that. Bet her with the same bill that traded hands so frequently between Clarence and Amos.

And you'd have won twenty bucks.

Perry, Dew and maybe twenty-five heavily armed and grim-faced soldiers came running down Woodbridge Street. The cavalry to the rescue. The men fanned out, working like the fingers of a hand, some pointing guns across the street at the boarded-up windows of Chelsea's building, some darting across that same street to the building next to hers, backs against brick walls, slowly inching to the corner, some continuing down the street, probably to surround the place. Dew and Perry ran right up to her.

'Margaret!' Perry said. 'We got the gate. Are you okay?'
He hugged her, suit and all, picking her right up off the
ground.

'I'm okay, I'm okay.' She hugged him back. She couldn't
believe how good it was to see him.

Dew scooted to the corner, peeked around, then ducked
back.

'Clarence said you saw Ogden?'

'And Chelsea Jewell,' Margaret said.

Perry's smile faded. A look of hatred filled his eyes.
Margaret instantly thought of the dead, angry stares of
the infected victims she'd had on her autopsy table.

'And hostages,' Clarence said. 'About fifteen of them.
And at least three gunmen armed with body armor, M4s,
sidearms and grenades. There could be more already
inside.'

Dew looked Clarence up and down. 'Human condom,
eh?'

Clarence nodded at Margaret. 'Blame her.'

'Hell, I wish I had one right about now,' Dew said.
'Margaret, what happened with Sanchez? You figure this
thing out yet?'

The sensation of relief vanished, replaced once again
by feelings of failure.

'No, I didn't,' she said. 'Try not to get infected, because
there's still no cure.'

Dew and Perry nodded.

'How about Gitsh and Marcus?' Dew asked. 'Doctor
Dan?'

Clarence shook his head.

'So we've got losses,' Dew said. 'Let's make them count.
Clarence, take Margaret and go to the football field at
Martin Luther King High School, about a mile up

Jefferson, you can't miss it. Murray dropped a MargoMobile there to set up an infection triage. There are also two Ospreys on the ground. If things turn dicey, you get her out of here.'

'I'm standing right here, Dew,' Margaret said. 'Clarence isn't my keeper.'

'Yes he is,' Dew said. 'And he's getting you out.'

'Have some of your men take her,' Clarence sad. 'I'm staying to finish this.'

Why couldn't Clarence just shut up and leave? Hadn't he done his job? Hadn't they sacrificed enough? She wanted out, and she wanted him with her.

'Otto, you *will* get the fuck out of here,' Dew said. 'Your mission is to protect Margaret, and I want her gone.'

Clarence shook his head. 'But Dew—'

'Shut your broken-toothed mouth. You've got your orders. Do you mind if we go ahead and save the fucking world? Perry, you go with them.'

Perry Dawsey actually laughed. A dark laugh, something he might have let slip back in a kitchen filled with three dead bodies.

'Fuck you, Dewie,' he said. 'Chelsea and I need to talk.'

Dew turned to look at Perry, tilted his head up to make eye contact. Perry's filthy blond hair hung in front of a face smeared with grime and reddish dust.

'You'll go *now*, Dawsey, and that's an order.'

'How many times do I have to tell you, old man?' Perry said. 'I'm not a soldier, and your orders don't mean dick to me. I'm getting that girl. The only way you can stop me is to shoot me, and this time I'll shoot back. With your own gun.'

Perry raised his eyebrows and lifted a pistol, not pointing it at Dew, more of a show-and-tell gesture.

'Sir!' A big black man, almost as big as Perry, ran up to Dew. 'Sir, someone is sticking a white flag out the front door.'

'Son of a bitch,' Dew said. 'Let's see if we can close this out. Nails, have half your men target the second-floor windows, the other half the ground floor. I don't want to kill any hostages, but I'm not in the mood to be shot at, either.'

'Got it,' Nails said, then started barking orders. Margaret had never heard a human being that loud.

Dew looked at Perry again. 'I suppose if I tell you to stay here, you'll just ignore me?'

Perry nodded.

Dew sighed. 'Fine, fuck it. Let's go.'

Perry's slow breaths steamed in the cold air, carried away by the breeze coming off the river. The helmet felt cold on his head, but his flak jacket trapped his body heat and made him sweat despite the freezing temperature. He gripped the .45 tightly and followed Dew around the corner. Dew carried an M4, barrel angled toward the ground. Jets still screamed overhead, their engine roars echoing across the cityscape. Far up ahead, the RenCen continued to burn like a tall, smoldering black torch, a column of greasy smoke angling up and trailing across downtown Detroit. Helicopters hovered all over the place, probably waiting for more of Ogden's men to show themselves.

Perry and Dew walked toward the building on the corner. The front door was open just a little, enough room for a stick with a white shirt tied to it to wave back and forth.

He saw Whiskey Company men all over the place, guns trained on the open door and the windows. If someone opened fire from inside the building, an instant bloodbath would ensue.

Dew stopped twenty feet in front of the door. Perry did the same, a step behind Dew, a step to his left.

'We're listening,' Dew said.

The door opened, and Chelsea Jewell walked out, carrying the flag.

Had it been anyone else, a soldier, a grown-up, some twitchy finger might have opened fire, white flag or no. But the image of a seven-year-old girl with beautiful blonde curls and an innocent face instantly made fingers ease off triggers, if only a little.

To anyone else she looked innocent, but Perry saw deeper. He saw a nightmare, something dark and self-serving, something happy to destroy anything that didn't give her what she wanted. He didn't care what he had to do, how far he had to go – Chelsea Jewell would never leave this place alive.

She walked ten feet from the door, far enough to stand in the debris-strewn, potholed street.

Perry stepped forward. Time to end this. A hand on his chest – Dew pushing him back. Perry wanted to shoot her, but he would back Dew's play.

'We wanna negotiate,' Chelsea said. 'My mommy needs help.'

'Tell all your men to throw out their weapons,' Dew shouted, loud enough so the men in the building could hear him.

Chelsea stood there, motionless save for the white flag still twitching in her little hand. Guns flew out of the building's broken windows and clattered on the sidewalk. Two came from the ground floor, just one from the second. Was that all Ogden had left? *Three* gunmen?

More silence.

'Where's Colonel Ogden?' Dew asked.

'He will come out now, with my mommy,' Chelsea said. 'She's hurt, she needs help.'

Perry heard Nails's bellowing voice. 'Squad One, move up!'

Soldiers of Whiskey Company stepped out from cover and moved forward, forming a wide half circle around Chelsea.

She turned and walked back through the door. Perry started to follow her inside, but Dew's hand on his chest stopped him again. She slipped inside, out of sight. Only a few seconds of tense waiting later, a man walked out. Ogden. He reached back and pulled something through the door. Something big, like a two-legged hippo. Gray. Wearing . . . pants?

Wait.

The man wasn't pulling that thing.

That thing . . . was *walking*.

Margaret watched an obscenity walk out of the building.

'What the fuck?' Clarence said. 'What is that?'

It was a woman. A woman horribly bloated to insane proportions. Her arms were swollen to the point where the skin stretched out thin and semitransparent like a balloon, or like the casing of a sausage sizzling away on a grill. Her stomach distended like a cartoon-character. Her breasts looked massive, misshapen, like beach balls. Her *face* was puffed up to the point that her eyes were nothing more than stretched, squinting slits. The woman couldn't see – that's why Ogden led her forward.

'Stay where you are!' Dew screamed. 'Ogden, stop or we shoot!'

Guns rattled as soldiers took aim. Ogden stopped. So did the woman. With a smooth, confident motion, Ogden reached into his pocket, drew out a grenade and pulled the pin. He jammed the grenade into the woman's bloated folds.

Dew fired. Ogden's head jerked to the side, and he dropped, lifeless.

Next came two long seconds, a pregnant pause. Margaret and the soldiers stared at the obscenely bloated woman standing next to Colonel Charlie Ogden's fallen body.

Someone started firing.

A dozen M4s suddenly erupted, bullets punching into the monstrosity that had once been the beautiful Candice Jewell. Each bullet kicked out a gray jet like the spray of a miniature fire extinguisher. She stumbled back a step, arms comically pinwheeling as she fought for balance.

And then the grenade went off.

A bang, no flash. A cloud of gray peppered with red, fleshy shrapnel.

The cloud expanded, billowing past Dew and the men who had surrounded Chelsea. It thinned as it spread, a translucent sphere growing more and more transparent. The soldiers turned to run, but the cloud engulfed them before they made it three steps. It blew past them seemingly hungry for the next man in line, and the next

The soldiers slowed, then stopped. Hands went to throats, to eyes, to ears. They scratched at themselves. They *clawed*. They screamed. They fell. They writhed and kicked.

The cloud billowed past Margaret, tiny spores covering her airtight suit.

Tears rolled down her face. This was it, this was the final stage. There had to be millions of the spores. Sanchez had caught the disease from a tiny puffball, maybe a thousand spores landing on his hand, and even though he'd washed the hand immediately, it hadn't mattered – the stuff penetrated almost on contact.

Every one of these men, including Dew, including Perry, was already infected with a dose at least a thousand times more concentrated.

She looked away from the men, looked at the air around her. The pollenlike dust drifted away, a grayish cloud carried by the wind. The spores were already starting to fall, but only slightly – they might travel a mile or more before they finally came to rest.

A mile would carry them into downtown Detroit, even beyond, spreading them across the tens of thousands of panicked citizens trying to hide from gunfire. Spores were far smaller than bullets, far more dangerous, and from those spores there *was* no place to hide.

People stumbled out of the house. The hostages. Clawing at their eyes and throats and ears, running in any direction, every direction. It wasn't just the wind that could spread the contagion – these people would take it much farther.

How many of them would leave the city in a panic? Find a car, a way out, and just start driving? How many would travel three or four hours before they fell asleep?

And how many of those would change into another gasbag, like Chelsea's mother?

She saw other civilians, stumbling out of buildings where they had hidden, hands rubbing desperately at eyes, digging at exposed skin. They ran in a panic, aimlessly scattering in all directions.

'Clarence, does your HUD say anything about suit integrity?'

He said nothing. He just stared at the carnage.

'Clarence!'

'Uh . . . no, nothing about suit integrity.'

Thank God. He was safe.

'We have to get out of here,' she said. 'We have to get to the decon trailer at the football field. Can you drive that motorcycle parked in front of the building?'

'Yeah, but what about Dew? Perry? We have to help them.'

Margaret swallowed. Dew writhed on the ground. Perry just lay on his back, barely moving. She wanted to go to them, but the cold, mathematical part of her brain knew the score.

'We can't help them,' she said. 'Do what I say, and do it now. If you don't, the world is fucked.'

Clarence looked at her, then looked back at the men crawling across the ground, at the people running into the city. It seemed to click home for him. He closed his eyes tight. Tears dripped down his cheeks. He opened his eyes, grabbed her hand and ran for the motorcycle.

PEOPLE HELPING PEOPLE

Get up, Perry. I need you.

Coughing.

Dust, the taste of smoke, the taste of dirt, the taste of . . .

(don't think about it)

. . . of scorched flesh. In his *mouth*.

More coughing.

But not just from the brick and dirt and smoke and wood and the (don't think about it) scorched flesh, coughing from something deeper, way down in his lungs.

Something that *burned*.

Perry knew. He felt stabbing pains all through his skin, his face, in his muscles and eyes. They were *inside* him.

It's time for you to join me.

It was her again. In his head. He'd thought the gate was the most beautiful thing he would ever experience. He was wrong. As rapturous as that gate was, it paled in comparison to the voice.

Come to me, Perry. Get me out of here.

So beautiful. He'd heard her before, but he'd been hundreds of miles away. Now there was no distance, no jamming, no grayness – her pure, raw power raged through his soul.

Perry stood and stumbled down the street. Men were all around, the brave guys of Whiskey Company, rolling on the ground, coughing, spitting up blood. They were all totally fucked.

Just like Perry.

And there, lying in the middle of the street . . . Dew Phillips.

Just relax and let it happen. You'll be stronger now. You'll be like me. Come to me, Perry. Protect me.

Perry shuffled toward Dew. The man was on his back, mouth opening and closing. He saw Perry and managed to smile, then shrug.

Dew knew the deal.

'Sorry . . . kid,' he said, his voice a hoarse croak. 'Looks like . . . we're not going fishing after all.'

Kill him.

Dew's face screwed into a pinched mask of agony. Perry knew what Dew was feeling, because he felt that same pain himself. The difference was, Perry and pain were long-lost buddies.

Dew's wave of pain seemed to fade for a second. He blinked rapidly, then coughed, bloody foam splattering onto his lips.

'Kid . . . get my radio. See if Margaret got out.'

Perry nodded. 'I will.'

Kill him. Do it now.

'I'm proud of you, Perry,' Dew said. 'Maybe you don't . . . have testicles . . . but you sure got balls.'

Dew Phillips actually laughed. Or started to, then he coughed up a little blood.

Perry saw his .45 lying on the ground. The one that had belonged to Dew for thirty-some years.

Kill him!

'Thank you, for everything,' Perry said. 'And I'm sorry about this, but I have to.'

Perry put the .45 against Dew's forehead.

'Kid? What . . .'

Perry closed his eyes, kept his hand perfectly still and pulled the trigger.

Then he turned away and walked toward the building.

Chelsea had called for him, *God* had called for him, and he had to obey.

RIDE TO LIVE

The black Harley Night Rod Special roared down the sidewalk of East Jefferson Avenue. Shell-shocked people ran out of the way, only too eager to flee from yet another potential threat – a loud-as-hell motorcycle carrying two people in black hazmat suits.

Bodies lined the sidewalk and the street, the corpses of people who had resisted the hostage roundup of Ogden's men. Clarence wove around those bodies, around cars that had driven onto the sidewalk and crashed into buildings, and around a few people wandering aimlessly, clawing at their eyes, their faces, their arms. Margaret saw traces of gray dust everywhere. As they drove, the dust thinned until she saw no more of it. They'd driven out of the puffball's expansive blast radius.

Now the only spores would be on their hazmat suits.

Even with the parking-lot-like traffic jam, the Harley moved along at a brisk pace, its obscenely loud engine a long-distance warning to anything that might stand in its way. Within minutes they saw the high-school football field on the left. Sitting on it, a MargoMobile and two Ospreys.

An icon illuminated on her heads-up display—wireless connection. Her suit computer had picked up the communication net from the new MargoMobile.

'This is Doctor Margaret Montoya!' she shouted as Clarence turned sharply on Mount Elliot. 'Prepare for immediate evacuation. Patch me through to Murray Longworth on this frequency *right now*, open the airlock door, then everyone *out* of the trailers and onto the Osprey. Get it warmed up. We're out of here in three minutes. *Do not approach me,* I am contagious.'

A block later they reached the football field's main gate. A guard had been there, but she saw only his back as he sprinted for the Osprey. Clarence drove the roaring motorcycle through the gate onto the field and stopped at the MargoMobile's airlock door.

As soon as the bike's engine died out, Margaret heard Murray's voice in her helmet speakers. 'Margaret, what's going on?'

She and Clarence sprinted for the airlock. She'd been running forever, it seemed, and every last muscle screamed in protest. She entered, and he shut the door behind them. The instant the air pressure equalized, she opened the door to the decontamination chamber.

'Margaret,' Murray said, 'answer me!'

'It's contagious,' she said through heavy breaths. She ran to the controls as Clarence shut the second airlock door. She hit the controls and the room filled with the bleach/chlorine spray.

'We know it's contagious,' Murray said.

'No, you don't get it.' She raised her arms and slowly turned, letting the mist wash over her. 'It's *airborne*. It replicates inside people, fills them up like a puffball till they burst.'

'Okay, how do we contain that? Where's Dew?'

'Dew is infected,' Margaret said. 'So is Perry; all of them are. There's nothing we can do for them, Murray, and if we have any hope at containing this, we need to act right now.'

Dead silence on the other end.

'Murray, did you hear me?'

'Yeah,' he said quickly, but in a voice that oozed total exhaustion. 'What do you want us to do?'

The mist shut off. Clarence opened the airlock door that led back to the entrance. Margaret swallowed 'You have to . . .'

Her voice lodged in her throat as she followed Clarence. He shut the door, then ran to the final airlock.

'Margaret?' Murray said. 'Talk to me.'

She felt tears pouring down her face, but because of the suit she couldn't wipe them.

'Option Number Four,' she said. 'You have to use Option Number Four.'

Dead silence. Otto pulled her onto the football field and started taking off her gloves.

When Murray spoke, his voice sounded thin, old. 'There's got to be another way.'

Clarence lifted her feet one at a time, took off her shoes.

Margaret shook her head. 'There isn't. The fireball will crank the temperature up so high it will kill all the spores for three or four miles around. They've probably spread a mile already. You have to do it. Now.'

Another pause. She disconnected the helmet from the suit but left it on her head so she could keep talking to Murray. She started tearing off her suit. Clarence did the same with his.

A new voice in the speakers.

'Margaret, this is President John Gutierrez. Do you realize that you're asking us to drop a nuclear weapon on Detroit?'

'Of course I *fucking realize* that! I know *exactly* what I'm asking, you *fucking moron*!'

Margaret couldn't stop the tears now, nor could she stop the sobs. She stepped out of the suit. She wore nothing but scrubs and the helmet. Otto grabbed her hand and pulled her toward the Osprey's open rear ramp.

'How much time to evacuate?' Gutierrez asked.

'You can't evacuate,' she said. 'If you don't do this right now, it's going to be too late. Look how it converted Ogden's men, how fast it took over and what it made them do. The spores have already spread all through downtown Detroit. Thousands are infected. The infected will radiate out of the city. These people are terrified. They're going to get as far from Detroit as they can; you can't stop them. Some of them will turn into these . . . gasbags . . . full of spores. We just watched it happen. The infection will spread everywhere. People will be converted into this collective organism – they won't be human anymore. If it spreads past Detroit, we're *fucked. Humanity* is fucked. You have to act now, Mister President, or it's out of our hands for good.'

'Where are you?' Gutierrez asked.

'We're getting on the Osprey at the football field.'

She ran up the ramp. It started to close behind her. Seven men were inside. They stared at her and Clarence, and instantly shied away, shuffling toward the front of the passenger section.

'Margaret,' Gutierrez said, his voice quiet and cold. 'Are you sure, *absolutely* sure this is the only way?'

'I . . . I am.'

Another pause, then Murray again. 'I'm telling the Osprey pilot to take off fast,' he said. 'You should be out of range when it goes off. What are the exact target coordinates?'

Margaret stared out for a second. All of Dew's men were gone. No one to paint the target. There was one way, though, to make sure the nuke hit the right spot.

'Can you get a signal from Dew's satphone?'

'Yes.'

'Drop it there.'

PERRY MEETS CHELSEA

Perry's body boiled inside. He and pain were old buddies, but his old buddy was making itself a little too welcome. His second infection, it seemed, would be just as much fun as the first.

He walked through the front door of the abandoned building. Two of Ogden's men were inside. They'd recovered their weapons. The spores didn't seem to affect them.

They let Perry pass.

Come to me, my protector.

He walked. The two men followed him, one behind each shoulder. Chelsea was on the second floor. He could sense her, feel her beauty, her power, her *divinity*. He walked up old stairs that creaked under his feet.

General Ogden said we'd have another hour or so before they shut down the city, so we have to hurry. We need a car. Then we can go for a ride.

He reached the top of the stairs.

Down the hall, standing in an empty, trash-strewn room of the abandoned building, he finally saw her.

Chelsea.

And his heart *ached*.

'I'm afraid I destroyed the gate, Chelsea.'

You have destroyed many things.

'No gate . . . what will you do?'

We're like a new person now. A superorganism. Isn't that a neat word? Can't you feel the crawlers working through your body? They will change you even more, Perry. We will escape Detroit, and then you and I will make the whole world play together.

He walked up to her. His feet seemed heavy, each step like dead-lifting a thousand pounds. Every nerve screamed with agony.

She could do it. She *could* take over the world.

Chelsea Jewell could be God.

You understand now, don't you? You understand how silly it was to fight all this time? Let's get a car and go get some ice cream.

Perry smiled down at her. So tiny, so fragile, so beautiful.

He snapped his right arm back into the soldier behind him. A pile-driver elbow smashed into the man's face, crushing his left cheek and fracturing his right orbital bone. The man on Perry's left started to raise his M4, but Perry pointed his .45 down and fired twice. Two bullets shredded the man's foot into raw meat. The man shivered, dropped his gun and instinctively reached for his foot. As he bent down, Perry put the .45 to his head and pulled the trigger.

Perry swiveled right to face the man he'd elbowed. Two shots, both bullets ripping through the man's chest. Before the body even hit the filthy wooden floor, Perry turned back and reached out.

His big right hand locked on Chelsea Jewell's throat.

He lifted her. She weighed nothing.

Stop it!

'No.'

No, Perry, NO! Bad Perry!

She didn't look scared. She didn't look evil, either. She looked like a spoiled child, a child who did whatever she wanted, *took* whatever she wanted.

He squeezed a little harder.

Fear crept into those angelic blue eyes, the realization that maybe she didn't control him.

You have to do what I say! I told you to kill that man, and you did!

'You didn't make me do it,' Perry said. 'I couldn't let him wind up like me. I had to help him.'

Footsteps rushed up the stairs behind him. Perry turned to face the open door, Chelsea still held out in front of him. The last gunman sprinted down the hall, M4 raised. He skidded to a halt when he saw Chelsea held in the air like a shield.

Perry aimed and fired.

The bullet hit the last man dead center in the forehead. He took one step back, dropped his gun, then lifted his right hand, weakly, as if he wanted to touch Chelsea's hair one last time.

The man fell backward.

He didn't move.

Perry looked at Chelsea. So beautiful. He understood that man's dying gesture of love, of affection.

Why would you kill me, Perry?

Hate tinged her ice-cold eyes.

Cold, like the eyes of a hatchling.

You're not like anyone else. I can see into your memories, Perry. No one accepted you for who you are, but with me you can be what you were born to be – a killer.

'Maybe that's what I was born to be,' Perry said. 'But it's not who I am anymore.'

It is, and you know it is. Why help them? What have these people ever done for you?

'One of them was going to take me fishing,' Perry said. Then he shot Chelsea Jewell in the face.

DEW'S SATPHONE

A soldier handed Margaret a satphone. She just looked at it. Clarence took it and answered.

'Agent Otto here.'

The voice on the satphone was crackling but clearly audible. 'It's Murray. I've got Perry. He wants to talk with Margaret.'

Margaret's body sagged in her seat. Perry was still alive? Not for long, not long at all.

'Okay,' she said, and took the phone.

More crackling, then the deep voice of Perry Dawsey. 'Hey Margo.'

She fought back the tears. If she cried too hard she couldn't speak. 'Hey,' she said. 'Are you . . . are you on Dew's phone?'

'Yeah,' Perry said. 'I got Chelsea. The voices have finally stopped, but . . . I don't think I'm doing so good. I've got those things inside me. It hurts. Bad. I think they're moving to my brain. Margaret, I don't want to lose control again.'

'You won't,' she said. 'They won't have time.'

A pause. 'Holy shit,' he said. 'Are you nuking me?'

'Yes.'

Laughter, cut short by a wet cough, then a groan of pain. 'Dew said I'm like a cockroach, that nothing can kill me. I don't think physics is on my side this time, though.'

Margaret let out a sound that was half cry, half laugh. Her soul *hurt*.

'Clarence with you?'

'I can hear you,' Clarence said, his voice also choked with sobs. 'You are really something else. Nobody ever been as tough as you.'

'Sorry about those Toby jokes,' Perry said. 'Truth be told, I was just jealous of you and Margo. I wanted to beat the shit out of something, and you were there.'

'I know,' Clarence said. 'It's nothing.'

'Don't fuck it up with her,' Perry said. 'I hope you know what you've got.'

'I do,' Clarence said. 'Trust me, I do.'

'Cool,' Perry said. 'Uh . . . how long do I have?'

Murray's voice. 'About fifteen seconds.'

'No shit?' Perry said. 'That's kind of fucked up.'

A pause. More coughing.

'Margo?'

'Yes?'

'Thank you for saving my life.'

B61 MAKES BINGO

The order came through.

Captain Paul Ward asked them to repeat it.

They did.

Paul said nothing.

His weapons officer, Lieutenant Colonel Maegan 'Mae' Breakall, sat right behind him. She was one of the few female crew members of an F-15E, and she'd achieved that position by being a team player and never questioning an order.

While Paul sat speechless, Mae also asked them to repeat it.

They did so, this time with a bit more force.

Captain Paul Ward then did something he hadn't done in his entire military career – he refused to obey.

No sir.

No sir, I will not drop a ten-kiloton B61 nuclear warhead on the Motor City.

Fifteen seconds later, air force general Luis Monroe came on the line. As if that weren't enough, President John Gutierrez joined in as well. One hell of a conference call.

Monroe explained, quite calmly, considering the situation, that if Paul and Mae disobeyed a direct order, it was an act of treason. Gutierrez added some motivation of his own – if Captain Paul Ward did not drop the bomb, like right fucking *now*, he would be directly responsible for a disease spreading across the United States of America, a disease that could potentially destroy the country, its people, and if they were really unlucky, the entire human race.

Paul and Mae had no idea how much of this was true, but then again, it wasn't their job to question orders. Their job was to *follow* orders, from any commanding officer – and when those orders came first-person from the air force's top man *and* the commander in chief, it was impossible to disobey.

Paul pulled back on the yoke, bringing the F-15E to fifteen thousand feet. As he did, the rest of his squadron kicked in the afterburners and headed out. The radio filled with chatter: the Ospreys, Black Hawks, A-10s, F-15s and every other aircraft turned away from downtown Detroit and flew at maximum speed.

Paul and Mae were alone.

About to drop a nuke on America.

Mae fought back tears as she entered information into the computer.

A B61 Model 4 tactical nuclear warhead is a kiloton-range weapon with a 'dial-a-yield' feature. Dial-a-yield allows aircraft crews to change the B61's output while in midflight. As ordered, Mae set in a yield of ten kilotons. She set the detonation point at one thousand feet, armed the weapon, then told Paul that it was ready to fire.

He flipped open the covering plate on the nuke trigger. He thought of his three sons back at Mountain Home Air Force Base in Idaho, wondered how many sons like them were down there in Detroit, how many daughters, mothers, fathers, brothers, sisters, nephews, nieces and cousins. And dogs. How many dogs were down there?

His finger gripped the trigger. His hand felt weak. He hoped that maybe, just maybe, he'd have an unexpected stroke and lose the ability to squeeze it.

Mae said, 'Do it, Paul.'

He squeezed.

He didn't have a stroke.

The trigger clicked home.

The twelve-foot-long B61 rocket fired, launching away from the F-15E at 750 miles per hour. As the bomb streaked toward the target, Paul went full throttle and shot away from Detroit at supersonic speed.

The seven-hundred-pound B61 dropped toward the city. The guidance computer tracked a signal emitting from near the corner of Franklin and Riopelle. The B61 wouldn't actually hit the ground, but if it had, it would have landed only twenty feet away from the satphone in Perry Dawsey's hand.

At twelve hundred feet, a gas generator fired, ejecting a twenty-four-foot nylon/Kevlar-29 ribbon parachute. In just three seconds, the B61 slowed from 750 miles an hour to 35.

It drifted down until it hit eleven hundred feet, where barometric pressure activated a firing mechanism that began a nuclear chain reaction.

Detonation.

In a millionth of a second, a fireball formed and heated the air to 18,000,000 degrees Fahrenheit, nearly twice as hot as the surface of the sun. This heat radiated outward at the speed of light, expanding and dissipating. *Dissipating* being a relative term, however, as the heat caused instant first-degree burns as far as two miles away. The closer to the detonation, the worse the burns. Inside a quarter mile of the blast, flesh simply vaporized.

Every spore within a mile of the detonation point died instantly. Those between one and two miles out lived for as long as two seconds before they burned up in infinitesimally small puffs of smoke. The five-mile-per-hour wind had carried some lucky spores as far as two and a half miles away – those took almost five seconds to cook, but they cooked just the same.

The plasma ball was really the whole point of the nuke, to create instant, scorching temperatures that would kill every spore, and it worked like a charm.

The rest of the nuke's effects were a bit of unavoidable overkill.

The Renaissance Center stood less than a mile from the detonation point. Star-hot heat radiated down, turning metal, glass and plastic into boiling liquid. Some of these liquids evaporated instantly, but the building didn't have time to completely melt and burn.

The shock wave came next.

The explosion's power pushed the air around it outward in a pressure wave moving at 780 miles an hour, just a touch over the speed of sound and twice the speed of an F-5 tornado, the most powerful wind force on Earth. The wave smashed into the melting glass, metal and plastic of the RenCen, thirty-five pounds per square inch of overpressure splashing the molten liquid away in a giant wave and shattering the still-solid parts like a sledgehammer slamming through a toothpick house.

The RenCen's main tower had seventy-three stories, the four surrounding towers thirty-nine stories each. Less than three seconds after detonation, all of it was gone.

The shock wave rolled out at the speed of sound, losing energy as it moved. It shattered Comerica Park, home of the Tigers, ripping the concrete stands to pieces and hurling chunks of them for miles. In the days that followed, three seats from Section 219, half melted but still bolted to their concrete footings, would be found in the parking lot of Big Sammy's Bar in Westland, twenty miles away. The curved white roof of Ford Field, home of the Detroit Lions, caved in like an eggshell stomped by a fat man.

A mile outward from the detonation point, the pressure wave smashed any building smaller than ten stories, broken pieces flying farther outward in a lethal, hurricane-class shrapnel cloud of brick and wood and metal and glass.

That same pressure wave picked up cars and flung them like Matchbox toys, spinning them through crumbling buildings, each Ford or Toyota or Chrysler its own whirling missile of death. As far as a mile away, the blast knocked burning cars onto their sides and roofs.

Detroit wasn't the only city to feel the effects. Across the river the fireball scorched most of Windsor. The shock wave tore through the city, leveling houses as far as a mile from the shoreline.

Everywhere people died. The lucky ones, close to the detonation point, evaporated in the initial flash, their shadows instantly burned onto sidewalks and walls. One woman was in the middle of drinking a Coke – the flash vaporized her, leaving a perfect silhouette with arm bent, head tilted back, can in hand. Farther out from the detonation point, you didn't vaporize; your skin just bubbled as the sudden heat caused the fluid in each cell to boil, expand and burst the cell membranes. Survivors would later describe the feeling as being dunked deep into a vat of boiling water. Most of those who lived through the initial fireball effects died from the pressure wave or were killed by building wreckage and various car parts traveling at five hundred miles an hour.

If you lived through all that, you had to deal with second- and third-degree burns, burning buildings and dead as far as the eye could see.

And if you lived through *that,* your body would feel the effects of radiation for years to come. The cancer rate in southeast Michigan would skyrocket.

The initial blast caused an estimated 58,000 deaths. Another 23,000 died within days as a result of burns and shock-wave-related injuries. Combined, the blast caused 81,000 deaths. In the five years that followed, another 127,000 would die of persistent injuries, cancer and other radiation-related causes.

In those years, through all the scandals and congressional inquiries and public outcry, President John Gutierrez, his staff, the Joint Chiefs, Murray Longworth, Margaret Montoya and Clarence Otto would ask themselves every day . . .

Was it worth it?

As brutal as it sounded, it was.

They had destroyed the spores, killed Chelsea and brought down the Orbital. They still didn't know what was supposed to come out of those gates, what the angels really looked like and what damage they might have caused.

They didn't know, and thanks to those who gave their lives, they never would.

In the weeks after the explosion, as FEMA, Homeland Security and a dozen other agencies and charities converged on the Motor City and its suburbs to help the survivors and bury the dead, two small, manned submarines began picking up the only solid enemy remains.

The pieces of the Orbital.

Nine hundred feet below Lake Michigan's rough surface, the Orbital's wreckage lay spread across the lake bed, a collection of twisted, warped and broken rubble.

One piece, however, remained mostly intact. This object had been engineered to survive such crashes, to endure almost any type of damage in order to ensure delivery of its contents.

That particular object was about the size of a soda can.

ACKNOWLEDGMENTS

My 'First Reader:' You always take one for the team.

'Team Sigler:'
- Julian 'Tha Shiv' Pavia and the hard-workin' cats at Crown Publishing. Y'all make this a fun party.
- Byrd 'The Natural' Leavell for constant support, guidance and story instincts.
- Scott Christian and J. C. Hutchins for vital advance reads that helped iron out some pesky wrinkles. You guys are nails.
- Mae 'RDQ' Breakall for being my brain.
- Paul 'Pulsar' Rogalinski, programming assassin.
- Arioch Morningstar, audio production machine.

Research and guidance:
- Jeremy 'Xenophanes' Ellis, my friend and amazing science adviser. This book wouldn't have happened without your brilliance.
- Doug Ellis for help with BSL-4 procedures.
- Paul Blass and Bill DeSmedt, who provided much-needed help with orbital physics.
- 'Slow-Lane-Express' for teaching me about semi-tractors and trailers.
- Robert W. Gilliland, Major, USAF, for in-depth Air Force knowledge and many years of friendship.

- Chris Grall, U.S. army veteran, for all the tactics, weapons, details and culture.

Thanks to all the men and women of the U.S. military for all that you do and all that you sacrifice.

EXTRA-SPECIAL THANKS WITH SPRINKLES ON TOP:
A most heartfelt 'thanks a frickin' lot' to Joe Dumars, president of Basketball Operations for the Detroit Pistons, for trading Chauncey Billups to Denver shortly after this novel went to the printer. At least now I can say that Dumars made me look like an idiot . . .

And finally, to my die-hard fans, aka 'The Junkies.' All of this is for you. The novel you hold in your hands brings us closer to the Sigler Ascension. Spread the faith, for soon the plaid tanks will roll . . .

E-mail the author at: scott@scottsigler.net.